OVER THERE

OVER THERE

A NOVEL

Jane Rubin

JANE LOEB RUBIN

To my patriotic grandfathers who served in WWI, my father and uncles who served in WWII and to those who ministered the wounded.

Praise for A Gilded City Series

Praise for *Over There*

"I am in awe of Jane's courage, on and off the page. What a privilege to spend time in the world she has created in *Over There*." — Bess Kalb, Emmy-nominated comedy writer and the bestselling author of *Nobody Will Tell You This But Me*, a *New York Times* Editor's Choice.

"Bravery and daring, compassion and patriotism are the forces that push and pull Jane Loeb Rubin's latest historical page-turner, *Over There*, and tug at the heartstrings. It is a captivating tale of three medical professionals who join the American Hospital Corps and American Red Cross during WWI. Gut-wrenching and heroic, Rubin's rich characters draw you into a world where duty calls, love waits, and surgeons, medics, and nurses are the true heroes forced to redefine their lives while saving others. The price tag of war is devastating and heartbreaking—but in the end, Rubin's evocative tale proves that love ultimately wins." — Lisa Barr, *New York Times* bestselling author of *The Goddess Of Warsaw*

"This informative, fast-paced historical fiction, *Over There*, is the third of a trilogy comprising 'The Gilded City' books, yet it easily stands alone. It was preceded by the author's other novels, *In The Hands of Women* and *Threadbare*. The book takes its title from the 1917 patriotic war song 'Over There,' by George M. Cohan. Taking place during The Great War, 'the war to end all wars,' WW1, the story moves between New York City, pastoral upstate New York, Paris, and the trenches at the French front. This is a highly recommended read, whether alone or as part of the series. The reader will learn much about this era with great detail paid to the particular challenges of surgery in the field, the misery of war, and the sparks of humanity, care, and hope during the most difficult times." — Miriam Bradman Abrahams is a writer and reviewer for The Jewish Book Council

"Jane Rubin has truly captured the horror of war and the dedication and selflessness of the medical personnel who also sacrificed so much to care for the troops wounded in battle. With superb writing, she weaves a complex story of World War 1, through the eyes of four members of a family of extraordinary people."—Harriette Sackler, Agatha-nominated short story writer

"A meticulously researched novel immersing the reader into the indelible impact of war on the soldiers and medical personnel in the war zone, as well as the families at home. In this emotional, engaging story, set during WWI, we follow the characters Rubin brought us in the first two books of her Gilded City Series. Read this evocative novel as a standalone, but be prepared—you'll be anxious to read the whole series."—Linda Rosen, bestselling author of *The Emerald Necklace*

Praise for *Threadbare*

"Rubin's novel, *Threadbare*, is a classic, delicious immigrant story with a twist. Set in 19th-century New York City—not the 20th—it's loaded with history, and its protagonist, Tillie, is a headstrong, visionary teenage girl. Although Tillie becomes a woman far too fast, her indomitable spirit prevails. Her compelling story is one of resilience in the face of discrimination, economic hard times, and epidemics—and it resonates for the 21st century."—Susan Jane Gilman, bestselling author of *The Ice Cream Queen of Orchard Street*

"In *Threadbare*, Rubin weaves a vivid tapestry of hope, heartbreak, and resilience amid breath-stopping challenges, opening a window to a trans-formative time in women's history."—Audrey Blake, USA bestselling author of *The Girl In His Shadow* and *The Surgeon's Daughter*

"Full of research and fast-paced storytelling, Threadbare explores many critical, ever-relevant issues, including poverty, childbirth, reproductive freedom, women's place at home and in the business world, rampant disease, immigration, and the value of community. Rubin's contrasting depictions of rural Harlem and New York City during this period are as vivid as her description of Tillie's frustrations, failures, accomplishments, and successes as a daughter, caretaker, wife, mother, partner, and businesswoman."—Miriam Bradman Abrahams, Reviewer, Jewish Book Council

Praise for *In The Hands of Women*

"The author deftly captures the social challenges for women of the era, when sexism restricted their access to the best protections that science could offer. One can't help but be impressed by the rigor of the author's research...The depiction of the era in which Hannah lives is so vividly instructive that it makes this a worthwhile read, especially at a time when its principal lessons seem on the verge of being forgotten."—*Kirkus Review*

"Rubin has written a fascinating novel, well-paced and brimming with historical detail. It's 1905 in New York City, a time and place of dramatic social changes. Hannah Isaacson has graduated from a major university with an MD in obstetrics, but faces widespread discrimination as a professional woman. She encounters chronic antisemitism, realistically depicted. One can't help cheering her on as she fights for decent health care for women, for equality within the medical profession, and for respect in her own personal relationships. Ultimately, *In the Hands of Women* is a compelling and heartwarming historical novel."—Libby H. O'Connell, Chief Historian Emeritus, History Channel, and author of *The American Plate*

ISAACSON
FAMILY TREE

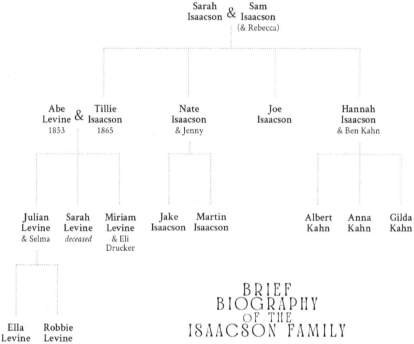

Sarah Isaacson & Sam Isaacson (& Rebecca)

Abe Levine 1853 & Tillie Isaacson 1865

Nate Isaacson & Jenny

Joe Isaacson

Hannah Isaacson & Ben Kahn

Julian Levine & Selma

Sarah Levine *deceased*

Miriam Levine & Eli Drucker

Jake Isaacson

Martin Isaacson

Albert Kahn

Anna Kahn

Gilda Kahn

Ella Levine

Robbie Levine

BRIEF BIOGRAPHY OF THE ISAACSON FAMILY

Tillie Isaacson emigrated from Germany to the United States in 1866 as a one-year-old. Her parents, Sarah and Sam, settled on a chicken farm in Harlem, NY, and had three more children: Nate, Joseph, and Hannah. Nate moved north with Sam and his step-mother, Rebecca to Sullivan Country when the farms in Harlem were leveled, making room for the city's expansion. He eventually took over management of the farm. Hannah, who was raised by Tillie on the Lower East Side, became a physician, a testament to the family's commitment to education, and later married Ben Kahn, a surgeon. Tillie's daughter, Miriam, studied nursing, later marrying Eli Druker, a surgeon. Their lives and values embodied the upward mobility of the Jewish immigrants through devoted family support, education, community, and business.

November 11, 1918 – Armistice - ELI

American Base Hospital 30—The Western Front

Fifteen hours without a break in sight, fishing shrapnel out of chests, bellies, arms, and legs. Head injuries were bandaged and sent directly to The American Hospital in Paris, hours southwest of the battlefield. My hands bloodied, barely washed between patients. Never enough clean water or aprons to make it through the horrific daily battle injuries. And the casualties hadn't ebbed despite the armistice reached this morning. The wounded kept coming. Men carrying stretchers calling for empty tables.

My nurse, Louisa, who had assisted me for months, was my shadow—a second set of hands that, within milliseconds, extended a retractor, a suction cup, and catgut suture. She was proficient in the silent language of an efficient operating room. Louisa was my second British nurse, moving with me to U.S. Base Hospital 30 from my Red Cross unit this past June. Her crisp, rapid elocution bolstered me when our hands were deep in a warm body, holding my attention like a tight clamp as I entered the deep well of fatigue following endless hours on my throbbing legs and feet, pulling me back to the present. Like others in my unit, I suffered the residual effects of repeated bouts of chilblains. Last winter, we worked in a frozen, tent-covered operating theater for weeks at a stretch.

Louisa's voice was barely louder than the clatter of bullets clinking as they dropped into the metal trays, or the screaming of the incoming wounded. "Almost finished, Doctor. I hear the battle is winding down for the night. No more casualties coming in. The end is near."

Thank you, God. "Any more news about the Armistice? Is the fighting over for good?" I was anxious to see my beloved Miriam, to find out if our love had endured the war and our hardships. I forced my concentration back to the operating room. "How many did we save today?"

Louisa drew a deep breath, wiping her brow with her forearm. "Let's see, we had four chests, one deceased, six bellies, three on the train heading to Paris for more surgery. One poor lad lost most of his intestines. My God, what a stench that was. The rest were limbs." She paused, then carried on. "Dr. Roberts took all the head wounds, lost five out of eight. Perhaps a bloody blessing. They had no faces left."

A wave of grief gripped me. After all these months, we had learned to think of these valiant young men, barely more than children, as nameless organ injuries. Could we have coped with the carnage any other way? But today, it hit me harder. Perhaps with the end in sight, my frayed emotions were surfacing.

In her clipped King's English, Louisa continued, "My best guess is you'll be back in New York by New Year's. Then you can see ...." She pulled away from our patient's body, the retractor in her hands dropping to the floor with a crash.

"Louisa, what the bloody hell?"

Then my world went dark.

I

PART ONE

"We'll be over, we're coming over,
And we won't come back till it's over, over there."
Over There, *by George M. Cohan*

Chapter One: Miriam

May 1917—Eighteen Months Earlier—New York City

I was convinced no man would ever want me as a wife. I'd been jilted for another woman before I turned twenty-one, traumatized by the deception, dubious of romance. Then I was stricken with disease, relinquishing any shred of remaining hope.

An outsider, one unaware of my history, might cast his eyes on Eli and me, standing under the chuppah, the wedding canopy, and comment that we made a handsome couple. But beneath my billowing lace wedding outfit, tulle underskirt, and over my delicate silk stockings, the brace dug deep into my right leg and thigh. I'd secured it that morning, pulling the buckle to the tightest notch I could tolerate, determined to stand tall and walk down the aisle without my customary limp. Knowing there would be chafing, I'd applied talcum and gauze, but not enough, fearing the powder would leave a trail on the carpet runner and draw pitiful attention.

I turned to look at my small family, sitting in the front pew. Everyone told me Mama would be with me in spirit, but my breath hitched in sorrow when I thought of her. Mama's absence beside Papa on the hard bench left a pit in my heart. Papa sat beside Aunt Hannah, whose eyes locked with mine. I knew we shared the same thought. She placed her right hand over her heart, nodding at me, sending the message Mama was with us, deep inside. I lifted my hand, placed it over my heart, answered her gesture, then turned back to Eli.

My toes tingled with pins and needles. Too much standing, too much preening all morning before the ceremony increased the pain in my right leg, my stance growing wobbly. Although I knew I'd be crippled the rest of my life, I wished polio hadn't left its vengeance on my leg. If only I could have been flawless for my wedding. I drew closer to Eli, seeking his reassurance and physical support. He was too good to be true.

Eli turned his eyes toward mine, once again trapping me in his loving gaze, whispering in my ear, "Are you holding up all right, my love? Let's find a chair for you soon."

Polio, a disease we hadn't encountered in the past, added its deadly presence in New York City the year before. I'd been working as the head nurse in the children's ward of Beth Israel Hospital in downtown Manhattan for five years when this new, terrifying illness hit like a firestorm. One day, we were caring for the ordinary maladies of asthma and fractures, then, as if overnight, children were pouring into the hospital with a trio of symptoms: high fever, vomiting, and shortness of breath. As we addressed what we thought were common flu symptoms, the disease raged into a more vicious stage, paralyzing limbs and, in some unfortunate cases, the lungs. After several months tending our youngest patients day and night, I succumbed. At first, I brushed off the headache, stiff neck, and fatigue, but when the body aches and weak limbs were too much to bear, I asked one of the doctors to examine me. By that time, I was confined to my own hospital bed.

Eli, better known around the wards as Dr. Drucker, tended to me day and night. We'd always had an affable, sparring friendship. Still, until I became ill, I had no idea the depth of his feelings toward me. As my fever lifted, I'd find him sitting by my bed, writing patient notes in his stack of thick charts, periodically looking up to study me.

One morning, I whispered in my raspy voice. "Don't you have better things to do than sit around the women's ward?"

He released a deep sigh. "Do you have any idea how worried I've been? About you?"

Up until that point, I had never considered he'd taken me seriously. I shook my head on the pillow, for the first time self-conscious of the rank smell of my hair and breath.

"Well, I was. I feared we'd lose you." Dr. Drucker cleared his throat, scanning his eyes about the room. His voice dropped to a whisper. "Then I would have lost you before having my chance for a dinner date together."

In all my adult years, the last thing I expected was to receive an invitation on my deathbed. I could barely choke out, "What are you talking about?"

He took my hand. "I'd been working up the courage to invite you out for months. Then, you almost died. You see, I had all the details worked out. You know, candles, soft music, wine, my best jokes."

My eyes warmed. Was I dreaming? Was this handsome man interested in me? "But I may be crippled from this horrible disease. Why would you want me?"

He squeezed my hand. "You silly, beautiful woman. Do you know anything at all about love?"

Love? Did he just say the word "love?"

Chapter Two: Hannah

Witnessing the marriage of my beautiful niece, standing beside her *bashert*, her love, under the chuppah, filled my heart with gratitude. Miriam and Eli had selected New York City's Central Synagogue on Lexington Avenue, with its blended congregation of German and Eastern European Jews, in their search for a more liberal, spiritual interpretation of Judaism.

If not for this joyous time, I could never have borne the losses. On the heels of my wedding to Ben a few years earlier, and the arrival of our precious daughter, Gilda, my life took an unanticipated, harrowing twist. First, I lost my elder sister, Tillie, my surrogate mother, and then a year later, almost lost Miriam, my only niece, to polio.

Miriam and Eli's marriage was the promise that life would go on. As her sole aunt, in the throes of my own pain, it had been my responsibility to pass along the valuable lessons Tillie taught me. I guided Miriam through her grief and its passing with the tenderness of a mother, supporting her as she forged forward. I dabbed my eyes, knowing the deep love Tillie had for Miriam, especially after the loss of Tillie's infant daughter, Sarah.

At the time of Tillie's passing, a disease like polio was my furthest concern. But a quick year later, Miriam faced the fight of her own young life. We were lucky. The good Lord held out his loving hands while we nursed her through the perilous challenge. For others, the disease, with its devastating symptoms, shot a bolt of fear through the city. We had no idea where it came from, nor how to treat it. What we did know, was it was contagious.

Now, watching Miriam gaze at Eli under the canopy, I concentrated on gratitude for all that was good in our lives, reaching for Ben's hand, gently squeezing, recalling when we'd shared our vows. I was a late-in-life bride, verging on thirty with a string of romantic blunders. Despite my academic prowess, I was well behind other women my age when it came to sizing up men. But our lives aligned, both ready to open our hearts. Ben, widowed and close to a decade older than me, was beyond his youthful years, with two school-age children and two decades worth of surgical experience.

Since our nuptials five years ago, the random gray streaks in his mop of ginger curls had transformed into a forest of silver. Then came the steel-framed glasses. I mused how quickly we age. Ben had been the anchor in my turbulent adult life, keeping me bound to the here and now, generously sharing his counsel with me, one of the few women physicians at Mount Sinai, and again in my role as Department Chair. For me, having waited what felt like a lifetime for genuine love, I didn't want to miss a moment with him.

I turned my attention back to my beautiful niece, Miriam, with her long chestnut waves, tall like her mother, standing straight and proud beside her new husband. I knew she worried about the future. Like Ben and me, her colleagues at Beth Israel were turning their attention to the war overseas, leaving in droves to tend soldiers in Paris and Red Cross field hospitals. Now, a month after President Wilson had declared war on Germany, it was only a matter of time before the irresistible magnetic pull hit our family.

Chapter Three: Ben

May 1917—New York City

I n the last two months, the beating drums of war had overtaken New York City. Even amidst the excitement of planning Miriam's wedding, it was nearly impossible to direct all my thoughts to the lovely couple now standing before us in the sanctuary. There was simply too much happening in the world to fully concentrate on the ceremony.

At work, daily meetings were held at noon in the Board Room of Mount Sinai Hospital. Since March, when America declared war on Germany, we renamed it the War Room. The conflict was having an immediate and growing impact on the hospital. Staff was shrinking in every department and role, as physicians, nurses, and orderlies left for France by the week. It was a constant challenge to reorganize coverage of the floors, operating, and emergency rooms.

With the prevailing call for experienced volunteer nurses and doctors, all New York City hospitals lost critical talent. Sprinkled throughout the hospital, tack boards held official Red Cross notices. Posted in every lounge and locker room, they called for medical support in the European conflict, now in its third year. Last month, the United States War Department added to the call, summoning every available doctor and nurse to join the effort. The French, our dear ally, were desperate for help, on the cusp of losing.

I sat at the large oval conference table, eating soup and crackers. George Blumenthal, the hospital president, sat beside me, devouring an egg salad sandwich, both of us waiting for the Chief Nursing Officer to enter the room. George, an acerbic middle-aged man who had been in his role for the last seven years, was spoiled by years of rapid growth, new hospital wings, and generous donors. We'd worked together throughout that explosive growth, and the war effort weighed heavily on him.

George turned to me, wiping his mouth with a napkin, "We need a new contingency plan. Tell me, are the doctors giving you ample notice? How fast are they leaving?" Without waiting for my reply, he continued to unleash his frustration. "That damn Wilson promised us he'd stay out of the conflict. So much for relying on politicians."

As much as I wanted to offer reassurance, I couldn't. Medical staff, primarily surgeons, were leaving at a steady pace, one or two each week. I said, "Wilson's side-stepped the conflict for as long as possible. Three years, George. Must I remind you of the sinking of the Lusitania? We lost one hundred twenty-eight Americans in that ghastly attack; innocent mothers and children drowned in that frigid water. Germany has our back against the wall."

He waved his hand, dismissing me. "I know, I know, I read the papers, too."

I continued, irritated that his sense of national pride was so low. I huffed, "So I need not remind you of Germany's refusal to honor their own Sussex Pledge, providing ample warning to merchant and passenger ships so people could safely disembark before an attack. And of course, you know the last nail in the coffin came when we intercepted that secret proposal from the German Foreign Secretary, Zimmermann, to his counterpart in Mexico, offering to join Mexico in an attack on the United States from the southern border. That shifty German had the gall to offer Texas, New Mexico, and Arizona." I lowered my voice. "What do you expect the poor man to do? We have a country full of Europeans who cannot visit their families, the trade routes are too treacherous, and now, coercing Mexico?"

He studied my face before speaking. "I'm not in the mood for a lesson in current events, nor am I interested in learning to speak German or Spanish, God forbid."

I had to hand it to the man; he might be overly concerned with pleasing the Board, but he knew when to lay down his sword.

George continued as if we never derailed. "Let's deal with the matter at hand, the medical staff. The young ones are our future, the mid-career our backbone, and the elders, our wisdom. No matter who leaves, the war has hit us in the family jewels."

I smirked. "We'll come up with something. Most of the physicians leaving are young. Also, we can hold off on elective cases, and work on a plan with the convalescence centers to move patients out of the hospital sooner, opening fresh beds." I chuckled, "Be glad, George, that we're not in England or France. They've been dealing with this for three years." I paused, considering a different tactic. "Have you checked how they've handled things? That may give us some answers."

George turned to me with a scowl. "I suppose I should. I'll get our financial officer on it right away. You know this will destroy our budget."

The hospital leadership throughout the city had never dealt with anything quite like the rapid attrition of medical staff. The last time the medical community answered a call to arms was at the end of the century, in the war against Spain. I had enlisted, along with several surgeons from Mount Sinai. But by the time I was to leave for training, the treaty was signed in Paris. Cuba had been liberated from Spain. That was years before my first marriage and the loss of my first wife, tragically killed in a carriage accident. It felt as if it were a lifetime ago.

Despite a thread of impatience for his preoccupation with profit, I tried to understand George's dilemma, offering, "I can ask the surgeons to move our patients out faster. The load is felt most heavily on the inpatient floors, where we need most of our nurses. It's a good thing they're not taking the married ones."

He harrumphed, "That will help. Maternity should begin slowing down soon. Can you ask that wife of yours to keep me informed? I want to know when the volume of pregnancies drops off." George made some notes in the column of his agenda.

I cleared my throat, irritated he barely remembered Hannah's name despite the fact she was running the Obstetrics Department. "George, if you're worried about money, I suggest you don't plan on making any this year or building a new wing. It's not going to happen. You're only going to drive us all crazy if you don't reset expectations."

He snapped back, "But the Board...."

I interrupted, "I refuse to believe the Board is more concerned about turning a profit than supporting our country at war. Stop worrying about your unblemished record and let us deal with the matter at hand." I drew a breath. "And pray our boys, doctors, and nurses help put an end to this quickly." I paused a moment. "And return alive."

He plopped backward in his chair, his face sagging with defeat. "Well, let's get on with it." In a loud voice, he spoke to everyone in the room. "I'm calling the meeting to order."

* * *

Since April 6th, when President Wilson declared war on Germany, Hannah and my discussions always referred to *them*, not *us*. After all, I'd just turned fifty and Hannah was a decade younger. By all measures, we should both be thinking ahead to retirement.

"Do you think Eli will enlist? Poor Miriam. She must be sick with worry." Hannah asked the evening before the wedding. "I'm glad you're close to the cutoff. And now that you've taken the position as Chief Medical Officer at the hospital, you're not operating quite as much as in the past."

I sighed, considering her rationale made the decision to enlist even stronger. Me, with a life's worth of surgical experience, should be in France, overseeing the surgeries and young physicians. But would they accept an older doctor? "We'll discuss it once they return from their honeymoon. I hesitate to raise it now and spoil their special time."

Would Hannah understand my pull to the battle? The loss of her sister, Tillie, left her shaken to the core, and then Miriam's bout with polio practically destroyed her. The thought of leaving Hannah with the three children, two of mine from my first marriage, whom she adopted without pause, and our Gilda, was almost unthinkable. But so was war. So was the slaughter of innocents on a ship. The insanity had to stop. There were some things a man must do, no matter his age.

* * *

Now, we sat together in the sanctuary of Central Synagogue with its stunning Moorish design, awe-inspiring internal arches, and brilliantly colored stained-glass windows, watching Eli and Miriam in their happiest moment in years. I squeezed Hannah's hand, pulling myself back into the joyous moment, hoping beyond all hope that their happiness would last.

Chapter Four: Eli

May 1917—New York City

I f only the world could stay calm for one damn minute. More than anything, I longed for more time with Miriam. Love and hope filled my heart as I gazed into her dazzling blue eyes under the chuppah, but beneath my deep emotions was a growing well of fear.

Although she and I knew medical personnel would not be conscripted, we agreed to table serious war conversation until we returned from our honeymoon upstate. After a terse discussion, we'd come to that decision a week earlier in my apartment.

By the time we'd become serious, we were well beyond the traditional courting ages and disregarded the social confines of younger couples, spending many evenings together alone in my apartment. Of course, we took precautions, but neither could deny our affection nor wait for marriage.

Miriam was stretched out on the couch while I massaged her withered leg, a regular routine. She propped it on my lap while we shared the details of our workdays, the upcoming wedding, and the dream apartment we hoped to find. Presently, Miriam lived with her father, Abe, near the Lower East Side where she was raised. Since Tillie's death two years ago, Abe had shrunken into an old man. At seventy-three, the scales had tipped against him. His losses outweighed his happiness, leaving him rudderless and lonely. In Tillie's final months, Miriam promised her mother she'd watch out for him. If needed, we would welcome Abe into our home.

The wedding, only one week away, was when I clumsily broached the topic, the singular subject we had tried to avoid. "The Chief of Medicine met this morning with the attending medical staff about covering the hospital during the European engagement." I was nervous, knowing I must serve, far more frightened than I was willing to admit aloud.

Miriam twisted her leg from my grip and sat upright, her enchanting eyes piercing into mine like the ocean depths. "What did he say? How many are leaving? Is he figuring out how to backfill?"

I squirmed, not knowing how to approach the news. Then I plunged in, hoping she could understand. "The Medical Corps is all volunteer for the time being. There is no talk about conscription. But darling, I must join. I don't feel right having our men over there without American doctors caring for them."

Her voice was even, far more controlled than I'd anticipated. "But, Eli, we're about to wed. This is too soon. Can't it wait?"

I shook my head. "They need medical personnel of every type, especially trained surgeons and nurses. The European casualties have been staggering, especially with that horrid gas and new weaponry they're using. They're called machine guns and shrapnel sprays out everywhere, ripping bodies apart. Now our boys will fight there, too. It's not right for me to stay back."

Miriam's face turned beet red. Her eyes drilling into mine. "Then, I'm going with you!"

What had I done? The last thing I wanted was to place my love in harm's way. She had already fought the battle of a lifetime with polio. I placed my hands on her shoulders. "There are many details to learn before making decisions. I'm sorry I brought it up. Let's enjoy our wedding and honeymoon to the fullest. Then I'll figure out my next move."

It took a lonely decade for me to find Miriam. I would not lose her now. My mind raced back to our first encounter.

I was a new surgical resident at Beth Israel Hospital in Lower Manhattan, finding my bearings, navigating the location of patient units and specialty departments, dependent on nurses, orderlies, and housekeepers for directions. My attending physician had asked me to look in on a young patient. I wandered the halls to no avail, searching for the correct unit and bed. Frustrated, I stood in the corridor with my hands on my hips, wondering if this was possibly a demented hazing ritual.

A beautiful young nursing student wearing a crisp white student cap approached me, sensing in the sixth sense of all nurses that I needed help. She looked so serene and gentle that I couldn't help but swallow my request for help, terrified to break her bewitching spell.

She smiled, surmising I needed help. "Are you a new doctor here?" Without waiting for my answer, she added with a teasing smirk, raising her lovely thin eyebrows, "Lost?"

I dumbly nodded, knowing I had revealed a vulnerability, conveyed a chink in my status as a physician. At Beth Israel, like most hospitals in New York City, physicians dominated the corridors, patient orders, and decisions. But at that exact moment, I didn't care I'd lost more than my hallway compass. I was trapped in her presence.

She spoke again. Those knowing eyes looked straight into mine. Her ivory skin and slender, tall form held me captive. "Tell me the patient and unit, and I'll show you the fastest way. I've worked here a couple of years and know all the shortcuts." She laughed lightly, reaching out her hand. "By the way, I'm Miriam Levine, student nurse. I graduate this year."

Oh, that radiant smile. Unprepared for the electricity running into my hand from hers, I managed to sputter, "Eli Drucker, surgery resident." Catching myself for my sloppy familiarity, I cleared my throat, "That is, Dr. Drucker."

From that instant throughout the next two years, my eyes sought hers whenever I stepped inside the hospital. I'd been hit by Cupid's arrow, and it never lost its grip. Miriam, far more buttoned in emotionally, disguised any feelings she might have toward me, always equally affable to all the nurses and physicians. In turn, I did my best to contain mine. It was widely expected that doctors maintain their demeanor, no matter how taxing. That is, until Miriam was stricken with polio. Then I unraveled, terrified I'd lose her.

Now, sitting on the couch together, discussing the war, I realized how brave Miriam was. She would exercise the same conviction serving her country that she demonstrated fighting her way back to health from polio. No one thought she would ever walk again, but they didn't know this woman like I did. As soon as her condition stabilized, Miriam was on the move. First, bed to chair and back to bed, then walking the hallway with wood crutches, finally limping with a clumsy brace, her permanently deformed leg dragging, determined to keep it abreast of her otherwise healthy body. During her convalescence, she would pin on her nursing cap and hobble to the children's unit wearing her patient gown and robe, comforting parents, sharing hope for their sick children. Despite my own reservations about becoming a wartime surgeon and my downright fear of trauma care, she had enough fortitude to bolster the two of us. Simply standing in her presence made me stronger.

Chapter Five: Miriam

May 1917

E li and I borrowed Uncle Ben's spanking new, red Model T and drove north into upstate New York for our honeymoon the morning after our wedding. We stowed our valises in the back of the car and drove north of Central Park through Harlem, almost out of the hubbub of the city. Throughout childhood, Mama shared stories of her younger years, growing up on a chicken farm in Harlem before her mother, Sarah, passed. The farm was later displaced far north to rural Sullivan County thanks to funds from Baron Maurice de Hirsch. In the years following the move, before Opa Sam passed, my older brother, Julian, would spend summers on the new chicken farm along with his cousins, a respite from the sweltering summer heat and humidity south in the city. Mama said I was too young, too much extra work for her stepmother.

It was difficult to imagine Harlem in those early days, with hilly, rocky terrain more suitable for raising livestock than growing vegetables. Opa's tales of cows and goats meandering the streets of Harlem and Central Park entertained all the grandchildren at our family get-togethers. Now the land was fully built, except for the stringlike parks hugging Riverside Drive. The leveled land supported three- to five-story brick buildings with a sprinkling of wood structures. Negroes lived in many of them, building their street level storefronts along the busier roads, a near perfect reflection of our Jewish neighborhood in the Lower East Side.

As we drove, my thoughts drifted to my older brother, Julian. He didn't attend the wedding yesterday. Although disappointing, I knew his life had become complicated after leaving for college. Month after month, he distanced himself from family, replacing us with his new friends, until there was no longer room for his past. After completing an actuarial degree at City College of New York, he married Selma, whom he'd met through college friends. They moved to Brooklyn, married privately, started a family, and forged new friendships. Julian crossed the Brooklyn Bridge daily for his work in downtown New York at Metropolitan Life. Still, sadly, despite his first-rate job and a handsome couple of children, the marriage lacked joy, perhaps strained by the day-to-day demands and Julian's unexplained late nights. Before long, they extracted themselves from our frequent family gatherings and each other, as if the East River and the Brooklyn boulevards were the dividing lines in their lives.

Before too long, Eli and I arrived at the ferry, loaded the car onto the barge, and crossed the Hudson River, driving northwest to the Liberty Highway. We unrolled the car windows and drank in the clean air. Laced with the perfume of blossoming trees and bushes, we passed groves of dogwoods and orchards of cherry trees. It would have been a flawless landscape if not for my watering eyes and fits of sneezing. "We may need to roll up these windows." I struggled with the window crank, wiping my nose with Eli's handkerchief. "The pollen is irritating me."

The first stop on our honeymoon was Opa Sam's chicken farm, now in Uncle Nate's capable hands. Since Opa's death, Nate had grown the farm into the second-largest kosher chicken producer in the county. The explosive growth in the city's Jewish population brought a constant demand for poultry and eggs. I smiled inwardly. No doubt we'd be eating chicken for dinner.

We arrived in the late afternoon, in time to unpack and help with dinner. Eli jumped from the Model T, more relaxed than I'd seen him all winter. His customary worry lines had melted off his face, replaced with a broad smile. "Your Uncle Nate had the right idea, living in the country, helping your grandfather with the chickens. It's peaceful. I could get used to this."

He ran to my car door, lifting me out in his arms, whispering, "I love you."

I kissed him back, scarcely believing how happy I felt. But unlike Eli, the quiet in the air left me off balance. I'd always found the strident noises and energy of the city invigorating. "It's quite beautiful, awfully quiet." I mused. Perhaps too quiet for me.

Nate's renovated farmhouse perched high on the property, catching the soft breezes that snaked through the rolling hills and valleys, diluting the stench of chickens and goats. We pulled up to the front door to unload. From that vantage point, we stood holding hands, marveling at the landscape: neighboring farmlands, silos, and Nate's orchard trees dotting the countryside.

Just then, Uncle Nate and his wife, Jenny, sprang out of the front door. Jenny ran towards me with her arms spread wide, calling loudly to me. "Is this my beautiful niece, Miriam? Come, let me look at you!" Her Polish accent was heavy despite having arrived in New York close to twenty years earlier. "God bless you, love birds." Jenny's eyes searched my body, sizing up the damage from polio.

The last time I saw Uncle Nate and Aunt Jenny was twenty years ago, visiting the farm. Now, they had two grown sons, Jake and Martin, who were strapping young men. In April, they left for military training. I was sure our stopover was a welcome distraction.

Aunt Jenny clapped her hands, abuzz with purpose. "Nate, show them to Jake's room," she said wistfully, her breath halting for the briefest moment. "I need to run to the kitchen. Dinner's cooking on the stove." With those few words, she hustled back inside, her ample behind swishing from side to side beneath her skirt.

I followed Eli and Nate, each lugging our heavy valises, bumping them against the walls on the way up the steps to our room. Standing in place, memories of visits to the farm flooded back, gathering eggs from the coop for breakfast, but shying far away from the red barn when Uncle Nate butchered. The panicked sounds of squawking chickens hung in my head for hours afterward.

The bedrooms were exactly how the boys left them, as if they'd gone on a weekend camping trip. Each had sports pennants tacked to the walls, small trophies on the dressers, and neatly made beds. Now, Jake and Martin were stationed in a military camp for three months somewhere in the Midwest, learning how to kill people instead of chickens. I could only imagine how Aunt Jenny's heart ached for the days when they were safely tucked into those two beds, harmless images filling their dreams.

I hurried down the stairs to the kitchen to help Jenny prepare dinner. At the base of the steps, I paused in the parlor, once again filled with memories of my childhood excitement traveling from the city on holidays to visit. Jenny had chosen wallpaper with a botanical print for the first-floor parlor, similar to Mama's, and decorated the walls with numerous wooden shelves crammed with family pictures and interesting *tchotchkes* from her early life in Poland. My eyes caught a framed sepia photo of Mama and Papa. Julian and Aunt Hannah, both school age, stood beside them. Only two or three at the time, I sat on Mama's lap, my hair a nest of ringlets, my eyes wide in shock from the flash. Beside our family photo, there was a framed picture of Jake and Martin in their uniforms, taken a few months earlier. How did they ever grow up so fast? Both were fresh-faced with the full smiles of eager young men. I said a silent prayer for their safety and turned to the kitchen, calling to Jenny on my way, "How can I help?"

My aunt was a short bundle of energy, a whirling dervish, darting about the small kitchen, her gray-streaked hair in a loose bun, yellow calico housedress much like the kits Mama manufactured during her twenties. A splattered white apron was tied tightly about her round middle, but billowed in front as Jenny's constant motion created a crosswind of its own.

She greeted me with another tight hug, huge smile, and instructions. "Come in. You can help with the peas. They need to be shelled. Picked them this morning. First of the season." She grabbed a few from the bowl, inspected them closely, and popped one in her mouth. "I may have jumped the gun by a week. They're still small, but sweet."

Carrying the bowl of peas and a medium-sized pot outside the kitchen door, I sat beside the compost bin on the landing. As I shelled the peas into the pot for cooking, my eyes drifted west to the horizon, watching the sun set. When was the last time I could see so much sky? As the sun dropped beneath the hills, painted clouds in scarlet, sunflower yellow, and indigo hues sharpened, their colors more vibrant by the second. I wished I could share the sight with Eli, but he was off touring the farm with Nate.

Ten minutes later, Jenny walked to the front door, ringing a cowbell and calling, "Wash your hands and come to the table. Dinner is ready." The men strolled up the rise, in jovial discussion, their boisterous laughter audible a half-acre from the house. Eventually, we sat down to a meal of roasted chicken, freshly baked bread, and peas. It was the most flavorful food I'd had in months.

Eli was quick to comment. "See, Miriam, even the country food tastes better. It sits mere minutes before being prepared, not days like in our marketplace, rotting in carts. Did you catch that sunset? Magnificent. God's paint pallet."

Did Eli want to move here, so far from the city? He'd never spoken about being a country doctor.

* * *

Two weeks later, we returned to Manhattan, after driving all the way to Niagara Falls, riding in the Maid of the Mist, and adoring each other every moment. Back home, we settled into Eli's tiny apartment, anxious to begin our new life as a married couple. Although the sun had risen hours earlier, I lingered in bed, sated from an early morning intimacy, sinking into our new mattress, linens, and married lives. I would enjoy each second of my marriage if every day began this way.

Although excited to shop for our next apartment, I craved to linger at this crossroad, relishing the splendor we'd enjoyed on our honeymoon, stretching it out as long as I could. But before discussing a new home, we had to settle the serious matter hovering overhead. Instead of a first blissful month of marriage, June lurked before us, like a darkened storm cloud charged with the force of thunder and lightning. Although we vaguely sensed the damage the war would unleash on our lives, it was impossible to place an exacting finger on its impact. The Medical Corps was tapping its toe, waiting like an impatient spouse. I sat up in bed, reaching for my cane. I wasn't in the mood just yet to strap on that awful brace and feel confined in a metal cage. I'd wait until we dressed for the day.

As I sat on the bed's edge, the delightful fragrance of toast and coffee drifted into our bedroom, enticing me. Unlike many men who first had mothers and then wives preparing every meal, Eli had no family to speak of, living alone long enough to learn the basics of cooking. I knew better than to take his skill lightly or make him wait for me to come join him. I shook off my blanket and wrapped myself in my amethyst robe, a wedding gift from Hannah. She had explained, "Purple is one of the three suffragist colors. The stores have been fashioning clothing in purple, green, and white to support the movement. It's all the rage in England where the ladies have taken over the men's jobs in factories and offices."

Eli's apartment was typical of housing near the hospital, designed for busy workers with efficiency in mind. Although it generously contained a bedroom and private lavatory, the remaining one-room space consisted of a small kitchen at one end, a drop leaf table in the middle, and two brown tattered upholstered chairs set by the windows.

Eli carried two plates with buttered toast and eggs to the table, turning back to the counter to pour our coffee, mine with a drop of cream, his, a heaping teaspoon of sugar. Once seated, he gazed into my eyes. "It's hard to be back, but we must return to reality. Let's eat and talk about what's next. Even though it's Sunday and I'm not due back to work until tomorrow, I'd like to stop at the hospital this morning and find out what's happened while we were away."

I sighed in surrender. The honeymoon was over. There was no sense putting off the inevitable any longer.

Chapter Six: Ben

May 1917—New York City

T he Monday following Miriam and Eli's wedding was work as usual for Hannah and me.

My schedule was packed with meetings. For half of them, the agenda concerned the war and its impact on the hospital, identifying wards we'd transition for recovering soldiers, redeploying nurses and doctors to fill staffing gaps, and selecting the most highly skilled to handle complex surgical cases in the absence of our customary staff of experienced surgeons. We were guessing. No one was around since the last war, and we had no accurate idea of what our returning soldiers would need, either immediately or during their months of rehabilitation. We drafted plans for every imaginable scenario.

Chatter of war filled the air. The physicians' lounge, nurses' stations, and cafeteria hummed with voices of excited and anxious staff speculating about battle results, husbands and relatives preparing to serve, and the terrifying trenches. We adjusted our daily staffing based on the continual drain of staff leaving for training camps and ships heading to the European Front. But I kept my intentions a secret from my colleagues and the hospital president. I hadn't yet run it by Hannah, either. I knew she'd be angry when I told her I'd decided to join the Medical Corps and leave with the next round of volunteers. Come hell or high water, I was determined to serve my country.

By mid-week, I embarked on a fact-finding mission. Leaving the hospital at lunchtime, I walked downtown to the army recruitment office to speak to the commanding officer. As I approached the headquarters near Times Square, I noticed young men dressed in everyday work clothes lined up out the front door and around the corner, some quiet, others speaking in their native European tongues. I jostled past the line into the building. Curious eyes studied my sharp-cut suit and official-looking stride. Inside, the hallways were smoke-filled as soon-to-be soldiers nervously lit cigarettes, attempting to appear older than their late teens. A woody tobacco smell permeated the air where they stood. Most held conscription letters, waiting to enter the intake office. Head high, I walked past them with a curt nod, hearing grumbling in my wake. I ignored their murmurs, proceeding straight to the front of the line.

At the rear of the room was a door with a plaque that read 'PRIVATE' in all capital letters. I knocked firmly. The heavy door opened immediately, and I faced the angry expression of a slightly younger man than me, cigarette hanging from his lips, smoke streaming out his nose.

Momentarily shaken by his lack of respect, I cleared my throat. "I'm Dr. Ben Kahn, Chief of the Medical Staff at Mount Sinai Hospital. I'd like a few words with your commanding officer."

The soldier stepped backward, his eyes appraising me in a sweeping manner. "What about?"

Again, his rudeness ruffled me. Perhaps I should have called first and avoided this underling, but my decision to walk down was spontaneous. I was accustomed to an extraordinary degree of deference from the physicians, nurses, and patient families at the hospital. His offensive nature triggered a long-buried anger I held towards doctors when they were disrespectful, speaking down to sick immigrants. I constantly reminded my youngest students that although their white coats may garner respect, it's not the clothing that makes a man, woman, or a great doctor. If I caught wind of any arrogance or disrespect to others, there'd be hell to pay. Apparently, the army hadn't spread that message yet, the power of rank going directly to this man's head. "Whom am I addressing? I would like to talk to the appropriate officer handling the Medical Corps."

The officer leaned his shoulder against the door frame, again eyeing me with a look of superiority. "I'm Staff Sergeant Reilly, in charge of recruitment. The Office of the Medical Corps is located downtown at Tompkins Square." He paused, studying me further. "They ain't gonna take an old geezer like you. I wouldn't waste their time."

Furious, I spit out my words, "We'll see about that."

* * *

Hours later, after enlisting with the Medical Corps, I rushed back uptown, hoping to make it home in time for dinner. Ordinarily, a brisk spring evening walk like this would have filled me with renewed energy. Instead, I knew the hours ahead would be difficult. I should have told Hannah my plans first. She wouldn't like the news. Perhaps I could twist the truth, present it as if I hadn't signed up yet, and avoid her anger.

"Hello, darlings," I shouted eagerly as I entered the apartment. I heard muffled greetings from the older children; their voices seeping through their bedroom doors. Naked and dripping from her bath, Gilda tore through the apartment and jumped into my arms. My God, how I adored that child.

"Papa's home! Papa's home," she cried out joyfully.

Hannah, two steps behind, scooped her up in the waving towel she held in her outstretched arms. "Come back here, you little imp. You'll make your papa soaking wet." She smiled.

"Hello, sweetheart," I said. I loved this world, my three children, and especially my extraordinary wife. I knew in my core it would be heart-wrenching to leave them. "Any chance dinner's still warm?"

"I waited for you. Let me get Gilda ready for bed, and I'll heat something for us. Perhaps you can read her a story while I fix our dinner."

I hung my coat in the foyer closet. "I'll wash up and meet you in her room." Tapping on Anna's door before poking my head in, I said, "How's my big girl?"

Anna was stretched out on her bed, wearing a yellow flannel nightgown. She had inherited my curly red hair, and a face sprinkled with freckles.

Glancing up from her book, she answered, "Hi, Papa. I'm finishing a seventh grade reading assignment for tomorrow. They moved me into the next grade for reading." She turned the book to show me the cover. "It's *Tom Sawyer*."

Albert, two years older than his sister, was completing his schoolwork when I knocked on his door. He had inherited his birth mother's dark hair and penetrating brown eyes. "Hi, Papa, want to see my mathematics test? I practically got everything right."

I examined his test. He was studying algebra in eighth grade. "Fine job, son. Keep up the good work."

Last stop, Gilda's nursery. I plopped down on the rocker, ready to read her favorite new book, *Appley Dapply's Nursery Rhymes*. Gilda was besotted with the brown mouse who stole food from the cupboard, a rodent that triggered a fit of giggles each time we read that page.

Hannah set Gilda in my lap. She was small, like Hannah, with a head of blond curls. Gilda hugged her tattered pink blanket and stuffed bear, immediately curling into her favorite position, snuggling deep into my chest, and popped her thumb in her mouth. I knew after five pages she'd be fast asleep.

Minutes later, I sat with Hannah at the dining room table. Although famished, I could no longer dodge my news.

Hannah sensed something was amiss, studying my face with knit brows. "Ben, what's going on? Your mind is elsewhere." She set her fork on the side of her plate and clasped her hands, waiting for me to speak.

I exhaled slowly as I always did before starting a major surgery, preparing to place the first incision in a precise location and then, without wasting a stroke, swiftly navigating around organs, my steady hands fixed on limiting collateral damage. I did not want to escalate the discussion and invite Hannah's dark anger. Anger that could silence us for days. "I hoped we could discuss the Medical Corps. I visited the intake office this afternoon to gauge their needs and future hospital attrition. The corporal in charge of our region spent a few hours speaking to me."

Hannah's eyes didn't shift a millimeter from mine, her body immovable as a statue, waiting for my next words. Why was she so difficult to read?

I reached for her hand. "As you know, it's been Armageddon over there, especially in France, where our boys are headed."

Her lips moved carefully. "What will they need?"

I straightened my back. I was in the meat of the discussion, but my next words would be critical, and the last thing I wanted was to hit a major artery and cause her hot anger to spew forth. "They're estimating between the medical ships, regional European hospitals, and emergency field care, the army will need upwards of tens of thousands of doctors and multiples more ambulance drivers, stretcher-bearers, and orderlies. Fortunately, most nurses already on European soil can be recruited from England and France. Their immediate need is for experienced surgeons capable of running the surgeries and supervising cases."

Hannah gripped my hand, her nails digging into my palm. Both of our dinners were growing cold. "So, they think there will be a blood bath?"

I sighed. "Darling, it's been a blood bath for years. The Allies are desperate for our support. That explosive artillery the soldiers are using sprays shrapnel everywhere, ripping apart bodies. And the gases the Germans have started using…." I paused. "Apparently, even the Allied armies are using the hideous stuff now. It's ghastly. There are no limits to how far they'll go. The gas wreaks havoc on the lungs and brain. Now American boys are headed over there."

Her jaw dropped in disbelief, just enough to allow a breath through.

I squeezed her hand again. "There's more. Apparently, for years, the big guns like Walter Reed, who have been studying the effects and treatment of gas warfare, the Mayo brothers, and Cushing, have been at The American Hospital in Paris helping, months at a time, making a difference for the soldiers. Everyone is…, but me."

There it was, out on the table. Time was ticking as I gave Hannah a moment to consider her response. My wife was no fool. Despite her reluctance to discuss the matter, somehow, she was prepared. Always five steps ahead, ready for any eventuality. That's why she had the best mortality statistics in the Obstetrics Department. But she wasn't giving me the satisfaction of letting me into her thoughts. I cringed as the realization hit. She already knew.

In barely more than a whisper, Hannah asked, "Ben, tell me the goddamn truth. Exactly when are you leaving?"

Chapter Seven: Hannah

May 1917—New York City

T he next day, in a fit of fury, I shot out of the apartment building to meet my friend and colleague, Ina, at the Biltmore Hotel for an early lunch. I craved an invigorating walk to blow off steam and someone sensible to talk with. Early that morning, I phoned Ina, arranging to meet her for a proper lunch, hoping by speaking together, I would gain a different perspective.

Although it was a long distance from my apartment on the Upper East Side to 44th Street and Madison, I decided to walk the entire way rather than hail a cab. These days, we never knew what we'd get, a horse-drawn carriage or a Model T, both fiercely competing for the taxi business, cutting each other off, with motors spooking the poor horses. Mayhem. Despite the cool spring air lingering in the morning, I broke into a sweat after ten blocks, with blisters sprouting on my toes even though I wore my most comfortable boots. When will shoe designers devise footwear suitable for women?

My painful feet compared little to my rage. I charged down the next ten blocks. How dare Ben enlist without discussing it with me first? I couldn't dissuade that man once he'd made up his mind. He thinks he's immortal, precisely like every surgeon I'd ever met. Didn't Ben realize life would go on after this war? That he alone, an older man, wouldn't determine the outcome of a global war? And what about our sweet Gilda, who won't remember him if, God forbid, he doesn't return? And our older children, who have already weathered so much loss after their mother's death? His sheer gall!

I turned east on 44th Street and slowed. Damn feet. I'd have to take a taxi home. Finally, I approached the Biltmore at Madison Avenue, breathing hard. Something about its mixed façade, its gravity and permanence, settled me. It was the ideal location to meet Ina, who would take the train into the city to Grand Central Terminal, another fortress immediately beside the hotel, with convenient entrances in the basement for nasty weather.

Ina had been my right hand, my confidante since the beginning of our careers, always supporting me through my most formidable challenges. In return, I fought hard for her too, guiding Ina through her education and career. Her life had blossomed nine years earlier after my release from Blackwell's Island Workhouse. Throughout that time, Ina remained loyal and steadfast, never doubting my innocence, even when so many were happy to see me rot in that dreadful place. Now, married to a lovely general practice physician, she lived outside Manhattan, in a picturesque neighborhood in Long Island City, Queens, commuting by train to her management position at Mount Sinai. She was living her dream. I envied the small patch of grass in her yard, where she'd planted the most exquisite roses to decorate her office all summer, while simultaneously disguising the acrid smells of the hospital. How I'd love to escape the constant clamor of the city.

Ina stood at the main entrance to the Biltmore on 43rd Street. Even against the stark granite façade of the first floor, she was recognizable a block away. Her beautiful blond hair was cut to a chin-length bob, her waves jutting out from around the edge of her hat, spraying outward in the city's crosswind like a pyramid. Ina always had a flair for the latest trends; however, since the war years overseas and the suffragists who'd marked their spartan influence on style, her fabric colors had darkened, veering toward utilitarian.

Although Ina's skirt was an attractive violet and gray tweed, her long, belted gray suit jacket conveyed that she was all business. For the last three years in England, while the young men had gone to war, women procured most jobs, and their clothing bore little femininity. Their toil kept the economy in gear, emboldening the suffragists, their influence growing, catching like wildfire on American soil. Ina, an active supporter of the movement, embraced the fashion outwardly expressing their principles. The war had pushed women into traditional men's jobs, motivating them to use their influence to drive the government closer to ratifying the women's vote. Now with hospital assignments growing in importance, she was careful to dress the part, toning down her old feminine flourishes.

Nearing the entrance, I waved. Ina returned my gesture with a broad smile of recognition. Looping arms at our elbows, we entered the Biltmore, heading directly to the main lobby, where we were greeted by an older bellman wearing a fitted red jacket adorned with two columns of brass buttons.

I asked, "Good morning. Any chance we can sit in the Palm Court for lunch today?"

He bowed deeply, casting disappointed eyes my way. "My regrets, Madam. With the staff reductions, we now serve all lunches in the main dining room. I hope you find it acceptable."

Ina and my eyes locked in disbelief. Only a month into the war, was this austerity the beginning of a new life in New York, a constant reminder our young men were abroad? In their wake, gaps were left in every hotel, restaurant, and factory. How would we support the enormous economy built at home? I was quick to answer for both of us, "The main dining room would be divine."

Although we sought the privacy of the lounge, we couldn't help but ogle at the artistry of the main dining hall, a spacious room filled with dark oak furniture, red carpets, elaborate drapery, and crystal chandeliers. The details were classic, with gilded ornamentation of birds and artfully displayed festoons draping the upper walls.

As we sat, the waiter handed each of us a menu.

Ina quickly glanced over the sparse selections, returning her eyes to the waiter. "What happened to your old menu? Is there another page?"

Dropping his head to the floor, he shyly lifted his eyes back to us. "I apologize. Last week, management decided to limit the selections to support the military needs. We must do our bit to ensure our soldiers are properly fed." He drew a full breath and launched into a well-rehearsed pitch. "We are offering two excellent options for today's fare: a succulent filet of sole roasted in wine and butter with pommes persillade, and a sautéed breast of chicken with fresh peas, accompanied by a delicious beef consommé, fruit cup, and garden salad."

I sat, realizing how New York had transformed overnight, even for the wealthy. Although the hotel façade was unchanged, life inside was braced for war, food shortages, and an all-hands-on-deck mentality. Nothing would be the same until we defeated the German army. My anger toward Ben wilted when compared against the sheer scale of President Wilson's decision to enter the war. Who was I to hold my life, my husband, and my family above millions of others? If one of the top restaurants in the city could make this sudden, drastic change, justifying their decision with their customary panache to its pampered guests, then I would find a way for the children and me to manage as well.

Chapter Eight: Miriam

June 1917—New York City

T hree weeks after our wedding, Eli and I waited in the queue at the Midtown Army Intake Center for nearly an hour. While we fidgeted in line, a soldier walked up and down the column of anxious medical volunteers, updating groups. We were not accustomed to waiting this length of time. Typically, it was the doctors who generally caused most of the waiting for others in the hospital and clinics. The war had turned the world on its head with a new set of rules. How well would we handle this distorted reality?

When the soldier reached Eli and me, his message was quick and terse. "At the intake desk, present your birth certificate, primary source credentials, and completed health form. Then go directly to the clinic for your physical examination. The next units depart for Europe in two weeks."

Dumbfounded, I asked, "That soon? When will we know if we qualify?" A niggling concern had sprouted in my gut. Would the brace be a problem?

"Yes, ma'am. That's ample time to make a will and say your goodbyes." He smirked with a curt nod, slight snort, and continued down the line.

There would be nothing warm and reassuring about serving in war. This was a nightmare come true. A cruel joke at the heels of our glorious honeymoon. I shuddered, would Eli and I ever return home, or would we be left behind on foreign soil, buried in the cold ground? This soldier did not appear to care either way.

Dark thoughts filled my head as we approached the intake table. With a chilly greeting, two silent soldiers eyed our documents and directed us through separate doors for physical examinations. Before parting, Eli leaned toward me, whispering, "Let's meet out front when we're through. Good luck."

* * *

The physician was a relic from the last century. He stood with a fishhook posture, wearing bottleneck glasses, likely resurfacing after years of retirement. Although he carried himself with an air of professionalism, I was repelled by his jagged, yellow fingernails and dusty smell. Would he touch me with those ungroomed hands? Where had the army found this man?

I changed into an examination gown and sat on a sheet of thin paper covering the cold metal table, my brace hidden in my clothing behind the white dressing screen. Although as a nurse, I knew it was unlikely I'd hide my disability, I still hoped with his bad eyesight, he wouldn't take notice.

The doctor cocked his head to the side. "Why do you want to serve? It's not safe over there for women."

I sat straighter. "It's my patriotic duty. Can we get on with this exam?"

His eyes swept down to my leg, dangling from the table, shriveled, and bent. "What happened to your leg?"

I said, "I had polio in 1916, but I'm good as new."

He shook his head with vigor. "Oh, no, you're not. Get dressed, madam. You're not going anywhere." His eyes ran down my arm, noticing my wedding band. "Married, too? Don't you know married women can't serve?"

I countered, "My brace supports me just fine."

He shook his head firmly.

"But…." I needed a chance to explain. He had no idea what I was capable of.

He screwed his face, raising his shoulders to his ears, "No. Are you daft?

34

Do you have any idea what war is like? You will be on those feeble legs for twelve hours without a break. And that's on a good day. Get dressed, and don't come back. You've already wasted my time!" He harrumphed, spinning on his feet, stomping out the door, grumbling to the staff at the outer table. "Who the hell sent a married cripple in here? Was that some sort of sick joke?"

My eyes welled with rage-filled tears as I scrambled to dress and leave. It had taken minutes to be cruelly insulted and denied. Storming to the front of the building, I waited for Eli, along the way, scattering a flock of pigeons outside the door, busy picking at breakfast crumbs on the sidewalk. How dare he treat me in such an offensive manner?

* * *

Hours later, at home, stomping about our little parlor, Eli tried his best to console me. "I know how important this is to you, but there must be other ways to serve."

I forced back tears, my disappointment and sadness near impossible to contain. "But I want to serve too, for better and worse, like our vows. We make a solid team. And I will miss you terribly." Tears broke through, streaming down my cheeks.

Eli reached for my hand, guiding me onto the couch. "Sit. I'm making a fresh pot of coffee. I'll bring some over and we'll talk sensibly."

I sighed, wiping my eyes on my handkerchief. What difference would more talking make? The dye was cast. I'd be a cripple stuck at home, worrying about Eli every minute of the day until he returned.

He brought over two steaming cups and set them on the coffee table. Eli said, "Darling, the staff at Beth Israel is draining fast. Over a third of the doctors, nurses, and others are heading overseas. This shortage may be your opportunity to rise here in New York and show them what you're made of. Beth Israel will be depending on what remains of its talent. It won't be easy managing all the patients."

I considered his words, never contemplating anything other than joining him in work, here or in France. "You're right, but I'd rather face the unknown with you than hold things together, alone."

He stroked my arm. "The war has gone on for three years. It's not likely to last much longer. And you know, it could take years to rise in the nursing rank and file under normal circumstances. Think of all the good you'll do. You and your Aunt Hannah won't be alone."

I scoffed, picking at a loose strand of thread on the couch. "Good? It's a drop in the bucket compared to saving soldiers' lives. That is the good I should be doing." But I knew he was right. I tried to shake off the whining. My childishness wasn't helping matters.

Eli pulled my chin upward. Our eyes met. "We are partners. We'll make the best of this dreadful war, and before you know it, I'll be on a ship back home and we'll continue where we left off." He drew me into his chest until I felt our bodies meld into a familiar, comforting oneness.

I gently pulled away, bucking up with a braver front. "I know you're right. How can I help you prepare?" Eager to make the most of our remaining two weeks together, I reached for my coffee cup and held it to my face, inhaling the smoky, vibrant smell. The glow of our honeymoon still heated my body. "Oh, Eli, what will I do without your lovely morning coffee?"

Chapter Nine: Hannah

June 1917—New York City

A month following the wedding, I met Miriam at Healy's Tavern. She'd called the night before, distraught that she'd failed the physical examination at the intake center. It was time to step forward and lend support. Knowing we both had the next day free, I suggested we meet in person. Healy's Tavern, one of our favorite meeting places, was midway between our homes in Lower Manhattan and the Upper East Side. When I arrived at noon, the tavern was already bustling with lunch customers.

I was relieved my niece would be staying in New York, a gift in disguise. Her father, Abe, required closer watching, and Miriam would move in with him while Eli was overseas. Since Tillie's death, Abe's health had declined, his balance unpredictable, and I doubted he was eating properly. Besides, if Miriam remained in New York, my responsibilities with the three children would be less isolating.

Healy's Tavern reeked of old New York with its rich red brick walls, dark tin ceiling, and massive wood bar at the back end of the room. The waitress recognized me, waving me into my favorite booth to wait for Miriam. While the minutes ticked by, I stirred cream into my tea, imagining O'Henry crafting *The Gift of the Magi*, scribbling furiously on sheets of ink-stained papers strewn across the table, writing in this very booth.

Moments later, Miriam walked in wearing a light wool wrap that caught my eye. Her brows were drawn with two worry lines, lips in a pinched frown. Not the happy appearance of a newlywed.

I waited for her to settle and order lunch, knowing Miriam's anger could be a difficult foe to slay. I finally said, "It looks like you and I will be keeping the home fires burning. How are you feeling about remaining stateside?" Although her disappointment was obvious, I considered it might help if she talked of her frustration. I was confident we'd support each other through the ordeal ahead. What she said next surprised me.

"I miss Mama. Why is it I think of her when I'm sad or upset? She didn't cross my mind when Eli and I were on our honeymoon. But now, I can't stop thinking about her." Her eyes drifted up from the table, meeting mine.

My heart dropped. She had caught me blindsided. "My sister was one of the bravest, steadiest women I knew, always able to pick herself up in her lowest times and still lend a reassuring hand when I needed her. It's natural to be thinking of her when the chips are down. She's been in my thoughts, too."

Miriam nodded. "Even at the end, she made the most of each day until she couldn't any longer."

The waitress set our sandwiches on the table and refilled the cups. "Is there anything else I can get for you right now?"

"I think we're fine," I answered as silence fell over the table, both of us steeped in our thoughts, taking our first bites.

My memories drifted back to that fateful morning only a few years ago.

* * *

It had been a hectic scene in Ben's and my Upper East Side apartment. Our nanny, Sophie, was whisking Ben's older children off to the Reform Jewish day school. I'd just finished nursing Gilda. At fourteen months, she preferred the enticing table food we ate, calling and reaching for toast with her grunts and crowing. But I was reluctant to stop nursing. I knew she was the only child Ben and I would have. At forty, I'd been blessed to have one. But I worried she'd steal away the last piece of my youth when I switched her to table food.

I set her on the rug, her dainty feet kicking. Gilda waddled around the apartment while I helped the other children collect their schoolbooks. "Come on, you two. Don't forget to put those lovely lunches I packed last night in your school bag. And I included Sophie's rugelach as a treat. Say goodbye to Gilda." It would inevitably take ten minutes to quiet Gilda's crying after they left.

Ben whizzed into the kitchen and, in one unbroken move, bent to kiss Gilda on the head, snatched a slice of cold buttered toast from the plate of leftover breakfast, and leaned toward me, pecking my cheek with a quick kiss. "I have a full day in surgery. Can we have a late dinner? Just you and me?"

Thank heaven, my afternoon was light. I had scheduled morning office hours in the Lower East Side Clinic and then hospital rounds at the Jewish Maternity Hospital, all downtown. Since negotiating the Women's Health Grant eight years earlier with Governor Hughes, I'd split my time between the Lower East Side and Mount Sinai's uptown maternity department while keeping pace with charts and data for the grant. The massive amount of work left me exhausted most days.

I caught his arm, squeezing it gently. "A late dinner together sounds lovely." I hoped he wouldn't be too late. My saving grace was I typically got to bed early, right after the children.

That was my life—too busy to think or dwell on problems. My daily agenda overflowed, consuming all my energy. Navigating the endless details with my young family and career absorbed every ounce of my energy.

Within seconds, the door latched, and it was Gilda and me alone in the vacuum our family left behind. Her eyes sought mine, silently pleading, "Now what?" Seconds later, her face would crumble in anguish, realizing with a devastating sadness that her entertainment was gone for the day. But today, the fates rescued me. At that exact moment, a loud drrring pierced the air. The hallway phone. Distracted from her impending howl, Gilda and I raced to the side table, reaching out to grab the receiver. Picking up my daughter in one arm and the bell-shaped receiver out of the cradle of our candlestick phone in the other hand, I replied. "Hello, Kahn residence."

Miriam cleared her throat, interrupting my reminiscing. "Hannah, where did your mind go? I'm trying to talk to you."

Shaken from the memory of that dreadful morning, I said, "I was recalling that awful day when we learned how sick Tillie, I mean, your Mama, was. Even years later, it's hard to shake."

Miriam's brows wrinkled, deep in thought. "I still think about that day, too. It was the beginning of a horrid time. I remember telling Papa to call you that morning. He was worried about the pain in Mama's belly. She'd been up the entire night vomiting and moaning. He was beside himself."

I slipped back in time to the phone call that came moments after the older children left for school, returning to the memory.

Abe's rapid breathing was audible through the receiver. He was barely able to talk.

I said, "Meet me at the Women's Maternity Hospital emergency entrance. I'm making rounds there in an hour, and I'll check Tillie first. Use warm compresses on her belly. Try to keep her comfortable."

Starting at the Jewish Maternity Hospital, where I feared appendicitis, I transferred Tillie uptown to Mount Sinai Hospital for exploratory surgery. But the fates had a far gloomier plan. As Ben observed from the galley, once the surgical team opened her and found a belly full of cancer, presumably originating in her reproductive organs, they quickly sewed her up. Nothing further could be done. Even though I, as a physician at Mount Sinai, could observe the surgery with Ben, I simply could not watch my older sister's ordeal. Ben was my eyes and ears, and I waited outside the operating theater with Miriam, Abe, and Ina. It was the beginning of the end.

Weeks later, we transported Tillie and an ample supply of laudanum to her home downtown to help her pass with a degree of comfort. Bereft didn't approach the emptiness I felt. Miriam and I sat by her side for hours each day, comforting her, propping her head while she sipped water, and administering more and more drugs to stem the vicious, unrelenting pain. As time passed, our gentle musing on past stories transformed into only Miriam and me sharing memories. Meanwhile, Tillie rested on the bed between us, listening, occasionally interjecting a minor correction in the story, but mostly dozing off. We had no idea how much she absorbed, but we were determined to fill her final time with the wonder of family, her heartfelt priority.

Supporting her body with gentle caresses, Tillie gradually shut down, shrinking into a diminutive version of her former self, her eyes sunken and skin gray. During those hours, while sitting quietly, I reflected on her generous role in my life, absorbing me, her little sister, into her tenement home as if I were the missing ingredient in her life, guiding me through my highs and lows, always determined to help me reach my full potential.

* * *

Miriam, as if hearing my thoughts, interrupted me again. "Aunt Hannah, you've been a wonderful aunt, and unlike Mama and you, who lost your mother when you were both young, I'm lucky I had mine for all of my growing-up years."

I looked at my unfinished food, my stomach souring. "I never knew my mother, but Tillie taught me well. I only wish I were as strong as she. She had a reassuring way of convincing me that everything would turn out all right."

Miriam tilted her head back, gazing at the intricate copper ceiling. "Uncle Nate is a lot like her. He has two sons in training camps in France, and it's business as usual on his farm. I don't know how he and Jenny keep their spirits up. Their family is so strong."

I tightened my lips. She was right. "We must be strong, too. And we must believe with all our heart and prayers, they will return to us when this war is over. Miriam, never forget, I'm here for you, always."

Typical of most medical workers, we found it more comfortable keeping the maudlin banter brief and slipped back into more non-emotional, factual topics.

I cleared my throat. "I still can't get over how the army arranged for hospital units to leave together and work as teams once they're deployed, like Johns Hopkins and the University of Pennsylvania. I suspect they'll be located near the American battlefields. Right now, there are Red Cross hospitals just a few miles in from the trenches." Although Ben had an inkling of his assignment, we'd no idea where Eli would be sent.

The waitress returned to our table and cleared the dirty plates. "Would you like more coffee? Dessert? We have fresh pie with early Georgia peaches, a slice of America." She paused, clearing her throat. "Lord, help our soldiers. My younger brother left for training camp a month ago. We're worried sick."

Despite the sober connection between our soldiers and pie, the thought of peaches after the long winter sounded delicious. Besides, a little sugar always cheered me.

Miriam shook her head, but I was determined. "That sounds lovely. One slice, two forks." A split second later, adding, "And a dollop of whipped cream."

Once the waitress left, Miriam asked, "Has Uncle Ben been assigned to a ship? I'm curious to learn how they're outfitted. How do they keep the soldiers in their beds when the sea is rough? I can just see them flying onto the floor." She chuckled. "He'll have to tell us when he arrives in France."

I was relieved Miriam had perked up. Like the rest of us, medicine and everything about it was in our blood, what we loved to think and talk about. There was wisdom in keeping an older surgeon like Ben away from combat. Barely shy of the age cut-off, the intake office saw his potential as a leader and surgeon, able to tackle more serious injuries needing sophisticated medical care. But Eli was another story. Young and vital, he could withstand the harsh elements of the Front. I was certain he would face greater adversity and danger.

"I think he'll be working on the ship *Comfort*. The army refitted a passenger ship, only ten years old. I believe it was called *Havana*. Now, it has an operating theater, an X-ray suite, and multiple patient care units. He'll be fine if they stay away from German torpedoes." That word, torpedo, made my skin crawl.

Miriam had stopped listening, her eyes fixed on a distant place, far from the restaurant where we sat. "All we know is that Eli will head to France. First to The American Hospital in Paris for orientation, then somewhere... far more dangerous." She flicked her hand in the air with a half-hearted shrug. "We won't know where for weeks. I figure it will be at a Red Cross field hospital close to the battle."

I felt her pain, her uncertainty. She was terrified for him. I shared the same message I told my patients when they were overcome with fear. I reached for her hand. "We're in this together. You are not alone." I took a deep breath, grappling for firmer ground. "In a few years, when the wounds of this war have healed, the four of us will visit Paris and see it at its glorious best."

Chapter Ten: Eli

June 1917—New York City

W hy in God's name did I enlist? I had covered the Emergency Room on a regular basis over the last ten years, but the few trauma cases I saw were simple, broken bones and minor burns. When we had a carriage accident or house fire, I was surrounded by a team of doctors helping sort through the victims and assisting in the operating room. I was entirely ill-prepared to take charge of a parade of battlefield trauma.

Miriam rose early with me each day, reviewing the Lancet articles I borrowed from the hospital library. Since the onset of the war, there had been a series of publications, all addressing new techniques in trauma care and infection. The machine guns and other ammunition used on the Front heightened the severity of injuries. I couldn't stop reading, terrified I'd fail. Two lousy weeks was all I had to fill my head with an entire body of knowledge. I needed a head start if I was going to save anyone.

This morning over coffee, Miriam peppered me with questions. "How are the wounds cleaned? They're coming in from the trenches, right from the filthy mud. How can you keep the operating field sterile? Do you have running water?" Miriam's face grew more troubled. The two lines between her brows deepened. "And who handles anesthesia? Or surgical recovery?"

I handed the pile of Lancets to her. "Take a look at these. This is what the British have documented as their newest methods since the start of the war.

44

Maybe some of your answers will be there."

At that moment, I wished beyond all reality she could come work at my side. The woman was brilliant. I'd been told throughout my career I had gifted hands, but knew surgical repair was only the beginning. The long road to recovery followed my end, and that's where nurses branded their mark, steering the patient clear of infection, managing pain and fever, restoring hope. I knew less than I should have of the intricacies of their realm of practice. I said, "The nurses have enormous responsibilities in the Evacuation Hospitals."

Miriam flipped through the pages, studying the drawings. "Oh my God, it's barbaric!" She sat deep in thought, then came another barrage of questions. "Tell me where the soldiers are taken after the battlefield." With the dispassionate eye of a scientist, Miriam knew exactly how to break the process into manageable bite-sized pieces.

She listened attentively as I laid out the flow of patients in detail. From time to time, she tried to interrupt, but I held out my palm, insisting she let me finish.

Miriam searched my face and said, "Let me get this straight. The wounded are first taken to a Dressing Station near the trenches and bandaged. Then they go to an Evacuation Hospital in the closest village, say five or ten miles west. That's where you think you'll be sent?"

"That would be my guess. I've read about the Evacuation Hospitals. Some house over four hundred patients after the end of battles." I looked hard at Miriam, my body sinking into the chair. "Good Lord. How am I going to manage?"

She tenderly placed her arm around my shoulders. "You will manage. But you'd better face it now; you're not going to save everyone."

I nodded, drawing a deep breath through my nose, and continued. "After we treat them, they either go back to the trenches or get transferred to Paris or England for more surgeries and postoperative care. All the serious head wounds are sent west and don't return to battle. I suppose the American soldiers will eventually return to the States on the hospital ships, like *Comfort*, Ben's ship, if that's where he ends up."

Miriam pulled her chair beside mine. "I wish I could be there with you. If you think about it a little differently, it is an opportunity of a lifetime. Medicine always advances during war. Imagine all you'll learn."

My eyebrows shot upward, horrified. "How can you say that? These men are in desperate straits. Do you think that by being a surgeon, I am going to make much of a difference? Especially with my limited skills?"

She pulled away; her eyes open in alarm. "What is it, Eli? What's worrying you?"

"I just…feel so unprepared." I tried to steady my breath, but I couldn't ignore the enormity of my assignment and my fear of failure. "I know nothing about head wounds. Next week I'm going to read more, but I've only handled a few cases in my entire career, and there are none on the operating room docket this week. My experience is from the chest down."

The corners of her mouth turned upward. "Don't be so hard on yourself, Eli. You have great hands and will learn. Besides, you'll come home a better surgeon than you'd ever become sticking around New York. Ben's been talking nonstop about all the great physicians who've worked there." She sighed. "You're going to learn so much. I hate to admit it, but I'm jealous."

She tilted her head, touching mine, her hair dropping on my shoulder. I inhaled the fragrance of her hair. Miriam's new shampoo, purchased for our honeymoon, smelled of coconut. My sadness grew. I drew a jagged breath. A wave of fear drove a shudder through my body. Despite the danger, I'd give anything to have her with me, to work with me, to keep me warm at night.

Chapter Eleven: Miriam

June 1917—New York City

One week remained before Eli and Ben's departure for Paris. I couldn't shake the mountain of sadness growing in my gut. I hated the idea of him leaving without me. Imagining the journey, I knew the two-week crossing could be bumpy in spring, and neither Eli nor I had ever been on a steamer. From the port, they were scheduled to report to The American Hospital in Paris for orientation and field training. Although Ben already knew he might return to the ship, *Comfort,* to provide transatlantic care during the war, we still had no idea where Eli would be deployed.

Upon arriving at Beth Israel at the start of my nursing shift, I immediately noticed that the number of doctors and nurses had diminished. The lobby and hallways felt half-empty. On any given day, there was a buzzing beehive of activity early in the morning. I turned the corner of the front corridor, heading to the coffee shop for a buttered roll and coffee, expecting the typical line of a dozen impatient workers. Instead, there was no line at all, and the attendant filled my order in no time. Inhaling the nutty aroma from my open mug, I shook off my trepidation. I made my way to my children's unit, listening to my footsteps echo, *kerplop, kerplop,* as I ambled through the internal maze of nearly vacant hallways and staircases.

After stowing my purse and sweater in the locker room, I entered the nursing station, expecting to receive patient reports from the night staff.

The nursing desk, usually humming with conversation and staff at this hour, was quiet. "Where's everyone?" There were only two nurses instead of the usual half dozen or more.

Nurse Sonia sat on her stool, charts piled high on her lap. She exhaled loudly, exhausted. "I'm glad you're early. This is it, Miriam. Just Ruth and me. The rest have gone to serve in France. We're hoping to get new graduates by summer."

My belly soured. How could the hospital run on such a thin, inexperienced staff? "Is this the case on every floor? Are the patients getting the care they need?"

"Who knows?" Nurse Sonia dropped her head to her stack of charts. "Let's go through last night's issues so I can get home and sleep. At this rate, we'll all be working double shifts."

The morning hours raced by. At one o'clock, the children on my pediatric ward had been fed, bathed, medicated, ambulated, and toileted, ready for a quiet hour of napping. At last, it was time for my lunch and to rest my leg.

I turned my patients over to the second nurse and left the unit, shaking off the strain in my shoulders, hoping I hadn't forgotten anything important. Between the two of us, we were each working a double load. Walking briskly to the hospital cafeteria, I sorted through my little patients, considering who we could discharge earlier than usual. Would they do as well? I turned the corner and nearly collided with the Chief Nursing Officer, Raisa. "Oh, I'm so sorry. My thoughts were still back on the unit."

She nodded. Darkened rings encircled her exhausted eyes, and untethered sprigs of grey hairs shot out from under her white nurses' cap. "There's too much change in such a short time." Straightening her uniform, she said, "Nurse Miriam, I'd hoped to speak to you today. May I join you for lunch? We'll bring our cafeteria trays upstairs to my office and speak privately."

Minutes later, seated at a small round wood table in her office, Nurse Raisa launched into the discussion. "I wanted you to be among the first to know that I will announce today I'm joining the *Comfort* hospital ship staff. I'll be leaving next week."

I set my sandwich on my plate, flabbergasted. A rush of envy shot through me. Why her and not me? "Who will run the hospital, I mean, the nurses? Who's left?"

Nurse Raisa studied my face. "Don't worry. This has been in the planning for quite some time, and I'd never leave without securing a safe plan. We'll be assigning three nurses to oversee the nursing end of the hospital. And Miriam, we'd like you to take the lead spot. Your group will work in shifts and fill in for patient care emergencies and shortages on the floors."

I tried to digest her words, but had so many questions. "Why three?"

Nurse Raisa brushed the crumbs into a pile on the table, then took a long draw of tea. Setting her ivory ceramic cup in its matching saucer, she said. "We expect more staff attrition and must ensure that we always have trained leadership, nurses who know the medical staff and inner workings of the hospital. Let's face it, what you witnessed today with staff shortages will only worsen as the American boys get deeper into the conflict." She set her cup in the saucer. "Graduate nurses won't hold a candle to those leaving to assist overseas. We'll have them work the day shifts until they are confident. Thankfully, they won't take married nurses. To answer your question, we need experienced nursing staff in the house around the clock."

That made perfect sense. I hadn't realized there was a no-marriage requirement until I went to sign up, and the newer young nurses, especially at night when the doctors weren't there, would need backup. "Where will I be assigned, and when will this assignment begin?"

"Tomorrow, you'll be assigned to the operating theater. Circulate and watch everything. We're anticipating losing more than half our staff from there." She sighed, "Additionally, we're preparing to transition two units for soldiers returning for care and have three months to prepare. The first order of business is to empty as many patient beds as we can. Every morning, after the doctors make rounds, the nursing unit managers will meet to review the census. This week, we hired a second social worker to make additional discharge arrangements. That will help with the staffing shortage in the short run. Fewer patients need fewer nurses."

The war effort was posing an enormous disruption to the day-to-day hospital functions. "How long have you been working on this? And what is your staffing plan once we begin to fill the empty wards with returning soldiers?"

Nurse Raisa wiped crumbs off her face with her handkerchief. "The Chief of the Medical Staff, the Hospital President, and I have been meeting since January, knowing this downturn in staffing was inevitable. But I'm not certain of the plan far down the road. The Red Cross must have considered a relief staffing plan. Who knows? They may bring nurses stateside for reprieves. The same nurses who've helped in the Allied hospitals abroad. Perhaps we can pull some of them into our staff." She sank into her chair. "It will depend on how long the conflict lasts. When our nurses come back to the States and the hospital is fully staffed again, working at our little hospital will feel like a walk in the park."

I spent the afternoon double-checking every patient chart on my unit, ensuring everything in the care plans, medications, and discharge planning was in order. I left follow-up concerns for the physician to review and address. Proper, thorough patient handoff was a hallmark of nursing excellence, hammered into all novice nurses from our first hour of training. Since my next assignment was the operating room, I would not see these small patients again. I didn't want to forget a detail.

* * *

That evening after dinner, Eli and I discussed complex fractures and limb amputations. He said, "There are far too many lost limbs over there. There must be more ways to spare them."

Thinking of my nursing experience, I knew the culprit was gangrene, a festering infection that, if not contained, could spread throughout the body and lead to death. The muddy grit in the trenches gummed onto uniforms and open injuries, a recipe for trouble. "From what you told me the other night about the Dressing Stations near the battlefields, the wounds should be cleaned immediately after removing soldiers from the field. The longer that trench filth sits in the open injury, mixing with blood and God knows what else, the more likely the soldier will develop an infection. Think about it, the trenches are filled with all kinds of contaminants, from horse manure to the soldiers'...." I saw no reason to beat the point any harder. He knew how disgusting it must be.

Eli nodded, his lips drawn into a firm line. "You make a good point. I'll push for an aggressive flushing station before bandaging. How else will we send our boys home with four limbs?" He stopped, his face pinched and his eyes full of fear.

I pulled my chair closer. "I wish I could be there to work with you. What is it, Eli? What's still eating at you?"

He sighed, repeating, "I'm just terribly unprepared."

I took his hand. "You keep saying that, Eli, but you will learn quickly. Believe in yourself. In a few weeks, you'll be an old hand."

* * *

That night, we made love with a fury, as if it were our last time. Fused, our hearts beating as one, neither wanted to part. War had heightened every aspect of our time together, our physical and mental connection. We'd become a passionate larger unit, connected in our brains and bodies. Cuddling in Eli's chest later that evening, fondling the brown curls covering his lean chest, I contemplated the near future. "I think I should move back with Papa while you're overseas. That way, I can keep an eye on him, and we can put this rent money aside and use it for a nicer place when you return."

He lay quietly, digesting my words. "That's probably best, but it makes leaving feel so permanent."

I kissed his neck, burrowing my nose behind his ear, inhaling his musky smell. I considered another round of intimacy. "You know that's not true. I'm just trying to be practical. It's the way I've always been."

"You are the most sensible person I've ever known. Just promise you'll save me a warm spot in this bed."

"There are no words to describe how much I'll miss you, darling. Just promise you'll come home." I slid my hand lower, roused by his response.

Chapter Twelve: Ben

June 1917—New York City

Saying goodbye was more heart-wrenching than I could ever imagine. Despite the banners and hundreds of waving flags at the Brooklyn Navy Yard, the ear-splitting brass bands playing *Over There*, and the excited soldiers marching in twos and threes up the gangway, my heart sank. What if I never see my beautiful family again?

My children's eyes were teary. Precious Gilda, with no insight into her emotions, cried in sympathy with her brother and sister. Hannah's face was frozen into a brave smile. I knew the steep price I was paying. My conviction to serve, patching up our men until the end of this atrocious war, was paramount. Scores of other families surrounded us, wives gripping their husbands in a final embrace, boys and girls saying their farewells, all of them, like Anna and Albert, growing up before their time.

Hannah had brought the children to wish Eli and me farewell as we boarded *Comfort* for France. The docks in Brooklyn were packed with so many well-wishers I feared someone might trip and fall into the harbor. Soldiers were boarding two other enormous ships. Eli and Miriam stood beside us, embracing one another fiercely, knowing it could be their last time.

"All aboard! All aboard!" roared the voice in the speaker. "Ships depart at 10:00 am sharp."

Hannah threw her free arm around me, holding Gilda in the other, squeezing me close, whispering. "Remember, you promised to come home to us." She drew a jagged breath, "And in one living piece." She pulled back to study my face.

I did the same, memorizing her lavender scent, startling green eyes, the same eyes that drew me in the first time we met years ago, and the faint crow's feet in the outer corners that had deepened from worry since I decided to join. This snapshot of her beautiful face would be imprinted in my memory, and with my family photo tucked safely in my wallet, they would all stay close to my heart during the months ahead. "You know how much I love you and our family. Remember, darling, we both have important jobs to do." I hugged her tightly for the last time.

She squeezed her lips together and nodded her head in agreement.

I crouched lower to embrace Anna and Albert. "I want you to help your Mama while I'm gone. Keep your eye on the ball in school. I want to hear great things in your letters."

Their teary eyes told me this painful separation would not be easily forgotten. They understood the importance of our separation but were wordless. Finally, Anna whispered, "I love you, Papa. I'll be a good helper." Albert echoed her words.

My neck tightened as I swallowed my tears. Having lost their natural mother when they were small, my older children had already experienced more pain in their young lives than they deserved. I hated subjecting them to more uncertainty. "I love each of you with my entire being and will come home as soon as this war is over. I'll try to write every week." I kissed them on their cheeks, pulling them into my chest.

Albert, now at an age when he often pulled away from my kisses, accusing me of treating him like a baby, held on tight, burying his head in my neck, sniffling.

"We are all frightened, son," I whispered in his ear. "But I have no choice; the German army must be crushed. There are times a man *must* do his duty."

Albert loosened his grip, wiped his face with the back of his hand, and like a little man, thrust his hand forward to shake mine. "Godspeed, Papa. Come home soon. I'll write to you every week, too." Children everywhere were afraid, growing up too fast.

I caught Eli's eye as he and Miriam parted. He sent back a slight nod. It was time for us to board. Throwing our duffle bags over our shoulders, we wormed through the crowd, away from our families, and walked up the gangplank. Once we reached the ship's deck, we turned one last time to look back. I spotted my family in the crowd of faces, their hands waving among the small American flags, already melting into a memory.

I placed my hand on my heart, then saluted the crowd.

Chapter Thirteen: Miriam

June 1917—New York City

T he pier shuddered as *Comfort's* engines roared, pulling away from the pier. The ship left mountainous surges in its wake, separating the past from the future, signaling a new period of our lives. Life without our men would leave a crater in our New York world, homes, businesses, and hospitals. Aunt Hannah and I must get busy filling the void or risk spending months handwringing, waiting, and worrying for our husbands to return. I gazed at the heavens above, the sky a cerulean blue, the sun warming the air through pillows of white clouds. Please God, keep our men safe.

Hannah's older children and I held hands as we left the pier, the ship disappearing around the bend in the East River on its journey east to dock again in Saint Nazaire, France. The trip across the Atlantic would be perilous. German submarines could torpedo any Allied ship in sight. The German army, a treacherous, faithless force, was disposed to killing indiscriminately, soldiers, women, even children, in their bloodthirsty quest to prevail. At best, it would be close to two weeks until we received the men's telegraphs of safe arrival. Could my heart last that long?

Aunt Hannah squeezed my shoulder, then placed her hand on the handlebar of Gilda's carriage. "There's nothing to be done now but wait. How about we cook dinner at your Papa's apartment? I'd like to check on him. How's he taking everything?"

I took the carriage from her, brushing a tear away with the back of my hand. "Let's switch. I'll push Gilda." I welcomed the clumsy navigation of the carriage on the uneven stone block road, its large, spindly wheels bouncing off every sidewalk crevice. Gripping the handles and steadying the buggy helped me shed the helplessness I felt.

Aunt Hannah continued as she placed her arms around Albert and Anna, "I'm sure your Papa would love to see the children. He's been lonely since Tillie passed. Perhaps it's a silver lining he has you back with him again." Hannah squeezed Anna tightly. "You'll be good company for each other. None of us should be alone in these times. Right, sweetheart?"

I swallowed hard, not wanting to explain how heart-wrenching it was to pack up Eli and my apartment and move our possessions to my parents' home, continually reminding myself that Eli wasn't dead, just leaving for a year or more. Stepping back into the world I'd left before my wedding felt as if I'd lost ground, returned to the starting line of adulthood. Mama would have told me to think of something happy and pull forward. I dug into my thoughts and reminded myself that I would save every penny I could squirrel away until Eli returned. Then we would find a wonderful new home and fill it with children. That is, if... *Stop it!* Snapping out of my sour mood, I answered, "We'll pick up something nice to cook on the way. And maybe a little cake for the children." I locked eyes with Albert. "How about you pick out dessert?"

* * *

Aunt Hannah and I stood side by side in the kitchen that evening, washing and drying the dishes. For a while, we were silent, all industry, intent on finishing dinner cleanup so Hannah could bring Gilda home in time for her bedtime routine. I didn't blame her. That child could howl like a coyote when she was overtired.

Draining the water, I said, "You were right. Dinner with Papa was a good idea. I think the trick is to keep busy. Staying productive is the way through this."

"There will be plenty for each of us to do at the hospitals. With so much staff gone, we'll work our fingers to the bone." Hannah whispered. "I'm a little worried about your father, though. When's the last time he saw a doctor?"

I shook my head. "Oh, you know him. He never complains. Since Dr. Boro passed, he doesn't trust anyone new. He thinks the young doctors are all in it for the money, that they order too many tests." I chuckled, "He said they shake him back and forth on the table until there are no coins left in his pockets."

Hannah persisted, tsking. "He's wrong. Most new tests give us more information about what we couldn't see before. I noticed this evening that his balance is terrible. He was gripping the furniture when he walked around. Can you bring a cane home from the hospital for him?"

I winced. "Why don't you discuss it with him? He won't listen to me." I'd repeatedly attempted those conversations and received a head pat in return. Papa preferred to view me as his darling little girl, discounting my decade of study and work in nursing. Were all parents like that?

Aunt Hannah snorted a burst of air, annoyed. "Well, it won't do him a bit of good if he has a heart attack or stroke and spends the rest of his days drooling in a wheelchair. Better to get him medicine now and avoid the misery later."

A tightness gripped my chest. I had to admit I'd taken my eye off Papa the last six months. With the wedding planning and uncertainty of the United States entering the war, my mind had drifted away from more mundane matters at home. Now, back in the tattered apartment, I saw firsthand the toll Mama's death and Papa's age had taken on him. It was clear, my job was here, caring for my father.

At seventy-four, Papa had become an old man with thinning gray hair, gnarled fingers, and a gentle slope in his stance. In my mind, he was always spry, playing on the floor with me as a child, interested in my schoolwork and future. He'd say, "Looks like you're going to follow in your Aunt Hannah's footsteps. You have the heart of a healer."

Mama had enjoyed recounting their first meeting. In his day, Papa was a dashing young man with a full head of dark hair, perfect white teeth, and a spine straight as an arrow. She fell in love with him the instant their eyes met. At that first meeting, Abe, my Papa, had taken a streetcar uptown to meet Mama at Opa Sam's chicken farm in Harlem, shortly before he moved to Sullivan County. Papa was sitting with Opa and his second wife, Rebecca, in their farmhouse parlor when Mama, a young girl of fifteen, made her grand entrance, practically tripping over herself when she saw his handsome face. And, if his looks weren't enough to woo her, his voice capped the deal. She described it as the dreamiest baritone she'd ever heard. Now, in his waning years, his voice hoarse and broken, those baritone notes could still be heard. That is, if one listened closely.

When they first married, Papa walked the fashion district selling buttons to dressmakers, carrying heavy bundles of sample boxes and orders to deliver, never flagging in his energy and good humor. Dressmakers greeted him with enthusiasm, checking his arms for fragrant bags of bialys and boxes of cookies from the bakery. "What did you bring for us today, Abe?"

Mama was always concerned his eye would wander. But it never did. In the months she lay dying, exchanging old stories with Hannah and me, she revealed secrets we hadn't heard. We were surprised to hear about sales meetings where she stepped out in front of him, determined to be noticed in her own right. In their marriage, Mama was the impatient one, challenging the boundaries, never happy to play the traditional wife role. Her determination to have her own business in a men-only world placed enormous strain on their marriage. It was a testament to his love that he helped her, and they endured. I wondered how many more secrets she had, ones that might help me in my marriage. Those she'd taken to the grave.

In the end, as he had always been, Papa was present for Mama, holding her hand, honoring and loving her as she passed. At that time, before my polio, I prayed someday I'd meet a man who loved me fully as Papa loved Mama.

Now, we were alone, the evidence of my all-too-brief married life stored in crates and barrels in my older brother, Julian's, empty room. I committed to sprucing up the apartment. I'd keep Mama and Papa's memories in the curio cabinet, but the clutter of chairs, low tables, and throw rugs had turned the apartment into an obstacle course. And with Papa's failing balance, it was a miracle he hadn't fallen yet. Yes, the time would fly. Between the apartment fix-up and work at the hospital, I'd be busy until Eli returned to me.

Chapter Fourteen: Eli

June 1917—Atlantic Crossing

Ben and I ambled up the gangplank onto *Comfort's* main deck, then followed directions from the ensigns to our assigned bunk rooms. I'd expected a room with two cots, much like the on-call rooms at the hospital. Instead, twelve of us were squeezed into a long, narrow room containing six pairs of bunk beds, three attached to each wall, our names set atop the mattresses. "It's a tight squeeze in here. Looks like they put me on top."

"By the time we hit the hay at night, we'll be too tired to notice. Let's hurry and unpack. I want to explore." He quipped back.

The harbor was calm, offering a chance to acclimate to the gentle rolling of the ship. Even though I grew up in New York City near the water, I'd never been on a boat of this size until today, and hadn't thought about seasickness. What if I couldn't stand the motion?

The medical team on board, over one hundred doctors, nurses, and stretcher-bearers, met in the cafeteria for lunch and orientation. The ensigns divided us by rank, and each group was led through the hospital ship on a top-to-bottom tour. My tour guide, a Red Cross doctor from Ohio, had been serving at the Front the last four months. The Red Cross hospitals had been in place since the beginning of the war. We would train with them and wait for the Medical Corps to catch up with their own Evacuation Hospitals close to the Front.

"First stop is lifejackets and lifeboats in the event of a submarine attack," said the doctor, a man in his thirties with hair shaven to his scalp.

One of the new nurses placed her hands on her hips, her face incredulous, "But we're a hospital ship. Won't they see the Red Cross markings?"

The doctor answered, "Forget it. The Huns don't care about red crosses, polka dots, or black stripes. They shoot torpedoes for sport."

My stomach turned sour, recalling the clipping I read earlier in the year when the Germans made it clear they'd attack any enemy, no matter who or what the conditions. I leaned toward Ben, whispering, "Who are we kidding? This ship could be the end of us before we land in France."

The tour continued. "Next stop, infirmary. Empty for now, but not for long," said the doctor. "And if you're wondering why I shaved off my hair, well, you will too when you see all the fleas and lice at the Front."

I'd never seen anything like it. Beds and furniture were bolted to the floors and walls; nothing stood on wheels as in a standard hospital. Several identical wards were scattered throughout *Comfort*, a ship capable of handling hundreds of wounded soldiers. I could only imagine men in all stages of recovery tied to the beds, so they didn't flip onto the floor.

"The condition of the soldiers we send home is shocking. You rookies have never seen anything like it." The doctor pointed down to the floor. "There's a central area for supplies and charting down below."

I held onto the steel bedframe as the ship picked up speed. Now in the open waters of the Atlantic, the craft was pitching, the sea taking us up, up, up, and releasing the ship into a free fall, crashing into the bottom of a swell. I broke a sweat, the stuffiness of the ward closing in on me, my lunch returning to my mouth. I no longer registered anyone's voice. I ran from the room to the outer deck and heaved over the railing, gulping in the sea air, desperate to resettle. I wasn't the only one at the rails. Searching right to left, there were three others, all as seasick and humiliated as I was. *Buck up, Eli. Get back inside. This is nothing.*

I finished the tour without further incident, and no one commented about my brief absence. The center of the craft, the most impervious to sea movement, was reserved for the operating and X-ray theaters, one on each floor. Still, I stood, shifting my weight from one foot to the other, turning to Ben, whispering, "You're supposed to hold a scalpel steady in rough seas? Lord, help the wounded men."

Ben, sensing my jitters, placed his hand on my shoulder. "Eli, we'll both get used to it. Think about what they've done here—a full-service hospital. It's damned amazing."

But his words did little to calm me. He would most likely be deployed to this ship working, spending weeks on end stateside. But for me, I was facing a more terrifying unknown, near the trenches, with no end in sight.

The remaining days were spent in classes, absorbing everything known to mankind about trauma. After a decade of surgical practice, I was reduced to a student, studying war medicine. Our instructors were a sturdy lot, Red Cross physicians and nurses on respite from the Front lines. It was hard to fathom that a rough sea filled with German torpedoes was considered a holiday. These men and women had seen the worst of the carnage. And as much as they attempted to temper their descriptions of injuries, I was increasingly terrified, finding it difficult to sleep at night, lying awake for hours, listening to the others snore.

After docking, Ben and I would travel by train to The American Hospital in Paris for further orientation. The Red Cross and academic hospitals, together with their medical students and residents from all over the United States, had been working at this prestigious hospital in Paris and at the Front since 1914, furiously seeking ways to improve infection control, anesthesia, and reconstructive surgery; dealing with the spiritless soldiers whose minds and emotions had been shattered by the battles.

At breakfast, the seventh morning on *Comfort*, Ben remarked on the deep circles around my exhausted eyes. "I'm getting worried about you. Want me to see if I can find something to help you sleep at night?"

"I can't take sleep medicine. We're approaching enemy waters and must stay alert if the alarm sounds." I grimaced at the picture in my mind. "Although it would be a relief to sleep through an attack. Nothing to fear or remember."

Ben shrugged his shoulders. "You need to find a way to get used to this. I hate to say it aloud, but I think it's going to get much worse from here."

I answered, not believing my words, "Well, at least we'll be on land."

* * *

By the Fourth of July and the grace of God, we arrived safely in France after nine torturous days at sea. We were told it was a smooth crossing, but for me, with my head in the toilet most days, it couldn't have been rougher. The saving grace was the absence of German submarines. Without patients on board, much of our extra time had been spent in class and practicing safety drills, only adding to my disrupted sleep, always on the ready to evacuate the ship.

Finally, the train reached Paris after a half-day ride and a quick taxi trip. Ben and I stood on the sidewalk, gazing in disbelief at The American Hospital. "Get a load of the size of this place," I said, rotating my body to capture the sheer scale of the buildings along the avenues.

Ben was as wide-eyed as me. "It makes Bellevue's one square block back in New York look like a sandcastle. I hear its nickname is The American."

I led us into the main entrance. "How are we ever going to find our way around?"

"On ship, I was told it grew from thirty-some-odd beds to six hundred beds and then jumped to two thousand in just a couple of years, all filled with soldiers requiring care of one type or another. It's a small city, with ward upon ward of wounded."

Once directed to our sleeping quarters, the first afternoon was free. Just under two weeks confined to walking the small transatlantic ship left us both restless, eager to stretch our legs. Ben said, "Let's take a walk around the city. We can eat at a local café and practice our French. Besides, it may be a while before we get another chance to explore."

Within two blocks of the hospital, I fell in love with Paris. The charm of the intricate architecture and wide boulevards, broken with glorious parks and gardens, was more picturesque than I'd imagined. The peonies, delphiniums, and campanulas were in full bloom, filling the air with nose-tickling fragrances. It was no wonder a deep sense of patriotism prevailed. Who could possibly hand this priceless historical city to the Germans?

We walked beside the Arc de Triomphe, stopping to admire its size and significance. "There's no monument in the United States that quite compares. It's a magnificent honor to those who died in their revolution," Ben said.

"We must bring our wives here after the war when the city is restored. I can't get over the sense of history everywhere I look. I'd always pictured a smaller, more provincial city. I could not have been more wrong."

Ben nodded, his eyes drinking in every inch of the gorgeous views surrounding us. "The Arc de Triomphe is the gateway in. The French are nothing if not a proud people."

After stopping for coffee and a pastry at an outdoor café, we strolled through the Luxembourg Gardens. I asked Ben, "Tell me what you know about The American Hospital. You've been reading the newspapers since 1914. How did it grow to a grand size in just a few years?"

Ben shoved his hands in his pants pockets, jiggling his loose coins. "All I know is from reading the *Daily Express*. With all the newspaper censorship, it prints the most details about the battles and medical care. It's where I learned so much."

I scoffed at myself. I'd been preoccupied with my life and career in New York the last three years. It was a good day if I read the headlines.

Ben turned my way, eager to dip into his well of knowledge. "The hospital opened soon after the turn of the century, I think it was 1906, mainly to offer American expats access to hospital care if they needed help. Some of the very rich donated building funds so their children playing polo would have a place to get patched up after a bad fall. Originally, it had twenty-six beds. Can you imagine?"

I was dumbfounded. How could a hospital possibly grow at such a speed?

As if anticipating my question, Ben continued, "As soon as the war began, the hospital was repurposed for the war effort, and a brand-new boys' school on the neighboring blocks was acquired to add more beds."

"My God, that must have cost a fortune. Where'd the French find the money?"

Ben shook his head. "It didn't come from the government. It came mostly from private donations, big and small. Some of the same families who donated in the first place, the Morgans, Vanderbilts, and that crowd, put in thousands, but the Red Cross raised a fortune back home and here in France and England for beds and supplies. And that's not the half of it. Most of the staff works for a pittance or volunteers. The French have been desperate for our support from the very beginning. Did you know we helped them start their ambulance service at the start of the war?"

I shook my head. Not only would I need to learn volumes about trauma, but my knowledge of the war was barebones at best.

Walking, block after block, it was impossible to ignore the many homeless and dismembered veterans wearing tattered uniforms, leaning on crutches against walls, begging for change. They surrounded every famous landmark and were stretched out on benches in the parks. Ben and I handed out our loose centimes for food and coffee, knowing that their needs stretched far beyond.

I digested Ben's words, proud that despite America's late official entrance into the war, we'd been supporting the Allied countries from the start, helping care for the wounded. "Now it's our turn to do our bit." I looked at an armless man sleeping on the grass. "But, Ben, what will become of these homeless veterans? They deserve better than this."

* * *

The following morning, another physician from the Red Cross, Dr. Conner from Boston, took us on a thorough tour of the facility. As we walked through endless corridors, he pointed out the organization of the patient wards. "We've bedded the patients by the type and severity of injury. The soldiers from France and England are mixed." He chuckled, "Maybe we'll finally learn each other's languages. One good thing to come out of the war."

We walked through the fracture ward. Traction devices were attached to each bed, an army of men wrapped in plaster. Bed after bed, hundreds of men were hoisted in all levels of suspension, unable to use the toilet. The stench from unwashed bedpans permeated the air. Finally, I could not hold my thoughts inside. "Why don't they keep the place cleaner? It stinks like an outhouse in here."

Dr. Conner tisked, "It was worse in the winter with the windows closed. Know any more nurses back home who'd be willing to come? We never have enough hands to keep up. At one point, a couple of years back before the last expansion, we were bedding men on the floor."

He had effectively silenced me. Unlike my smoothly run Beth Israel, each day at The American would present a new challenge.

Next were the chest and belly wards, most men lay half covered and feverish with nurses and orderlies scrambling from bed to bed to change bandages and administer medications. The sheer volume of devastation left me dizzy.

From the first building, we crossed the street to another where soldiers with head and facial injuries recovered. Like the other wards, hundreds of men with heads and faces wrapped in thick layers of white gauze lay in bed, some tied to the frames. Ben parted from the group and began walking through the ward, stopping to speak with an occasional patient. Moments later, he returned to us. "There are so many complex injuries. Who's handling the surgery?"

Dr. Conner nodded. "I oversee this ward. I originally came with Dr. Cushing from Harvard when I was a resident. He helped set protocols for the brain injuries. Since then, I joined the Red Cross to stay on.

Ben's arm swept across the ward. "We don't know enough about head injuries in New York. I'd love to speak with you more about your findings. Can function be restored after these devastating injuries?"

I leaned toward Ben, softly commenting, "There's a massive amount to learn." I couldn't help but imagine their conditions when they were pulled off the battlefield. "I've been studying trauma for the last month, but had no clue it was this tragic."

The next day, we ate sandwiches and coffee at lunchtime behind a partitioned section in the cafeteria, listening to the Chief of Surgery overview the critical medical discoveries since the war began.

"We've made three notable advances: ambulances, anesthetics, and antiseptics. Let's take each separately." The Chief elaborated, discussing the importance of speed from the battlefield to medical care, and with the introduction of both motorized and horse-drawn ambulances, significantly more lives were being saved. In addition, with the introduction of blood transfusions and X-ray suites, soldiers were stabilized before bleeding out, and surgeons could locate shrapnel that was impossible to see from the patient's exterior."

Ben raised his hand. "I couldn't help but notice the vast number of amputations. Is there something we can do to spare more limbs?"

The Chief cleared his throat. "That brings us to the third, antiseptics. Our field surgeons face two problems. First, the trenches are filthy. That's putting it in gentlemanly terms; filth like you could never imagine without seeing it firsthand. There are rodents, death, disease, human and horse waste throughout the trenches and battlefields. The bandaging stations on the edge of the battle never have adequate water and antiseptics. Wounds are often bandaged, dirty, and left for the Evacuation Hospitals to deal with."

Miriam warned me about that situation. My hand shot up without hesitation. "What is the second problem?"

The Chief tilted his head to the side and rolled his eyes upward, sighing deeply. "Old and tired doctors don't want to spend the time and effort to save limbs. They want to save the maximum number of lives, but that often translates to fast amputations, moving the patients through at a quick clip. Remember, surgical speed in the field is crucial. You'll have unimaginable decisions to make. The pressure is mindboggling." He looked down, hesitating before continuing. "None of us were born to play the Almighty. But in war, the job of the surgeon is to save as many lives as we can."

Ben and I were dumbstruck. There must be a better way than turning the surgical suite into a butcher shop. But we held our tongues. We would talk more in private.

Later in our room, Ben's eyes were ablaze with agitation. "These soldiers here in this city of hospital beds and the scattered homeless made it off the battlefield alive. The War Office didn't tell us what percent died, but last I read, since the war began, the mortalities were approaching one million. To hell with *Comfort,* and ferrying wounded soldiers home. I'm staying in Paris. This is where I'm needed most."

I was left with two inescapable thoughts. First, fear or not, my decision to help our men was the right one. I was confident I would learn enough medicine to save lives. But to do that, I needed more time to train, here at The American Hospital with the best surgeons in the world. "Ben, how do you suppose I get permission to spend more time in Paris? I want additional trauma training before heading to the trenches."

He shrugged. "It's not a bad idea, but it sounds like they're desperate at the Front."

As things turned out, I was one of many requesting the same delay to the Front for the exact same reason. Most fresh physicians shared my concern about trauma inexperience. But instead of insulating us at The American Hospital, where we could methodically build surgical trauma skills, we were sent to assist the surgeons in the field hospitals surrounding Ypres. We would learn fast and under fire at the Front. The British army had secured the Messine Ridge, and a battle to retake Ypres was imminent. With it came a desperate call for additional surgeons. I packed my bags the next day, placed my wedding photo atop my clothing, drew the duffle bag cord securely, and climbed aboard the train heading to the Western Front.

Chapter Fifteen: Hannah

June 1917 - New York City

Like a knife cutting through time, our life at home was sliced into two parts—before Ben left and after. The sweet harmony and normalcy of our old home, balanced with two parents in charge, had turned into a nest of moody children. They sensed the shift, acting out their fear and anger. I knew they were afraid. Their teachers reminded us they were not alone; truancy and fighting among the boys grew daily. Young girls cried over petty disputes. Both Anna and Albert had lost their usual interest in studying.

I tried to patiently let the days pass and give them room to adjust. The school year was almost over. With summer, I hoped the children would relax and stop feeding off each other's fears. I sat with them at dinner most nights, attempting to draw us tighter as a family. But there was no way to calm Albert. It didn't help that Ben's first letter from Paris was far from the elixir needed to reduce tension in the house.

At dinner that night, Albert sat opposite me in Ben's seat. I had assigned it to him while Ben was away, hoping to build his sense of importance, but it was having the opposite effect. He was near hysterics, nostrils flared, his arms flailing. "What if Papa doesn't come home? Half the boys in my grade have fathers who left for war. We all know some won't return."

Stunned by his comment, I asked, "Why are you bringing that up now at the dinner table? You're upsetting everyone, Albert. We'll talk about it

69

later."

He jumped from his seat, shouting, "I don't care that we're eating. Why aren't you more upset? Don't you love Papa anymore?"

Anna's eyes clouded with tears, pleading, "Could that happen? What will we do if he dies?"

Hearing the words aloud made my ears ring with a harshness I could not accept. "Of course, I love your father. But I refuse to think that way. He's not a soldier and is not in France to fight. He'll be stationed in Paris, far from the battlefields, helping the wounded. Besides, I shared his telegram with you, that he made it through the most dangerous part, the trip across the Atlantic. He arrived safely in Paris last week."

Albert crossed his arms, his eyes turned to his plate, staring blankly at his cold chicken and peas. "I'm not hungry."

Anna chimed in, pushing her chair away from the table. "Me neither."

Gilda cried, fully aware things were amiss, reacting to the charged emotions around her.

I struggled to pull them out of their moods, but my nerves were raw, too. "I miss him, just like you." I paused, seeking a way to lead them out of their panic. "I have an idea. Let's all share a story about Papa. He's probably missing all of us right now."

Although at first it was like pulling teeth, we took turns sharing memories. Before we knew it, a hesitant smile swept across Anna's face, recounting the time they went ice skating in Central Park and Papa deliberately slipped on the ice to show her falling didn't hurt. I then added to her story, reminding her that after skating, I'd examined his leg, and he had a tender purple bruise. Finally, we all sang one of Gilda's favorite bedtime songs, and she called out, "Papa's song, Papa's song."

We sat, finishing the meal, far more settled until I announced, "Albert and Anna, I'd like both of you to spend an hour on your schoolwork tonight. School is almost over, and I'd like to end with strong grades. I'll check your work after I get Gilda to bed."

Albert snapped back, his earlier calm shattered, "You never checked my work before. Why now? Don't you trust me?"

I shot back, my voice stern, standing eye to eye with him, "Because your teachers tell me you haven't been completing your assignments. You know full well your father expects you to keep up your grades. We all have a job to do. Your job is school."

Albert picked up his plate and silverware and stormed into the kitchen, crashing everything into the sink.

"Come back in here, Albert. I'm not done yet." I forced my voice to soften. "I'm going to post a letter to Papa at the end of the week. I would like to include a short note from you and Anna along with mine. Gilda will draw a small picture."

Anna spoke, recovered from Albert's outburst, "Can I draw a picture, too? I've been practicing flowers."

"Of course," I answered. "I'll ask if he can send a telegram reassuring all of us that he is settled in, and all is well. "Will that make you feel better, Albert? For all I know, he may have to pull some strings to get permission to write a telegram."

Albert's eyes filled, his anger diffusing. "Yes, I'd like that."

I leaned toward him, my eyes full of understanding. Innocent as children or, like me, full of adult dread, we were missing him. "Me, too. But I can't promise. I have no idea what it's like there. In the meantime, once school is over, I'll take you both to Uncle Nate's farm for the summer. It will do all of us some good to get out of the city."

Anna pleaded, "Mama, can you spend the whole summer there with us? Do you have to come back to work?"

I smiled. Anna was always two steps ahead. "Darling, I wish I could take more than two weeks off, but Gilda and I will get underfoot. Besides, my patients need me here. Uncle Nate will give you morning chores, and you'll swim at the pond in the afternoon. It will be lovely."

Albert said dryly, "I can't wait."

Was that feigned excitement or an inkling of joyful anticipation I heard in his voice?

Chapter Sixteen: Miriam

July 1917—New York City

L ate June marked a month and a half since Eli left for France. The
city sidewalks, filled with women, children, and the elderly, were
the only clue that life in New York City had changed. The men
had evaporated into the war machine overseas, and we were left behind,
grappling with a new reality. The air had warmed, and the sun's rays were
sharp. I pulled my straw hat tight, using the brim for protection. Walking to
the hospital, I felt pleased with the work I'd completed in Papa's apartment.

The weekend after Eli left, I spent my time ridding Papa's apartment
of hazards, rolling the carpets, putting them in storage, and polishing the
parquet flooring with a careful eye for edges that could catch the toes of
his shoes. The heavy brocade drapes from winter were removed, and all
the windows were washed until they glistened in the natural light. Then
I hung the white summer lace curtains Mama had bought years earlier.
I cleaned the settee and Queen Anne chair upholstery and switched out
Papa's bedding for the lightweight quilt in greens and yellows sewn years
ago by my step-grandmother, Rebecca. If only I could change the wall
covering. Mama loved the Victorian botanicals. Her choice had been wall
after wall of heavy green leaves. But the fashions had changed since she
first decorated in 1890. I promised myself that after Eli returned and we
found our new apartment, I would decorate the walls with gentle yellow
bouquets set against a striped background on the paper. It will remind him

of Uncle Nate's farm, his favorite stop on our honeymoon.

By the time I finished, I knew Mama would have been pleased. The apartment, while considered large when they first moved in, looked twice its size with the clutter and dark colors removed. Perhaps I'd discuss new wallpaper with Papa, but it would need to wait until after the war, when the workmen returned.

Papa may have been old, but he was no fool. He watched me apply the finishing touches, moving small tables out of the traffic flow and replacing the lace armrests on the chairs. "*Bubala*, what do you plan to do now that you've turned our home inside out?"

I approached him with care, determined to respect his pride. "I'm going to be working long hours and may not be home with you often. I'd like to find someone to cook meals for you and perhaps accompany you on a walk every day."

He waved me off. "No need, I'm fine on my own."

I'd expected this initial reaction. He was a proud man. "Of course you are, but Mrs. Nadelmann on Six needs something to do. I ran into her daughter yesterday, who asked if I had any ideas for her mother. She's a great cook, and this might be a good arrangement for all of us."

He eyed me appraisingly. "You think I need a nursemaid? How much does she want?"

I sighed, "Of course not, but I worry you'll be lonely when I'm at work, and I want you to eat properly."

He stormed, "How much?"

"Oh, Papa, stop shouting. Only the cost of food. Can't you let anyone help? Mama spoiled you, and she'd be very disappointed you're making me worry at work when I have so many sick patients to care for."

He shrank in his chair, rubbing his fingertips in thought. Finally, he lifted his eyes to mine and, to my great relief, nodded.

* * *

The hospital was a madhouse. With no ebb in patients and fewer nurses and doctors, we struggled daily to keep pace, sending many patients home or to convalescent homes earlier than we were normally comfortable. I began every shift in the Nurse Executive Office I shared with my partners, Esther and Julia, inventorying the new and discharged patients, any unanticipated issues, and unresolved problems. The three of us came from different medical backgrounds, but between us, we had an in-depth knowledge of the entire hospital. Esther had spent five years in the emergency end of the house, or so we casually called the hospital, and was an expert at triaging illnesses and injuries, assigning the sick to beds, the operating room, and the X-ray suite. Julia had worked in adult care for the last twenty years and knew as much as the physicians about heart attacks and other nonsurgical conditions. And my experience in pediatrics and now surgery, rounded out the patient services. We each took an eight-hour shift, staying longer most days to fill staffing holes on the nursing floors, routinely surviving on less than six hours of rest. It was exhausting. How could serving overseas be any more taxing than this?

Dragging my hungry, weary body home after my first double shift, I noticed a sheer envelope on the side table inside the front door. It was marked, "OAS", On Active Service—no postage. The postmark was stamped "Paris." It was the first letter I'd received from Eli. A wave of relief ran through me. Hopping with excitement, I almost lost my balance. I took a deep, steady breath, a technique I'd learned while recovering from polio, and hobbled by Papa's room, opening the door a crack to ensure he was sleeping comfortably, holding the letter to my heart while I walked into the kitchen to sniff out the leftovers Mrs. Nadelmann left behind for me. I fixed a small plate and carried it to my bedroom.

Moments later, supported by pillows behind my back, I sat on my bed, savoring Eli's letter while I picked at cold chicken from a plate balanced on my lap. His letter was already two weeks old.

July 4, 1917
My dearest Miriam,
A day doesn't pass without thinking of you. I gaze at your picture

before I sleep and again when I wake to remind myself there is true beauty in the world, and it awaits me after this conflict ends.

We arrived at The American Hospital in Paris today, and I will remain here (more on that behemoth of a hospital later) for one week before shipping out with scores of other doctors and nurses for the French field hospitals. You see, the Red Cross has been running many of these hospitals for quite some time. The American field hospitals won't open until General Pershing is ready to send our boys into combat. He's been adamant U.S. soldiers receive six months of training, at least two on U.S. soil and three or four here in France, before they head into battle. Trench warfare comes with its own skills—none of which our boys have. He also wants them to fight together as a unit. In the interim, American doctors and nurses will work with the Red Cross, treating Allied soldiers.

I had a brief orientation in Paris to learn more about trauma and new advancements. Otherwise, I'd have no hope for many of the wounded. I am told they arrive in our makeshift field hospitals in dire shape, barely clinging to life. Our job, my job, is to tilt the balance in their favor and get them on a train to Paris for more repair.

I don't want to alarm you, but reports at home are understated in magnitude. We've been getting the bare facts back in the States. See if you can pick up the war paper, Stars and Stripes, written by the U.S. soldiers. You might get a truer insight.

I expect I'll be working from dawn until the last injury most days. God knows if I'll ever sleep. But I will save those last waking moments to think of you and your warm, loving body. For now, my mind replays my first impression of the wards, scores of injured soldiers lining every unit. Their young, forlorn faces. For those we lose, the great sadness inflicted on their families is immeasurable.

Perhaps I'm too tender-hearted, but I am who I am, and knowing I have your love keeps me forging ahead, helping me face tomorrow.

Did you notice there was no stamp on the envelope? Mail is free for men-at-arms. If only they could deliver it to you faster. One day, our

planes will cross the North Atlantic without refueling in Greenland,
and mail will fly from my pen to your heart. My next letter will come
from the trenches.
   With all my love,
   Eli

I set the letter on my nightstand and turned out the light, thinking all the while about Eli's words. I knew he tempered the news, not wanting to frighten me. How horrid the truth must be if the newspapers were doing the same. I wondered how far his field hospital would be from the trenches. Would he hear the artillery explosions? How I wished I could be there to help and reassure him. It was his tender heart I loved so dearly, one he revealed to very few. I knew many doctors had hides so thick one couldn't help but wonder if there was a beating heart beneath their skin. But not Eli. All that carnage must be terrifying, its impact on the men and their families—beyond anything I could remotely imagine.

   Lying there, drifting into sleep, his words startled me awake. The Red Cross! Why hadn't I thought of that? I had given up after that damn doctor dismissed me at the Medical Corps Intake Center. Would the Red Cross take me? Would they get me over to France? But what about Papa? Could I possibly leave him on his own?

Chapter Seventeen: Ben

July 1917—Paris

I n no time at all, I fell into a routine. Grateful Hannah and the children were tucked away safely in New York City, far from the fighting, I pushed them to the back of my mind, shifting my daily thoughts and energy to the surgical challenges awaiting me.

My long career had been spent in the realm of general surgery, mostly dealing with the abdomen and broken bones. With the massive number of facial and head wounds arriving from the battlefield, hundreds at any given time, it was a once-in-a-lifetime opportunity to learn something new. The patients who made it to Paris were the survivors, the ones who passed through the filters of death on the battlefield, bandaging stations, and transit. Our job was to give them a decent chance at normalcy, no doubt a daunting, at times impossible undertaking.

Immediately after Eli left for the Front, I spent my days in the surgical observation area, watching the skillful hands of the reconstructive surgeons. Dr. Gillies had left Queen's Hospital in London, his own head and face hospital, to demonstrate his new grafting techniques in Paris. I watched from my bench in the gallery, observing his delicate work rebuilding faces, noses, and cheekbones from transplanted bone and skin grafts from the thighs and buttocks. I was so absorbed in his surgical prowess the hours flew by while I furiously took notes, skipping lunch most days. I didn't want to miss a crucial step. After one week, I was determined to join his team. Their techniques would be invaluable at The American after he left and later in New York.

Friday afternoon, after a ten-hour session in the operating theater, I followed Dr. Gillies into the outer hallway. Tall and slender with a mop of unruly brown hair, Dr. Gillies, a man in his forties, leaned his body toward mine. As he studied my face, his eyes, edged with bushy brows, held an intelligent intensity.

I extended my hand. "It's an honor to meet you. I'm Ben Kahn, Chief of Surgery at Mount Sinai Hospital in New York. Your work is brilliant."

A slight smile crossed his lips. "A Yank. Welcome. We could use your help, here and in the trenches." He paused a moment as if unsure he should say more. "I must ask, and I mean no disrespect, are many of the chaps they've sent your age?"

I hesitated a moment, for the first time feeling old and outclassed. I forged on, laughing lightly. "No, they found me in the ancient forest of surgeons who can't seem to hang up their aprons."

He joined me in laughter, giving my hand a firm shake. "I meant no offense."

Now it was my turn. Would he accept an "old chap" like me? "Although I expect you to fill your team with young bucks who have a career ahead of them, my hands are steady, and I'd like to join your team while you're in Paris, if you'll have me." I hesitated, clearing my throat. "Both to help our men here, but also to bring your methods back to the States after the war and improve what we offer burn patients and facial wounds in New York."

His smile, beneath a moustache barely covering years of poor dental care, broke across his face. "Let's catch some supper and talk." He looked at his wristwatch. "The cafeteria is open for another hour."

We filled our trays with stew and roasted vegetables, heavy fare for a warm July evening. I asked, "Do the French eat like this year-round?"

Dr. Gillies shrugged his shoulders. "Don't really know. Only been here a month, and they serve something different each day. They sure cook better than the Brits. French cooks can make leather taste good."

My curiosity sparked. "Where are you from? You accent is unusual."

"Ah, you picked up straight away. I've been working on fixing my New Zealand accent for years. 'Tis where I grew up. Came to the Queen's country for medical school. Cambridge."

It amazed me that he traveled half the globe to learn his craft, unlike me, who never left the little island of Manhattan for my years of education and work, until now.

That evening, I wrote to Hannah, filling her in.

My beloved Hannah,

I have learned that in the horrors of war, opportunities arise. As of tomorrow, I will be joining Dr. Gillies' surgical team, first as a gopher, then as I prove myself, as a full surgeon. Before I operate, he insists I meet the patients on the floor, become fully acquainted to the point of friendship. I admire how concerned he is for their well-being. He has removed all mirrors, claiming they are more of a deterrent than help. I need to learn what kind of lives the men are returning to and help set their expectations. Some are comfortable using masks and can't tolerate more surgery. I will cull those patients out and send them to the prosthetic unit.

I feel like a resident again, young and thirsty to learn. His work with burns and facial reconstruction is well documented in The Lancet. Although everyone from the States who comes here does so to lend help, so many doctors are like me, seeking new skills to improve care when we return. This is a once-in-a-lifetime chance to work shoulder to shoulder with the greatest doctors from all over the globe.

Speaking of which, Cushing's team from Harvard is returning this fall. I hope to follow him around when he arrives. His advanced care of brain injuries has already saved many.

Tell me the news of the hospital and give Albert, Anna, and Gilda an extra kiss for every day I'm away. I'm saving yours for when I return.

With my eternal devotion,

Ben

Chapter Eighteen: Eli

July 1917– Western Front

After a week at The American Hospital, I was among forty-eight U.S. doctors, nurses, and stretcher-bearers who boarded a stripped-down train in Gare L'Est, the main military train station in Paris. Duffle slung over my shoulder, I entered the men's bunk car. I spotted an orderly smoking a cigarette, blowing the fumes out the open window, and asked him for a tour.

He flicked his cigarette butt out the window. "Be happy to, mate. You a doctor? Where from?" He extended his hand. "Orderly Cummins here," he said in his Irish brogue, offering his small pack of Bull Durhams. "You want a smoke?"

I shook my head despite the alluring smell of tobacco.

Cummins had a hint of whiskers. Built like a lanky adolescent, he couldn't have been more than eighteen years old. "The British manufactured most of the trains, first for their boys and then for the French. Can you believe they only had twelve trains at first? With the thousands of poor lads getting dragged off the field, they've been building them ever since the start."

"Do the German aircraft leave them alone?" I asked.

"God no. The Huns take shots even with the red mercy crosses painted on the roof."

There wasn't a safe corner in this entire country, I thought as we strolled through empty cars, all with collapsible cots bolted to the train walls, soon to be unlatched later for the wounded. Much like the hospital ship, the train was outfitted to operate like a full hospital, keeping the soldiers alive until they reached a safer location. Now, three years into the war, with all the kinks worked out, they had a smooth system in place.

Cummins leaned against the sliding cabin door at the end of the car. "There's nothing like the sight of these trains filled with wounded. We put the head wounds and shell-shocked in a separate car from the others. They're either screaming or silent as night."

As he talked, I imagined those men on their way to Paris, still bloodied, scared beyond reason, wondering what ill deeds they'd committed in their young lives to deserve such a hell-like fate. I exhaled uneasily, eager to move on. "Anything else?"

"Just the kitchen and staff bunks. We cook for the long rides, the ones going to the Channel for boat transfers back to England. You'll get sandwiches and coffee today."

I shook hands with Cummins and walked back to my travel car, settling in for the five-hour ride to Ypres. From the train station, I would be driven to the Evacuation Hospital and expected to see the wounded right away. The Battle at Messines Ridge was winding up, and those casualties were ambulanced directly to the local hospitals.

The train pulled into the station at one in the afternoon. The disembarking process appeared chaotic, but was, in reality, quite organized. My medical team was directed straight away into automobiles for the Front. As we grabbed our duffle bags and climbed down the steps onto the train platform, we were greeted by scores of moaning wounded, lying in stretchers, waiting to be carried aboard. Behind us, inside the train, we could hear the cots clanging and banging in a percussive rhythm as they were released from the wall, relocked with a clip into their open positions. It was clear they'd gone through this drill many times.

Soldiers directed me into the back seat of an extended Model T. Without a pause, it set off for the Evacuation Hospital, bouncing over the pitted roads. I thought my head would snap off from all the jostling. Dr. Martin, a surgeon from the Cleveland Clinic team in Ohio, who came to the Front on behalf of his Chief Surgeon, Dr. Crille, sat beside me. His assignment was to obtain an earlier view of the wounds making their way to the larger, more sophisticated hospitals in France, England, and The American Hospital in Paris. Martin was trialing limb repair procedures. The volume of amputees now filling the sidewalks of London and Paris was mounting, alarming the public. We were all seeking a better solution.

I asked with as much tact as I could muster, "What do you expect to see that you can't see in Paris at The American?"

He shrugged his shoulders. "Dr. Crille is frustrated with the volume of amputations. His team has developed an antiseptic approach that may make a difference. I'm on a fact-finding mission to see whether using his advanced cleansing technique immediately after injury will reduce gangrene and save more limbs."

I thought back to Miriam and her suggestion of a flushing station. Perhaps Martin could use her idea. I cleared my throat to get his attention. "My wife's a nurse stateside and she was curious about the wound cleaning. Are there flushing stations close to the Front? You know, at the Bandaging Stations?"

Martin scratched his jaw. "A nurse, you say…yes, she has a point. We could sure use more trained nurses here. Hang onto that idea for now. It's a good one."

The car pitched and bounced down the rutted road. Martin struggled to hold his hand steady while he lit his cigarette. "If you'd like to work with me, we can test Dr. Crille's approach together. I could use a second surgeon."

I nodded; my lips drawn tight in determination. Despite my trepidations about limb repair, something I'd never attempted, working with Martin might be the right place for me to start. We bumped along for another hour, Martin detailing the surgical steps he planned to use while I memorized his instructions.

As we approached Ypres, the green spring flora vanished, leaving in its place charred trees, stumps, and dust from the roads—all vestiges of prior battles. The villages had been leveled, turned to rubble, priceless edifices destroyed, stained glass windows shattered. The country markets had disappeared along with the cheerful crowds of families and passersby. The only sign of life was an occasional disoriented-looking man or woman stumbling about. A mule. A chicken.

Finally, I asked, "What the hell happened here? Aren't the front lines miles to the east?"

Martin's brows crumpled. "Don't you know the Germans advanced to forty miles of Paris when the war began? It took everything the French and Brits had to muscle them back east to the trenches. Thousands of men died. Many villagers, too."

Shocked, I'd never considered the impact of war beyond the medical. Entire communities, centuries of civilization reduced to rubble, leaving a whisper of the life that came before. Where had all the people gone? Exhausted and discouraged, the French had sacrificed their homes, lives, and futures to save their country. Every meter of soil recovered from the Germans was a small reclaiming of destroyed land. A sobering victory.

My stomach turned with apprehension. Would our troops be ready for the trenches in time to win? Already two generations past the Civil War, none of our boys had ever seen battle. Their practice with guns amounted to little more than shooting cans off rocks. With the required six months of training, General Pershing was running out of time. Could the ragged British and French hold the German army at bay that long?

Turning into the center of Ypres, I heard distant explosions, crackling artillery, frantic horses neighing. Martin sat alert, eyeing the eastern roads. Plumes of smoke rose in the eastern sky. The smell of burning gunpowder and sulfur permeated the air. Another layer of dust added to the filmy air and road. Through the haze ahead, the outline of a large building appeared. Its façade was pockmarked with shell holes; chunks of the roof were sheared away.

As the car drew closer, the rumbling erupted into an ear-splitting cascade of explosions. Horses reared in fear. Honking motorcars tore down the hill from the eastern battle into town. Men screamed orders. There was a frenzied beehive of activity on the gravel sidewalk in front of the stone edifice. Orderlies unloaded stretchers from motor ambulances and horse-drawn carts, setting them on sawhorses and the ground, waiting for doctors and nurses to inspect the wounds. Nearby, bodies awash in blood lay silent, attracting a swell of flies.

As my eyes grasped the apocalypse, the coppery smell of blood filled my nostrils, suddenly turning my stomach. I opened the car door and heaved onto the road until I was empty of lunch, gulping for air. My ghastly nightmares over the last two months were a meek version of what lay before me.

Martin, unaffected by the carnage, gave my back a reassuring pat. "Takes a while to get used to this." He held out his cigarettes, lighting one for himself. "Here. Have a smoke. It'll help settle you."

My first cigarette. I'd always thought smoking was a filthy habit, but now, in the thick of battle, somehow it calmed me. "My first."

"But not your last. You can trust me on that," Martin said. "Stick close, doughboy. These soldiers are coming in from the Ridge. That battle should be winding up. Let's hustle inside and get assigned. We'll see where they need us first."

I drew a swig of water from my canteen, rinsed my mouth, and spit it out on the gravel. Shaking off my queasiness, I followed Martin into the building. A nurse met us, her smock smeared in blood, face splattered in crimson. "Reinforcements from Paris, I suspect? About time! We're still getting wounded from Messine Ridge." She pointed to the corner of the room. "Drop your gear over there and come with me. Tables are about to turn. I need help sorting the incoming. I'm Nurse Helen." She hurried past us.

There would be no gracious introductions, fanfare, nor teatime. Martin and I grabbed aprons to tie around our waists, ready for her instructions.

We followed at her heels, quickly examining the men. Cards were set on each stretcher. The wounded were ranked by urgency, body organ, and some who sadly awaited the pile of deceased bodies. It couldn't have been more opposite to the hours spent diagnosing and recording Time of Death back in New York. A thought plagued me. What if we are wrong? There didn't appear to be any double checks.

A crimson hand caught my wrist. The soldier cried out, *"Yankee Docteur, sauve ma jambe!"*

Nurse Helen answered, *"Nous ferons de notre mieux."*

"What did you say?" I asked.

"We'd do our best." Nurse Helen handed a tourniquet to Martin while she cut away the soldier's pant leg. "Get this on him, he's bleeding like the fountain in Trafalgar Square."

The three of us bent over his leg. Barely anything left to save. It was sheared through most of the muscle, clinging onto his knee joint by a few bone fragments and a stringy sheet of muscle and tendons. Mud encrusted the wound. Could it be saved?

Nurse Helen muttered, "Too little to save."

But Martin shook his head, shouting into the operating area. "The bone and blood vessels are intact. We're bringing this one in. Get ready to put him under." He turned to the soldier and said, "Time to say your prayers."

* * *

We finished our cases hours past dinner. My hunger came and went while we concentrated on the leg. Once flushed and debrided until there was not a spot of filth, I began retracting muscle while Martin delicately inspected the blood vessels, working his way around the torn muscles and bone. We repaired layer after layer of the limb in a brave attempt to save the soldier's leg.

Our operating table was an island in a sea of pandemonium. Frightened, wounded men carried in and out of the operating theater, calling to God and their mothers, in English and French, to whomever would listen, begging to be saved. I lost my concentration, dizzy from the clamor, twisting my head around, watching the frenzied circus.

Martin, fully focused on the patient, shouted, "Eli! Eyes on the leg. Nowhere else. We save one patient at a time. Get it?"

Calm passed through me as I mentally cut out the noise, concentrating on our small piece of the maelstrom surrounding us. *You can do this. Eyes on the leg. Eyes on the leg.* Mid-afternoon turned into evening, and with it, the heat in the building rose, making the air hard to breathe. Sweat poured from my body into my clothing and surgical cap until it could be wrung out. With no available nurse to wipe my brow, I resorted to my sleeve. Soon, my face was covered in smeared blood.

As we closed the skin, Martin stepped back from the table. "We've done all we can. Let's keep him here to recover for a few days before sending him to Paris. I want to see if Crille's approach with the antiseptics keeps infection at bay. He may not get full use of his leg and will need a cane, but if his prayers were heard, he'll keep the leg."

Despite my bloody costume, a surge of satisfaction filled me. But that feeling didn't last long. The Surgeon Commander of our Red Cross hospital, Dr. Clarke, stood by his patient at the next table, glaring at us. He barked as our patient was lifted off our table. "Big cheeses! Now we've got a line out the door. Keep them moving through." He turned to the orderly at the door. "Get the next one onto their table. Those two big shots are wasting precious time."

Chapter Nineteen: Miriam

July 1917—New York City

T he case was taking an eternity. I shifted my weight onto my healthy leg, hoping the pins and needles would dissolve if I changed my stance. Dr. Silver was as slow as a turtle in the operating room.

"Close off the stump, Doctor. The blood vessels are sewn tight," Dr. Silver instructed Dr. Bell, the Beth Israel resident. "It's a shame the man lost his foot. With his weight, he's going to have trouble getting around."

Before starting the case, I had gathered the gauze wrappings for the wound from the supply closet and set them on a cart by the wall of the operating room. I wheeled the cart directly beside the table. Mr. Krinsky was our first case that day, and it had taken all morning to amputate and repair his stump, the longest amputation procedure I'd witnessed to date. Deep infection had seeded in his right foot despite our past efforts, soaking and ministering medications. Sadly, his left foot didn't look much better and could be facing a similar fate.

Diabetes was a death sentence. His wife had tried putting him on the standard starvation diet to curb disease progression, but he wouldn't cooperate. The man craved food day and night, scouring the cupboards when everyone else had gone to bed, eating the worst dreck from street vendors, all to satisfy his relentless cravings.

The resident and I set to work, stretching and sewing muscle over the exposed bone, then closing the skin on top. "Do you think he might benefit from a prosthetic foot?" I asked, hoping the surgeons had a postoperative plan for the poor man.

"I don't know. Let's first see how this stump heals. In the meantime, find out where prosthetics are sold in the city," Dr. Silver answered.

What are these doctors thinking? They better start figuring out how to handle missing limbs, and fast. By year's end, they would be dealing with scores of otherwise healthy, young soldiers returning from France with missing arms and legs. I made a mental note to discuss this topic with my nurse leadership team. Our surgeons had their heads in the clouds. As usual, the nurses would need to think beyond the operating theater and hospital for them. I imagined we could have a prosthetic service located here at Beth Israel.

We finished bandaging the remains of Mr. Krinsky's lower leg, and the orderly wheeled him into the recovery area. I headed to the basin at the side of the operating room to wash.

Dr. Bell was at my heels. "Silver has another case and told me to meet with the family. Would you mind talking to the wife with me? I don't think she's going to take the news well. She was hoping we could save the foot." Bell looked at me pleadingly. "A female touch wouldn't hurt."

What a coward! I forced a smile. "Of course. Her name is Mrs. Krinsky. She may want to know more about his recovery and how to help him. Isn't diabetes the central problem? How do we get that under control? If you discuss his underlying disease, then perhaps he'll be able to keep his other foot." After all his training, he should have learned to see his patients and families as actual people.

He shrugged his shoulders. A smirk crossed his face. "I have no idea about diabetes. I'll leave that to the internist to explain. They're supposed to handle those diseases. Our job, in a nutshell, is the surgery."

I huffed. What a crass attitude. It seemed as if all the talented doctors had gone to France, leaving behind a skeletal crew of second-rate physicians, all in a hurry to get on with their days. How could Bell care so little about the plight of his patient? Furious, I dried my hands and left the operating room, walking beside him to the waiting area where Mrs. Krinsky was sitting with her adult children.

As we approached her chair, an expansive but impressively short-statured family jumped up in unison as if connected by a rope. Mrs. Krinsky stepped in front of the cluster, her arms reaching out to us, hoping for good news.

Dr. Bell, in an apparent rush to announce the outcome and depart, said, "Mr. Krinsky is resting comfortably in the recovery area."

At that point, Mrs. Krinsky threw herself into his arms. "Tank you, tank you, bless you." She quickly pulled back, imploring in her Slavic accent, "He still has foot, yes?"

Dr. Bell took two steps back. "Er, I'm afraid the foot was too far gone. He's better off without it. Nurse Drucker will take it from here. I'd like to go check on him." Without waiting for her response, he spun around and headed down the hall to the charting room, not the recovery area where his patient rested. The family, of course, had no clue.

I drew a deep breath, my nostrils flaring, furious with Dr. Bell's spinelessness, and said, "Please sit, and I'll go over the plan with you."

The basic medical facts prompted tears from every family member. While Mrs. Krinsky sobbed hysterically into her handkerchief, two of her daughters wrapped their arms around her. I waited for my words to soak in and for their eyes to shift back to mine. Although it broke my heart to hurt them, they needed to know the truth. At this rate, their Papa would not be around too much longer. His disease was fatal and progressing with great speed.

Stunned, the family arranged themselves around Mrs. Krinsky. Finally, it was silent, everyone hanging on every word, until one of the sons asked, "Can we see him now?"

As soon as his words spilled out, the entire family cried out, a chorus of, "When can we see him?"

"When, when, when," echoed in my ears. After my quiet concentration in the operating room, the cacophony of the family made my head throb. Attempting to retake control, I extended my hands, pumping them up and down, the sign language we often used with non-English speakers, and said, "Let me explain how he's feeling and what will happen next."

I took Mrs. Krinsky's hands, holding them gently. "We're in this together. Diabetes is a very difficult disease to manage, but for now, he's through the surgery and resting." Addressing the others, I said, "I will take your mother back to see him for only a moment, but after that, take her home, make dinner, and get some rest. Come back in the morning, and your father will be ready for a short visit. Keep your spirits up. He is going to need your love and support."

Mrs. Krinsky and I stood, leaving her children behind in a buzzing knot of concern. We walked down the hall to the recovery room. "Just a short visit, no more than a kiss on the cheek, and then you go home and put your feet up. It's been a long day for you."

She stopped, placing her hand on my cheek. *"Tank you, darlink. Tank you."*

Simple kindness put families at ease, even under the most trying circumstances. And knowing they weren't helpless, that they would have our support with Mr. Krinsky's recovery and his remaining time on earth, one that could be full of hope and love, gave them purpose. Eli was a natural at the compassionate side of medical care. Why was it so difficult for these surgeons?

* * *

By late afternoon, after getting the Krinsky family on their way, I rounded with the lead nurses on each patient unit and checked the Emergency Department for complex, unscheduled admissions. Afterwards, I returned to the Executive Nursing Office for the change of shift report. The office secretary had left a small pile of messages on my desk. The slips of paper were held in place by a metal paperweight, a small sculpture of two humble hands in prayer. How apt a symbol, I thought as I shook off my fatigue, hoping to make it home for dinner with Papa, the first time this week.

Taking each message one by one, I began calling the floors to follow up. All went smoothly until I called the second-floor ward. The head nurse was beside herself.

"A problem with the husband? He showed up drunk and tried to hit her?"

90

I repeated after the nurse on the other end, who reassured me the police had been called and the problem was resolved for the moment. "You made all the correct decisions. Call security right away if he shows up again." It seemed that these types of violent incidents had grown in number since the war began. Everyone was on edge.

The next few were simple reports concerning flies, jammed windows, and water temperature. The warm summer weather always brought a litany of complaints, the most common of all, flies. I called the workshop in the basement and asked for more fans and flypaper to distribute throughout the house, and a routine check on all the trash cans, window jambs, and screens. Finally, my eye caught the last message from Mrs. Nadelmann. "Call home."

* * *

Mrs. Nadelmann answered on the first ring. "Oh, Miriam, I hate to disturb you at work, but I'm concerned about your Papa."

A wave of dread weighted me in my chair. My voice panicked, "What's wrong? Tell me!"

Mrs. Nadelmann began crying. "I've been waiting all afternoon by the phone for you to call."

"Calm down. Take a deep breath. Tell me if he's all right." I tried to breathe. Maybe hiring an older woman was a mistake.

I heard her fill her lungs. She said, "We had a nice lunch, egg salad, pickles, and challah—a little mayonnaise on the side. I tasted everything, and nothing was spoiled. You have a good icebox."

"Mrs. Nadelmann, what happened?" I asked with growing urgency.

"We talked while we ate, then took a stroll around the block. All was fine. Abe stopped and chatted with Moishe at the deli. They were both laughing at jokes. Then we came home for his afternoon nap."

I might have had more patience with her verbal meandering if we weren't talking about my father, but my impatience split through, and I raised my voice. "Mrs. Nadelmann, can I speak to my father?"

"Oh, no, dear. That's the problem. When he woke up, he wasn't right."

"What do you mean, wasn't right?"

"He can't talk. His lips move, and he grunts, but no words come out."

Oh my God! He's had a stroke. I shouted into the phone. "I'm dispatching an ambulance. Have him ready to go!"

II

PART TWO

"We are the dead. Short days ago
We lived, felt dawn, saw sunset glow,
Loved and were loved, and now we lie,
In Flanders fields."

Excerpt, In Flanders Fields—John McCrae

Chapter Twenty: Hannah

September 1917—New York City

I thought I'd never get out of the apartment this morning. Between Albert's foul mood and Gilda's fussing when she saw me dress in my customary belted work suit, it felt like I'd already spent a long day at the hospital before setting foot out the door. I finally trudged to the third floor of the hospital, entered my office at Mount Sinai, and turned on the lights. Was it my imagination, or did the corridors smell of urine? I thought cynically, *where were the housekeepers? In France, too?*

Glancing at the thick appointment book on my desk, I saw a jam-packed day, probably with no break for lunch. Last week, the administrators had pulled my assistant to help with, what I was told, more critical areas of the hospital. So, I was left managing without any support. Maternal services always had to claw for every dollar, with a disproportionately low budget. Now, I was stranded on my own with a full caseload of patients. Every day, I prayed for the end of the war.

I called the Labor and Delivery Unit, wondering if any of my patients with advanced pregnancies had been admitted before dawn. The phone rang and rang. No answer. I'd have to run up and see for myself.

I was winded after running up the stairwell to the sixth floor, aggravated but not surprised to see an empty nurse's station. Searching for the attendant, I checked the linen and equipment storage closets and found a nursing student refreshing towels. I said, "Good morning. Where's the charge nurse?"

Seeing me, she stood straight, adjusting her cap. "Good morning, Doctor Kahn. The last I saw Nurse Edna was in Delivery Room 4. We had a rush of laboring women early this morning. It was something about the moon, they said."

I sighed. From the beginning of my training at Johns Hopkins in Baltimore, I'd heard enough old wives' tales from patients to fill a two-inch textbook. When would the superstitions end? And from a nursing student, no less? In a voice more strained than intended, I said, "Study your books. It's not likely the moon had much to do with it. Let's hope they were all full-term."

As directed, I found Nurse Edna at a patient's bedside in Room 4. Opening the door, I signaled for her to join me in the corridor. Once out of earshot, I said, "Good morning. Can you give me a rundown of patients on the unit? Do you have ample support?"

Nurse Edna grunted in frustration, shaking her head slowly, "We have a unit bursting at the seams and are down to half our staff, like most floors around the hospital. They all took off to serve in the war.

"It's the same story in all the hospitals," I said.

"A few mothers are Dr. Shaw's patients, so he's been tied up with them. But we have no anesthesiologist, so we're delivering the old-fashioned way. As you can imagine, mothers aren't happy without pain medications." Her shoulders and chin sagged like a rag doll as a hysterical scream erupted from a nearby room. "It's going to be a long day."

"I'm sure you're right about that. Are any of my patients on the floor?

Her eyes, already bloodshot with fatigue, appealed to me. "Not yet, but we can use your help if you have time to spare."

I thought through the list of patients in my appointment book. Who could be postponed? "Let me reschedule my afternoon patients, and I'll be up after lunch. But call immediately if there's an emergency."

Back at my desk, I circled patients in my calendar book who could wait to see me and made calls, confirming no immediate issues, and pushing their appointments later in the week. After half an hour, I'd moved all my afternoon patients, clearing my way to help in Labor and Delivery.

By the end of the morning, without the help of a receptionist or nurse, I was dizzy from handling two jobs. In the brief moments between patient exams, I answered the phone, ordered labs, and scheduled follow-up appointments. Finally finished, I made tea and ate the sandwich Sophie had slipped into my briefcase a few hours earlier. She knew me well. If I was hungry enough, I'd find a moment to wolf it down.

Mindlessly chewing my cheese sandwich, I decided I must speak with Ina about securing more support. How dare the administrators take staff from the women's departments first? Most of us had stayed home while the men left. And many of my patients had been left pregnant by their husbands, who were now overseas. It would be several months before the birth rate dropped. Was this the ultimate farewell gift to the women of New York? For them to give birth without our customary support and then raise their children without a father at home.

* * *

Arriving in the delivery suite ready to assist, I was immediately directed to a patient room. I washed and introduced myself to the nurse and patient. Mrs. Berger had been in labor all morning, exhausted from the pain and her screaming. From the foot of the bed, I examined her. It was almost over. "Time to push, Mrs. Berger. Your baby's crowning."

She grimaced. "I can't! The pain. I want to die."

I placed my hand on her lower belly, waiting for the next contraction, ignoring her words. "Catch your breath a moment and follow my instructions." A moment later, her muscles contracted. I shouted, "Now! Push. Push. Push."

She succumbed to the overpowering urge and bore down as hard as she could, simultaneously squeezing, while roaring out in a convulsive fit. "I'm gonna kill my man if the Huns don't get him first!"

The baby's head appeared. Almost through. "Take a few deep breaths. I see a head of brown curls. Let's meet your child on the next push."

Moments later, Mrs. Berger's baby slid from her body onto the warm towel. In seconds, he found his voice, his squeal cutting through the moaning of other mothers on the floor, a heart-rending reminder of the joy following such extraordinary pain.

"You have a lovely boy and he's a good size, too." I cut the umbilical cord and wrapped the infant, handing him to his mother. "Excellent work."

Mrs. Berger held the child to her breast, kissing his head, grateful tears dripping down her cheeks, her anger forgotten. Looking up over the infant, she asked, as if I held all the answers, "Do you think he'll ever meet his Papa? He's been gone three months."

I caught my breath. Having birthed Gilda, I knew the torturous feat she had just experienced. Birthing babies without anesthesia was not for the lily-livered. But what do I tell her? I smiled back. "Take a picture when you get home and send it to your husband. He shouldn't have to wait until the war's over to see his little boy."

My words calmed her and gave me a new idea that might reduce the apprehension these war mothers felt. I would add it to my list of discussion topics with Ina. Besides pleading for more help in the women's units, I'd request a photographer to take pictures of mothers and babies and mail them to their fathers in France. At the hospital's expense, of course. It was the least we could do to lift morale.

* * *

Hours later, when I returned home, I walked in to find Sophie putting dinner on the table. She had held off the children's meals, and everyone was hungry. The savory aroma of roasted chicken awakened my stomach while evoking childhood memories of my Papa and his poultry farm. We ate chicken most dinners on the farm and later at Tillie's home on the Lower East Side. But this evening my children were famished, wiggling about in their chairs, tired of waiting. I called out, "Dinner smells lovely. Let me wash my hands, and I'll join you." I grabbed the mail on the sideboard before entering the lavatory, noticing a military letter from Ben and a note addressed to me from the school. I brought both to the table.

"Chicken, again?" Albert complained, his face pinched in annoyance. "Why do we always have to eat chicken? I'm sick of it."

I clenched my teeth, annoyed at relinquishing my joyful feeling. I had rushed home to make it in time to eat together. Why wasn't Albert ever happy to see me? We all missed the variety of dinners we were accustomed to.

Sophie began to apologize, but I interrupted. "No, Sophie, this is not your fault. Albert, you know full well that the city has food shortages, especially beef. Stop complaining. You're not a child anymore."

Albert shoved his chair away from the table, its legs scratching against the wood floor, and stood abruptly. "I'm sick of hearing about the war. Why are we fighting anyway?"

Anna began to cry. "I miss Papa. When is he coming home?"

Infected by the mood, Gilda began crying, too.

I set the mail on my plate and walked behind Albert, placing my hand on his shoulders. "Look around you. See what you've done? Everyone was about to enjoy a hot dinner before your outburst. Settle down, fill your belly, and be grateful for our lovely meal together. Many in this city don't have our blessings."

His eyes darted to my plate. "Is that a letter from school? And is the other from Papa?"

I stood firm, realizing he'd handed me my last weapon in this argument. "Sit down and we will read them after dinner is done, not one moment before."

He sat and pulled his chair into the table, lips tightly drawn, appeased. But he did not take his eyes off the letters.

After dinner, Sophie took Gilda for a bath, and I opened the letter from the school, scanning it quickly. I exhaled sharply. "Albert, they would like to meet with me to discuss your outbursts. What is all this fighting with the boys? I don't understand."

Albert eyed me while Anna sat silent. "I'm defending Papa."

I scrunched my face. "I don't understand. Why do you need to defend your father?"

Anna said, "The other boys call him a coward because Papa isn't in the trenches fighting with their fathers."

My heart sank. Little by little, this war was chewing away at our decency here at home. New mothers in the delivery room, preoccupied with their infants, would never meet their fathers and classmates at school, so worried about trench warfare, they couldn't concentrate on their lessons, instigating homegrown skirmishes instead. Only a couple of months into the conflict, we were experiencing food shortages. How much more collateral damage would we experience before the war was through? Only a fool could think this terrible conflict was confined to Europe. We were fighting on the home front, too.

In a hurry to dismiss the school note, Albert pointed to Ben's unopened mail. "Would you read Papa's?"

I picked up Ben's letter, but before opening it, said to Albert, "We're not done discussing your fighting. We'll talk about it later. I need time to think." I used a knife on the table to open Ben's letter and read it aloud.

> *August 5, 1917*
>
> *To My Precious Family,*
>
> *It is almost four weeks since I arrived at The American Hospital. Every week or so, one of your letters makes it to me. I've received three so far and reread each one before I turn in at night. That way, I sleep with a full heart.*
>
> *My days are busy from the moment I wake until late at night when I rest my head on the pillow. I fall asleep thinking about each of you and am saddened by the treasured times I'm missing. Will you have grown so much I won't recognize you when I return home?*
>
> *As I mentioned in my last letter (I hope you received it), I am working with Dr. Gillies' team, caring for soldiers who've had extensive head and facial injuries. These are the men who live to make it to us for reconstructive surgery. Sadly, there are those who don't make it to Paris. We use many innovative techniques to improve the appearance of these brave men so they can return home with pride. There's nothing*

quite like it in New York, so I hope to add a department at Mount Sinai when I return. This will give our burn patients far more hope.

Dr. Gillies takes an unusual approach. He removes all mirrors from the ward, knowing that the men's appearance after surgery and during healing can be devastating. Instead, he ensures everyone on his team continually engages with each patient, getting to know them and working to build their confidence so they can seek a productive life when they return home, even though they may be severely maimed.

Anna interrupted. "What does 'maim' mean, Mama?"

"Injured beyond full repair," I answered.

She tilted her head to the side. "Not 'good as new' as my doctor says?"

Albert interrupted. "Yes, dummy, let her finish reading."

I sighed. "Albert, you know better than to speak that way. Now apologize."

"Sorry," he mumbled.

I continued,

I am surprised by the number of American Red Cross volunteers here in Paris. So many young men and women have been in France for months, even years, helping in the war effort, mainly behind the trench fighting. One of my patients, Bill, William Conover, from Philadelphia, worked as an ambulance driver. His ambulance was a specially outfitted Model T that could carry three stretchers to the Evacuation Hospital on one run. A few months ago, his ambulance was hit by mortar fire and tumbled over the side of the road. Fortunately, it was empty, except for him. If it hadn't been for the next ambulance driving behind, he could very well have been left for dead, but the brave drivers worked like mad to pull him from the wreckage, and now he is here with me in Paris. We're rebuilding his left cheek and eye socket, so he will look presentable with a patch. Pirate patches are in fashion here at the hospital, as shrapnel has a way of finding sensitive areas of the body to injure.

"Ick, that's disgusting," Albert shouted,

I glared at him. "That's enough. Do you want me to stop reading?"

He looked down and shook his head.

Bill and a group of his pals had taken a year off from Harvard to help in France, thinking it would be the adventure of a lifetime. I'm sure he had no idea of the extreme danger. To me, he's a hero. Over the last year, he saved countless lives, packing the wounded in his ambulance and driving them to safety. Now, he will go home with a permanent reminder of his sacrifice.

He told me his girlfriend stopped writing, so we try to keep his spirits up. Letters from the States are good medicine. Anna and Albert, perhaps your classmates would like to participate. If you'd like, I can send some other names of American soldiers who could use a lift in morale, and your class can write to them while they heal. Knowing the children of their country both honor and miss them works a special type of magic in their attitudes and healing.

Hannah, as much as my heart aches for all of you, I am where I'm needed most right now. I know your strength will keep the family knit together and guide the children through this terrible absence. Please give them extra hugs and kisses from me, and tell me your plans for the holidays. Any chance you'll be going back to the farm?

With all my love,

Papa

I gently set the letter on the dinner table, sighing as my heart hurt for Ben. A moment later, I watched Albert, studying his sad face, his eyes hooded and full of shame. Anna's face was wet with tears. "What do you think about Papa's idea?" I asked.

Anna wiped her cheek with her dinner napkin. "Why would his girlfriend stop writing to him? That's so cruel."

Albert grumbled, "Because he's ugly now. His face was blown off."

"Maybe she's just scared to look at what happened to him," Anna retorted, her voice rising in anger. "He was trying to save people, Albert." She turned to face me, fear crossing her face. "Would you still love Papa if that happened to him?"

I bent my head to the side, amazed at Anna's depth of understanding and Albert's obtuseness. "What do you think? Do you think our beauty is only on the outside of our bodies?"

They both shook their heads slowly.

"Albert, your father may not be fighting in the trenches, nor should he be at his age. But he's ministering to men who are miserably hurt, helping them recover and improving their appearance so they can be happy when they return to their families. Let's pray he never has to repair any of your classmates' fathers."

Albert looked at me, beginning to assemble the pieces of war. "Could that happen, I mean, to my friends' fathers?"

"War is a terrible thing for people of every age, but it's the worst for children like you because you must find a way to manage a new fear, far worse and more real than pretend monsters in your closet. The boys in your school have let their fear bubble up until they practically explode from worry. Instead of admitting they're afraid, they call each other names... and pick fights." I took a moment to let my message sink in. "Your father is very brave to be in France, fixing the wounded, and the other boys' fathers are brave, too. God knows how much danger they face every day. Papa needs us to stay strong while we wait for him to come home. Do you think you can try harder to do that? For him?"

Albert nodded, finally understanding. The anger left his tone. "Yes, Mama. I'm sorry. I'll talk to my teacher about writing letters to his patients. Maybe that will help the soldiers."

"I will, too," echoed Anna. She sat for a moment and then turned her moist eyes to me. "Mama, could you find out if there are girls with no faces? Maybe we can write to them, too."

Chapter Twenty-One: Ben

September 1917—Paris

With a furled newspaper tucked under my arm, I strolled across the courtyard to my cluster of patients sitting beneath the horse chestnut trees. I called out to the British and French soldiers, "Top of the morning, bonjour!" I was greeted with a grumpy mixture of hand flips and grunts. It had been a miserably hot night in the hospital, and I assumed they'd had little sleep.

Today was Saturday, the sixth successive day of September temperatures in the upper nineties. Longing for a breeze in the courtyard, I couldn't wait to get out of the suffocating hospital. In a few hours, Paris would unleash its midday heat, driving the patients and staff to their wits' end. Far more vicious than New York summers, the hospital wards felt like furnaces, dragging everyone's mood down. Staff and patients were cross with one another despite the nurses' best efforts to open windows and arrange fans for a faint breeze. The smell of sick humans, a uniquely putrid mix of bodily odors, also attracted a platoon of flies.

After breakfast and daily physician rounds, the nurses wheeled my parade of patients outdoors into the courtyard for fresh morning air, and if they could tolerate it, modest exercise. Most sat in their wheelchairs drinking water and tea, some with straws, others with spoons. We were always encouraging the men to drink more. Those with damaged or missing jaws were at constant risk of undernourishment and dehydration.

To maintain my sanity when I wasn't scheduled in the operating room, or in the procedure area inspecting and debriding wounds, I joined my patients outdoors in the shade. Not only was it the only reprieve from the intolerable heat in the wards, but interacting with the soldiers gave me unexpected insights into their personalities, helping me understand them in surprising ways.

My ambulance driver, Bill, was the only American in a crowd of a half dozen mummy-like figures, some with eyepatches and others with entire bandage-wrapped heads. Although I knew there'd be more like Bill joining the head ward once American troops hit the trenches, he held a special place for me. If the times had been different, I could have been wearing the patch, missing my right eye and upper cheek. Like Bill, I'd been eager for adventure during college. The exhilaration of war led many young, courageous Americans to volunteer. Not a combat fighter by nature, Bill, like many of his American contemporaries, drove ambulances to support the Allies. But nothing could protect him from incoming fire. Bullets were indiscriminate, ravaging anyone and anything in their paths. No matter, the Germans didn't care, ambulances, hospitals, trains were all targets to them.

Dropping onto a bench beside the group, I opened my newspaper. "Has anyone seen the latest?" I asked. Discussing war news was the opening topic of our morning chats. It somehow softened the men for the subsequent discussions, the more heartfelt, important topics.

"Does it say anything about what's happening in Russia? I hear they have their own civil war going on," called out a patient in a wooden wheelchair.

"Let me see if I can find the story." I rifled through the pages, scanning each, pretending I hadn't already read the entire paper cover to cover. "Ah, yes, here it is." I began reading the article aloud. At the rate things were going on the Eastern Front, it was a matter of time before Russia threw in the towel. They had an internal war upending their country.

Loud groaning came from my right. Daniel, one of my British patients, brutally injured, had lost the better part of his lower right face and with it his speech. He grunted through his bandages. A soldier handed him a pencil and paper. While he scribbled furiously, I watched him write. I read his message to the group. "Bad for us. Huns will send their soldiers west."

A chorus of agreement ensued. Bill muscled in, "Pershing is running out of time. He's getting fresh troops by the day from the States, and it's time to send his first round into battle. That'll scare the Germans good. Don't worry, fellas, we've got you covered."

Murmurs of approval followed. It amazed me that despite their wounds, their suffering, their limited futures, they continued to rally behind the cause. The commitment to victory bound them together tightly.

Out of the corner of my eye, I noticed one unfamiliar patient in the cluster, sitting in a wheelchair two yards behind the others. I was certain my surgical team was not caring for him. From the looks of his bandages, his body appeared intact, but he'd suffered extensive head wounds. Dressings had been wrapped around most of his face and head, leaving open slits for his mouth, nose, and one eye. A tuft of blond hair sprouted through an open space at the top. He remained silent.

For the next half hour, we worked our way through the news, one headline at a time, until the air grew still. It was at this point of the morning that I turned the conversation to matters of home. "Speaking of news, has anyone heard from family or friends?"

The men sat quietly, sipping their drinks, shuffling their slippers in the dry brown grass. Finally, Daniel wrote on his pad. "I'm good at maths. My mum thinks I should study accounting."

I looked at him straight on, right in the eyes. "You are blessed with one fine mother. She's watching out for you. How do you feel about her idea?"

He kept scribbling while I read, "She wants me to have a purpose. She knows I'm sad."

Bill yelped, igniting the crowd. "Damn sure she's right. We gotta all have a purpose when we go home or we'll be hiding from the world, hitting the drink."

My chest filled with excitement. At that point, an air of magic transformed the men. These brave fellows still had fight left. One after another, they shared ideas and new dreams for professions: mechanic, factory worker, farmer, writer. I listened, awestruck, to these incredible men talk about purpose, about finding work and meaning again. An inner voice, one that never gave up, called to them, pulling each to find a reason to forge forward. It was the next step in clawing their way to recovery.

I lost my sense of time until my belly rumbled with hunger. An army of nurses descended from the building to wheel the men inside. Lunch time. As some of us walked back into the hospital for our midday meal and medications, Bill sidled up to me. I turned to him, "What's on your mind, son?"

He paused a moment and whispered, "Don't look now, but have you ever heard the new guy say anything? I noticed something odd, no chart at the end of his bed."

It was common for patients who were not part of my service to drift toward my group. After all, I worked hard to keep my men talking, and they'd developed a magnetic effect, drawing others to our circle. The pull to heal was a powerful, contagious force. And since the head and face cases tended to stay the longest for multiple surgeries, they had more opportunity to form bonds.

I raised my shoulders, my hands open. "No, I haven't. But you know, sometimes it takes a while for speech. And Bill, you should not be snooping in anyone else's chart. What's up?"

Bill leaned into my ear, his voice lowered to a faint whisper, "There's a reason there's no chart. Watch out, Doc. I heard him mumbling in his sleep last night—in German."

Chapter Twenty-Two: Miriam

September 1917—New York City

After the guests left Papa's final Shiva, Hannah and I sat frozen, holding hands, indifferent to the noise of her children filling their plates, eating, and playing running games around us. Hannah said, "You've been through so much these last few years. Do you think you'd feel better moving in with me? We can bolster each other's spirits. I can't think of better company, especially with our men away."

I shook my head. My life, every book, every souvenir, every reminder of Mama and Papa, even the few from my honeymoon with Eli, were in this apartment. I couldn't possibly leave. "I'll keep your invitation in mind, but not yet. I'm still in a fog and need to settle. Besides, I'm so busy at work that coming home to a quiet place is soothing." I caught myself wishing I had kept that thought to myself. "I mean no offense, Hannah."

She took my other hand in hers. "I know you're busy, and it's true, my home is a noisy place, but it's full of life." She watched the children for a moment. "Let's make sure we have at least a couple of meals together every week."

Mulling, I asked, "Don't you think it's a bit strange that my brother, Julian, never stopped by? I wonder what's going on with him."

Hannah tsked in disgust, "I told his wife Selma. She said that he moved out before leaving for France. Things are not working out with their marriage."

I sat in Papa's apartment surrounded by more platters of food than any one human could possibly eat. The aroma of savory meats, stuffed cabbage, sweet kugel, and apples, fragrances that once reminded me of joyful holidays, now smelled like death to me, making my stomach sour. No time is ever good for a father to die, but smack in the middle of the Jewish New Year, when my husband was away in France, was the worst.

Despite the early hints of autumn, September remained suffocating in the apartment straight into the Holy Days of Rosh Hashana and Yom Kippur. The icebox could only hold a small fraction of the food trays mourners brought. It would spoil fast, and I knew Mama never would have let it go to waste. One more wretched thing to do. Hannah suggested I call the Settlement House and arrange for someone to pick it up.

Mama and Papa, together in Heaven. Somehow, the thought comforted me even though I'd stopped believing in Heaven years ago. Back when I was stricken with polio, people would talk about finding peace in Heaven, even while sitting at my bedside. Instead of feeling peace, I felt judged. Poor, virginal Miriam, barely getting a taste of life. Perhaps things would go better for her in the afterlife. My resentment drove me to fight harder. Giving up on life in my early twenties was inconceivable. How dare they throw their pity at me like I was some starving waif on the sidewalk! Through my slitted eyes, I sent darts of anger their way, wishing they'd leave me alone.

But now, with Mama and Papa both gone, I had no fight left. Sitting alone, with Eli thousands of miles away, loss held me in a tight grip. How could the hole in my heart feel so heavy, so paralyzing?

* * *

The next day, after the food was delivered to the Settlement House, the quiet in the apartment unnerved me. I decided to return to work at Beth Israel, taking a leisurely stroll. When I arrived at my shared office, Esther and Julia were sorting through a long list of patient-related issues. Esther rose, offering a quick hug. "I'm very sorry about your father, but I'll admit, it's a relief you're back. It's been so busy, and we're constantly short-staffed. Julia and I have been working twelve-hour shifts. With you back in the mix, an eight-hour shift will feel like a vacation."

I looked about. The small office was in shambles. No one seemed to find time to file reports or return the stacks of patient records to the Medical Records Department. Dirty cups and food crumbs were scattered on the round wood conference table and desk. "Where's our secretary? This place is a disaster area," I complained.

Julia grunted. "Same story as everywhere around here. She was pulled to help at the nurse's stations on the inpatient units." She added with a sarcastic tone, "The edict came down from above. All administrators must fend for themselves."

I began gathering the dirty cups, setting them on a cafeteria tray. "I just dug out of a scene like this at home and can't work or think in this mess." How could my office mates possibly think that this disarray would be an appropriate welcome back after losing my father? There were plenty of people looking for work out there. Was everyone fending for themselves?

Julia jumped from her chair, pulling the tray from my hands. "Don't clean our mess. I'll take care of it before I leave today. Let's go over the patient problem list. That's far more important."

Brushing my annoyance aside, I pulled out a pad of paper. "Let's sort through the open problems, and I'll get right on them." The problem-solving I once found challenging and enjoyable had lost its luster. Was it my sadness losing Papa, or did I no longer belong here?

The list was long, ranging from patients with persistent fevers and flu-like symptoms to angry families. But there was one situation that stood out, a young woman who'd attempted suicide after receiving the dreaded telegram. Her husband had been killed in France. The chart notes hit me in a visceral way, sending goosebumps up my arms. That could have been me. Would I survive losing Eli? I decided to tackle her first.

Mrs. Azarov lay in the last bed of the fourth-floor ward with her eyes closed. Her face was pale as a sheet, eyes deeply shadowed, her auburn hair splayed across the pillow, matted and stringy. I drew the curtain, separating her from the twenty other women in the room.

Lowering myself into the visitor chair, I took her hand in mine, understanding the depth of her sorrow, as I was living in a world filled with my own grieving.

Her eyes slowly opened, drifting from my face and then to our joined hands, snatching hers out of my grasp.

Surprised at her refusal to accept my empathy, I shifted into my formal role as a nurse. "Good morning, Mrs. Azarov. I'm Nurse Miriam, one of the Chief Nurses at the hospital. I'm here to help you."

She met my words with silence.

I pushed on. "I understand you're going through a terrible time."

Like a trap door opening, her mouth moved, and words tumbled out in a jumble of anger and sadness. "Terrible, you say? Ha! My life is over. Adam was everything. We'd only been married six months, and I'm expecting. Now he's gone." Sobs erupted. "Forever."

I was shocked. The nursing notes hadn't indicated she was pregnant. I couldn't fathom anyone attempting suicide with a life, half her husband's, growing inside her body. What kind of desperation could lead someone to that extreme?

I handed her a handkerchief.

She drew a shaky breath. "I'm only twenty-two, widowed, and now with child. Does it get worse than that?"

Her sadness pulsated, but it didn't match the emotion I felt. I'd give my right arm to be carrying Eli's child, to have something of his essence living inside me, infusing hope and joy into my empty life. A child would give me a reason to climb out of bed every day. But instead of sharing my plight, I tucked my private thoughts inside and asked, "Mrs. Azarov, tell me about your family. Do you have parents? Sisters?"

"A younger sister who lives with my aunt. My parents are dead."

I knit my brows, wondering if she was ready to consider other solutions. "May I speak to your aunt? Perhaps you and I can talk afterwards. For now, you need rest." I poured a fresh glass from the pitcher and sat with her while she drank.

By day's end, I couldn't shake my thoughts about Mrs. Azarov's pregnancy. Eli and I had been careful during relations, knowing he was going overseas, afraid to complicate our lives any further. Now I regretted our caution. A baby brought hope into the world. With my lonely days consumed with fear for Eli's safety and sadness surrounding Papa's death, a baby would have buoyed me, its joy an emotion of which I was in dire need.

An unfamiliar hollowness and fatigue followed me the rest of the evening; my walk home, leftover Shiva food for dinner, changing into my nightgown, brushing my teeth, all my actions wrapped in a shroud of sadness. Could I conjure enough energy to return to work the next day? My head pulsed with thoughts of Eli, his touch, his friendship, his counsel. I lay in bed replaying our honeymoon, his funny quips, the sound of his laughter, what a child of ours would look like, while tears fell from my eyes, etching a path down my cheeks, dampening my pillow.

In the wee morning hours, I woke with a jolt, with a new wave of clarity and determination. Had the old Miriam returned? I knew at that moment I would find a way to France. With Papa now buried beside Mama, and Ben and Eli both overseas, I'd find a way to join them. Who in their right mind would turn away a nurse?

Chapter Twenty-Three: Hannah

September 1917—New York City

"I'm telling you, it's too soon." I said, "You're still grieving."

Miriam stared at me, stone-faced, sitting on her apartment couch. "I'm not asking. My mind's made up. I'm going to speak to the Red Cross next week. If that doesn't work, I'll take a ship to South America. I hear they're still sending passenger steamers to France through Marseille."

I was floored at her recklessness. I gripped my emotions and tricked them into a corner, refusing to react directly to her impulsiveness. My voice was controlled, if not a bit laced with honey. "Darling, it's been only three weeks since your Papa passed. You know it's too soon to decide anything momentous. Besides, what will Beth Israel do? You're invaluable to them, helping run the hospital."

Miriam shook her head. "There are two other Chief Nursing Officers. They'll handle it without me. Besides, there are a few nurses ready to take my place."

Insanity, that's what this was. My niece had borne the brunt of too many losses; proper use of her leg, death of both parents, and a new husband at war mere weeks after their marriage, right at the cusp of their lives together. Strong as she was, she must be coming unraveled.

"Did something happen at work to bring this on? Are you feeling unwell?" I asked, reaching out to take her hand.

She recoiled, laughing indignantly. "I'm not sick. Stop acting like this is polio. You know I'd always planned on joining Eli." Miriam collected herself. "Now that Papa's gone, I have no reason to stay here."

I knew she'd regret this decision, and it was my responsibility to stop her. "Miriam, you're running a big hospital. Why do you insist on minimizing such an important job?"

She sighed, exasperated, shaking her head. "You know my job is a drop in the bucket compared to what our men are sacrificing in France. Didn't Ben say his hospital in Paris has two thousand beds, all of them full? Don't you think we should all be there with them?"

I scrunched my brows. "And, then, who would care for the children?" I tried to draw her into a hug, but she shifted away, out of my reach. "You're not thinking straight."

"There's nothing logical about this war. Nothing!"

I struggled to understand how she was putting the pieces together in such a cockeyed way and what I needed to say to set her straight. Maybe saying nothing was best.

She continued her rant. "Hypothetically speaking, if the children didn't exist, wouldn't you go? I mean, as a doctor, wouldn't you want to do everything in your power to help our boys over there?"

Her words rang in the air, suspended in their power. She had a point. Then I considered my pregnant mothers and their appreciation for a set of skilled female hands. Could I leave them behind? Finally, I said, "Honestly, I'm not sure. I know I'd be apprehensive about leaving my patients. Some of us must remain behind and take care of everyone else. But promise me one thing."

Her voice flattened. "What's that?"

I stared into her resolute eyes, wondering how to break through her determination, remembering the day over twenty-five years ago, when I was still a high school student. Tillie, her mother, trying like mad to pull me out of my grieving for a lost friend, allowed me to assist her midwife deliver Miriam into the world, an infant who howled at the top of her lungs before her entire body left the womb. I had an inkling the day of her birth she would be a challenge. I reached for the last shred of guilt I could conjure.

114

"For the sake of my duty to your devoted mother, please do not make a move for another month. It's too soon to make a decision you might regret."

Chapter Twenty-Four: Ben

September 1917—Paris

After hearing Bill's report in the courtyard, I rearranged my plan for the day. The top priority was getting to the bottom of Bill's mysterious patient. Having seen the devastating damage inflicted on our men, I couldn't be lulled into assuming any patient was harmless, particularly a heavily bandaged mummy. What evil might be lurking under all that cloth?

After helping the nurses wheel the last patient of my unit back to the ward for lunch, I dashed over to the Central Administration Office to investigate. The office was in the original hospital structure on Bd. Du Château, a stone and brick building, constructed to care for a few dozen wealthy American expat patients. Since the war began, the building had been converted into meeting space and offices designed to accommodate the central functions of the now sprawling military hospital interlacing the streets of Paris.

Oversized floor fans were running in the vestibule, swishing the blistering air about the room. I approached two French uniformed soldiers manning the office door. Both were fully dressed in uniform, beads of sweat shining on their foreheads. I announced, "Dr. Ben Kahn from the Head and Face Unit. May I enter?"

A soldier half my age barked back at me. *"Les papiers d'identité."*

The hair on my neck rose. How ironic, an officious soldier worrying about me, an old doctor taking the time to introduce myself, when he should be concerned that deep in the wards, in the guise of a wounded patient, danger could be lurking. Unlike the British, who would die before forgetting their "pleases" and "thank you's," these French soldiers bordered on disrespect, perhaps overcompensating for the fact that their mates were dodging bullets at the Front while they had cushy jobs. At Mount Sinai, I had grown spoiled by the degree of respect I garnered. Younger doctors, nurses, and orderlies all knew my position and name and made a point of politely greeting me when we crossed paths. Here, in a war-torn country, it was easy for soldiers carrying deadly weapons to get cocky. With growing irritation, no doubt fueled by the incinerating heat, I reached into my white coat pocket, pulled out my identity papers, and handed them to the guards. "May I now enter?"

After passing the papers back and forth and inspecting the documents for an absurd amount of time, they handed my papers back and signaled for me to enter. Once inside the dark paneled room, a uniformed soldier looked up from behind his desk, speaking in English. "Lance Corporal Morton here. How may I help you?"

I said, "My name is Dr. Ben Kahn. I'm an American surgeon on the Head and Face Unit. I need to check a soldier's identity."

"Is the patient one of yours, sir?" the Lance Corporal asked.

I shrugged my shoulders. "How is that relevant? I need to know his name and review the chart." Why was he so curious? I was a staff doctor. What was it about these administrative soldiers? None of them looked old enough to shave. Besides, weren't they aware we Americans had joined the effort to help them win? I wondered if things would change once American boys began pouring in on stretchers.

"Is he on your service, sir?" he repeated in his refined British accent.

"Not that I know of. He is a new patient on the unit with my men and without speech." Why was I defending myself? I flushed with a growing anger. My voice rose. "Who's in charge here? I'd like to speak to him immediately."

Although the soldier held my eyes, I detected a slight twitch in his brow. "Let me see if he's available." Climbing from his chair, he grabbed a crutch from the floor behind his desk and braced it under his arm. When he stood erect, I noticed his left pant leg was pinned to his upper trousers behind the knee. My stomach dropped.

"Where are you from, soldier?" I asked, nodding at his leg. "Battle injury?"

"Cornwall. Yes, sir, Flanders' injury in 1915," he answered while hobbling to the door across the room. Turning to regard me further, he added, "Sergeant Major Anderson is in command."

I reached out my hand and shook his. "My deepest gratitude for your brave service." I knew he could have been discharged home, but he stayed. It was clear he was determined to help the cause any way he could. Like my patients said. "We must have purpose."

His sad eyes latched onto mine. "Thank you, sir."

Moments later, I was led into Sergeant Anderson's office and introduced by Morton. "What brings you here, Doctor?" Anderson asked in his clipped English. Was that alcohol I smelled? This early in the day?

I shared Bill's suspicions about the silent, bandaged man. "I have several concerns I think we should address. Of course, safety is number one. If this patient is a prisoner of war, he should be moved to a secure location. After all, we conduct numerous procedures using instruments, and we wouldn't want anything sharp finding its way into his hands."

Anderson, a short, bald man in his late forties, struck me as tired, fed up with the war and all it entailed. He feigned listening attentively, nodding his head from time to time, but his eyes did not connect with mine, and I feared his mind was occupied with other matters. "I see," he said.

His lack of concern compelled me to push harder. "What is your procedure for a situation such as this?"

Anderson cleared his throat. "My dear sir, of course, we know enemy soldiers are in the hospital. We use them in exchange programs for our own injured men held in Germany."

"Do you keep them in a secure ward?" I pressed, eyeing him closely.

He sat straighter, realizing I was determined to pursue the matter. "Of course we do, except for the head wounds. They fare better when cared for in the special Head and Face Unit."

I ran my hand through my hair, growing more frustrated. "As a surgeon, I always want to see patients do well, but I'm also concerned about the safety of our Allied patients. How have you vetted this man? I'd like to speak directly with the physician in charge of the case. Can I see his chart?"

Anderson stood. "I don't know offhand, but you can rest assured that he has been cleared for your unit. We have procedures. As for the medical chart, I can have that for you tomorrow after morning rounds if you stop back." He walked around his desk to the door and opened it, waiting for me to follow. A tight chuckle escaped his open mouth. "Is he even conscious?"

I stood, scowling back. "I will be back tomorrow, but in the meantime, I'll alert the nurses to keep a close eye on him. He's most certainly conscious."

Departing Anderson's office in a fury after a half-hearted handshake, I headed back to the floor, determined to flesh out my own answers. Until now, I was convinced, after my decades of work at Mount Sinai, I'd seen every shape and form of procrastinating bureaucrats. But I was floored by this new type, the military pencil pusher, likely counting the hours until he was off duty and could head back to the officer lounge to indulge in shots of dark rum and beer. Or were his bottles kept deep in his desk drawer?

Ten minutes later, I entered my building and climbed the steps to the third floor. By the top, my body was drenched in sweat. The head nurse, a middle-aged French woman who spoke impeccable English, was squirreled away in a small office, sorting through an ungainly stack of paperwork and filing reports in the sleeves of patients' charts. I knocked gently on the door.

"Sorry to disturb you, but I have a few questions about the patient in Bed 10." Glancing at his bed, I saw it was empty. My heart thudded. "Where is he?"

She pointed to the window bank. "Probably having a stretch. He seems to have a touch more energy today."

I released my breath, calming myself. "Who's his doctor? Do you have the chart?"

She lifted herself from her chair. "Dr. Kahn, he's one of the classified patients, if you know what I mean."

My voice rose as my incredulity grew. "If the patient is a German prisoner, where is the guard?"

She spoke evenly as if I were a child. "Please calm yourself. He has been cleared. No guard is necessary."

I was anything but calm, my patience with the military process had all but vanished. But more immediate was my concern about the safety of our own men in the unit. Within my first days on the unit, I'd come to understand the unpredictable nature of head wounds. While the brain healed, behavior could become erratic. A patient could suffer wild mood swings, one minute calm, the next combative, swinging wildly at the nurses as if they were reliving the shooting in the trenches. My temper flared. "What's the doctor's name? When's the last time he checked the patient?" I thought a moment. "I've never seen a physician caring for him."

She shrugged. "In all due respect, I think you're overconcerned." She lifted her eyes to mine, registering my irritation. "But I'll request his doctor come by today so you can confer."

I spoke through my teeth, attempting to regain my composure and appease the nurse. "Please do. In the meantime, I'll change his dressing and check the wound for you."

The nurse said in an even voice, "Thank you. That would be a big help."

As I turned, I asked, "By the way, what's his name?"

Having returned to her paperwork, she twisted back to me and muttered, "Friedrich."

* * *

After examining the most recent admissions, ensuring they were resting comfortably, I made my way to Friedrich, who by that time had returned to his bed. He lay on his back atop a light cotton blanket.

I still recalled remnants of my parents' German that I used with immigrant patients from time to time in New York. Perhaps speaking in his tongue would help Friedrich remain calm. *"Guten Morgan."*

He snapped his head around to see me with his uncovered eye.

I told him my name, *"Ich bin Doktor Kahn."*

No response.

120

I wondered if he had heard me. Raising my voice, I tried again, speaking German, telling him that I would examine him. *"Friedrich, Ich werde dich untersuchen."*

He remained silent as I unfurled the bandages wrapped around his head. After learning he hadn't been tended for days, I'd expected dirtier, stained gauze. But as I unwound the dressing, it remained mostly white, little oozing or blood. How long had he been lying here, pretending to be seriously injured? I proceeded, speaking to him in German, "Friedrich, let me take a closer look at your wound. Does this hurt?"

Silence.

Bill, who had been watching from his nearby bed, sat at the side of his cot, leaning forward on his forearms, curious. "I hope to hell it hurts. Did he get it as bad as he dished it out to the rest of us in the trenches?"

At the sound of Bill's mocking voice, Friedrich stiffened, breathing rapidly, grunting.

The last thing I needed was for Bill to unsettle Friedrich. "Bill, drink your water. I'm handling this."

I faced Friedrich. "Relax, son." Although I doubted he knew English, I was convinced he could recognize my reassuring tone.

But my soft voice did not help calm him. Friedrich began writhing as if in pain, grunting and groaning, pushing me away.

"I'm not going to hurt you," I said, as I held his arms down.

But in his panic, he wrestled one arm from my grip, sliding it under the mattress. Out of the corner of my eye, I saw a glint of light reflecting off a metal object.

In a blink, I realized he held a scalpel, drawing it backward, poised to impale me. Time stopped as a primal bolt of fear raced through my chest. I reached for the hand with the scalpel, ready to smash him in the face with my other hand. Red flashed through my head. Kill him!

Before I could make a move, Bill sprang from his cot and in two lightning-fast steps dove between Friedrich and me, absorbing the extraordinary force of the attack. The scalpel plunged into Bill's neck. "Animal!" Bill screamed, sliding between Friedrich and me, reaching the handle of the scalpel. He pulled the scalpel from his neck, then drove it repeatedly into Friedrich's chest. Blood squirted from both their wounds, intermingling in a pulsing red fountain of gushing blood.

Within seconds, the other soldiers were screaming, hoisting themselves from their beds to pull Bill off Friedrich and set him on the floor. Then, like a pack of jackals, they pummeled Friedrich, bracing his arms back, locking him to the bed while he hemorrhaged from his chest.

Friedrich screamed, *"Scheißer! Scheißer!"* Then nothing.

I kneeled beside Bill on the floor, pressing towels on his neck to stop the bleeding. "What's he saying?" I asked no one in particular.

"Fuckers." A soldier shouted in his British accent. "That's what the Hun's calling us."

I helped the men lift Bill back onto his bed, anxious to inspect the wound more closely. Blood spurted from the puncture entrance when I lifted the towel. He was losing blood fast. Friedrich must have hit his carotid artery. Every second brought him closer to death. "Call for the operating room, now!" I shouted, knowing in my gut it would be impossible to save him.

Within seconds, an orderly raced into the ward with a gurney. We lifted Bill onto it, reversing direction, heading for the operating room, me riding atop him, pressing down on his wound. Bill grew paler by the second. I turned back to look at Friedrich, knowing in my gut I would have killed him if the others hadn't. For the first time in my long life, I understood with excruciating clarity the savagery of war, a terrifying instinct lying dormant precariously close to my surface.

* * *

Bill bled out before we could begin surgery. Friedrich must have been proficient at anatomy, because severing the carotid artery, the primary vessel to the brain, was a bull's eye for a soldier, a quick death, one only a butcher or soldier would know.

There was no time for the reality of loss to set in. Once Bill was pronounced dead, I hurried back to the ward to check on the rest of my soldiers, still wearing my bloodied coat. By the time I got there, Friedrich's body had been removed. The nursing staff was cleaning the area and helping the soldiers who fought Friedrich remove their bloodied gowns, changing them into fresh ones. But crimson-stained or dressed in pristine white, the hour could not be undone. Without a moment's hesitation, this ward of men, all healing from devastating wounds, rose to defend their wounded brother.

I stood at the doorway, taking in the scene before me. A mixture of sadness and pride washed over me. One by one, they eyed me, brows rising, seeking news of Bill. I announced, "Bill is dead. He...." My voice faltered as it struck how important he'd become to me and to all the soldiers in my unit. "He saved my life."

A British soldier, wearing a face mask to cover his missing cheek, shouted out, "The German bastard's dead, too! We got him good."

A round of cheers rose in the room. These men were still fired up. It would be hours before they settled down. I nodded, "Yes, you did. I'm in your debt, soldiers." I walked through the ward shaking each man's hand. "That's more than enough excitement for the day. Please settle down and try to rest."

I turned on my heels and walked to the Head Nurse's office.

She was standing at the door jamb, her forehead creased in shame. "Doctor, I'm so sorry. We should never have missed that."

I huffed, still stunned from the calamity. "You're not the only one, Nurse. It was a comedy of errors, if I can be so crass to use the phrase." I spoke softly.

She looked at the floor and exhaled loudly. "We'll be needing you for a meeting at 4:00 in the old building to review the incident."

I rubbed my stubbly cheek as a mixture of frustration and sadness surfaced. "I tried to warn everyone, but no one took me seriously. Now he's gone." I sighed, attempting to steady myself. "Please tell me there are no other prisoners on this floor. Our men deserve better."

She looked straight into my eyes. "There are no other prisoners on the floor. Unfortunately, the wheels around here turn slowly, but perhaps this incident will put some speed into the process."

* * *

Major Robert Bacon, a tall, middle-aged, portly man, dressed in a fine suit and pocket watch, was accustomed to being heard. He slammed his two hands on the mahogany conference table, shouting, "An enemy soldier has no place in a hospital unit full of defenseless men and sharp instruments!"

He had everyone's attention. There would be no shirking from the gravity of this death. The Major, a prominent founder of The American Hospital along with the Vanderbilts and Morgans, was responsible for raising millions of American dollars together with the Red Cross to expand the hospital for the war effort. Not only did they donate money, but most of his gilded set also volunteered personal time, offering their expertise and connections to acquire needed services, supplies, and equipment.

His fierce blue eyes swept around the massive rectangular table at the twenty or so attendees, one by one, pulling each into its grip before moving on. "You better have a damn good explanation. How in hell's fire will we explain this to his parents? That their boy," he quickly glanced to the paperwork before him, "Bill—ahem, William Conover, a kid who'd volunteered for the ambulance service who'd already lost half his face in service to his country, was killed by an enemy soldier, and while convalescing here at The American, the preeminent Allied hospital on the Continent?" Punctuating his message, he slammed his hands on the table again. "And we'll need to answer to the Board and the Vanderbilts on this one."

The heat in the room was suffocating; the air hung with disgrace. No one wanted to begin. The room remained still until he spoke again.

His eyes shot to Lance Corporal Morton, whom I'd met earlier that morning outside Sergeant Anderson's office. Morton sat with his back ramrod straight, holding a pad of paper and pen. "We'll start at the beginning. You, with the pen, don't leave anything out."

Corporal Morton nodded, pen at the ready.

The next hour was spent circling the table of doctors, administrators, and nurses who recounted the movements of Friedrich's unconscious body from a month earlier, when he was unloaded from the hospital train in Paris. I lost count of the times I heard the words, *followed military procedure, military procedure....* Listening to each person explain their part, it became clear the calamity had turned into a child's game of hot potato, throwing the blame to others, no one owning responsibility.

What a farce. I'd seen "cover your ass" behavior throughout my professional life, especially when patients died in surgery, but the excessive blaming after Bill's stabbing was a full octave higher than any chorus of denial I'd ever witnessed. With so many involved in Friedrich's care, the finger-pointing was nothing short of operatic. My head was ready to explode, but my better judgment told me to wait.

Eventually, it was my turn. After recounting the steps I took that morning, I stopped, looked hard into the Major's eyes, and said tersely, "As Chief of Surgery at Mount Sinai back in New York, I'm acutely aware of the importance of clear procedures and adherence to them. But therein also lies the problem." I let my uncomfortable words settle into the room. Words the military did not like to hear.

Major Bacon opened his hands, his brows knit in annoyance, his strained voice laced with irritation. "Enlighten me."

I cleared my throat, refusing to bend to his intimidation. "Although procedures fit most circumstances, they never, ever fit all. Those very procedures, designed with good intentions, become obsolete and sometimes dangerous. Procedures must always be tested against the rules of common sense. When such a large assembly of professionals responds automatically with the word, *procedure,*" I swept my arm around the table, pointing to each person, "and no one stops to challenge decisions when the facts no longer add up, well, that's when catastrophes happen, as to our patient, Bill."

Major Bacon was staring at me now. He cocked his head to the side, readdressing me in an even tone, "Where did the process break and what do you suggest we do about it?"

I inhaled deeply, slowly releasing my breath, hoping to relax the mood in the room. "The breakdown came when the patient's status changed, and his brain began to heal. He transitioned from unconscious to conscious. That was the time to return him to the prisoner unit. Bill, as we all knew him, our American, was the first to notice. You see, these patients don't stop being soldiers when they're injured. Bill's instincts were as sharp as a tack. He reported to me this morning that he heard Friedrich talking in his sleep last night," I paused, "in German."

Again, the room hushed. The only sound we could hear was the ticking of the pendulum in the grandfather clock casing.

I continued, "Bill was the only person alarmed because no doctor or nurse had been examining the German. You see, their beds were across from one another. That morning, when Bill reported his concern to me, I immediately alerted the chain of command, administrative and medical. All refused to take immediate action." Again, I let the information sink in. "Every person I spoke to was unfazed as they reported a moment ago, because they were following *procedure*," I said, emphasizing the word "procedure," letting its negligent sting settle.

The Major stared at me. Others in the room squirmed in their chairs. "Continue."

"Based on the inept actions of the last twelve hours, I suggest two changes. The first is recovering enemy soldiers are kept in a locked, guarded unit. If their treatment dictates they leave the unit for additional care, X-ray, a procedure, or to convalesce in a specialty unit such as mine, they are accompanied by a guard around the clock."

The Finance Officer cut in. "Do you have any idea how expensive guards are? We have no budget for that kind of excess."

I answered solemnly, "No, I don't know, and frankly, I don't care. My job as a doctor is to save lives. That's why I'm here." I knew I should have stopped, but this moron had finally pushed me over my edge. "This morning. We lost two," I pointed to myself, "almost three if our American casualty, Bill, hadn't sacrificed his life." Try as I did, I could not stop my words from spewing out. "Tell me, sir, what's a soldier's life worth? I suppose we could save a lot of money, keep you on budget, if we left everyone on the battlefield to die."

The Finance Officer looked down at the table.

Major Bacon cleared his throat, tapping the wood with his forefinger. "Of course, we are here to save lives and return our soldiers home." He turned to the doctor who had moved Friedrich to my unit. "This would never have happened if you'd stayed on top of your patient's status. It appears you turned his care over to nursing and hadn't seen him for days. Is that correct?"

The British doctor glanced up from the table. "Yes, sir, but..."

Major Bacon barked back. "No more excuses. Given your duty to care for the German, it seems only proper that you write the telegram to Mr. Conover's family explaining his death." Major Bacon finished his last words with a snort of air. "And, Dr. Kahn, I want you to draft your recommendations and have them on my desk first thing tomorrow."

I answered, "Yes, sir, but I'd like to make another request."

Bacon glanced at the wall clock, his finger again tapping on the table. "What now?"

"I'd like to write the telegram," I said, my face unmoving, frozen in seriousness.

Everyone in the room sat straighter, eyeing me in disbelief.

I continued, "This morning taught me a grave lesson, something I hadn't realized." I pointed to Morgan. "Morgan, he knows, having fought in Flanders."

Bacon's bushy eyebrows shot upward. He pulled on the side of his mustache. "What's that, Doctor?"

My eyes moved around the table, the grandfather clock by the wall rang five times. It was the end of the hour, the end of the meeting. My voice was firm. "Before today, I'd never felt the savagery of battle, unrestrained violent men bent on killing each other. I know Morton will never forget, but I'm not sure how many of the rest of you have fought in hand-to-hand combat, fighting for your life. Any?" I waited.

No one moved.

I dug in deeper, "Our perception of our brave soldiers rings hollow when held against their fight, their drive to prevail, to survive. Words alone don't give their noble service justice." I paused, drawing a deep breath, slowing my speech. "I had a small taste. An enemy patient tried to take my life, to stab me to death. He didn't care who I was or that I was trying to help him. Bill, always on a soldier's alert, without a second thought, made the ultimate sacrifice."

Major Bacon nodded his head, staring deeply into my eyes.

I stood. "It would be my honor to inform his family of his selfless patriotism, his final act of bravery."

Chapter Twenty-Five: Eli

October 1917—Ypres, Belgium

Martin shook me awake. "Come on Eli, you have time for a coffee and chow if you get your ass out of bed. I'm heading to the mess hall now."

"You're the ass," I muttered, clinging to my dream, one that fled before I could remember. But from the looks of my undershorts, it must have been a very good one. "Meet you there. Need to hit the latrine." I sat up, rubbing crusted eyes, wrapping my blanket around my body as I yanked on my pants and sweater. When did it start getting cold?

After three months in Ypres, the summer heat had ebbed, only to be replaced by cold nights and rainy days with no end in sight to the fighting. The number of wounded and dead pulled off the battlefield increased by the day despite the encouraging news announced over radio waves and in newspapers. From my bloody corner on the Front, I would have guessed we were losing ground. Where were the sturdy, corn-fed American boys we'd been promised?

Word from the officers was that across the continent, Russia was throwing in the towel, cooling the fighting on the Eastern Front, consumed by their country's Bolshevik revolution. They'd begun working on a peace treaty with Germany. That meant only one thing: the Huns would send their troops to the west, strengthening their forces opposite our trenches.

Since I arrived, our dilapidated Evacuation Hospital had doubled in size, now holding hundreds of men, many of whom would be sent to Paris or England for further care. A few returned to the trenches. Far too many were buried in the Ypres military cemetery.

Ten minutes later, we sat together mopping our eggs with a heel of bread, slurping down tea. "For the life of me, I'll never get used to drinking tea instead of coffee," Martin said. "If my family saw me sipping this stuff, they'd think I'd gone to the moon."

I chuckled, admiring the way Martin could joke about anything, knowing full well we were looking at a tsunami of patients today, just like practically every day for the last few weeks. Finishing the last puddle of egg yolks, I said, "Let's round on the limbs we saved this week and make sure they're holding up. I dread having to put any of those boys back on the table."

With the advanced scraping and flushing procedures, known as debridement, together with concentrated antiseptics, Martin and I were saving a considerable number of limbs that ordinarily would have been amputated. Certainly, enough to persuade Dr. Clarke, our superior officer, to grant the two of us more elbow room, more time for each patient on our table. Never in my life had minutes in the operating theater been measured by other lives lost, by soldiers lying on cots in line at the door waiting for their turn. How many would die while we repaired a limb? What an insane measurement.

Moments later, Helen and I stood by Cadet Collins, who was writhing with fever. We'd operated on him two evenings earlier. As a last-ditch effort to save his right arm, we'd reattached damaged blood vessels. It was a tough call. Normally, if the arteries were damaged, we'd amputate. We knew Collins had waited hours on the open battlefield for rescue, lying in the filthy mud in no man's land behind the barbed wire. It wasn't until nightfall that the stretcher-bearers could reach him without getting themselves shot. Somehow, we convinced ourselves to try saving the limb.

Martin turned to Nurse Helen, "Unwrap it. We need to examine. But I don't like his looks, fever and all."

She peeled the cotton wrappings off his arm, the repulsive stench of rotting flesh leached out from under the bandages, permeating the air. "Good God Almighty, it's gangrenous." She covered her nose with her wrist and peered at Martin, seeking his assessment.

My stomach sank. Now the poor lad would lose his entire arm. If we hadn't tried so hard to save it, the amputation would have been at the elbow. Now he'd be left with a short stump off his shoulder. That is, if he lived.

Martin sighed, "Let's get him taken care of first thing before the wounded start pouring in. I'll find an anesthesiologist and get a table ready."

I was left standing beside Nurse Helen, watching Cadet Collins. Through his feverish haze, he knew what lay before him.

He shouted, spit spraying from his mouth, "Liars, all of you! If the Huns don't kill us, you do. You call yourselves surgeons? You told me you'd save my arm, and now I'll be left with nothing."

His words shot through me like the machine gun bullets that had destroyed his arm in the first place. He was right. Do no harm, do no harm. The very first day, the very first lesson in medical school was the Hippocratic Oath. How could I justify experimenting on these poor men? With a stump, he'd have far less function.

I glanced at Nurse Helen, judging her reaction. She looked back at me, her brows drawn tight together, her eyes lit with urgency, "What are you waiting for? Shouldn't you be getting inside and washed for surgery?" She huffed, rebandaging Cadet Collins's arm, settling him. "It will be fine, soldier. You will live to tell your story."

I ignored her, standing frozen in place, gazing down at our feverish patient, transporting myself into his body, his soul, knowing he was right. I had no idea how to fix these broken men and was completely helpless in the operating room, willing to try anything to save a limb. Now look at the mess we'd made of the poor boy.

Nurse Helen grabbed my forearm, leading me outside the door. "Had his arm hung in there, you'd be cheering like you won a rugby game. Just like you did yesterday with those legs you saved."

I tried to absorb her words, but instead, they slid off my skin, not penetrating my horrible mood. This poor man had a long way to go to get out of here. His rotting smell was the scent of death. It wasn't as simple as his first surgery. Now he was fighting for his life. One day I was a hero, saving a leg, the next day, a murderer. It shouldn't feel so random.

She shook my arm, locking her eyes with mine. They softened as she took in my turmoil. "This is no time to feel sorry for yourself. We have hours of work ahead of us. Buck up, Doctor. We can talk about it later."

I knew she was right. I closed my eyes and conjured Miriam's calming face, thinking about her last letter, *"I can only imagine how overwhelmed you must feel. Remember that 'these are the times that test men's souls.' You will prevail and return from the devastation you now face. I will wipe every tear, every crease from your brow, until you are fully healed, at peace beside me."*

* * *

Miriam's words cycled through my head, propelling me through the endless day. When I wasn't in full concentration over a patient, I thought of her fight with polio, how she clung to life like our soldiers, not knowing if she'd survive. Having already treated infected children, she knew the course polio could take. She'd watched their small bodies shrink as their muscles withered, finally gasping for air when the disease invaded their lungs. She knew the angel of death was beside her as her body mimicked their symptoms. How did she remain strong? She'd shown me the depth of her bravery every day until the polio ran its course. And here, in Ypres, I knew she would have faced this chaotic bloodbath with a level of courage I could only pretend to muster. For me, I waffled between confidence and cowardice by the hour. But not Miriam. She never questioned her purpose.

We finished the last operation for the day, an easy wound to the upper arm, the shrapnel miraculously missing the brachial artery and humerus. He was lucky and waited outside the operating room until the more pressing cases were completed, his injury bound in cotton wrap. When the stretcher-bearers carried him inside, he was smoking a cigarette. "Doc, is this goin' send me home?"

I understood right away. Only the insane wanted to return to the trenches. Those few were the rare men who bonded so resolutely with their fellow soldiers that their loyalty prevented them from leaving. But, three years into the war, most of the remaining soldiers had lost too many mates. Today, they were left fighting among troops of panicked strangers, otherwise decent men who had turned into wild savages, spending every waking hour ducking and dodging, forcing themselves to follow maniacal commands, charging into machine gun fire, spearing men with their bayonets. Who in their right mind would want more of that?

Without the line out the door, we could slip into a less frenzied pace as we repaired his arm. "Time to put him to sleep," I said to the anesthesiologist. Both Martin and Nurse Helen stood around the table as I took the lead. "This guy got lucky. His arm should have full function." I pointed my bloodied finger to the unbroken highway of vessels and nerves. "Look at this. The nerve is practically intact. Do you think he'll be sent back to the trenches? Can't blame him for wanting a ticket home."

Nurse Helen clucked her tongue. "Who knows? If the Yankee recruits are ready, they may send him home, but up to this point, all the soldiers who can walk and shoot get sent back to the Front once they've healed."

Martin winked at me. "Don't slip and cut his nerve. He won't be able to shoot his gun. That'll get him sent home in a jiffy."

Did surgeons do such things? "Not me. He'll have to take his chances. I'm just getting the hang of these repairs. Not going to blow my scorecard now."

Martin and Nurse Helen laughed. She chimed in, "Never considered you'd do it. Not in a million years."

While Martin closed the wound, I looked at Nurse Helen, diligently mopping the man's arm, preparing the bandaging. The picture of efficiency. Not a delay from her end anywhere. She glanced at me, and her hazel eyes caught mine, soft and confident. Disarmed, I cleared my throat, steadying myself, and said, "Nice job today, Nurse. Let's hope he lives to use that arm of his."

What was in that look of hers that knocked me off balance? Was it admiration? Had I finally crossed over from the sweaty surgical pup to a bona fide battlefield surgeon? Or did she feel sorry for me, holding on so dearly to my ethics?

* * *

A week later, I woke before dawn in a cold sweat. The same nightmare had returned. In my dream, I envisioned operating as quickly as my hands would move while dying men, stacked outside the hospital entrance, cried out for help. The pile of wounded men continued, mounting by the minute, all suffocating in the carnage. Operating as fast as my hands would work, I could not keep pace with the flow of desperate, dying soldiers, each expecting me to bear the hands of God.

When would this blasted war end? Every wretched day was another marathon. My old drive for excellence was replaced with a sense of near-reckless urgency. Moving cases along as quickly as I could, I stitched torn, frightened men from dawn when the artillery started until well after dark when the wounded in no man's land were retrieved by our brave stretcher-bearers. The constant metallic smell of blood stayed with me day and night while the percussive rat-a-tat-tat of shrapnel dropping into the specimen pans throughout the operating room echoed in my ears. The men's screaming tore at my nerves. In my brittle state, I wanted to holler back into their faces, "For the love of God, would you all shut the hell up?"

There would be no more sleep for me. I sat upright and checked the clock, four thirty a.m. I may as well get up and shower before the next deluge of broken men. As I shook the dream from my head, I remembered that today I would eat alone.

Yesterday, I'd accompanied Martin to the station and watched him board the last train back to Paris, leaving me in command of the limb-saving initiative. Martin was returning to The American Hospital together with our forty surviving limb repairs. He planned to remain there for the next three months. In his wake, I was assigned to replace him as the lead surgeon on the limb project. The sight of Martin tipping his cap as he boarded the train could have taken my spirits down, but instead, I felt myself fill with a sense of command. I'd mastered the vital project he began and, for the first time, could add my own touches.

A fresh replacement from Harvard in Boston, Dr. Philip Harrington, arrived on Martin's incoming train to take my old job as assistant. Philip, as I heard he liked to be called, with his Ivy League education, was arrogant. He had a thing or two to learn. My belly was already roiling in anticipation. Now, with only three months apprenticing with Martin, I was the senior. Between this new spoiled chap and the grave responsibility I held, it was no wonder my nerves were shot.

After months of working together, Martin and I had fused into a well-oiled machine. We'd cut our surgical time in about half, still more than an amputation, but not by much. No one could accuse us of wasting a second. Speed improved outcomes. To save time at the start of each case, we brought a turkey baster into the operating theater, squirting clean water, bathing the wounds thoroughly before finishing debridement of the area with a small scalpel, reducing the opportunity for infection. From then on, our hands moved in rapid unison, inserting plates and screws onto splintered bones, suturing layers of tendons, ligaments, and muscles, and then finally joining skin. Splints and dressings were applied last, protecting our work, the soldier's full limb. I knew I'd surpass Martin's skill; we had learned fathoms over a short period of time, but would I hold a candle to Martin as a new mentor, or, for that matter, could Harrington catch up to me? I could only pray he did not slow me down.

This morning, after the endless Ypres offensive that resumed last month, there was no time to waste. The Americans had still not yet joined the battle, and I feared this showdown would go on for months. Both sides were racking up casualties at an alarming speed, only further demoralizing the soldiers. But I couldn't think about that right now. I had to concentrate on preparing for a long operating day. Like Henry Ford's assembly lines, our supplies and bandages must be stacked meticulously beside the patient table to run the operating room efficiently.

Dawn had come, the late August sky clear for its last few moments. I finished my breakfast and headed toward the latrine. Swish...Rumble... Crack. Swish...Rumble...Crack. The artillery explosions began, filling the distant sky with smoke and soot, the sound waves reverberating in my ears. It would be another twelve hours before the air settled, when we would again see the sky's true color. I cringed, sweat beading on my forehead. The incoming wounded would be arriving soon.

My eye caught Harrington ahead of me, running into the latrine. He had the right idea. I fell in behind him. It might be hours until our next rest break.

Within seconds, a woman's voice yelled through the door, "You boys in there? Drucker? Harrington? Wind it up. Incoming!"

"Yes, sir," we grunted in unison from within the makeshift stalls. We may hold superior titles, but Nurse Helen was the indisputable commander of the operating room.

Ten minutes later, the first round of mayhem hit the hospital. Outdoors in the open with Harrington at my side, we sorted through the wounded arriving on stretchers and set on blankets while I hurriedly explained the triage process and labeling. Our first patient was an unconscious soldier with monstrous wounds. I peeled open his jacket. His chest was torn to ribbons. The ribs so shattered, I could see his shivering lungs. "Black Tag," I said.

Harrington handed the card to me, then ran to the garbage barrel beside the operating room door, heaving.

Remembering that was me a few short months ago, I yelled out, "Catch your breath. I need you here, Harrington...now!"

My eyes shot to another soldier, barely conscious, holding his right arm against his chest. "What's your name, soldier?"

"Liam Humphrey with the British Fifth." He gasped in pain, releasing a deep belly grunt. "Doc, please save my arm. I'm a righty."

"Let's take a look." I grabbed the scissors and cut away his jacket and shirt sleeves. "Harrington, with each injury, finds reasons to save the limb rather than reasons to amputate. This forearm bone is splintered, but the vessels appear viable. He's our first case." I then glanced down at Humphrey. "We're going to try to save your arm. Say your prayers."

Humphrey made the sign of the cross on his chest with his left hand, mumbling, "Hail Mary, Full of Grace. The Lord is with thee...now and at the hour of my death."

I'd come to recognize the prayer. Growing up Jewish, I first heard it after I arrived in France. Humphrey was trusting in God and in me to take him to the next step in his life. Mary, a mother figure, brought comfort along the journey. But who knew if anyone or anything heard us anymore? My hunch was they did not.

While the stretcher-bearers brought him inside, Nurse Helen, Harrington, and I identified two other limb repair patients and one chest for my line-up.

Moments later, Humphrey was under anesthesia. We began cleaning the wound. I caught Harrington eyeing the other tables, his attention distracted by the commotion, the multiple cases in the very same operating space as ours. He said, "I've only seen one case in the operating theater at a time. This is nuts!"

I barked, thinking of Montgomery's words only three months ago. "Eyes on the arm. I don't want to see you looking anywhere else while we're working or you're outta here. Got that, Harrington?"

He huffed, "Yes, sir."

We completed our morning cases shortly after noon. Nurse Helen stepped back from the table as the orderlies carried our last patient into recovery. Her forehead was covered with a syrupy mix of sweat and blood. "You both have time enough for a fifteen-minute latrine and coffee break."

Nurse Helen, with her unflagging spirit, had many of Miriam's qualities. Although the two women didn't remotely resemble one another in appearance and had opposite dispositions, both were tough as nails in a crisis. Helen was fair, short, and freckled, with a combustible temper, exactly what I envisioned of the Irish fighters; while Miriam was tall with thick dark hair, calm as a still pool of water in a crisis. The only physical feature they shared was their penetrating, disarming eyes. But Miriam was thousands of miles away.

At 1:30, we resumed surgery. I asked Nurse Helen, "What's the OR tally so far?"

She answered in her clipped English. "In total, one hundred ten patients went through the operating room. Twenty-seven in the morgue, two were bellies from our table, bled out. Sixty-two from recovery were packed

137

for today's hospital train to Paris. They included seventeen head wounds, thirty-eight belly wounds, and seven amputations. That leaves twenty-one more to stay here with us tonight."

"How many of those are limb repairs?" I asked.

She sighed audibly, "Only our three. So far, they seem to be holding up."

I turned to Harrington with a huff. "No one else is even trying. They just amputate. What are they so afraid of? Our mortality rate is the same as theirs." Shifting back to Nurse Helen, I asked, "The others?"

"Eleven are minor and will return to the trenches in a week. The others are awake but non-responsive. They're calling it 'shell shock.'"

Harrington grunted. "Sounds like 'fraidy cats to me. Coward's way out."

Nurse Helen snatched his arm, spinning him around to face her. Leaning back to glare upward into his face, she challenged, "You think they're cowards? Want to spend a week in the trenches and see what it's like?" Her freckles lit up like embers of fire. I'd never seen her so angry. "Not one is a coward. Their brains quit on them, terrified beyond belief. Don't you know it's a living hell out there? Even the brave ones shit in their pants."

The operating room went silent. Judgment filled the air. Harrington stepped away from the operating table, shaking his head, his eyes hooded in embarrassment. He'd been warned to keep peace with the nurses, and on his first day, he tripped over his words: "Apologies, Nurse. I didn't mean to upset you. I was out of line."

"Now, that's a bit of hard truth," she snapped. "I've been here for eighteen months, and my most petrifying nightmares don't come close to what these brave young lads endure every single day. Show your respect or find another table."

* * *

My feet were swollen and throbbing by nightfall. With autumn upon us, the days were shorter, and so was the bright operating light. Fishing for blood vessels was nearly impossible under spotty electrical lighting. If lucky, we could grab a free stretcher-bearer to hold an extra torch. Cases took longer, and I hoped the men would fare as well as their fellow soldiers who'd been repaired earlier, during better light. As my last patient was slid off the table onto a stretcher and taken to Recovery, Harrington looked to me. "Done for the day?"

I nodded, "Go find some grub before the canteen is locked up for the night."

On his way out, Harrington called back over his shoulder, "It looks like we're the last to leave." His words dissolved into the night air.

I sighed with a grunt, turning back to Nurse Helen, who was washing off the table. "Don't you ever wear out? You know, you are the inspiration that keeps me going."

She pulled off her blood-soaked apron and dropped it in the wash bin, her voice soft. "Of course I'm exhausted, but I have two brothers in the fight up north, and they get no rest. I see their faces in every lad I touch." She looked at the floor, her shoulders quivering. "Lost my eldest brother at Flanders Field at the beginning of the war." Helen's voice broke, "Along with sixty thousand others. Such a lovely name for an abominable place. He's buried there."

Her impenetrable eyes glazed over with sadness. I'd never seen her falter in the months we'd worked together, but now, vulnerable, unmasking her deep emotions, she became a siren, calling to me. How could I not comfort this brave, driven woman who saw every soldier as a brother? I extended my arms and drew Nurse Helen to my chest. Barely reaching my shoulder, she sobbed, soaking my shirt while I held her against me. Moments passed as she collected herself and drew a final jagged breath.

My body grew warm with longing. It had been months since I embraced Miriam. I'd all but forgotten the power of human touch. At first, I thought compassion for her consumed me, but it guilefully shifted to desire. I could not restrain myself another moment. She reminded me so much of my indomitable Miriam. I leaned down to her face, kissing her cheeks, then her damp lips. Gently at first, but fully enough for the demon within me to exit his warren, shutting the door behind, tempting me to ignore my vows. I knew she wasn't Miriam, but I craved her, nonetheless. I pulled Helen closer, kissing her mouth more deeply until our breaths caught, my body drumming with desire.

She pulled back. "I'm so, so sorry, Doctor. Didn't mean for that to happen."

I drew her back into my arms. "You give me hope and warmth in this miserable place." I was helpless in my need, kissing her neck, inching my way upward to her lips, gripping her entire body to mine, both of us yearning for each other. This time, she did not resist.

* * *

I woke from a dreamless sleep. My body was calm while my head raced. Opening my eyes, it all came back. The night before. A reckless, sumptuous kiss. Helen's nocturnal visit to my tiny room in the back of the church. A church turned hospital was an ironic place for an affair. The titillating pleasure. I sighed deeply, wondering what I would do next.

I had mounted a racehorse charging full speed into calamity. Why had I joined this wretched war in the first place? I thought back to last spring when I was full of vigor to play my part, patching up America's youth as they faced this miserable conflict. I wanted to be with Ben, serving with Europe's and America's great surgeons, to do my part and show Miriam I was as strong and determined as the soldiers. Now they were filling the hospitals and morgues. What happened to my convictions?

I adored Miriam with all my heart, but I never could have imagined spending every waking hour covered in blood, choosing who would live or die. It was the ultimate nightmare. Then to have temptation of the purest delight set in my path. Who in their right mind could resist?

When I arrived in Ypres, I'd been issued a kit bag with a razor, towel, toothbrush, and condoms. I laughed when I first saw the square wrappers, thinking how lucky I'd be if somehow Miriam made her way to me. Now I was thankful they'd been issued. What did the commissary know something I hadn't? Did all the rules of civility go out the door in wartime?

I threw back the covers, bracing myself for the blast of autumn's chill. War, a forbidden hell where the law of survival reigned, I'd continue to do whatever it took to make it to the other side of the carnage. So be it if I must break a few rules on the way.

Dying soldiers would be arriving at the hospital doorstep in the next hour. There was no time to waste. I needed every minute to prepare.

Chapter Twenty-Six: Miriam

October 1917—New York City

E ncouraged by my dreamy inspiration, I took a cab to the midtown Red Cross office the following day, wondering why I hadn't thought of going to them in the first place. Walking through the door, a spring to my step, I observed a well-oiled operation, a depth of experience absent when Eli and I visited the Medical Corps office, where staff tripped over each other in a race to set up their recruitment office.

The Red Cross staff was comprised of polished professionals. They'd been recruiting physicians, nurses, ambulance drivers, and stretcher-bearers, deploying them where each was most needed, for the past three years. The office was lined with photographs of their efforts through the war. Front and center hung a large, framed picture of their Mercy Ship, the first to send physicians, nurses, and medical supplies to France. Beside it was a photograph of a hospital train paused in a remote location, loading patients in wheelchairs and stretchers, nurses and soldiers climbing aboard beside the injured. Awestruck by the expressions of determination on their faces, I scarcely heard a woman's voice calling to me from across the room.

"Miss, can I help you?"

I turned about and smiled, "Oh, yes, I'm here to enlist. I'm a surgical nurse."

The woman wore a crisply ironed outfit, conveying her importance, a gray cotton long-sleeve dress with a red cross appliqued on the sleeve, a white full-body apron with a matching red cross, and a white nursing cap with a third red cross stitched in the center. Her warm eyes scanned my body from head to toe. They twitched when she reached my legs.

I took the first steps, approaching her, drawing her eyes away from my leg brace. "Good morning, my name is Nurse Miriam Drucker." I extended my hand, explaining my role at Beth Israel, emphasizing my vast job responsibilities.

She waved for me to follow. "I'm the Nurse Director, Nurse Lennon. Let's sit somewhere private and talk." She led me into her small, tidy office, closing the door behind us, then repositioned the wood guest chairs so they faced each other. She lowered herself into a chair, straightening her cotton frock and apron, and pointed to the chair beside hers. "Nurse Drucker, please sit."

Something about this interview, perhaps that we were even having one, struck me as odd. I waited for her to begin.

She cleared her throat, studying me calmly, one brow lifted, then cocked her head to the side. "Nurse Drucker, perhaps you can explain why you're really here today?"

I pressed my lips together, curious and somewhat annoyed at her question. "I came to enlist. To help in France as a nurse." I smiled slightly. "I thought I mentioned that to you in the lobby."

Nurse Lennon sighed. "There's no dainty way to say this, so I will be direct. From what you're telling me, you have an extremely vital job running Beth Israel, and from the looks of things…." Her eyes shifted to my laced shoe and exposed brace. "You have an impediment that would make serving overseas quite difficult."

Determination crawled up my chest, and I drew in a fortifying breath. I did not want to argue, but I had to find a convincing response. "Yes, you are quite correct. My position is very important, requiring me to work long days, much of it on my two good legs. But many individuals in my family are working as physicians in France, and I'd like to be there to support our troops and their efforts."

Nurse Lennon pinched her lips, nodded, and sat quietly for a moment before adding, "You must understand. We can only send the able-bodied overseas. We can't have you becoming a patient there, too."

"But…."

She cut off my words. "There are plenty of important roles stateside. The Red Cross has grown at lightning speed, with new chapters in every state in the country, and we're desperate for strong leadership at offices in Upstate New York to organize our recruitment efforts. I'm sure your talents would be well received."

My voice rose. I would not be sent to a remote countryside office. "With all due respect, that is not how I'd like to serve. It would be far less than what I do now." My annoyance was making it difficult to think straight. Breathe, Miriam, breathe. I thought quickly, "It would be a shame to forego an experienced operating room nurse in France, where the need is so desperate."

Her face turned red. "Not if you collapse on the floor, and we must send you directly home!" She sniffed, annoyed. "And your impertinence won't get you far with the Red Cross, no matter your position at Beth Israel."

I gathered my paperwork, stuffed it into my satchel, rose from my chair with as much dignity as I could muster. "In my years at Beth Israel, I've yet to collapse against a wall, on a chair, or God forbid, on the floor. I'm sorry I wasted your time today. Personally, I find it absurd that my stellar qualifications are not up to par for serving our dying men in France."

She gazed at me, her face stunned. "I'm worried about you, Nurse. Isn't anyone in your family looking out for your welfare? You have a critical position at Beth Israel. You don't need to be in France."

My hand was already on the doorknob as I straightened my hat and twisted back to her. "The army has no compunction about sending our young boys to those perilous trenches to get torn to ribbons. My husband is a surgeon there and tells me the situation is desperate. If I'm willing to take my chances to help them, then you should be willing, too. That's all this is about."

Nurse Lennon studied me further. "I will discuss the matter with the Red Cross Commander, but I warn you, it is doubtful he will permit it." She gave me a quick nod. "You may not believe me, but I'm trying to protect you."

The effect of her words unsettled me as I rushed out of the building and stormed across town to Hannah's apartment. I had anticipated spending my day off packing and arranging to leave for France. Instead, a cauldron of fire burned within me. I needed to speak to someone who could understand.

* * *

Sophie was settling Gilda in the carriage along with her beloved, tattered blanket and doll as I approached Hannah's building. Still annoyed, I tried to calm my anger as I reached the corner of Fifth Avenue to cross. I waved and called out to greet them.

She turned about and waved back, waiting for me to cross the street.

I hurried across, dodging a pile of fresh manure. "Those cars' engines and horns may be noisy, but I will never miss these disgusting piles of horse dung."

"It's a lovely morning for a stroll. I thought I'd take Gilda to the park while the sun was warm, and we'd collect leaves. We'll press them later." Sophie said, ignoring my mood.

Gilda sat in the pram holding her doll. "Auntie Miriam, come too!"

Bending to kiss Gilda on her cheek, I asked Sophie, "Is Hannah home? It's her day off. I have something important to run by her."

Sophie pointed to the upstairs window. "Yes, she's still upstairs, preparing to meet Ina for lunch."

I cupped Gilda's soft cheek in my hand. "I will take you back to the park this weekend, my love. Would you collect some red and yellow leaves for me?"

Gilda nodded with a delighted face, her smile full of gleaming little teeth, her cheeks rosy.

Waving to the doorman on my way into the building, I started up the stairwell.

He called to me in a loud voice, "Ma'am, I'll get the elevator for you. It might be easier on your leg."

145

A new wave of anger coursed through me. Why is my leg all anyone sees? I am so much more than a crippled leg!

Hannah was gripping a hatpin between her lips when I opened the door. Her hair, once blond and wavy, now showed strands of gray, giving her small stature a stately appearance. Although she always had a stylish flair, I knew she was making an extra effort to impress Ina, her fashion idol. Hannah's hair was pulled back in a low chignon while the brim of her felt hat bent softly over her forehead. The brown and gold in the hat fabric accented her drab brown tweed belted suit. Despite the utilitarian flavor of war fashion nowadays, Hannah and her friends always impressed me with their additional flair for style, a feather in her hat, an attractive brooch on her jacket.

Hannah was the only naturally slender woman in our family. Unlike the rest of us who grew wide looking at pastries, she could eat anything she chose and never gain an ounce. Inwardly, I chuckled that in her middle years, Hannah still cared about her appearance, her clothes impeccable and well assembled. But she did, especially when it came to Ina, the fashion queen of Mount Sinai. Hannah wouldn't want to appear dowdy beside her old friend.

Catching my breath from the brisk climb up the stairs, I asked, "I hope you have a few minutes to talk. I'm so frustrated I could scream."

Hannah searched my face, her brows drawn. "What happened? I'm about to walk to Grand Central and meet Ina for lunch. Do you care to join us? We can talk on the way."

I sighed, "I'm sorry to intrude on your day off. I'll walk with you. We'll see how I feel about lunch when we arrive. Right now, I have no appetite for anything short of a freshly sharpened sword."

Only two blocks into our walk and my rant, Hannah chastised me. "You know that Nurse Lennon was right. Why can't you let it rest?"

I huffed in annoyance. "You don't understand, either. I'm fine to go to France. It's only my leg, not my entire body. I know my limitations!"

Hannah lowered her voice. She was trying to handle me like a porcelain doll. "No responsible physician will ever sign off. There's far too much risk."

Et tu, Brute? My head was churning, and I wondered if I could stow away on a ship. Then no one would have to sign anything.

Hannah stopped in her tracks. "I know you too well, Miriam. What is going on in that head of yours? I certainly hope you're not thinking about doing something reckless."

My God, am I that transparent? "I'm just thinking if I could find a way to The American Hospital, Ben could vouch for me."

"Oh, Miriam, slow down. You've just lost your father, your husband's been gone for months, and we're at war. It's natural to want more control in your life." She took my hand in hers as we walked. "Eli will be home before you know it. Our boys have been there for months and are ready to join the fight. Besides, the Germans are exhausted."

Should I tell her? Probably not, she would only worry more, but I couldn't stop myself. "Don't be so sure. Eli hears the Germans will be doubling their troops on the Western Front now that the Russians have retreated to handle their own insurrection."

Hannah's eyes widened in surprise.

"You know that means this could drag on longer than we figured."

She sighed in resignation. "I hope you're wrong. The children, particularly Albert, have been a wreck, and things at home are worsening by the day."

I squeezed her hand, realizing I was not the only one struggling. Since she adopted Ben's two children, Hannah's life had been surprisingly idyllic. But back then, Ben was always home in the evening helping, adding a second dose of love, and in Albert's case, male authority. "Tell me. I'm a big girl. There's no need for you to struggle alone."

She stopped and faced me, her face pale with fatigue. "I was called to the school last week to discuss Albert's behavior. He's been fighting on the playground." She paused, lightly clearing her throat and sighing again. "Apparently, the fighting has been a growing problem in his grade. Not only Albert. The boys are terrified their fathers won't come home."

For a moment, I was lifted from my own problems. Having spent most of my career caring for infants and children at the hospital, my heart immediately went out to those boys. "How old is Albert? I should remember, but I've been so distracted lately."

"He just turned fourteen. I'm surprised you don't remember. His Bar Mitzvah was only last year. Thank God Ben was here for that." Hannah began walking, our pace picking up.

I chuckled. "I know the school fighting is serious, but the rambunctious behavior is normal. You do know boys his age are quite physical. With all their body changes, they act like randy animals in the wild half the time."

The corners of Hannah's mouth turned up, and she shook her head. "I hadn't considered that. It must be feeding into his monstrous attitude. I could use Ben now, more than ever."

My eyes scanned the buildings as we walked. I couldn't help but notice the sizable number of construction projects curtailed, new edifices unfinished in midair, likely to remain in that state until our troops returned. The children came back to mind. "How's Anna? Is she acting up, too?" If she were, Albert's behavior might concern me more.

Hannah hummed for a moment. "She's the loveliest little girl I've ever met, except for Gilda, of course. Anna is very mature for her age."

"Is she talking about her fears? How would you know if she's keeping it bottled up?"

"She's talking about her Papa, but with more insight. And I believe she's chosen to remain positive as he's encouraged them to in his letters." Hannah made a firm nod. "It's best that way."

Thinking about the children prompted a new thought. Injured children caught in the fighting would need nursing care. That's it! Working in a children's unit would be my next ploy, that is, if I could find a way to France.

* * *

The months crawled by. Autumn, with its vibrant hues of crimson, ginger, and gold leaves, had ended. Now December, winter had arrived in its crystalline splendor, readorning the streets and buildings of New York, replacing the dead fallen leaves with its first light frost. Smoke poured from

148

the rooftops as furnaces and radiators labored around the clock, warming households. Blanketed horses pulled carriages amid the bustle of cars filling the avenues, passing vendors bundled in wool coats and scarves, roasting chestnuts, their nutty fragrance filling the air.

It was a freezing Monday morning, a week after Chanukah festivities had come and gone. I wrapped a wool scarf around my face and head, warding off the strong crosswinds sweeping through the open streets as I hurried to work. My wool coat, long and warm, was once Mama's, one of her favorites. She had owned it for years, never frivolous with her clothing, always valuing good function and comfort over fashion. Her old clothes were a source of most arguments in my home.

I was raised after my parents had both sold their garment businesses—Papa's buttons and Mama's tea dress kits. They had moved on, purchasing residential and commercial buildings. But they still bickered about clothing as if their livelihoods depended on it. Mama would scold Papa for bringing an unnecessary garment home as a gift. "Oh, Abe, where on Earth am I going to wear such a frilly hat? We don't live on Fifth Avenue."

Papa didn't care, he only wanted the best, the most fashionable for Mama, even if she wore the garish hat around the apartment and never out the door. But as much as he adored her, he also understood her sensitivities. Mama didn't want to flaunt their good fortune while so many from her old neighborhood in the tenements still struggled to make ends meet.

But when it came to boots and coats, Mama's decisions prevailed, reminding my brother, Julian, and me, "I don't want you ever to feel the cold we once lived with day and night, only a coal stove to warm our entire apartment. You must bundle up and stay warm. It will keep you healthy." So, in winter, woolen hats were tied tightly over our ears and coats were buttoned to our chins, no matter how much our skin pinched. Every year, Mama brought our wool coats to the tailor to let down the sleeves and hems, and move buttons, affording another year of use. It didn't matter that she and Papa could afford new, more fashionable coats. To Mama, wasting money on food and clothing was simply abhorrent.

With thoughts of Mama ringing in my head, I pulled the sheared beaver collar of my coat tightly around my ears and dug both hands into my matching muffler. Oh, how I wish my parents were both still here with me. It's never quite the same when they only live in one's heart.

The red and green displays decorating store windows for the Christmas holidays were uplifting, but also a sober reminder of the chairs circling dinner tables around the city that would sit empty as our men fought in France. Every scene evoked thoughts of Eli as I imagined him alone in a cold makeshift hospital near the battles, hands half frozen, legs stiff from standing for hours, struggling to save his patients. Eli's letter last week left me hollow and more determined to find my way to France.

> *My dearest Miriam,*
>
> *I worry the mail isn't making it across the Atlantic. I write twice a week but haven't heard from you in nearly a month. I pray you haven't given up on me.*
>
> *There is no way I could have anticipated the deplorable conditions in which I work. The weather has turned cold and grows colder by the day. The winds are torturous. I fear the men in the trenches will suffer from frostbite. Supplies are sporadic, scarcely enough to make it through to the next train delivery. Some of the roads are impassable. German aircraft shoot at anything moving.*

The next line was blacked out by the censors. I imagined he was sharing his location.

> *XXXXXXXXXXXXXXXXXXXXXXXXXXXXXXXXXXXXXXXXXXXXX.*
>
> *Now I see our boys, too, torn to shreds, petrified. I wonder if any of us will survive to witness the end of this nightmare. Sometimes I wonder if the Germans considered the apocalypse they were creating. Do they not value life and peace for their own countrymen? Their soldiers, whom we occasionally treat at the hospital, are equally battered.*
>
> *Ordinary men with decent values have turned into savages. That is, until they're injured. Then they become terrified children calling for*

their mothers in every language. "Mamma, Mamman, Mama...." Agony and fear sound the same in all tongues. This war is sheer madness.

I know I sound hopeless and lonely, but there is one shred of good news. My operating skills are a universe beyond what they were when I left New York. I have learned to sew together limbs that would have previously been lost. Everyone here whispers in my ear that I'm the best in my unit. That must count for something. The heap of legs and arms behind the hospital in the limb crate grows slower due to my team's work.

I feel the weight of sleep bearing down and will end this letter thinking of you as I drift off. I'm thankful you are home, safe, keeping our bed warm. I hope you're not missing your Papa too much. I wish he were there to keep you company during this difficult time.

Sending all my love and prayers for an end to this living nightmare.
Eli

* * *

For the past two months, since being denied by the Red Cross, I'd been searching nonstop for an alternate way to reach England or France. With barely a passenger ship venturing into the treacherous seas, I'd given up traveling under the guise of a passenger visiting family abroad. No one was visiting anyone in Europe these days. The military crafts were monitored, and security was as tight as a drum, officials fearing sabotage. The options had dwindled.

In the meanwhile, I'd followed Hannah's advice and reengaged with nursing colleagues at the hospital. We were busy preparing procedures for the influx of injured American soldiers soon returning for care. The plan to discharge patients to convalescent homes had been working like a charm, clearing close to thirty percent of our long-stay beds. Not only did it open beds for new patients, but it took pressure off existing staff, improving their morale. The patients' families were happier too, preferring a patient visit in a calmer atmosphere, a more natural transition home. The convalescent centers allowed more visitors, home-cooked food, and personal items. Many patients dressed in street clothes for the day. All in all, it was a good decision.

Perhaps Hannah was right. There was plenty of important work stateside. That still didn't calm my fears for Eli and concern about him weathering the Spartan winter conditions. But the more I spoke about my worries, the more I realized I was not alone. Beth Israel was full of soldiers' families who worried as much as I did. As I listened to their concerns, my isolation began to lessen.

* * *

It was seven a.m. the following Monday when I walked into my office with a cup of fresh coffee and a toasted bagel. I had thirty minutes to receive the night report from Julia, then head to the operating room to fill in for the day. While I was tied up in surgery, house emergencies would fall to my next in line, Nurse Rachel, the head nurse in Emergency.

Julia rattled off a list of problems I could hand off. None seemed terribly urgent. All the while, I thought how trivial my triage list was compared to triaging the wounded at the Front.

Before going to the operating room, I stopped to see Nurse Rachel in Emergency and handed her the list of matters, mostly trivial: Mrs. Favin didn't like the food and wanted her daughter to cook her meals, the ward wasn't warm enough, Mr. Kassen wanted his wife to bring his own blanket and pillow to the hospital, and so forth. I wrote, *NO*, in capital letters beside the last item as it might introduce lice or scabies into the hospital. *How was I supposed to take any of this seriously? Lice and scabies were endemic at the Front.* Nurse Rachel and I reviewed actions for the more serious problems before I made my way to the operating room. I trusted she would handle everything with her customary compassion and efficiency.

Heading to the surgical suite, I couldn't help but scorn at how the average New Yorker had no clue what was happening overseas, how ghastly it was.

If they did, would they complain so much about food and pillows? I hustled downstairs to the locker room, listening to my footsteps echo in the empty stairwell. When I arrived, the other surgical nurses were already donning aprons and hats.

"What cases do we have today?" I asked.

The senior nurse, Erma, a stout woman in her fifties who had worked for decades at Beth Israel, answered, "Just the usual, nothing we can't manage. We'll have both operating rooms going. Miriam, why don't you work in Room 2?"

I walked to the paper schedule thumbtacked to the door. Dear Lord, Room 2 was Dr. Silver's operating room. Not him again. He was a snail, singing to himself off-key from the beginning to the end of every case. His first patient was a tonsillectomy scheduled to start in a half hour, and the second, a hernia repair. How could he block an entire day for two such simple cases? Cases that in capable hands should fill only half a morning. I exhaled in a loud huff. He made such a fuss about nothing.

Nurse Erma turned my way. "Why such an attitude? Do you have a problem with Dr. Silver?"

I waved my hands in front of me. "It's just there's pandemonium on the floors that could use my attention while Dr. Silver is singing in the operating room."

"I understand, but remember, we've lost close to forty percent of our surgeons, and we must keep the remaining doctors happy, or we won't have any left."

The last person I wanted to irritate was Nurse Erma. She was a master at fixing problems in the operating room. One never knew when they'd need her help. "You're right, maybe there will be time between cases for me to catch up with the inpatient problems," I answered, forcing a smile.

As expected, the morning dragged on. It was the longest tonsillectomy I'd ever witnessed. The saving grace was the child fared well under the anesthesia, and there was no excessive bleeding.

Dr. Silver, pulling off his mask, smiled, appearing pleased with his results. He glanced at the wall clock. "Looks about time for an early lunch break.

Let's get the child to recovery, and I will speak with the parents. See you back here at 12:30 for the hernia."

Fifteen minutes later, I was just about to dash out the door to check on the inpatients when the telephone in the operating theater rang. I picked up the receiver. "Operating Room, Nurse Drucker."

I heard rapid breathing from the other end. "Who is this?" I demanded, in no mood for pranks.

"I'm sorry, it's Rachel. I need you in Emergency, right away!"

My voice rose. "What's going on? Tell me."

"There's been a train derailment at Grand Central. I don't have any more information. No numbers, no severity. My guess is they're alerting all the nearby hospitals."

My heart leapt with nervousness and anticipation. This was my calling in life, bringing calm and order to chaotic situations. "Rachel, we can do this. I'm heading down right now. In the meantime, no staff leaves the unit for lunch. Bring in sandwiches and check that your supplies are well stocked. Alert X-Ray and the Laboratory, and make sure their staff also stays in place."

My next call was to the Hospital President, notifying him of the accident and the need to handle the press. As with all traumas, the administration would step back and give the doctors and nurses a wide berth to maneuver, ensuring we were insulated and receiving the supplies needed. Their job, in part, was to manage outsiders, keeping the press away until we had solid information. Seconds later, I limped into the second operating room. Nurse Erma was washing her hands at the sink, her morning cases finished.

I placed my hand on Nurse Erma's steady shoulder, leaning into her ear. "There's been a train derailment at Grand Central. I need you to prepare the operating rooms. Surgeons and staff should stay in place and be prepared."

She stared at me in shock. "But the surgeons and nurses just left for lunch."

"Get them back. Bring in lunch if you must. Push off all elective cases. I'll be in Emergency sorting out the impact."

"But...." Nurse Erma started.

"No buts. I'm counting on you. I'll call with an update once I know

154

more specifics." With those words, I threw on a clean apron and shuffled as quickly as my legs could carry me upstairs to the Emergency Department.

By the time I arrived, ambulances were pouring in. Police, drivers, and patients holding their scant belongings were clogging the entryway. The air was filled with screaming: patients calling for help, irate police demanding attention, and ambulance staff shouting for support. Nurse Rachel leaned over a bloodied patient, applying pressure to the wound, ignoring all around her. It was pure chaos.

I was accosted by a red-faced police officer who shouted directly in my face, "Who's in charge here?"

I pulled away, staring him in the eyes. "I am. Do not shout in my face! Blow your whistle and get everyone's attention."

Four blasts of his whistle were all it took to get everyone's attention. The room fell silent.

I pulled a wooden chair to the center of the floor. "Help me up on this chair," I ordered the officer. He steadied me as I pulled myself up above the crowded room.

My words rang loud and clear. "We will assign each patient a severity level. The most severe cases will be taken by our staff immediately to an exam area. The others will wait their turns, here in the front open area." I pointed to one of the new nurses, wearing her hair in a braid down her back. "This nurse will stay by the entrance and make sure everyone is properly cared for while you wait."

A deep voice cut through the crowd, demanding, "Don't you know who I am? I need a doctor now."

Stepping off the chair, I leaned into the police officer's ear. "I don't care who that man is. No one gets preferential treatment. We must take care of the most serious cases first. Can you handle him?"

He nodded firmly, appearing pleased to have direction and a semblance of order. "Yes, ma'am."

Within seconds, the room was restored to its usual hum of activity. Over the next five hours, we treated over sixty patients from the derailment, ranging from head injuries and complex fractures to cuts and bruises. Nurse

Rachel and I triaged the patients and assigned an additional nurse to remain in the waiting area, applying pressure to wounds needing suturing and icing broken limbs. A secretary from the main office moved from patient to patient, helping register and taking addresses for sending telegrams to family members out of town. The X-ray department ran constantly, helping to prepare studies for the patients requiring surgery and bone setting. Their staff was in a constant panic, worried the X-ray machines would overheat and blow a fuse.

A sense of satisfaction filled my spirit. *Maybe this is where I'm meant to be after all.*

I walked back to the operating room late in the day to check on the surgeries. Julia, my Chief Nurse partner, had returned to the hospital by early afternoon. While I oversaw the Emergency and X-ray Departments, she handled the operating room and inpatients. Julia was picking supplies from the closet and lining a wheeled cart to resupply the operating room.

"Thank God you came back in. What's the status?" I asked.

She brushed a few loose strands of hair from her face, tucking them neatly under her cap. "Finally, calm, but it's been the wild west all afternoon. Dr. Silver is struggling with a case right now, massive internal bleeding. I don't know if the patient will make it."

Alarm shot through me. Dr. Silver was fine for tonsils, but a massive belly bleed? Did the woman stand a chance? "Are there any other surgeons who can help him?"

Julia shook her head, her eyes full of the answer I dreaded. "You know as well as I the best surgeons are in France."

I left her in the hallway, opening the door to the operating room just in time to hear Dr. Silver's shaky voice announce, "Time of death, 5:32 pm."

Nurse Erma looked up from the body, her face somber and exhausted. I roped my arm around her shoulder. We both watched Dr. Silver, his head sagging to his chest, leave the room.

She said with resignation, "In all my days, I've never seen anything like this. Such madness, so much bodily damage."

I studied her bloodshot eyes and squeezed her tighter. "Let me help. I'll get the body ready for the morgue and see about contacting her family. Clean up and go home."

* * *

The operating room had finally emptied. All that remained was the corpse and me. The silence was saturated with the stunned souls of the departed, mostly young people with no clue this day would be their last. A metallic smell of blood drifted upward from puddles on the floor where the patient had bled out. I gazed at the exposed face. She was a young woman, close to my age. Her face was as white as the plaster walls, unmarred, a small blessing for her parents. Cleaning her cooling body, I thought about the words I'd use to tell her family she was gone, no longer part of the mortal world. I wondered why she was on a train from Pittsburgh to New York in the first place. To start a new life, a job?

With those thoughts in mind, I scanned the room for her personal possessions, hoping to get a clue of her identity and contact information. But there was no sign of a purse or valise. Pulling the sheet over her body and face, I headed to the Emergency Department, hoping the staff had stored her belongings.

When I arrived, Rachel was helping the housekeeper mop the waiting area. "No stragglers?" I asked.

She looked up from her mop, weary lines outlining her face. "Thank God, no. Hell of a day. How was it in the Operating Room?"

I frowned. "Not great. Erma was scrubbed in with Dr. Silver, and he has no idea how to manage trauma. He lost a few, including a young woman this afternoon—couldn't stem the bleeding from her internal injuries."

Rachel shook her head sadly, "It's like everyone keeps saying, the best surgeons are overseas. So sad this is who we have left to care for the rest of us."

I didn't want to complain. I'd had enough mediocrity for the day and knew at some level I must remain professional. "By the way, I'm looking for personal items to notify her family."

Rachel pointed to the closets behind the nurse's station. "Check the supply closet on the left. We tried to gather everything and store it there for safekeeping. I was planning to sort it out this evening."

"Good idea." I stood in place, facing her straight on. "Nurse Rachel, excellent job today." I spun around and walked to the closet. It was a jumble of coats, small valises, and purses, all thrown atop each other. As I picked my way through the pile, glasses, coins, handkerchiefs, and train tickets fell out of pockets. Three purses lay on the floor. I carried them to the nurses' charting area and opened each, hoping for an answer. The first purse was the size of a small suitcase and overstuffed. I dug around and pulled out a large leather wallet containing folded receipts and a library card for a Mrs. Thornberry. There were four photos, each of an older woman holding hands with what appeared to be restless children, none standing long enough to face the camera, one with his tongue out. Replacing the items in the purse, I moved to the second, a plain brown leather handbag. It contained a Chinese Newcomer's membership card for an Ella Wong. My deceased woman was Caucasian.

I sighed, hoping the third would reveal a clue to the body upstairs. Shifting the purse in front of me, I examined it closely. It was a small, hand-tooled brown post bag with a top flap, buckled closed. I imagined a woman traveling for business, perhaps a family matter such as settling a will, planning a quick stop, and then returning home. Turning the purse upside down, four items fell onto the counter: a small wallet, a comb, a lipstick, and an envelope. *I'll bet I guessed right. A short visit, then back home.*

Opening the wallet, I saw my corpse's picture and identification. Sarah Rosen, 15 Juniper Lane, Pittsburgh, Pennsylvania. Birthdate May 15, 1890, the same month and year I was born, twenty-seven years ago. *This could have been me.* I shuddered. I was sure she never saw a disaster like this coming. I emptied the envelope, unfolding the papers, and scanned the content. A wave of goosebumps swept across my skin. *Oh my God!*

Red Cross deployment papers to Paris. Sarah Rosen was a nurse, and Jewish, like me. She was scheduled to board the Navy's Mercy Hospital Ship later this week. Upon arrival in Paris, orientation at The American

Hospital in Paris, then transfer to work on an ambulance train. Sarah was going to the Front!

III

PART THREE

"Here today, gone tomorrow."

Chapter Twenty-Seven: Hannah

December 1917—New York City

C lick, clack, click, clack. My steps were brisk as I walked home from the hospital. The days were short, temperatures dropping fast. The new incandescent lamps lit the sidewalk, their erratic current flickering. I charged ahead, determined to have a relaxing dinner with the children.

Of all years to have a freezing cold December. Was the weather in France this harsh? Tonight, I'd write letters to Ben and Eli after dinner and send each of them a package of wool socks with a sweater. Perhaps Albert and Anna would include notes, too. Who knew if it would all make it across the ocean? But I had to try.

It occurred to me a few steps from the apartment door that I hadn't spoken to Miriam all week. We had a brief call before the train derailment days ago. She must still be digging out. I'd give her a ring when I got upstairs and invite her for dinner this weekend. By then, the commotion at Beth Israel will have died down.

Upstairs, moments later, I dialed her number. The phone rang and rang. I let it ring ten times, my limit. I'd try her again in the morning.

Setting the receiver back in the cradle, my eye caught a stack of mail on the credenza. I sifted through, hoping for a letter from the men and noticed an envelope addressed to me, in what looked like...no, it couldn't be, Miriam's handwriting. She never wrote letters to me, only telephoned.

Ripping it open, dread in my heart, I dropped into the foyer chair and began reading:

My dearest Aunt Hannah,

I know this won't come as a complete shock, but I'll tell it to you straight. Right now, I'm crossing the Atlantic on my way to France. I boarded the Mercy Hospital Ship last Friday from New York Harbor, heading for St. Nazaire. The decision was sudden. I could have spoken to you before leaving, but I chose not to, afraid you'd try to convince me to stay, and then feel guilty you hadn't succeeded.

You were right about spending a few months in New York after Papa died and concentrating on my role at Beth Israel. It helped show me how important my work at home was, especially after the derailment. If this opportunity hadn't come my way, I would have stayed put until the end of the war. But the chance to go to France came and there was no doubt in my heart I had to take it. Let me tell you the events of the past two weeks leading to my decision....

My heart was pounding in my chest as I read about the train derailment. Since very few patients were brought uptown to Mount Sinai, Beth Israel, and Bellevue bore the brunt. But I was floored when I read to the letter's end. Miriam had always been a willful child, but never in my wildest dreams would I have predicted her next actions.

... As I said, her name, now my name, is Sarah Rosen, RN. You can reach me at The American Hospital in Paris by that exact name. I changed her home address on my new papers to your address. When I arrive in Paris, I'll find Uncle Ben and write to Eli so they both know my situation. I don't want my family to worry I've vanished into thin air.

I notified Sarah's parents of her death before I left, and they will come to New York to identify the body and take the real Sarah home for a proper burial. But I kept her identification and enlistment papers with me to use as my new identity. The family won't need them and will think they were burned in the wreckage. I also sent a note to Beth Israel in my real name explaining that I had an opportunity to join the Red Cross in France and would return after the war. I'm trusting you to keep everything confidential. The last thing I want is to stir up trouble.

Sarah's papers instruct her to report to The American Hospital in Paris for orientation and training after reaching St. Nazaire. Afterwards, she is assigned to serve on the evacuation trains, transporting patients from the hospitals near the Front to Paris. Although I would like to work by Eli's side, this assignment may suit us better. He'll be reassured his limb repair patients are in good hands until they arrive at The American. We'll work as a team.

As for Eli, I'll write once I arrive. I don't want him worrying about the crossing. If I have any pull with my assignment, I'll try to hop a train to Ypres and surprise him. If not, I'll post a letter when we get to Paris.

Pray for a safe passage, and I will send a telegram when I arrive in France. Until then, give the children hugs and kisses and keep one for yourself.

Love you dearly,
Miriam

My heart continued to thud. I sat a moment, then the tears came. How could I be so blind? She slipped right through my fingers.

Sophie called out, "Is that you, Dr. Hannah? Is everything all right?"

I rose and walked into the kitchen with my tear-stained face. "Miriam has left for France." I poured myself a glass of wine, muttering under my breath. "This war is going to be the death of me—without even one bullet shot my way."

Sophie wrapped me in her arms. "Try not to worry. She's a clever girl. She wants to help the wounded."

I unwound myself from her grasp and handed her my untouched wine glass, pouring myself another. "You're God sent. I don't know how I'd keep my life together without you."

One by one, the children came into the kitchen, all surprised to see us sitting and drinking. Albert stared at me, wide-eyed. "What's going on? When's dinner? I'm starving."

Anna, at his heels, tilted her head to the side, her mouth agape, "Did something bad happen? Is Papa hurt?"

I pulled Anna into my arms. "He's fine. It's just… I'm a bit stunned. Aunt Miriam joined the Red Cross and is heading for France. She's somewhere in the middle of the Atlantic right this very moment."

Albert's face ignited with excitement, his eyes sparkling with admiration. "She's fearless!"

I sat Gilda on my lap. "Albert, there's a thin line between brave and reckless. Let's pray she doesn't get hurt."

Anna wiggled out of my arm and faced me with her soft eyes, her dark lashes wet with her own worry. "Papa will protect Aunt Miriam."

Her twelve-year-old voice sounded like an older woman reassuring the child in me. Who was this extraordinary little girl, with insight so far beyond her years? Did a life of turmoil, first the loss of her mother, living with her grandparents until Ben and I married, adjusting to a new family and sibling, then finally her father leaving for war, force her to mature too fast? Or was she destined to see the bright side, betting her cards on fairy tale endings? Did we adults in her life, who faced every storm together with Albert and her, provide enough cover so she could grow unscarred from her losses and disruptions? If so, how did that explain Albert's continual surly behavior?

I arranged Gilda on my lap and gazed at Anna, this red-haired daughter of Ben's, who resembled him to a fault. "You are right, sweetheart. Aunt Miriam will be fine with Papa. I'll telegram him in the morning and tell him she's on her way."

Anna smiled, "Tell him I miss him."

My stomach rumbled with hunger. "I will be relieved and happy when everyone is back home with us. But for now, let's help Sophie set the table."

Chapter Twenty-Eight: Miriam

January 1918—Paris

Atlantic crossings were always unpredictable in winter, but I had no idea what that meant until it was too late to change my mind. For a week and a half, we were caught in a storm cycle, vicious spears of dark water ripping across the open deck, sending any freestanding object overboard. Fourteen-foot swells, sinkholes of voracious water, threatened to swallow our ship. Advancing against fierce winds that whipped up at night made any thought of strolling the upper deck for fresh air impossible. The romantic fantasy about ship travel I'd privately entertained throughout childhood was shattered. Hiding in our stuffy, crowded cabins, at times holding on for dear life, we fought unrelenting seasickness, many of us missing meals for days.

The words "unrestricted submarine warfare" echoed in our heads, adding a layer of mental dread to our weakened bodies. Daily evacuation drills kept us on alert in the event of an attack. The nurses in my bunk room were petrified, crying in their beds, not even attempting to muffle their sobs. For me, crying provided no relief from the anxiety. Instead, I lay on my side, writing letters of regret to Hannah that I planned to mail once onshore, my handwriting jagged, at times illegible from the ship's pitching.

Three weeks later, we finally docked in Saint Nazaire. The applause circling the deck was deafening. Everyone, spent and relieved. With wobbly legs, we scrambled off the ship. No one was willing to spend an extra second aboard. I dropped my letters in the trash, no longer regretting I made the journey.

The ride from Saint Nazaire to Paris was a bit over a half day by train. Once in Paris, we expected a week of training before deployment to the Front or to the hospital trains. We were soon to learn that plan had changed.

I gasped when the cab pulled up to the front of The American. Both Eli and Ben had written about its size, but there was no substitute for witnessing its sheer magnitude with my own eyes. It was a fortress of carnage and healing, multiple times the size of Beth Israel, consuming blocks upon blocks of Paris. How could mankind impart such cruelty and evil? I stood, frozen from the cold wind, twisting my body right and left, absorbing the many buildings in the hospital complex.

The nurses from my ship's berth called out to me as they walked ahead to the main door. "Sarah, are you coming? We'll freeze out here!"

The spell was broken. Eager to get down to business, I followed the pack of nurses into the main building, where we were directed to the cafeteria. We dropped our duffle bags and valises in a pile by the door and sat together at the far end of the room where a classroom-style arrangement of long tables and chairs awaited us. I sat, rubbing my thigh where the brace had dug.

An Officer Jackson introduced himself and began, "Welcome, weary travelers. I've heard you had quite an initiation during the crossing. Winter can be like that, but fortunately, no submarines or casualties. Trust me, that would have been much worse."

A chorus of groans erupted from the audience of sixty-some-odd nurses, doctors, and stretcher-bearers.

He continued. "My heartfelt thanks to all of you for joining the Red Cross effort in France. Our soldiers, our boys, need your help more than ever." He paused for a round of applause designed to lift our exhausted spirits. "Our job is to answer the call, a medical need that we cannot always predict ahead of time. As such, in the last month with the freezing weather at the Front, the combat has stemmed, and by God's good grace, casualties are fewer. However, we anticipate this trend to be short-lived."

A middle-aged man, who had identified himself on the Mercy ship as a surgeon, raised his hand, calling out, "I'm Dr. Hartman, we need to talk. It was my understanding...."

Officer Jackson interrupted Dr. Hartman, holding out his outstretched palms, attempting to quell the sea of rising hands. "Please, everyone, hold your questions. Kindly let me finish."

He continued, raising his voice above the murmuring, "Later today, after you settle into your assigned rooms and have tea, my team," he extended his arm to the uniformed men and women sitting at the adjacent tables, "will return to their tables to meet with you individually for your orientation and interim assignments here at The American. We will assign you to hospital wards that meld with your current expertise."

Hearing his words, the audience settled back in their chairs, appearing relieved.

"While you are temporarily assisting at The American, medical teams from the Front will join us, both to see how their patients are faring and for well-deserved furloughs. You'll have a chance to meet many of the nurses and physicians who you'll eventually join at the Evacuation Hospitals and on hospital trains. Spend time getting acquainted, as they'll give you a clear picture of everything you need to know heading east, what to bring, and the challenges you'll face. For now, rest up, and learn as much as you can here at this great hospital."

He paused, drawing a deep breath before continuing. "There will be times you may question your decision to serve. Please don't. We absolutely can't win this war without you, and our wounded are desperate for your skillful care. It *will* make a difference." He let his message settle and said, "On my left, you can pick up maps of the facilities and your bunk assignments. Keep the maps handy, you'll need them. I'll see you back here for afternoon tea at 3 pm."

I rose from my chair, walking away from the crowd, avoiding the rapid scrambling toward the table with the maps and room assignments. There'd be plenty of time for me to get situated, and I did not want to risk a further injury to my leg. Instead, I hobbled to the coffee station to fill a cup and sit a while longer. My brace had been a constant irritation since leaving New York, likely from the ship's pitching on the choppy seas. The chafing on my thigh had progressed from red, raw skin to small, ruptured sores in several areas. I would need to get the wounds properly cleaned and bandaged before infection set in.

It took one sip of coffee to remind me I was far from home. The strong beverage was thick and bitter, a nuttier smell, clearly a different drink from any New York City cup of black coffee I'd ever tasted. I rose to pick up a sugar cube from the canister on the counter. Thank goodness they're still getting sugar in the city. Turning away from the condiments, my eye caught the profile of an older doctor wearing steel-framed glasses with a head of gray curly hair. He turned toward me. I squelched a yelp. "Well, hello there, Dr. Kahn. Greetings from New York City!"

His face broke into a delighted smile of joy, and was it also relief? We stepped toward each other, careful to keep our hug short and professional, not revealing the true extent of our relationship.

He shook his head, unable to break the smile, whispering. "I could flog you, young lady, for your recklessness, but I'm too thankful to see you safe and in one piece. Your Aunt Hannah has been sick with worry. Once you have your coffee, we'll send her a telegram so she can finally settle down."

I shrugged my shoulders, snorting air through my nose. "It shouldn't have come as a surprise to anyone. I've been talking about finding a way here for months."

Uncle Ben huffed. "Do you have any clue how dangerous it is? And for women?"

I smirked, creasing my brows. "Of course I do. The crossing was terrifying. But this is where I belong now, helping in the war effort." I sat back in my chair and laughed with a sense of false resolve. "But if you had warned me about this dreadful coffee, I might have stayed home."

He stared at me, his face softening. A slight smile pulled up the corners of his mouth. "Very funny, you crazy woman. Right now I'm damn thankful you made it here alive." He took my hand in his. "Is there anything you need?"

170

I melted. It had been so long since anyone had comforted my nerves in such a manner, had asked me such a basic, caring question. "Seeing your face, seeing family is all I need at this moment." I sat quietly, thinking, "But I'd appreciate it if you could peek at my leg later. It's been through the mill the last couple of weeks on the ship." I winked, "And don't forget, my name here is Sarah. Calling me Miriam could get me in quite a pickle."

* * *

Uncle Ben carried my suitcase to my room, offering his arm for the three-block walk to the women's dormitory housed in a separate building several blocks apart from the inpatient units. The block of buildings was originally constructed as a boys' school, acquired by the hospital before ever opening in its true intent. Each room was fitted with two bunk beds, one on either side, two small closets, and a shared bathroom in the hallway, doubling the occupancy originally intended. Not an inch of space was spared as the hospital continued to gobble up every adjacent property to house more casualties.

At the door, Uncle Ben handed me my suitcase. "Why don't you take a moment to settle in and get acquainted. I'll wait for you downstairs, then we'll find a private place to check your leg. If you're up for it, I'll take you on a brief tour before tea. You'll soon see that it takes practice to learn your way around."

There were three women about my age unpacking when I entered. All beds had been claimed but one, an upper bunk. My stomach twisted thinking of the difficulty hiking myself up and down the bunk bed with my bad leg. Disappointed, I decided to manage the best I could and accept the leftover bunk without complaint.

"Hello, it's nice to meet you. I'm Sarah Rosen from New York," I said, announcing my presence. "The trip here was so awful, I was holed up in my cabin practically the entire time, and I didn't meet many people."

They stood nodding and met my eyes, scanning my body, and like everyone else, their eyes stopped at my brace. A short blond nurse said, "My goodness, Sarah, I don't know how you managed it on that roller coaster ride at sea. Would you like to switch beds and take my lower bunk? It might be easier to climb in and out. My name is Gloria, from Connecticut."

My face melted into a smile. Relieved and grateful, I said, "I'll take you up on your kind offer." I set my suitcase beside my new bunk bed.

The two other women introduced themselves. Pat from Rhode Island was tall like me and had kind hazel eyes. I knew the soldiers would adore her. Willa, with her chestnut braid and slender frame, lived in Philadelphia. She and her thick Irish accent immediately captivated me, reminding me of New York City and the volumes of European immigrants. "I'm looking forward to getting to know all of you. I'll unpack a little later. A friend from home is waiting for me downstairs."

As I closed the door behind me, I overheard Pat whisper to the others, "I can't imagine how she convinced the Red Cross to let her join with that bad leg and all." She added with a disdainful edge, "And isn't Rosen a Jewish name?"

I hurried down the steps. Those kind hazel eyes were a ruse.

* * *

By the end of the tour, Uncle Ben had persuaded me to join him on the Head and Face Unit while I waited for my assignment, convinced it would both expand my technical skills and open the door to new opportunities when we returned to New York after the war. He knew the city needed a dedicated burn and facial reconstruction unit and wanted to build his vision at Mount Sinai. As a matter of fact, he'd already begun corresponding with the President of the Hospital and Board of Directors to begin raising money for such an effort. After a week in Paris, I could see his vision quite clearly and was excited to support his plan.

At first, I thought he was looking to keep me close to him, keeping an eye on me, but I couldn't have been more wrong. With my newly acquired surgical skills, together with years running inpatient services, reconstructive care offered a new, exciting frontier, one missing from most hospitals, and would be critical for the men returning home with extensive head wounds.

I couldn't have been happier than working with him on his unit. The hours quickly slipped into days, then a week. I wrote to Eli, telling him about my arrival in Paris and plans to work with Ben. Immediately after, I sent a similar letter to Hannah.

December 26, 1917

Dear Aunt Hannah,

Despite the unfortunate discovery that my stomach and ship travel don't mix, I am very happy I braved the crossing—and lived to write about it. Although my leg took a beating from the rough seas, the sores have been healing due to excellent ministering here in Paris by none other than Uncle Ben.

I had no accurate idea how bad things were. For France, Britain, and Belgium, the war has been an endless parade of bloody battles, most barely gaining an advantage for either side. Weary, hopeless soldiers, many without arms and legs, are scattered about the city. Some too drunk to stand. I wonder what happened to their families and homes. Are they too broken to return to those they left, or have their villages been wiped off the map? It is terribly sad. If we had known the extent of destruction, would the U.S. have waited so long to help? Many doctors, nurses, and ambulance drivers did not wait, they've been here for years, working with the Red Cross as volunteers.

Back in New York, we are completely removed from the true horror. More than ever before, I stay tuned to the news, to the many newspapers and radio. The news coverage in France is far more extensive than what I was accustomed to.

Uncle Ben is a remarkable doctor. He has a true gift in the operating room. But, moreover, his loyalty and dedication to the men in his unit are unmatched. Even in this goliath hospital (nothing at home comes close to the size of The American), everyone knows his name and extends the respect he has earned. You would be very proud of him.

But he pines for you and the children, mentioning your name in every other sentence. My arrival may have heightened his homesickness. I don't think he'll be able to let any of you out of his sight once he's back home.

Day after day, the original plan for my transfer to the evacuation trains gets delayed. I've heard that most of the medical staff at the Front will be issued furloughs to Paris over the next few weeks. I'm hoping Eli will get one as well once he knows I'm here. I sent a letter to him, but haven't heard back. I'd give anything to see the look on his face when he learns I'm in Gay Paree! In the meantime, I'll wait patiently. There's no shortage of work to fill the time.

Give yourself and the children a big hug from me

Love

Sarah (Miriam)

I set down my pen and folded the paper, licking the seal. I'd drop it in the post box on my way out tonight. I had only moments to grab my coat and meet Uncle Ben downstairs. We were taking a cab to a charming café for dinner.

Chapter Twenty-Nine: Eli

January 1918—Ypres

N ew Year's Day, I was startled awake by a tingling sensation, a hand fondling the hair on my chest. The fog of sleep lifted while Helen moved closer, curling against my naked side, reaching below. She popped her head under the scratchy, military-issued blanket, talking to my lower parts. "Good morning to you, too. From the looks of things, you were dreaming of me." Helen laughed, climbing atop me.

If Helen only knew. Lying in bed with my eyes closed, I was lingering on the tail of a dream about Miriam, whom I hadn't heard from in weeks. One year ago, New Year's Eve, the night of our engagement party, five months before our wedding, was everything this year was not. No nightmarish parade of wounded and dead, no flavorless food, no exhaustion. Celebrating our engagement with family and friends at the Waldorf and dancing to Billy Murray's big band hits filled me with an all-encompassing sense of happiness. When we snuck back to my apartment after midnight, no one blinked. After all, we were both approaching thirty, well beyond the confines of a young courtship. Me half-running, Miriam hobbling on the slick, frozen sidewalks to my apartment, we laughed at our impulsiveness, grasping each other, barely restraining our desire.

This New Year's Eve had passed with little celebration or regalia, none of the dancing to big bands, French champagne, or fancy roast beef dinners of my past. Instead, ambulance drivers and medical personnel huddled for

175

warmth outside the hospital, rubbing their hands together over outdoor fire drums on the cobblestone streets where the wounded were lined up for triage earlier in the day. The eerie quiet was broken by the notes of a French ballad threading through the freezing air. A melody flowing from an ambulance driver's harmonica accompanied by the percussive crunching sound of soldiers tamping out their smokes. For lack of entertainment outside, Helen and I slipped away to my quarters to celebrate the only way we knew how.

* * *

Minutes later, dressing together, buttoning the front of her uniform, Helen broached a different topic, her words hesitant. "Darling, I received my furlough papers yesterday. I'm traveling home to see my family for a few weeks. I'll hop a hospital train to the Channel and cross on a hospital ship."

I half-expected this, not entirely surprised by the news of her leave. After all, she'd been stationed in Ypres far longer than me. Other doctors, nurses, and soldiers departed on furloughs throughout December as the fighting ebbed. Nevertheless, a rush of envy tugged at me. Time with Helen was my single reward for tolerating this endless, arctic existence. It would be hell remaining here without her. I groped for a solution. "What if I could swing a few days off myself? Would you be interested in Paris? We can stay somewhere away from the hospital to ensure our privacy." I didn't want word getting back to Miriam's Uncle Ben.

She twisted, facing me, her dress half open. "Eli, you know this can't go on forever. Have you forgotten you have a wife at home? Besides, I haven't seen my parents in over nine months. They're worried sick about me."

I sighed, silently acknowledging my two worlds. I knew Helen could never be part of my future. Even my dreams were still of Miriam. But it was also a fact that daily thoughts of Miriam had diminished over the months in France. Helen was here, in Ypres with me, a breathing, vibrant, passionate human being. What if I died in France? Damn it to hell, why couldn't Helen support me in this godforsaken place? Did I have to suffer the loss of companionship altogether?

I steadied myself, pulling my thoughts back to Helen, stroking her hair, tracing my finger down her uniform. "All I can manage right now is feeling alive every day. Lord knows, I had no idea what I'd signed up for, how we would drown in death. This…," I pulled her body into mine, burying my face in her silky slip between Helen's small, warm breasts, begging, "…is what's keeping me sane."

* * *

The news of Helen's furlough broiled in me, demanding quick action on my part. I could convince her to stop in Paris before visiting her family if only I could secure a leave. Waiting patiently for a furlough would never work, I was too low on the seniority list. If the fighting resumed, I'd be dead in the water.

Since late November, the days passed with relentless freezing temperatures despite the sparkling clear blue skies. Every morning, after sleeping in two layers of clothes, my joints were stiff, my feet constantly throbbing. With little break in the weather, out in the open trenches our soldiers also suffered, but in new ways, arriving at the hospital with high fevers and frost crystals on their hair and eyelashes. We sent trainloads of ailing men to the larger hospitals in Paris and England, many with trench foot and compromised circulation. Despite our best efforts, amputations once again rose. An equal number were stricken with typhus and influenza. Pneumonia, death's front door, was rampant, a heartbreaking conclusion for men whose bodies were never grazed by shrapnel. We burned their filthy clothing, crawling with fleas and lice.

As my surgical work ebbed, I was transferred to general medical patients, caring for those who could not be treated with a scalpel. I missed the quick decision-making and action of my operating table, finding the care of chronically sick patients tiresome. I fantasized about closing the unit entirely, sending these suffering men off on trains to somewhere else. I no longer cared.

I grabbed breakfast right after Helen left my room and rounded on the soldiers in the hospital. Two had died during the night, and I telegrammed their families, a heartbreaking start to 1918. By 2 pm, I finished my clinical work and crossed the street to the makeshift headquarters, located in a row of stone buildings. One end of the block had been sheared to the ground, exposing the foundation and a skeleton of walls, a hint of the structure above. The other buildings remained intact, completely unscathed by artillery. Before the war, a thriving pharmacy, indoor market, and tailor's shop inhabited the space. They were long gone. I'd no idea where to. The displacement of people and commerce was beyond the limits of my imagination.

Now inside, the large front spaces that once held products and displays were now filled with long tables and unfurled maps of the Front. In the back of the room was a rabbit warren of interconnected offices, each with a rear door to the alley, perfect for privacy and a quick, undetected escape.

I knocked on the Commanding Officer's door, a French man in his fifties, whom I occasionally passed in the mess tent and on the sidewalk.

"Entrez." The Commander sat behind a desk, reviewing papers and drinking a steaming cup of coffee. Despite the quiet on the Front, his face looked concerned. His low-slung jowls and deeply etched grooves along his frown lines looked as if they hadn't held a smile in years. Shifting his eyes up from the piles of paper, he glared at me through his steel-rimmed glasses.

Despite his lack of gentility, I reached out my hand. "Good morning, Commander. Dr. Drucker, American surgeon, New York City. I don't believe we've formally met."

He shook my hand quickly, answering in his heavy French accent. "I know who you are. Let me guess, you want to return home and leave us...how do you say it? In the lurch?"

I stepped back, startled. "Oh, no, sir." Was this the risk he faced when he issued furloughs? Soldiers and medical personnel disappearing into thin air? Abandoning their posts?

He continued accusing me, a sharp edge lacing through his voice, "Not enough glamour for you? You know the war is not over."

I smiled, shaking my head, convinced he'd be relieved once he heard my request. "No, Commander. I'm only here to ask for a furlough before the fighting starts again." This time I paused, my smile gone, stating firmly, "It's not over until we crush the Germans."

The Commander sat back in his chair, eyeing me from head to toe. "How do I know you'll return?"

I was right. The Commander's concern was desertion, and for good reason. Before the American troops arrived, the French had a hell of a time hanging onto their soldiers. Upon arriving in June, Martin shared that the soldiers had been leaving in droves, weary of the battles, defeats, and carnage, advancing a few feet in one battle only to lose it in the next. Many of the men, even officers, had given up in despair, disappearing into the night, never to be seen again. The desertions had become epidemic until the Americans came and injected a strong dose of cowboy optimism.

I placed my hands on my hips, standing tall. "I guarantee I'm not abandoning my post. I am only asking for a reprieve from this charming village." I waited for him to crack a smile. "Could I get a pass to the capital for a couple of weeks? I intend to check on my limb repair patients at The American while I'm there."

The Commander's face relaxed. "You're the arm and leg magician I've been hearing about." He sat for a moment, staring at my face. "And you give me your solemn word to return in two weeks?"

I extended my hand again. "I'll shake on it. You have my Yankee promise."

He nodded. "Do you have a moment to talk about your results? My son lost a leg in battle two years ago. He's home now in Paris with his mother, but the Germans made a frightful mess of his leg, *gaussément,* simply terrible."

I settled into a wood armchair missing its left arm, typical of the furniture the townspeople had left behind. If the Commander didn't keep a sharp eye, it would soon be firewood. After listening to his son's unfortunate story and our process in Ypres, the Commander pulled out a form, scribbled on the lines, and handed it to me. "Thank you, Doctor. Our boys deserve the best we can give them." He sat back wearing a downcast, solemn expression, his hand stroking his chin. "Leave your lodging information at the Administration Office at The American. Know that you'll be called back immediately if the Jerrys decide to take another round."

I couldn't wait to tell Helen.

Chapter Thirty: Ben

January 1918—Paris

What in tarnation is wrong with these young people? Who in their right mind runs into a burning building? And that's what war is, an inferno of human destruction. For three weeks after receiving Hannah's telegram, I was wild with disbelief, furious the girl had taken such extreme risks. But when I saw Miriam, now calling herself Sarah, and her familiar determined face, I immediately calmed.

I'd accepted the fact I wouldn't see my family for months, even years. I'd buried my longing, only allowing myself to think about them when I wrote my weekly letter. Seeing Miriam touched me in a familiar way I'd worked hard to bury. Her bright young face and enthusiasm for helping the wounded bolstered me from the first day she magically appeared in Paris.

Now, working beside her in the face ward, I can't imagine how I managed on my own. Only two weeks into her assignment, she knew more than I did about my men, medically and otherwise. And I had been treating them for months. As we made rounds that cold morning, I asked, "How did you know Private Stanley's uncle was a carpenter? I had no idea."

She smiled with the same enigmatic expression she used as a small child, as if I were from another planet. Miriam laughed brightly, "Uncle Ben, I mean Dr. Kahn, part of our plan is to help give these men a leg up with their futures. They know they need a plan when they return home, but not all of them can figure it out on their own. After all, half of the soldiers aren't yet twenty. Before leaving for war, they hadn't thought much beyond their first kiss. Now they must."

I studied her determined face, admiring her insight and how she resembled her mother, Tillie, who raised and protected my wife. Tillie had cushioned Hannah's falls, helping build her into the confident doctor and mother she became. Tillie was a rock, the backbone of our family. In a pinch, her flock of family and friends counted on her for sound advice. Miriam embodied the best qualities of her mother.

Miriam continued explaining as if her work were as simple as peeling a potato. "Private Stanley comes from a long line of craftsmen in Wisconsin. His father passed two years ago, and he has four younger brothers and sisters. He wants to help his mother support the family when he returns, not become another burden. Stan told me all about it while I changed his bandages."

Still flabbergasted, I pressed, "But he's one of forty-two on my service, and you know them all. How did you learn so much so fast? And so many don't speak English."

She tsked, readjusting her Red Cross-issued cap. "What red-blooded boy doesn't want to spill his story on a Sarah from Ohio, the girl next door? Besides, sending them home feeling whole is half the reason I came."

I raised my brows, having never considered that a young nurse might provide the chemistry to get these men talking. "Miriam—er, I mean Sarah— you must tell me immediately if any of them get randy with you. I will not tolerate disrespect, head injury or not."

A sweet, tight-lipped smile crossed her face. "Oh, I've been asked on a few unusual dates, but nothing handsy." She laughed. "One of them invited me on a hayride! If it weren't for Uncle Nate's chicken farm, a city girl from New York like me would have no idea what a hayride was."

Her words struck me. Ever since the Americans joined the war, I'd come to appreciate our extraordinary U.S. geography. From my tiny corner in New York City, I'd never thought much about the way others around our country lived. After the American troops arrived, I began keeping a log of the different states my patients called home and, in many cases, nationalities, as new immigrants filled the rank and file, too, still struggling with their English. When I inquired why they enlisted, they all said the same words, "I'll be a citizen when it's over."

I showed Miriam my small leather journal with the information I'd collected. "I've been jotting down the different colloquialisms these men use, so make sure you share anything unusual with me." I added, "Many of these boys have never traveled more than twenty miles from home until now. War makes for a distorted introduction to the bigger world."

She shrugged with a deep sigh, "I suppose a nightmare for most, especially our unit."

Curious to hear if she'd received new orders to leave for the evacuation trains, I asked, "What's the word from the Front on your deployment? Any updates?"

Miriam sat in a nearby metal chair near the nurse's station and tilted her head back in frustration. "They don't expect the fighting to pick up until the ground thaws. There's little combat, at least for now. The powers that be want my nursing team to remain here, training at The American until the action picks up."

"Anyone comment on the brace?" I asked.

She shrugged. "Of course, but then they see how unstoppable I am. Once I've snuffed out their concerns, they returned to their work corners. I'm never sure if their questions are in my best interest or not. You know, some people just like to make trouble."

I nodded in agreement. "No one could ever fault you for your commitment and intellect, but you still must take care of yourself, just like you aptly counsel the men in our ward."

She sighed. "Now that you mention it, I've been thinking it might be wiser for me to stay put in Paris with you. Our work is terribly important, and after that sea crossing, well...I hate to admit, I'm not sure my leg could tolerate months rattling around on a train."

* * *

I left Miriam in her chair at the nurses' station and headed to the operating room. We had two patients scheduled for skin revisions. Their scarring was shrinking as it healed, pulling at the skin and forming ghoulish expressions on their faces. My treatment goal was to avoid painful skin grafts by releasing the tension in the scar tissue. Over the last months, we typically ran through this cycle of healing and releasing numerous times. We took the men back and forth between the ward and the operating theater, stretching skin, reworking the tiny sutures. It was an exercise in stamina for these brave men, most of whom never complained. Gillies had confided to me that many of his patients had upwards of thirty surgeries.

Knotting the last stitch, I thanked the scrub nurse who'd stood patiently beside me during the delicate, tedious revision.

"Beautiful work, Dr. Kahn. You took a ruffled cheek and smoothed it flat. Do you think this will be his last revision?" she asked.

I set the surgical scissors on the instrument tray. "I hope so, but we won't know until he heals. Some of the boys mend better than others. He'll still need an eye patch when this is through."

She was quick to respond. "At least it's not a mask like the other surgery we had earlier today. That poor lad lost his nose and eye." She paused before continuing. "What do you think about Dr. Gillies' offer to accept British patients at his hospital in England? Queen's Hospital, I believe."

I knew Dr. Gillies offered to keep an open door for my patients. At Queen's Hospital, he had an army of physicians, dentists, and mask-makers at his disposal. "We can ask the men with more extensive mutilations, but I'll bet they won't want to go."

"Why is that, Doctor?"

I squeezed my lips together, considering the best way to describe their connection to The American. "The men in my ward are tight, a brotherhood. They know they're accepted and understood here. The surgery and healing are torturous. Day after day, they support each other with a fierceness, like a den of lions. For them, that's as important as what their faces look like."

Later, when I returned to my room, a military letter lay on my desk. I had only a half hour to clean up and change before taking Miriam for dinner at the Café de Flore, a four-and-one-half-mile ride from the hospital, a cozy restaurant where we could review patient issues and speak openly about family.

I laid out my clothing and sat on the edge of the bed, opening the letter with my finger. Hannah was forever scolding me for using my hands carelessly. "What will you do if you get a paper cut? It could keep you out of surgery until it heals." I smiled at the memory. The letter was from Eli and dated a week ago.

> *Dear Ben,*
>
> *The fighting has dropped along with the temperature, and our hospital is beginning to transfer patients to the bigger facilities away from the battlefield. I'll be hopping a train along with fifteen repair patients next week for The American. I plan to stay in the city for a two-week furlough. I hope all is well with you and that you'll have time to dine with me and discuss the latest innovations on your Head and Face Unit. News of your good work is reaching us here in Ypres.*
>
> *Until then,*
>
> *Eli*

This was the best news I'd had all week. I couldn't wait to see Miriam's expression when she read the letter. It had been half a year since she'd seen her husband.

Chapter Thirty-One: Miriam

January 1918—Paris

The ice crunched under my feet as I hobbled toward Uncle Ben, who stood by the street corner. "It's freezing out here. How far away is this place?"

He strode toward me and reached for my arm, offering to help me navigate the slippery sidewalk. "Hold on tight, Miriam, the streets are a sheet of ice. Don't want you to fall now that your leg has finally healed."

His strong arm was what I needed. "Where are we going?"

Reaching the corner, he waved for a taxi and said, "The Café du Flore. It's a fixture in Paris. Been around for decades."

"Have you been there? Do they serve hot food?" I felt my belly rumble. Thinking back, I didn't recall breaking for lunch. It was always so busy and shorthanded on the floor. We climbed into the rear seat of an idling black Peugeot. A hand crank was stationed beneath the front hood in the event the car stalled.

Ben's lips curled into a smile under his heavy mustache, setting off a twinkle in his eyes. "Once, with other officers. What a treat. The tastiest omelets on this side of the pond. And their soups are the stuff of dreams."

The thought of fresh eggs cracking over a bowl, a fork whipping them into a lather, and the sizzling of butter in the hot pan filled my head. In only a few weeks, I missed the daily cooking clatter of home.

He cleared his throat, smirking with mischief. "I have a surprise for you."

I sat straighter, a thrill filling my chest. "What is it?"

He pulled a letter from his jacket pocket, handing it to me. "This arrived today. Eli's coming to Paris."

My heart thumped so hard I could scarcely breathe. "It's too dark in here to read. What else did Eli say? Does he know I'm here?"

Ben paused. "I think he sent it a week ago. Your letters may have crossed in the mail. Come to think about it, he didn't mention when he'd arrive."

I bounced in my seat, excitement lacing through my body. This was the best news I'd heard in months. "Maybe I can surprise him!"

The taxi drove into the 6th arrondissement, approaching the corner of Boulevard Saint-Germain and Rue Saint-Benoît, chugging so loudly we could barely hear each other. The café awning was sloped in the middle, weighted down with snow and ice. Dim table candles dotted the interior, casting soft rays through the large picture window, sending arrows of light onto the deep sidewalk. I envisioned those streams of light illuminating crowded small tables and guests "people watching" while they sipped their wine or coffee during the warmer months.

Uncle Ben helped me exit the taxi. From a distance, the tantalizing smell of freshly cooked food filled the cold air. A pack of mangy street cats hovered by the building's edge beside an adjacent alley, mewing, begging for scraps. "Those poor starving animals. Uncle Ben, let's not forget to bring bread for them when we leave."

He was silent.

I lifted my eyes from the cats to him. "Uncle Ben? What is it?"

He set his hand on my back, firmly turning me away from the café, startling me. "We're going somewhere else."

I pulled back. "Why? It smells divine." I followed his gaze inside the café, trying to understand why he suddenly changed his mind. I froze in place, my blood turning to ice.

Straight in front of us, only a couple of feet separated by the plate glass window, sat Eli at a table. Across from him was an attractive woman, smiling, extending her hand. A hand that Eli lifted to his lips, ardently kissing. He abruptly stopped as if he sensed a dangerous current running through the air. Lifting his face to the window, he stared. His eyes locked with mine, widening, horrified.

At a complete loss, I shook my head from side to side; my heart in free fall.

I felt Ben pulling my arm, but my feet were cemented to the sidewalk. "I'm taking you back. I'll deal with him later."

* * *

Aware of the low, soothing hum of Uncle Ben's voice, I could not separate his words, the phonemes fusing together in the back of my head. I could only register Eli's image. Caressing another woman's hand. Kissing it. How could it be? Impossible. Or was it?

The jarring picture of them in a remote café hit me like a sledgehammer. In complete shock, empty of emotion, I struggled to digest their image. Losing grip of my surroundings, I was sucked into a shell, detached from my world into a nightmare that would not quit. I never thought I could be jarred into such a stunning withdrawal.

Uncle Ben shook my arm. "Miriam, can you hear me? Honey, look at me. We're in my room at The American."

I turned my head, watching his lips move, forming words. Words I could no longer decipher. What was he saying? I shook my head, then closed my eyes as my world returned to its haze.

I heard a banging at the door and moments later, men arguing in the hallway.

* * *

I teetered in and out of an amnesiac state for days. Each time the fog lifted, the reality of them together returned. Eli's loving eyes, kissing her fingers. It was as if a jagged spear had been plunged through my heart. I gasped for air, fighting my way back, but continued to slip back into my quietude, sinking within myself until the deep ocean of hiding shrank to a puddle

188

and I couldn't hide there any longer. By the third day, the voices around me were no longer a drone of modulated sound. The incessant humming had formed into recognizable words, my memory of the evening crystal clear, imparting a painful sting each time I replayed the vision. Little by little, I faced the gloom, sobbing into my pillow, expelling the shock like a venom to banish from my system.

By the week's end, Uncle Ben entered my room in his daily cheerful state and sat at the foot of my bed. He softly closed the door against listening ears, studying my face, his baritone voice settling me. "How's my niece this morning?" He took my ankle, buried under the covers, and gently squeezed. "You look calm."

I nodded at him. "Much better, but embarrassed." I drew a deep breath and began to cry. "I should have known he'd never stay faithful to me. I'm a cripple, damaged goods."

Uncle Ben recoiled, raising his voice. "Don't you ever say such a thing. You are beautiful, brave beyond measure, and smarter than the whole lot of us combined. This has nothing whatsoever to do with your leg."

"I still can't believe he's a cheater. I thought he was above that."

Uncle Ben cleared his throat. "If it makes you feel better, he's a complete mess, hanging around here every morning, leaving letters for you. Have you read any?"

"Yes, I've read them all." I settled my head on the deep pillow. "I should speak to him before he returns to the Front." My voice trailed off. "God forbid something bad happens before we clear the air."

Uncle Ben scoffed. "There you go, Miriam, putting the responsibility on yourself. You have nothing to feel guilty about. If you care to listen, I advise you to see Eli when you're good and ready. Honestly, I don't know why you're not angrier at him."

I was so lucky to have Uncle Ben here, filling the hole Mama and Papa had left behind and loving me for being my exact self. But I was too depleted to fight. I just wanted the avalanche of pain to end. "I'm ready to speak to him. If he comes back later today, we'll talk, but he might not like what I say."

He wrinkled his eyebrows together. "How are you feeling about the future?"

I exhaled sharply. "I don't have an answer yet. I want to hear Eli's version and ensure he knows how much this affair has unglued me. I'm not sure I can ever trust him again."

"That seems fair. Perhaps even a bit noble from your end."

My eyes pleaded with his. "The problem is, I still love him and will worry when he returns to the fighting. He needs to know that much."

Chapter Thirty-Two: Eli

January 1918—Paris

T he night Miriam saw me with Helen, after Ben tossed me on the sidewalk, I slunk back to my hotel room to finish things. But Helen knew what was coming and had left hours earlier. It wasn't her nature or job to stay and assuage my guilt. Instead, she left a note on the dresser. The woman had class.

> *Eli,*
>
> *We knew an end to our love affair was imminent. I will always carry the guilt of hurting Miriam the way we did last night. I hope you can mend your marriage. I expect nothing less from you.*
>
> *I am determined to transfer to another Red Cross hospital. If our paths do cross, I insist on a strictly professional relationship. Otherwise, you will not see or hear from me again. Please do not attempt to find me.*
>
> *Helen*

She'd made the end easy. Helen knew better than to hold on, hoping I'd choose her. We both knew from the start we were a salve for each other, as temporary and intense as the battles. But I'd never forget the fury of our lovemaking, the desperation to cling onto something equally powerful as the carnage mounting around us. Such a steep price to pay for a quick ride in heaven.

* * *

I slept poorly that night, waking every hour or two, consumed with remorse. A cad! That's what I was. How stupid. How selfish to believe I could cheat without consequences. No sense calling it anything else. A cheater, wounding the very person I loved most, the woman I spent close to two years infatuated with. Her look of disbelief, seeing Helen and me, then revulsion, would be forever imprinted in my mind. What the hell was wrong with me?

I'd never experienced the true nature of shame, its dishonor. Always a hard worker, I made my family proud. I'd been an honest man and a rule follower. Even at Beth Israel, I was careful never to exploit my position or take advantage of the nurses, especially Miriam. The fear of losing her to polio is what threw me to my knees. What was it about this devil of a war that tempted me with relentless force, enticing me to throw away everything precious?

The first morning after Miriam saw me with Helen, I knocked on Ben's door at six a.m. As surgeons, we woke with the birds, ate a quick breakfast, checked in on our patients, then washed for the operating theater. I was determined to catch him before his day began.

Ben answered my knock with a scowl, staring into my face with a sleepless, dark expression. "What do *you* want?" he snarled. Ben stepped into the hallway and shut the door behind him.

I looked over his shoulder at the door. "Where's Miriam? Is she in there? Where did you sleep?"

He barked at me, then looked about, lowering his voice. "On the floor, you moron. Things aren't right with her. She's climbed inside herself."

A whip of anxiety struck me. "What do you mean, inside herself?"

"She doesn't seem to hear me. Just curls up in a ball, rocking. She's finally sleeping."

"My God. Shell shock?" Every day, men were carried off the field suffering from similar psychological torment. How could I inflict that on her? Tears filled my eyes. "I feel terrible."

"You? You feel *terrible*?" His deep, gravelly voice shook the air. "Who the hell cares how you feel?"

My body filled with shame, trying to absorb his words. I couldn't raise my eyes to meet Ben's fury.

He leaned into my face, ignoring my question, spitting out his words, his eyes a pool of darkness. "All the while you've been thousands of miles away from home, schtupping that woman. A nurse? Someone at your hospital? How long has it been going on?"

I released my shaken breath. "No, it was recent. Nothing serious. She left before I got back to the hotel last night. It's over." I tried to reclaim my calm. "I want to see my wife."

Ben leaned his shoulder against the white plaster wall. "That's not a good idea right now. My greatest concern is that she won't snap out of her state. Seeing you, unable to register your words, might push her inward more." He stopped speaking, knit his brows, and gazed at me curiously. "What's your experience on the Front with this disorder, shell shock? How do you get the soldiers to rejoin the living?"

A deep chill ran through me. I'd no idea of Miriam's fragile state, her shallow emotional reservoir. What the hell happened to her in the last six months? Now I was at fault for pushing her into the beyond. I struggled to think how the nurses cared for these soldiers in our hospital, men whom I avoided, their behavior too peculiar. I tried to picture their beds at Ypres and the nurses who tended them.

Breaking from my memory, I said, "Tenderness. The nurses were gentle, coaxing them back to the present with talk of home. And they gave backrubs and fed them rich broths for added nourishment and…." I thought for a moment, envisioning the ward filled with traumatized men. "And they got sweets. Some soldiers came around and began reconnecting, normalized, while the others, well…." My words halted. "…Were sent here, to Paris, for further care."

Ben stroked his whiskers thoughtfully, "I'm assigning her to a private room. I'll report that she's caught an infectious flu and needs a week of nursing care. I know a nurse I can trust to help her."

"When can I see her?" Hesitantly, I added, "I'm terribly ashamed."

Ben glared back; his eyes still wide with anger. "When I say so. Presently, she's my only concern, not you. That woman put herself in harm's way for you, a frightening Atlantic crossing. One that added injury to her leg. She even took a dead nurse's name. All to help in the cause and to be at your side."

A dead nurse's name? I gasped, "What name?"

Ben shut the door in my face.

* * *

Each day in Paris was a repeat of the day before, first checking in with Ben for a status report on Miriam, rounding on my patients, then walking the streets of Paris, seeing but not registering any of its beauty.

Every morning, Ben dutifully updated me, and I was sent on my way. On the third day, he had hopeful news.

We walked together to the cafeteria. At seven a.m., there was a line at the grill, doctors and nurses calling out their orders to the cooks behind the counter, clanking silverware onto their trays, preparing for a rushed meal.

Carrying our food to a table in the corner of the large room, we sat apart from others. Ben set his tray on the table, placing his plate of eggs and potatoes in front of him as he sat. "I always knew Miriam was a smart cookie, but how she runs my floor is a sight to behold. The patients call her Saint Sarah. She goes the distance for every one of them."

I scrunched my face, confused. "Saint Sarah? Isn't that a Christian thing?"

Ben rolled his eyes back in disbelief. "You don't know. I keep forgetting you never got her letter. You must have left for Paris with that woman before it arrived at your hospital." He set his fork down with a clank. "There was a train derailment in Grand Central a month ago. She took on the identity of a dead nurse, one who died at Beth Israel, Sarah Rosen. Rosen had been heading for France with the Red Cross. Then, the rough seas knocked Miriam about so badly she, a/k/a Sarah, could barely walk when she arrived in Paris. It took a week to get the sores under control. Now her leg is mostly healed. No one knows her as Miriam, so be careful what you call her. As I've said, your wife has made great sacrifices."

I could no longer eat my breakfast; my belly was in knots. Here, I was doing everything in my power to soften the ferocity of war for myself, starting up an affair with Helen, while Miriam was putting every part of herself, including her identity, on the line to find a way to serve. I must make this right, not for me, for her.

I wasn't surprised Miriam had turned Ben's unit around. I could picture my wife winning the soldiers' hearts overnight, as she had with patients and families at Beth Israel. The same way she won mine. She had an intoxicating mix of calm, competence, and compassion, a rare trio of virtues. And it didn't hurt that she was the brunette version of Botticelli's Venus. So soft, so beautiful, so magnetic. But Ben hadn't yet shared her mental status. Why was he holding back? I probed further. "Ben, has she improved? Is she back in her right mind?"

He nodded slowly. "Yes, she's coming out of it. Your suggestions were helpful, particularly the back rubs. A gentle touch is powerful medicine. There've been a lot of tears."

I forged on, needing to know what she remembered. "What is she saying? Did she talk about that night?"

Ben sat back and stared into my eyes. "She remembers, but I'm not pushing her. Miriam will talk when she's good and ready. She gave me the fright of my life. So, Eli, stop pressing me."

I crumbled inside, pleading, "Look, regardless of my behavior, she's my wife, and I love her. I'm returning to the Front at the end of the week and can't leave Paris without seeing her and making things right."

Ben shook his head firmly, enunciating slowly, "Not today. Miriam knows you're here. I'll tell her you want to talk, but no promises. For now, I don't want to tip a delicate balance in the wrong direction. Quiet, undisturbed rest is what she needs most, not you begging her for forgiveness." While my appetite had vanished, Ben picked up his fork and finished his eggs.

I trusted his word despite my sense of urgency to apologize. In a crazy way,

I envied Miriam, having Hannah and Ben in her life with their unwavering devotion. Although it was well past Miriam's childhood, her aunt and uncle wrapped their love around her, all while anchoring the entire family. I didn't have such a mooring. My parents died years ago from tuberculosis while I was in medical school. Ironically, they'd worried I would become infected, working with sick people day in and out. Instead, they were the ones who caught the dreaded disease, dying together in their shared bed with an illness that had plagued the city for decades. I was left with a younger brother they'd sent to live with distant relatives in Chicago months earlier. Since then, he and I had lost contact. Now I was alone, except for Miriam and her family, that is, if she was willing to take me back.

Knowing how protective he was, I took Ben's words to heart. I would follow his instructions and stop at the hospital each morning for an update. In the meantime, there was much for me to do at The American. Besides checking my transferred patients, I wanted to see the renowned Head and Face Unit. Four years into the war, Dr. Harold Gillies had reached international prominence, and Ben's ward was the showpiece of The American.

"Do you have time to give me a tour of your floor? The Unit has quite a reputation at the Front. The face and head wound repairs are well beyond our surgical skills. It was all we could do to administer the most basic care, keeping those men alive long enough to move them to Paris on the ambulance trains. I'd love to see your work."

For the first time, the corners of his lips turned up. "Of course." A fragile truce.

* * *

After rounding with Ben on his unit, I spent most of the day visiting my patients on the surgical recovery floors. The number of amputees was breathtaking, row upon row of beds filled with recovering soldiers—missing arms, hands, and legs, typically only one limb, but for some more unfortunate, multiple limbs. Walking down the inner corridor, I heard my

196

name. Turning, I saw Liam Humphrey, the soldier who had begged me to save his right arm.

I barely recognized his face, but his Liverpool accent was unmistakable. In contrast to the terrified, filthy soldier he'd been when we met, I found a young, handsome patient with bright blue eyes and a head of clean, black, wavy hair. He shot a full smile my way, his freckles sparkling, extending his bandaged right arm for a handshake, slowly bending his fingers. "Nice to see you, Doc," he said with his nasal enunciation. "Remember me, Liam, with the British Fifth?"

His handshake, though still weak from nerve damage, was a manly grip, brightening my spirits. "Of course I remember. You told me you were a righty." I recall thinking at the time of his surgery how a handshake was the mark of a man. Although its importance symbolized strength and integrity, its loss was nearly impossible to replace.

His voice dropped. "I'll be heading home with all my parts in a few weeks. A whole man. The feeling in my hand is slowly returning every week. I can write a short letter now." Liam sighed, "I'm sad for the rest of these lads. I was a lucky one. Too bad they didn't all have you as their surgeon."

I looked around the ward. At least fifty patients were wrapped in white gauze and plaster, only a few with all four limbs. Liam's miracle was not about me. It was about him. I was merely an instrument. Looking into his face, smile, and confidence to direct his life forward inflated me with purpose. "You pushed me to save your arm, and I'm glad I listened. Where are our other men? Are they doing as well as you?"

He sat on the side of his bed, pointing to several patients in the ward. "There is a whole crop of us. All yours, with fixed legs and arms. The envy of the unit." He dropped his head. "A few got infections and are gone now, but most of us made it through."

I shook Liam's hand before leaving, my determination renewed. I'd repair as many injured soldiers as I humanly could.

Chapter Thirty-Three: Miriam

January 1918—Paris

The door opened softly. Eli entered, standing on the threshold. Was he in or out of my life? Teetering at the precipice, immobile, I realized he was leaving the decision to me. I lay still, searching his face.

Eli looked different. Six months at the Front had left him pale and thin. His brown wavy hair was shorn tight to his head, and he no longer wore a mustache. I'd never seen his eyes look so hollow, as if he'd returned from a trip through Dante's Circles of Hell. When was the last time he'd slept?

I pointed to the empty chair beside my bed and conjured those days two years back when he sat by me as I fought the grip of polio.

He removed his hat and lowered himself slowly into the chair, never taking his misty eyes off me.

Extending my hand, he gently took it in both of his. Tears fell. "Miriam, I'm ashamed and don't know how to make things right. I, I, I…."

"Stop," I interrupted, my voice gravely from disuse. "I don't know you anymore. Why did you cheat? Was it the war, or would you have eventually hurt me this way? Was it simply a matter of time?"

He blurted out, "I can explain…. I think."

My voice rose, breaking with a growing fury. "I'm not really ready to hear your excuses. Honestly, Eli, I wonder if you ever truly loved me or if you were just looking for a lame pup to call your own." I gulped down my anger, feeling it burn in my throat. "I feel like a fool, coming all this way to help you, help the men."

He sat back in the chair, quietly wiping his eyes with a handkerchief. "I've been to your ward and met your patients. They call you Saint Sarah. You've won their hearts in the short time you've been here."

"It's a bit overboard, but they are desperate men. They've lost everything but their lives." I sat up, arranging the pillows behind me. "Is that all I'm good for, desperate men?" My fatigue pulled me backward. I wanted to rest, be at peace, not argue.

We sat quietly before Eli spoke again. "I never meant to hurt you this way. And, yes, in all honesty, at the time I did feel desperate and concerned for myself. It's unimaginable at the Front, a disgusting, bloody parade of broken bodies. At that moment, I was selfish. I needed someone to hold and comfort me."

I gasped, not expecting such a harsh truth. Could I ever trust Eli again?

"I'm not proud of what I've done, and I know you deserve better than me. But the problem is, you are so deeply entrenched in my heart that I can't let you go. It would absolutely destroy me. I can only pray for a shred of hope you will find a way to forgiveness." He bit his lower lip, waiting for my response.

Wordlessly, I watched his face.

"If it would help, we could return to New York now and rebuild our lives," he said.

The heat in my body had been mounting with his preposterous excuses. "Now you want to break your commitment to the Medical Corps and the men whose lives depend on your skills. Does a commitment hold any value to you? Any at all?"

His forehead folded, vexed. He'd not expected my reaction. "Of course it does, but I'd do anything to keep you. I'd give everything up, right now, for you!"

Was this what I needed to hear? I knew it wasn't enough, but I handed him an olive branch, knowing I needed more time, lots more time to decide what I wanted for myself. I shook my head, my hair splayed on the pillow.

"What I want is for you to stay out of harm's way and survive this terrible war. Use your talent to save more men. They need you. Our lives are but a drop in the bucket."

He lifted his eyes to mine, whispering, "Is it over for us? Is there no hope?"

My eyes filled with tears. Was it love or pity I felt? I wasn't sure. "If you're asking if I still love you, the answer is yes. But if you're asking about our future... if we both make it home alive... well, I need more time...."

He sniffled, "Then there's still a chance?"

I nodded, my eyes fixed on his, lips in a severe line, dubious at best.

He stood over me, then leaned to kiss me. I turned my head away, and he clumsily kissed the hair above my ear. "Rest. Get your strength back. Please let me know if you need anything. Anything at all." He gazed into my eyes. "I promise I'll make you proud. Proud I'm your husband."

With those words, he turned and left my room, leaving me pondering the meaning of words like "forgiveness," "sacrifice," and "love."

Chapter Thirty-Four: Eli

January 1918—Paris

After seeing Miriam, I ventured into the city, walking for miles, another world away from the Front. Strolling aimlessly, I observed scores of soldiers, no longer able to fight, strewn about the sidewalks, all homeless, limbless, begging. My chest filled with fury. How could a country expect its boys to defend the borders with their lives, then cast them aside, broken on the street for all to witness, to pity rather than honor?

I stopped to light a cigarette, its acrid smell camouflaging the stench of fresh manure from the horses, indiscriminately expelling their waste on the street. A weak voice drifted toward me from a frozen garden on my left.

"American? Spare a cigarette?"

I glanced at a ragged soldier in the grass, wrapped in a filthy blanket. "Of course." I lit a second smoke and set it in his left hand. His right arm was amputated at the shoulder. I knew his story. It probably didn't matter whether his arm was salvageable or not. He was likely caught in the battlefield hospital's maelstrom, then the chopping block assembly line.

Seeing Liam on the ward at The American and now this bandaged soldier cemented my conviction. Our surgeons must work harder to repair the wounded. I knew it would be easier to persuade the powers that be if they witnessed the difference it made in a soldier's life. We were all told reconstructive surgery took longer than an amputation, that other soldiers would die waiting for their turn on the operating table. But it wasn't all that tricky. The steps were simple: clean and excavate the wound, check for good blood supply to the extremity, and layer the tissue in the repair. It was the least we could do to respect their sacrifices.

I strolled along Rue de Rivoli, securing the buttons on my coat, shielding myself from the bracing wind blowing off the Seine. I saw the glorious Notre Dame piercing the Paris sky. Thinking of the wounded who poured into my operating room, I couldn't help but see the irony, the ludicrousness— worshiping a God and his goodness while slaughtering our fellow man on the battlefield. From my vantage point, France's grand cathedrals that took lives and centuries to build did little to stem man's capacity for evil.

Before long, I found myself in the 3rd arrondissement, the Marais, with its narrow winding streets. Once a Jewish ghetto, it still housed a predominantly Jewish community. It was a marvelous sight, replete with medieval charm, narrow cobblestone streets, hidden courtyards, and gardens. I'd read of a new synagogue built at the start of the war in Art Nouveau style, and knew it was somewhere in the vicinity. Turning onto Rue Pavée, I saw the structure in the distance, popping out like a misfit, plopped into the blocks of centuries-old construction. By the front door of the sanctuary sat a box of yarmulkas. Although I knew my military cap was an adequate head covering, I removed it nonetheless and placed the yarmulka on my head, slipping into an old, familiar feeling, recalling attending services with my Papa as a child. I walked into the sanctuary and sat, closing my eyes, conjuring those distant childhood memories. Without realizing it, I fell asleep.

A man cleared his throat, waking me with a start. My eyes burst open, and I stared into the face of a bearded rabbi, his prayer shawl wrapped around his shoulders. "American? Jewish?" he asked in halted English.

I nodded, unsure if my French or Yiddish would suffice for much of a conversation. He appeared to be wondering the same thing.

"*Parlez vois francais?* Yiddish?" he asked.

"*Un peu. Je suis un médecin à Ypres.*" I explained. We continued our conversation in my broken French and his minimal English, stopping to clarify and laugh at our abysmal pronunciation and choice of words.

He asked, "Would you like me to recite a healing prayer?"

I shook my head, "I don't deserve it."

He sat, staring at my face. "I can see in your eyes you're distressed. How can I help?"

I looked at him, ashamed to tell him my truth. My eyes moistened with tears.

He reached out, holding my forearm, and said softly, "War is an ungodly thing. Men are forced to engage in unthinkable, cruel acts. You may feel your weight lift if you speak about it. Just between the two of us."

An unrestrained force broke in my chest, and I blurted out, "I cheated on my wife. She discovered us. Now I may lose her." I struggled to hold onto my composure, but the tears came anyway. We sat. The minutes ticked by. "We got married a month before I left for France." I raised my eyes to him, seeking guidance.

The Rabbi nodded his head in understanding, his lips forming a tight frown. "I'm sorry to hear your story. In this terrible morass, you had a temptation you could not resist. You know what you did was wrong." He sat straight in the pew. "Let me ask you this. If the situation had been reversed, what would it take for you to forgive?"

I was startled, blinking away the thought. Was my Miriam capable of such a sin? "I don't know the answer to your question. It's hard to imagine."

The Rabbi stroked his beard. "If your love for each other is enduring, there's a road back to your marriage. You must demonstrate your remorse and willingness to sacrifice. And of course, honor your vows. Healing takes time."

I wiped my nose on my sleeve and asked, "Then there's hope?"

The Rabbi's eyes met mine. We sat quietly, reflectively. Finally, he said, "As long as there's life, there's hope." He patted my arm and rose to leave. "I will say a prayer for you. In the meantime, demonstrate your love of God by caring for our wounded men. Right now, they are the ones you are here to serve. As for your marriage, be the loving husband you promised to be and give her time."

Chapter Thirty-Five: Hannah

April 1918—New York City

"This damn war! My family's falling apart." I dropped my fork on the starched, white tablecloth, directing my furious words at Ina. She was sitting across the lunch table at our biweekly date at the Biltmore.

"Eat your lunch, Hannah. When's the last time you had beef? Don't waste it."

Ever since receiving Ben's letter in early February, I'd been fuming, unable to sleep. Now, even with the start of April, the hopeful signs of spring, daffodils abloom in every patch of grass, my anger at Eli had not ebbed.

I cut my roast beef into small pieces, savoring each as long as possible, the Bearnaise sauce adding its lemony, buttery flavor. Was that a hint of tarragon I tasted? It was a rare treat to see beef on the menu. As usual, Ina, my voice of reason, was right. Best to keep my thoughts in the here and now. But Eli's hurtful recklessness continued niggling at me. And Miriam's response to seeing him with that other woman, damn troubling.

"How many soldiers do you imagine break their vows?" I asked over the sound of silverware clinking on porcelain plates. "Would you be able to forgive your husband?" I knew my remark was uncalled for. It was wrong to drag her innocent husband into this dilemma. Should I assume Ben was any different than Eli? "I would never forgive Ben after all we've been through."

Ina set her fork down. "As far as I'm concerned, my husband is behaving himself. And Ben doesn't deserve your anger. He's an amazing man and doctor."

Why was I such a mess over this? Mad at the world. Could this trigger an investigation into the real Sarah Rosen? Then what would happen to Miriam?

"I choose not to think about the *what-ifs* right now. The world has gone mad, and I'm trying to keep my head on straight." Ina said as she cut a small piece of overcooked meat. "What I want to know is how Miriam is faring. Is she improving? That young woman has been through the mill."

I sighed, my eyes misting. "She's my greatest worry. Miriam imagines she can brave anything that crosses her path—in the name of love, in the name of country. But the woman's only human, and now we know just how frail she is under that tough exterior."

Ina continued peering at me. "But what are you hearing from Ben? Is Miriam working in his unit again?"

I reached into my purse, pulling out the letter Ben sent to me. It was dated three weeks ago. I read aloud:

March 13, 1918

My dearest Hannah,

Finally, Paris is showing signs of spring. The ice has melted, and although the air remains cold, buds are peeking out on the tree branches. Unfortunately, it also means the fighting has resumed in full force. I'm happy to share that many men on my ward were discharged to convalescent homes. For some fortunate others, they returned to their families. I hope their parents help guide them toward meaningful lives. Some of the American boys will be sent back to the States for further surgeries. For those with extensive deformities, it will be quite a challenge. The public already views them with fear and trepidation.

The emptied beds are filling with a fresh crop of wounded soldiers. The catastrophic weapons that both sides use never cease to amaze me. As if this "war to end all wars" will truly be the end of fighting, forever. I'm not remotely convinced. I don't think so much bottled-up hatred can be buried so fast.

Ina interrupted my reading. "You know, he's a special doctor to work on facial injuries day in and day out. For many, it would be depressing."

"That he is. Listen. There's not much more."

I know you want to hear happy news about Miriam, and indeed, she's made strides, but her recovery has been slow. She's back working in the unit, and behaves like her old self while tending her patients. The woman never makes a mistake despite her misfortune. But when the day is done, she is despondent, often skipping dinner, and is now painfully thin. I wish she'd get angry, scream, and yell. Instead, she seeks a private place, reading Eli's non-stop deluge of letters and sulks. I know this because I've gone looking, discovering her in stairwells, outside in the cold on a bench, or alone in the corner of the cafeteria. My companionship is all she has, that is, besides her patients, whom she dares not share her problems.

Ina interrupted again. "That poor girl. No friends there, either? What about the other nurses?"

"I know. She wrote in an earlier letter that she feels ostracized with her brace. Her awful roommates don't want her there and have dropped the hint that they aren't comfortable sharing a room with a Jewish girl. Besides, they think she won't keep up, and her work will overflow onto them. Of course, it's never happened." I said, "Listen to the rest."

Eli's received two more passes to check on Miriam in Paris since that awful evening, but knows her condition is delicate. He checks in with me first. Her brief catatonia scared him back to his foxhole as it did for me. We tread carefully, as her emotional destruction is the last thing either of us wants. For now, he is patient, remorseful, consumed with guilt.

All of this has given deeper meaning to the expression, "taken to the edge." Most of us have no idea where our "edge" lies. War takes us beyond our slumbering nightmares into a world so horrid and vicious some cannot recover. We are seeing this condition in the listless men sent to us for mental care. Miriam must have been physically and emotionally predisposed, losing both parents, drained from the ocean crossing, and then caring for our horribly mutilated patients. All her hopes were set on reuniting with Eli. Seeing him stare into that woman's eyes was her last straw.

Once again, Ina cut in. "It makes me think how quick we were to underestimate her, thinking nothing could blow her over. She's as human and frail as the rest of us. Finish reading."

I'd considered sending her home on a hospital ship, but, honestly, I think she is better off here, working through her trauma and helping the men. Trauma nursing is her calling and fills her with a purpose she can't satisfy at home. She's an absolute saint with our faceless men. I pray she continues to heal, returning to her feisty self before long. But it has been a game of patience.

In the meantime, I've encouraged her to answer Eli's letters and let him know how she's doing. He is worried beyond belief. Rebuilding their bond, however impossible it feels now, will take unwavering work on his part. Eli appears to realize that truth.

In the meantime, I have all in good hands. Pray for the end of the conflict. With our American boys over here, it will, God willing, end soon.

With love to you and the children,
Ben

Ina shook her head, staring at our empty plates. "That poor girl. Her heart shattered, thousands of miles from home, wondering if she could ever trust her husband again. She's lucky to have her strong uncle in Paris to anchor her."

I snorted. "It's galling. This war has taken the lid off every decent shred of humanity. I had no idea men could be so evil. Knowing Eli, he would never have hurt her this way if he hadn't been taken to his limit, too. I hate to have compassion for him, but the temptation must have been overwhelming in the thick of so much unrelenting carnage."

Ina sneered, her large eyes narrowed. "Eli's lucky he isn't my husband. If I found out something like that was going on, there'd be no warm bed to come home to. And I don't give a devil's ass what he's facing over there."

We finished our lunches in silence. I'd skipped the part about the Red Cross, the near miss concerning Miriam's identity. I had told no one in New York about her stolen name. Her emotional break and need for isolated rest almost pried open her big secret. Who knows what would have happened if the battles hadn't resumed, sending hundreds of newly wounded to The American. Before anyone could take the time to investigate, Miriam had jumped back into her uniform, working at a superhuman pace on her patient floor, back to her tough self. Any investigation was tabled. Hopefully, forgotten.

* * *

On my days off, I'd made a point of meeting Anna and Albert after school, and we'd walk home together. I thought those hours gave us extra time to talk. But since the New Year, Albert refused to walk with Anna and me, charging ahead to meet up with his pack of schoolmates, throwing snow and ice balls at each other.

Time and Ben's absence were having opposite effects on the two children. Whereas Anna sought more projects at school to support the troops, packing cartons of wool socks, nonperishable salted meat, and candy for the soldiers in the trenches, Albert's behavior grew more rambunctious, bordering on violent. Insults, mean-spirited teasing, and arguments spewed from his mouth from the moment he rose in the morning. I was at my wits' end trying to deal with him. Nothing seemed to work.

That afternoon, waiting on the sidewalk, I spotted the principal exiting the building alongside the younger children. Despite the mild weather, he wore his warm coat and gloves. I strode toward him, waving my hand in greeting. "Good afternoon. Any chance you have a moment to talk?"

He recognized me immediately, nodding his head. "Glad to run into you, Doctor. I was about to pen a note to some parents, including you."

My stomach sank, waiting for the next shoe to drop. I said, "Then I'm glad we can speak in person. What's happened?"

His face wrinkled in consternation; his brows furrowed. "Many of the boys are out of control, not only Albert. They're turning the classroom into a boxing ring. It's no longer a pleasant place for learning. The teachers are beside themselves with the fighting. We've never been faced with a situation like this before."

My shoulders dropped. He was stating the obvious. What was he going to do about it? I'd run out of ideas.

He continued, his voice even, matter-of-fact. "I say if they want to fight, we let them, burn off their anger with sports. At least for now."

I gasped. "You must be joking. Allow them to fight in school? How is that a solution?"

He raised his palms, quieting me. "Hear me out. To begin with, boys in this age group are naturally very physical. Add the war and their fear for their fathers to the mix, and it creates a highly combustible situation. Rather than try the impossible, to stamp it out, I'd like to channel it, beginning with aggressive physical fitness, running, pullups, and sit-ups. You know, exactly what the soldiers do in their training camps. Presently, they only get fresh air breaks outdoors."

I envisioned the auditorium, rows of boys exercising, running around the city blocks. Interesting idea.

"It's not a new concept. Many schools around the country have gymnasium in their curriculum, modeled after the finest boys' schools in Europe. Then, if that doesn't tire them out enough to sit in their chairs, we'll come up with competitions."

Perhaps he had something. Albert was a simmering kettle of water about to burst into a full boil. Something needed to be done to help him. Then I thought about the girls; were they all as placid as Anna? "Will you have a similar program for the girls? Some of them must be feeling the tension, too," I asked.

He nodded. "We're working out those details. It will come, but I'd like to address the immediate crisis and get the boys settled down. If we don't, I fear they'll become ruffians and find new ways to get themselves into trouble. Especially once school is out."

Chapter Thirty-Six: Miriam

April 1918—The American Hospital, Paris

"How are you feeling, Sarah?" The strident chorus of my nosey roommates rang in my ears every time I crossed paths with them. Those three nurses could not resist needling me.

Now, in April, months after Eli returned to the Front, I rose before dawn for the workday, firmly pushing their questions off, injecting a cheerful tone in my voice. "That was the best night's sleep I had in weeks."

Despite my return to day shifts and to my bunk room, Eli continued to dominate my thoughts. Why couldn't I erase the nagging image of him with that horrid woman, gazing into his eyes? I tried to make sense of his actions but could not, especially after he'd fawned over me for close to two years, convinced I was his one and only. Eli, my Eli, the husband I'd lost sleep over every single night for the last year. The man to whom I promised my life, my body, my soul on our wedding day.

I was drowning in the conversations I held with myself, struggling to plan my next move. Should we stay married? Or was this a cautionary lesson about trust? For the first time, I had doubts about his character, despite his visits and words of contrition. I'd always had an inkling Eli had a broken part, needing me the way he did. Was it becoming orphaned young in life, and not trusting love unless he was holding it in his hands? Or was it, as he said, the bloodbath at the Front, leaving him shaky, making split-second decisions about who would live or die?

What made Uncle Ben so different? He stood by Hannah, by me, like a granite monument after having lost so much in his life. If I could only stop this damn noise in my head.

Thank God for my patients. They were the only antidote to the turmoil. Caring for the men helped distract me from thinking about a future with Eli. As dire as their injuries were, they appreciated every moment I spent ministering their wounds and spirits.

I knew the Christian soldiers had special names for me. They called me their angel, and others named me Saint Sarah. There was even one man missing the lower quadrant of his face who stroked the crucifix on his chest when I was near, calling me Mother of God, slurring his words with his partial tongue. Some Jewish soldiers referred to me as *bashert*, their true love, soulmate.

Many cried as I applied cool rags to their foreheads and necks to stem their fevers. For them, I was the "fixer," the gentle hand helping them heal, keeping their hearts beating. Forging forward for more days on earth for a few, finding new dreams for others, and helping too many gently slide across life's divide to their final breath. In return, they restored my sense of purpose. Sadly, even though I could help my patients, I had no clue how to fix my marriage, the most broken part of my life.

After returning from my week off, a couple of patients confided to me that they'd heard my roommates making snide comments behind my back when they filled in for me on the floor. "Doesn't Sarah know this is a Catholic country and there's no place for a Jewish nurse? Is she blind? Can't she see Notre Dame outside the window?" I chose to ignore them. I now had bigger fish to fry.

Unlike other nurses, I never feared the emotional toll of nursing, busy planning an exit after snaring a doctor, building a more conventional life. From the start of my career, my work with children, the trusting bond I formed with my little patients and their parents, always filled me with a sense of purpose, particularly after the polio outbreak hit New York. Knowing I couldn't fix everyone, I rocked and comforted the children every free hour I had until some passed away. I believed it was my role to help each patient heal in his own way, including facing death with acceptance and calm. Wasn't that what Eli did for me when I was stricken by disease? Where did that part of him go? Surrounded by so much death and despair, did he lose his way in the terror and smoke of battle?

Now, four months after seeing Eli and that woman together, I rose for the workday. I quietly pushed off my roommates' swarming, knowing it was false concern. Every morning, they studied me for a change in my demeanor. If I'd believed their concern was benevolent, I would have shared more, but they were the same people who tried to remove me from my post. They were obsessed, watching every move I made. My ruse, pretending to be Sarah Rosen, was almost foiled. I never in a million years saw their subversion coming. The events of February replayed in my head.

While Uncle Ben placed me in a private room for a week to convalesce in quarantine, my roommates peppered him with questions about my health, never fully sated. They were a sinister trio, looking for any way to get rid of me. This led to an unexpected visit by Nurse Hornsby on the Head and Face Unit weeks into February, after I'd returned to my duties. Nurse Hornsby, The American's Chief Nursing Officer, entered the unit near the end of my shift while I was occupied changing bandages and checking my patients' wounds.

I bent over a soldier, singing the folk song *When Irish Eyes Are Smiling*, while I peeled bandages from his head. He was an Irish American who had sustained a terrible brain injury. I'd learned singing stimulated the language function of the brain, and so I sang. He lay calmly in his bed, placing complete trust in me, attempting to hum along.

Startled by soft footsteps from behind, I jumped. My patient grunted, sensing my surprise. I turned to face Nurse Hornsby. "Good morning. How can I help you?" I asked as pleasantly as possible, knowing there must be a purpose for the visit.

She set her hand on my shoulder. "Please don't let me interrupt you. I heard you had a severe flu and wanted to see how you were feeling. All better now?"

A voice called out from the neighboring bed, behind the drawn drape.

"Thank God, Saint Sarah is back. We barely survived the last nurse. What a brute."

I laughed for the first time since the incident. "Oh, Private Crawly, you all managed just fine. She's one of my roommates, and I better be hearing a good report on your behavior."

The corner of Nurse Hornsby's lips curled up in amusement. "I see your patients like you." Her eyes drifted to my brace. "But tell me, how are you feeling? Still up for the job? Your roommates are worried about you."

I taped the end of the bandage securely on my soldier's head and pointed to the charting desk. "Let's speak in the office."

After washing my hands, I followed Nurse Hornsby into the small room behind the nursing station and shut the door until it clicked. "I'm fit as a fiddle. But I'm curious why you've taken your valuable time to check on me. Do you check on everyone who's had a bad cold?"

She averted her eyes, turning her head to the men. "Sarah, you are a valuable nurse in this hospital and have one of the most challenging units. It is quite clear the soldiers feel safe in your care."

I studied her face, tired and heavily lined. Dark, sleepless circles beneath her eyes. "I'm sorry to concern you. You have the biggest job in the hospital—thousands of injured men with no end in sight."

Her features softened. "Thank you, I appreciate your understanding, but your roommates thought you might want to go home where you can care for yourself better."

Those damn witches, a nest of troublemakers. I scoffed lightly. "It never seems to end with them. They're way off base. I don't quite know what their issue is with me, but from the start, they didn't like sharing a room with a Jewish woman, nor with someone requiring a brace."

Her eyebrows rose. "Really? Why didn't you report this to me sooner?"

I smirked. "If I were to report every time I'm insulted because I'm Jewish or when I'm undervalued because of my leg, I wouldn't have time to get my work done. I'd rather let it go." Despite her empathy, I was nervous and wanted this put to bed. The last thing I needed was for her to begin digging in my file, following up on the real Sarah Rosen.

She nodded slightly, still pressing. "Tell me, Sarah, what draws you to this unit? In the past, we've had a hard time keeping nurses here."

This time, my smile was genuine. Now I was on firmer turf, sharing my deep convictions. "These men are the bravest, strongest soldiers I've ever met. The brutality they've endured is unimaginable, but they still forge ahead. I can bring my best nursing skills here while still learning more. Each man needs extensive care, knowing with his deformities, the life waiting ahead will be vastly different from what it was when he left home." I thought about my reasons for choosing the profession and why I felt comfortable, searching for words Nurse Hornsby would understand. "Nursing has always been a calling for me. It's far more than a job, and here at The American, in this unit, I can see myself doing a great deal of good."

She reached for my hand. "I wish all my staff would pour so much of themselves into their jobs. Certainly, many do, but there are too many nurses hunting for doctors to bring home and marry after the war. I only wish the Red Cross had weeded them out ahead of time. They're generally more work than help around here."

If she only knew my doctor husband, Eli, was my greatest disappointment. At that moment, I wished I'd never married him.

Chapter Thirty-Seven: Hannah

April 1918 - New York City

Finally, the semblance of calm. At least for the moment. It was late April in New York, almost a full year since the men left for France and close to five months for Miriam. The children, each a year older, had grown considerably. All the days Ben missed could never be recaptured. Gilda, now three, was a chatterbox, offering a running commentary on the world around her. Did she remember her father? His soft eyes and the red hairs on his arms that she enjoyed tugging with her tiny fingers. Certainly, she knew of her Papa as a character we spoke about every day, but I wondered if her actual memories reached back far enough to recall the two of them reading books and rocking together before bed, or the funny rhymes he made up when they were out walking.

Like Anna, Gilda resembled Ben with her curls and freckled face. She had my petite frame and found the goings on around her amusing, engaging all in her delightful laughter. Perhaps it was just as well he couldn't see this stage of her life. If he saw what he was missing, it would surely break his heart into pieces.

Anna had forged a deep bond with Gilda, and I hoped they were forming the life-long sibling relationship Tillie fostered with me. Who knew what lay ahead and how much they'd need to rely on each other?

That Anna never failed to surprise me with her generous spirit. This past winter, she assembled girls from her class to knit socks for the soldiers. By the end of the project, they'd sent hundreds of wool socks in red, white, and blue to the trenches through the American Red Cross.

As for Albert, he'd made a few favorable strides, but with the early days of spring, his aggression had turned into mischief. On April 2nd, I received another call from the principal, interrupting my busy clinic at Mount Sinai. "Dr. Kahn, I need you to pick up Albert at school. He is suspended for the rest of the week along with two other boys."

My stomach dropped, expecting a new surge of violence. The gymnasium classes had been working so well, I'd almost forgotten his angry outbursts. I asked, "What is it this time?"

His voice was strained, exasperated. "A few teachers and I drive to work. Last evening, after a full day of silly, April Fool's jokes around the school, we left for home only to discover our cars all had flat tires. The boys confessed to letting the air out."

I couldn't stifle the giggle escaping my lips. Although I agreed Albert was taking an April Fool's prank too far, I was relieved it was a harmless gag and not a fistfight. But he would still need to be punished.

He barked through the phone, "I fail to see the humor. And I hope you're not encouraging such tomfoolery at home."

I answered in my most conciliatory tone. "No, sir, I was only relieved he wasn't mixed up in more violence. Wouldn't you agree that this type of behavior is more predictable for his age group? But I am very sorry for the inconvenience he created for you." I thought of a way to further appease him. "I cannot pick him up until after patient hours. Could you place him at a table in the front office, and I will collect him on my way home? I'm sure he will not enjoy separating from his pals, and he'll only have your staff and his assignments to keep him company for the day."

The principal cleared his throat. "That's a start, but he will still receive the suspension. I must exercise my authority over the boys, in particular. Otherwise, this school will run amok. And I suppose you make a good point. This type of prank is a bit more to be expected. No human harm. Perhaps the gymnasium program is working."

That afternoon, I arrived home with a sullen Albert, punished in his room for the weekend. A letter from Ben awaited us, dated three weeks earlier. It was never all good or bad news, but the mix in this letter left me troubled.

March 20, 1918

My darling Hannah,

Finally, the deep chill of winter has thawed. Miriam has sprung back to her full self, virtually running my ward, and has also picked up another unit in the same building. Talent is impossible to hide, particularly during wartime. She requested the limb repairs so she could monitor Eli's patients. Ironic how life's twists and turns express themselves. Their efforts to reconcile their marriage a reattachment of its own kind. Let's hope it's salvageable. A great deal of love still seems to be left on the platter. Seeing her spirits rise and her indomitable force resurface has been a relief of the largest measure.

In the meantime, the war has taken on a fevered force. Now with Pershing's men sprinkled among the French and British forces, the fighting has escalated. We're hearing of high mortalities and an increasing volume of wounded arriving in Paris daily. The American generals have demanded our men be sent to the newly erected hospitals manned by American doctors along the Front. There is a fear they will not receive comparable treatment in the British and French-run hospitals. Personally, I think it's rubbish, but we will eventually learn if the bias is true. As for Eli, I understand his assignment will change as well. I'm waiting to hear the details.

I am eager to learn about your efforts at Mount Sinai, establishing designated units for returning soldiers. We've learned so much, albeit at an unfortunate high human price. But our learning will help others in the future. Please advise if there is something more I can do from this end.

You have no idea how I treasure news of home. I read your letters right before I turn out my light, thinking about the wonderful memories we've shared and studying the pictures you send. Will I recognize everyone after so much time has passed? Tell me, were my eyes fooling me, or was that hair above Albert's mouth?

Give the children hugs and kisses, and Albert, if he deserves it, a swat on the behind. I miss you all.

Love,

Ben

Chapter Thirty-Eight: Eli

May 1918—Ypres, Belgium

I thought I'd never miss the cold of winter, but the never-ending parade of wounded since April was a horror like no other. Scores of men every waking hour were ambulanced to our hospital, in a flood of screaming, bloody bodies spilling out their insides over their stretchers onto the cobbled streets. Harrington and I worked like fiends, racing through the laborious steps to repair limbs—legs, arms, hands, feet. I knew it mattered. I saw the difference in the men at The American, but still, so many were dying right outside the door. Now, with Nurse Helen off working in a distant field hospital, we were also hampered by the new nurses in training. But that was the least of our trouble. My operating table was still considered an experiment, a concession to a self-involved American surgeon.

After a month back at the hospital and another grueling day in the operating room, I approached Surgeon Commander Dr. Clarke in the mess hall. He had authority over the operating theater from my first day. "Can I join you for dinner? I have an idea I'd like to share with you."

Dr. Clarke, a veteran British surgeon from the Second Boer War, looked at me with disdain. "Don't you Yanks know that mealtime is meant to be enjoyed in quiet? Can't it wait?"

I looked at my plate, a meal difficult to discern, gray meat swimming in a nondescript sauce, overcooked green beans, a dry slice of baguette. A sad excuse for French cuisine. I answered with a smile, "From the looks of my plate, it may be more advisable to take this fine fare with a generous side dish of distraction."

He caved, a light smile escaping his lips. "What is it, Drucker? What does the Yankee big shot want now?"

Searching for an approach to refocus on the injured men and not me, I shared my experience in Paris, the homeless amputees on the streets, the envy of soldiers with amputations toward our limb repair patients in the recovery wards of The American. Watching his expression, I saw I had his attention. "I share your concern about the additional surgical time and the human cost for those waiting to get onto an operating table, but as you surely agree, we must do more to help these men have better lives after the war ends."

He snapped, "What do you suggest? As far as I can tell, it's a game of Russian Roulette."

I fixed my eyes on his. "You're partly right, but if I can triage for two tables of repairs instead of one, put Harrington as lead on the second table, and bring two of your new surgeons to work with us, we can probably save twice as many limbs," I said. "I do believe Harrington is ready to take charge of his own surgeries."

"How do you figure that? And how many more will die waiting on the other side of the door?"

Pleased I had his attention, I spoke deliberately, explaining my rationale. "I've learned a great deal since I arrived. I can better tell what limbs will hold up to surgery, which means I can triage more specifically."

He set his fork on the table. "How can you tell, beyond the obvious?"

"There are several factors that support repair: a predominantly attached limb, intact blood flow, minimal bone and blood loss, how much filth is ground into the wound, and the amount of time the soldier was left waiting on the battlefield. Sometimes hands and feet hold up, but they are much trickier."

He nodded, "What else?"

"The sure hand of the surgeon, thorough wound cleaning, minimized bleeding, and speed." I considered my list and added, "Of course, our patients with multiple other wounds don't fare as well."

He continued studying my face, his brows tightening with doubt. "I'll tell you what. You have ten days to prove yourself with two tables, and I will give you a couple of our best new surgeons to work with. Some have approached me, chomping at the bit to learn from you."

A wave of relief spread across my chest and shoulders. "Thank you. I know you and I both want to help as many of our boys as we can."

"You got that right. So, if the numbers don't support your grand theory, we speed things back up and return to fast amputations."

* * *

How I wish I'd studied French with more gusto. Although my ability to read the language was acceptable, my speech and understanding were abysmal. Even after a year, the challenge continued to set me behind in my conversations with other doctors and nurses. The names of battlefields of the cities along the Front were a jumble of noises, Passchendaele and Aisne, strings of sounds impossible for my tongue to form. So, the letter on my bed that May evening, months after our two operating tables trial began, met me with both confusion at the pronunciation of the location and relief to be working with English-speaking medical staff.

In three weeks, I would be transferred to a new American-run hospital, Base Hospital No. 30, a few miles south of Ypres on the Western Front, still close to Paris and Miriam. The worst-kept secret out there was that for the first time, American troops would be entering a battle in an entire American unit in Belleau Wood on the Marne River. Base Hospital 30 would receive those casualties. I'd be leaving behind Montgomery, now a seasoned trauma surgeon, and two protégés, our experiment a resounding success.

For the last few months, Miriam and I sent each other letters, steering clear of the topic of my infidelity, but the act, the scalding memory of my deceit, continued to hang in the air invisibly tucked between the sentences of her newsy accounts of the surgical floors at The American and her polite closing lines of concern for me. Although she signed, 'With Love,' her notes lacked the romantic warmth and sultry suggestions of earlier letters. With great difficulty, I respected her need to remain at arm's length, so I mirrored her tone, pushing only as hard as I thought she could bear.

Her most recent letter caught my attention in an unexpected way. She described a growing problem on the non-surgical units, an ailment no one had ever seen.

> *Keep your eyes sharp for men who appear ill, feverish, with a hacking cough. The illness presents like an influenza despite the warm season. We've been receiving a growing number at The American, all terribly sick. At first, we thought the respiratory symptoms might be from mustard gas, but later realized it was an extremely contagious flu. Eli, be cautious. Whatever it is, the affliction is proving to be deadly. Our sickest patients experience massive nosebleeds, terrifying suffocation, and pneumonia. At present, the hospital is advising face coverings for nurses and doctors who tend to these men. Please let me know what you're seeing in the evacuation hospital.*

With haste, I hurried to the Commander's office the following morning, letter in hand. I knocked at his door.

An angry voice barked, "Who the hell is it? Better be important."

I took a deep breath, turned the knob, and faced the storm. "It's Dr. Drucker. If you wish, I can come back after surgery."

He pointed to the empty, armless captain's chair across from his desk. "No, no, don't do that. Might as well see you now before any more bad news comes in." He pointed to the east, the battlefield. "It's insanity out there. Tens of new hospitals are springing up along the Front, likely hundreds more before they're through. They're trying to mobilize the hospitals to follow the battles. How the hell do they expect us to keep the men alive if we jostle them about?" Stopping his rant, he took me in with his bespectacled eyes. "What do you want, Drucker?"

My head spun with the list I needed to cover. But I harnessed my thoughts, taking one at a time. "First, I'd like to speak to you in more detail about the hospital support strategy. As you know, in a couple of weeks I'll be transferred to American Base Hospital 30."

He stood, banging his palms on his desk. "That's God damn news to me! Who will take your place?"

I opened my arms. "Relax, it's covered. Montgomery and two additional surgeons are handling the limb repairs. They've been trained."

He sat back down with an irritated thud. "What else?"

I'd almost forgotten the letter I was holding. I held it up. "Oh, yes, sir, this came last night in the post. My wife is a nurse working at The American and warned me about a serious influenza outbreak coming into Paris with the soldiers. Apparently, it's respiratory. A rough ride. What have you heard? Should we be taking precautions here?"

The commander was silent, folding and unfolding his hands. "I've heard nothing official from above, but, yes, we are seeing a growing number of cases from the battlefield. I don't think it's anything to worry about. It's probably from all the goddamn fleas."

The poor man was at his wits' end with the unit mobilization. I hated to add more weight to his swollen burden, but if Miriam's information was accurate, we may be in for more than German artillery or flea-borne illnesses. I thought back to New York only three years earlier, when everyone pooh-poohed the early cases of polio. I nudged him further. "With all due respect, sir, as a doctor, I suggest we keep careful numbers on these cases and quarantine the sick. If this is the beginning of something serious, best to nip it in the bud and contain the spread." I considered ending the conversation there, then decided to proceed while I had his audience. "They're asking the nurses at The American to mask while on those wards, and I suggest we do the same. We can't afford to have staff fall ill."

He glared at me. "Any more good news?"

I shook my head, rising from my chair, forgetting the other items on my list.

Chapter Thirty-Nine: Ben

July 1918—Paris

I was back in the conference room at The American, sitting in front of the grandfather clock, its ticking loud enough for everyone to hear, a constant reminder of time passing, the mounting months of an endless war. More than thirty doctors, all in charge of specialized units, filled the room, waiting for Major Robert Bacon to enter with his weekly announcements. Typically, the air would be pulsing with the drone of men's conversations, speculating what we should expect from the battlefield. Instead, with the suffocating July heat and humidity, the air was saturated with the god-awful smell of men's sweat. We were barely able to breathe.

Young Lance Corporal Morgan hobbled in, leaning on his crutch with one arm and carrying a clipboard of papers and a small bag of chalk in the other. "Major's moving this meeting to the courtyard. We've set up chairs in the shade. Please assemble there now. We begin in five minutes."

Two men behind Morgan waited until the room emptied, then lifted the chalkboard, lugging the cumbersome apparatus outdoors, holding it upright to prevent it from swinging side to side on its swivel joints.

A cloud of relief snaked through the door as we relocated to a shady corner of the courtyard. Rows of elm trees lined the eastern edge of the burnt grass square, casting enough morning shade to shield one-third of the open space. I sat near the front, waiting. Morgan was leaning on the chalkboard, drawing the Western Front, a simple white jagged outline representing over four hundred miles of trenches, seven hundred fifty thousand French, British, and now American troops. The sheer scale was unfathomable. This plain white line grossly understated the massive explosion of violence. I waited, hoping to hear promising news, closing my eyes, absorbing the gentle breeze threading across the courtyard. I prayed it was a sign of hope that an end to the carnage was in sight.

Moments later, Major Bacon strode outside, breaking my meditation. He wore a beige cotton single-breasted belted jacket with four front flap pockets, the new summer uniform for officers. Still far too warm for the day's heat. He furiously dabbed beads of sweat off his forehead with a white handkerchief. We stood, the soldiers in the crowd saluting.

The Major straightened his jacket, gazing at the doctors, "At ease. Take your seats."

Once we were settled, he began. "We're entering a vital turning point in the Allied strategy, one that will ensure victory this year." He paused. "But as you might expect, it will come at a considerable human cost."

He had our attention. While we waited for his next words, I listened to the whirring bees hovering over the small white flowers scattered throughout the clover beneath our boots.

"General Pershing will begin deploying American troops as entire fighting units along targeted areas of the Front." He turned to Morgan. "Mark the approximate locations with white X's. You don't need the specifics at this point."

We watched, captivated, while Morgan drew X's along the trench line, one after another.

The Major told Morgan, "Now mark the evacuation hospitals with stars, and then I'll explain.

As Morgan drew in stars, Major Bacon continued, "We will locate evacuation hospitals in critical areas near the battles. Every hospital can be expanded with tents to hold hundreds of wounded, all accessible by train to Paris and the Channel to England. There will be two neurological hospitals for the headwounds and shell shock." He twisted away from the chalkboard, his eyes surveying the room. "As you can see, this will be an effort of historic proportions, both for the troops and hospitals, certain to win this insipid war and get our boys back home, once and for all."

How will they ever outfit all those hospitals with the proper number of nurses and doctors, or supplies? It appeared as if the entire globe was on fire. I turned my body to check the other Department Chairs' responses. Without exception, they were whispering to each other, their faces full of disbelief.

As if anticipating my concern, he continued, "Pershing has stipulated he must have American hospitals for his troops. Based on our work here in Paris, he's convinced American care is better. Who knows? But in any case, we will answer the call." He began drawing circles around some of the stars on the map. "The U.S. hospitals will be in the circles and pull American nurses and doctors from the Red Cross hospitals where they currently work. Some will transfer east from The American here in Paris."

I immediately thought of Eli. He would be part of that mobilization. Would I be sent too? What about Miriam?

Major Bacon swept his open hand in the area between the white trench line and hospital X's. "Throughout this interior area, we will have smaller mobile hospitals within five miles of the Front, capable of moving north or south in tandem with the troops. All on a week's notice. This way, we give our wounded maximum coverage and reduce the hours to receive proper care. If the soldiers don't return to the trenches, they get transported west to the Evacuation Hospitals."

Mobile hospitals meant mobile wounded, the most difficult to protect. I raised my hand.

Bacon caught my eye. "What is it, Dr. Kahn?"

I stood. "This is masterful planning, but what about the wounded in those mobile hospitals? How will we move them without incurring more injury?"

A few grunts of agreement rose from the crowd. The doctors in the meeting looked about, checking each other's reactions. The plan bordered on lunacy.

The Major nodded. "Anyone not returning to the Front will be transferred to an evacuation hospital by ambulance or train in a matter of days. Many will come here." He stopped and drew a deep breath before continuing. "That brings me to my next point. Listen carefully now. For this plan to work, we must begin clearing out beds here, at The American, to make space for freshly wounded from the Evacuation Hospitals. They will be arriving by ambulance trains in droves. I don't want to say it twice. There *must* be beds. The Americans just secured additional trains to transport their soldiers to Paris."

Hands darted into the hot air.

Major Bacon gazed over the crowd, and the arms shooting up by the second. "I'll take your questions now; one at a time, please." He pointed to a man in the back.

"Major, it has been difficult finding convalescent homes for our patients. Where do you expect us to send them?"

"To their country of origin. Where else? We have notified the city hospitals in the States to be prepared," he snapped. "All major hospitals in the U.S. have received correspondence to that effect. They should be aggressively clearing long-stay beds to local convalescent homes in their cities and towns to make room for incoming casualties as we speak."

I wondered how much Hannah or Mount Sinai knew about this. They'd had discussions for months, all speculative, even before I left a year ago, but hospital leadership was notorious for arduous planning. Execution was another matter altogether. Stateside, the wheels turned far slower than on a battlefield. Thousands of wounded men would be headed to New York alone, the largest city in the country. If my memory served me, there were close to thirty hospitals in the greater city, each with between one and two hundred beds, save for Bellevue with far more. Only six thousand beds to service both the current population plus incoming military patients. An impossible feat.

Then, of course, the unmentionable, this new influenza that was wreaking havoc in the trenches. Without a second thought, I raised my arm, joining the beehive of burning questions. Eventually, he got around to me. "Kahn?"

"As I'm sure you're aware, we seem to be fighting a new microscopic enemy. Every day, we see more cases of influenza and pneumonia entering the hospital. The mortality rate is close to twenty percent. It's a highly contagious strain, and we've begun grouping sick patients together with careful masking by all staff. How will this impact the discharge process?"

Heads snapped back to the Major, all keen to hear his answer. It appeared I'd struck a chord. I watched Major Bacon. For the first time since I set eyes on him months ago, he began to fidget, adjusting his belt and jacket cuffs, likely contemplating the best way to quell our concern.

He cleared his throat. "Medical Command is aware of the issue. We will send those soldiers to the States in clusters to keep infection contained. But there is no official word beyond those instructions. Presently, it is critical that our beds get cleared. That is the top priority." He raised his voice, its booming timbre echoing in the courtyard. "Keep your eye on the discharge process. Is everyone clear?"

Chapter Forty: Hannah

June 1917—New York

I n my many years living in New York City, I couldn't recall a more dreadful June. It was an inferno. We all held our breath as American boys entered the appalling trenches to show their might, knowing many would not return. With a two-month break in school, I decided to send Albert and Anna to their Uncle Nate's farm, hoping they'd be useful there and away from the fearful mood of the city.

Two days after school let out, I packed the car and headed northwest to the farmlands of Sullivan County, sharing the front seat with Albert and stationing Gilda in the rear with Anna. Arguments erupted within minutes. As usual, it played out in the typical sequence. One child was unhappy, and the bad mood cascaded until everyone was miserable. This time, it started with Gilda, who was thirsty and whining, immediately irritating Albert.

Albert yelled over the engine drone and whistling wind pouring through the windows, "Anna, can't you shut her up?"

I squeezed Albert's arm firmly. "Enough of your impatience. I don't like your language." Turning to the back seat, I reminded Anna where I'd packed refreshments. "The basket with her water thermos is on the floor."

Albert shot back, "I don't want to go to the farm. All my friends are staying in the city. We had plans."

My patience strained, I said, "A fifteen-year-old boy cannot be left roaming around the city all summer. It spells trouble. Besides, it's much cooler on the farm with the big pond for swimming. And besides, has it occurred to you that your uncle might need a hand at the poultry farm while his boys are in France?" The word "France" uttered aloud shot a bolt of fear through my body. I couldn't fathom the fear Nate and Jenny must feel with their older boys now stationed there, facing battle.

Albert sat fuming, his arms crossed tightly, forehead scrunched. "Maybe I'll just run away and join the war. I hate it here, waiting for Papa to come home."

Anna gasped so loudly from the back seat I heard it over the car noises.

I calmed my voice. "You'll do no such thing. Your poor father would never forgive me, nor get over his disappointment in you for pulling that kind of stunt. Try to think about it differently, Albert."

His voice was hoarse with frustration. "What do you mean?"

I took a deep breath, considering how to explain his frustration in a way he'd understand. I knew he wanted to take some type of action. "Consider supporting the war effort another way. So many farms in the U.S. are shorthanded, their strong men in France. It's near impossible to keep their businesses going through the year. By pitching in, you are helping your Uncle Nate and his family. When your cousins return, they won't need to work as hard to rebuild the business."

He sat quietly, his body sinking into the seat. "But Aunt Miriam snuck over there. I keep thinking I could, too. I want to help us win. You know, I look older than my age." He showed me his arm muscle. "I'm strong with all the exercise in my gymnasium class. And I've started shaving."

My heart raced. Was that what Albert wanted? To sneak into the army? War must seem heroic and bold to a boy, a great adventure. Did the recklessness come with the body hair? After two decades treating women, I was at a loss when it came to fifteen-year-old boys. One thing was certain: he was clueless about the carnage.

I forced myself into the narrow conversation, keeping it about him and not the perils of war. "Your call to help is brave and patriotic. You'll be old enough to join when you graduate upper school. But remember, the farm is critical for the war effort. Did you know Uncle Nate is a poultry supplier for the army training camps? As they say, "an army marches on its stomach."

"You never told me he was supplying chickens."

I'd hit gold. "Well, he does. Uncle Nate worries every day about his boys serving in France. Albert, you're built like a man, and trust me, your Uncle Nate can use your muscle around the farm. Standing around the city parks with other boys does nothing to win the war or help the soldiers. All it does is give parents more to worry about."

He sat quietly while the Model T chugged along, leaving the city roads behind. Appearing finished with the conversation and eager to switch the subject, he asked, "Have you gotten any more letters from Papa or Aunt Miriam? Anything new happening over there?"

I smiled inwardly at the frail truce. "As a matter of fact, yes. A letter came from your aunt yesterday, I was waiting to read it together." I pointed to my purse set in front of his feet. "Go ahead and take it out. Read it aloud to all of us, but you must speak loud and slow so we can hear you over the engine."

Moments later, we were engrossed, listening to Miriam's news.

My dear Aunt Hannah,

I've been waiting for a moment to get word to you. The wards have been so busy that I've been sleeping on my feet and haven't had a half hour to write. All I can say is I am forever thankful you are out of harm's way in New York.

In the last month since the American troops joined the British and French in the trenches, the fighting and casualties have exploded. The number of battlefields along the Western Front is staggering, miles upon miles, beyond any reasonable imagination. New mobile hospitals have shot up and move in tandem with the troops as battles shift north and south along the trench line. Many of the wounded are eventually sent to us at The American for more extensive treatment before they head home.

That brings me to my news. Uncle Ben and my work (and, of course, many others), all based on Dr. Gillies' techniques, are now viewed as the future for burn and reconstructive care. The Medical Corps is designing several new mobile hospitals for head and facial injuries to bring the immediate procedures closer to injured soldiers. They are pulling experienced staff from The American to work in the mobile units. I've been reassigned, leg brace and all, to lead nursing at one of them (presently, I can't tell you where). Although Uncle Ben will remain in Paris, some other (younger) physicians and nurses on my unit will join me. Although, on the one hand, it's regrettable we need such hospitals with the hideous weaponry both sides are using, I'm honored to be chosen to lead the charge. I hope the soldiers will have better results by administering our newest methods immediately after injuries occur.

Albert set the letter on his lap and turned to me; his eyes lit with excitement. "Mama, does that mean she's going to be near the battles, the trenches?"

So shaken by Miriam's news, I didn't answer. *Tillie must be rolling in her grave! She'd skin me alive for letting her daughter slip through my fingers.*

"Mama, did you hear me? Will she be going to the trenches?"

I shook off my thought. "No, Aunt Miriam will be miles from the fighting. She's going to work at a hospital, not on the ambulances."

He persisted. "But I read that the German planes were shooting at hospitals and trains, too."

My nerves had frayed. I couldn't engage Albert in any more discussion. "Is there anything more in the letter?"

He turned back to the paper on his lap. "Where was I? Aunt Miriam's writing is so small. Oh, here."

But that's not the worst of things. Uncle Ben and I think men are coming into the hospitals from the Front with a severe influenza. At first, it was just a trickle; now the sick arrive en masse, with violent coughing and pneumonia, their skin blueish, struggling to breathe. The strangest part is that no one up the chain of command wants to hear about it. Sure, they've let us isolate them, and everyone in the room wears a mask, but they're ordering us to send them back to the States and make room for the newly wounded. My fear is they will wreak havoc along the way, passing the disease to others in trains and ships. God knows what the potential spread could be once it hits American shores.

Please keep your eyes open, and if you can convince your hospital president, set up an isolation ward for these poor men (and women, too). I pray the illness turns out to be nothing, but from what I've seen on the ward, these poor souls become desperately sick, struggling for air, their ears and eyes bleeding from all the strain. As you can see, I'm worried this is a new chapter of this hideous war. If you begin to see an influx of admissions, please don't brush it off as a nasty cold.

Enough doom and gloom for now. It's time for me to turn out the lights and get a few hours of rest before we start again.

Write back soon and fill me in on the family. I miss you all so much and could use some good news!

Love,

Miriam

My sweat had turned cold, sending shivers down my back. Now I was worried on multiple fronts. First, Miriam's physical safety near the battlefield put her closer to the bullets, but her news about the mysterious flu left me more concerned. How would I bring information like this to the hospital leadership without having them dismiss it offhand? As a department chair, I knew we hadn't received official notice from the City Health Department.

I continued to drive, barely noticing the pastoral scenery as I struggled to think who in the city might know more about this influenza. Then it hit me. I'd need to start at Bellevue, the charity hospital, the most likely to receive sick soldiers, and the very hospital where my old enemy, Roger Holloway, worked. The same man who tried to drunkenly rape me in Baltimore while I was a young medical student and who detested me for redirecting state money away from the grandious construction project at Bellevue. Instead, it was used to construct a maternity hospital in the Lower East Side and various women's health projects. As much as I cringed at the idea, I must go there when I returned to the city.

* * *

The late afternoon sun was slipping behind the mountain range when we arrived at Nate's farm. It was a world opposite our city life, quiet, breezy, with the sweet smell of nature everywhere. It was difficult imagining a war unfolding thousands of miles away.

The chicken farm was a remote part of my childhood, one I barely remembered after moving in with my sister, Tillie, in her Lower East Side apartment when I was barely five. Once I began college, I spent occasional school breaks at Papa's farm during his last years of his life, making up for lost time and absorbing the type of childhood I might have had if my mother hadn't passed when I was so young. Nate, ten years my senior, had always lived with Papa on the farm even after it moved from Harlem to Sullivan County, eventually taking over the business when Papa passed.

Nate strode up to our car as we parked on the gravel driveway, wearing a broad smile. "It's so wonderful to see you. How was the drive?" Not waiting for an answer, he hugged me, then Anna and Gilda. My goodness, what are you feeding these girls? They're growing like our beautiful rose bushes." He turned to Anna. "Have you grown thorns, or are you still sweet as ever?"

She giggled, delighted with his attention.

Albert shot out his hand, announcing, "I'm here to help you this summer."

Nate stood in amazement. "Albert, is that you hiding in a man's body? I barely recognized you!" He threw his free arm around Albert and drew him into a hug. "Too grown to give your old uncle a hug?"

Just then, Jenny waddled out of the house, her white apron catching the breeze, her arms outstretched, flapping. "Velcome, Velcome, my darlinks. Dinner is cooking!"

For the first time since Ben left for France over a year ago, I felt the powerful warmth of family. The sensation radiated through me so fast and thoroughly I felt my knees buckle.

Jenny immediately saw the change in my stance and threw her arm around my waist for support, leading me into the house. "Oh, poor dear. You're carrying such a heavy load all by yourself. I'm so glad you've come to the farm. We vill all help each other."

Out of the corner of my eye, I saw Albert observing me. His face appeared confused, brows drawn together as if, for the first time, he realized he wasn't the only one struggling, that despite my forced calm, the war was taking its toll on all of us.

Aunt Jenny had thrown a tablecloth over the picnic table on the back lawn, far from the hot kitchen and dining room inside. After setting our suitcases in the upstairs rooms, I helped carry platters of chicken and cooked vegetables to the table while Anna brought out the plates and silverware.

As we set the table, I remarked, "How lovely to eat outdoors on a summer evening. This is much more civilized than struggling to enjoy a family meal in a piping hot apartment kitchen."

Anna gazed at the horizon. "We can watch the sunset and beautiful colors in the sky. I can barely believe there's a war across the sea."

Her words captured my thoughts, but I knew the serenity was hollow. Every farm in the area had sacrificed at least one son to fight. Both of Nate and Jenny's older boys were now in France.

Situated around the table, savoring the fresh dinner, I asked, "What do you hear from the boys? Are they together?"

Jenny piped in, "They won't tell us too much. We know they've been deployed to the trenches since their training. We're lucky to get one letter a month from them. My guess is they don't want us to worry. All we can do is pray for their safety and that the war ends quickly."

Albert, listening attentively, said softly, "I'm here to help while they fight. You can count on me." He filled his chest. "And, Aunt Jenny, the chicken is delicious."

We all turned to this new, mature version of Albert.

"You are becoming a man. Your Papa would be very proud of you, son," Nate said.

Albert sat straighter, answering, "I want to help."

I smiled inside, watching the relationship between uncle and nephew take form. Albert's anger was beginning to transform into an adult understanding that war was serious business. A male figurehead was just what the boy needed.

Nate smiled as he asked Albert, "Do you know how to ride a horse?"

Albert shook his head, his eyes downcast with embarrassment. "No, but I'm willing to learn."

"And you will, starting this week," Nate answered. "Our neighbors are training field horses and mules to be sent to France as war horses. Farms in the state deliver their animals to him next door and every month a pack of around forty is sent to France. The horses drag ammunition wagons to the Front and the wounded back to hospitals. Animal heroes, that's what they are. He trains them for the work they'll do in France."

Albert set a fork full of food on his plate with a clank, his face alive with excitement. "I've been reading about war horses. There are thousands of them from the States and Canada over there. Will there be Clydesdales next door to train? I hear they're gigantic."

Nate's belly laugh made all of us smile. "Son, those horses are raised in Scotland, not the United States. Most horses and mules we send are strong, healthy farm animals accustomed to pulling heavy loads."

"I hadn't thought about the horses or where they came from," I said. My main concern had been the humans sent to France.

Nate set his hand on Albert's shoulder. "They need more help with those animals than I do with my small chicken pens. Their son, Adam, is around your age. He'll show you the ropes. A perfect job for a strong, young man as yourself."

Albert's handsome smile delighted all of us. "I can't wait to start!"

Anna piped in, "Then I'll help with Uncle Nate's chickens. Do you have a special pen for the babies?"

Chapter Forty-One: Eli

August 1918—Base Hospital 30

"Dr. Drucker, over here! We need your help," shouted a fresh-faced medic in the clearing outside the hospital. "What should we do with this one?"

I took one look and knew. The body was shredded from a barrage of machine gun fire. He was unconscious, bleeding from too many places to count. "Black Tag. Give him morphine if he wakes up. He's finished."

The American medical response team had come straight off the boat from the States with no experience in military trauma. It would take weeks to get them up to speed. I said, "Stay close to me and you'll get the fastest lesson on earth in triage. Where are you all from?"

"The Philadelphia Emergency Team. We came together." The medic pointed to the nine or so nurses and medics examining incoming wounded. His voice was uncommonly high-pitched. "We've been working together for years."

Years? My disbelief grew. How old was this kid? Certainly, too young to shave. How could the team possibly understand trauma medicine? As far as I was concerned, they were as green as grass. Still, they knew each other, and all spoke English. That was something. "Today, you'll have a crash course in battlefield triage. Good triage determines how many of our boys live. I promise, it's like nothing you've seen back home."

They watched me closely. The tune, "Three Blind Mice," kept running through my head. Would they hold up under the massive pressure ahead, or scatter and hide? I hoped they were tough, fast learners. I pointed to three nurses and four stretcher-bearers from their Philadelphia team, then turned to the medic. "Get them and stay with me. We'll work this round together. Then you'll each take someone new by your side and train them in the same way."

Each Philly newcomer was fully engaged, ready to work hard. By the end of an hour, I had them assessing blood loss and respiration, applying tourniquets, and tagging the colors on the injured with a moderate degree of accuracy.

I pointed around the field. "Pick a new partner and work together." I patted the shoulder of the sharpest in the group, the slight medic with the high-pitched voice. "You, come with me. We're going to line up our limb repairs. The rest of the stretchers will be brought into the operating room according to severity. Other surgeons will handle their care. Name?"

Her back was straight as a pole as she looked me in the eyes. "Dr. Louise Caulfield, sir."

I stumbled backward. My eyes widened with surprise.

Watching my reaction, she shot me a crooked, cocky smile, "I was hired to come as a contract surgeon and yes, I'm a woman."

I shook off my surprise, thinking about how Miriam snuck into the medical war machine only months ago. Undoubtedly, there were other women just like Miriam, determined, single-minded, patriotic. I collected myself and said, "No problem from my end, Doctor. Would you like to learn limb repair? I'll need a second surgeon to help me. Although it does require a degree of brute strength."

She smiled back, her straight white teeth glistening, shining through the blood splatters on her face. "I'm strong. Grew up on a farm. And that's why I'm here, sir. To serve."

"Terrific. Wash up well, and I'll meet you inside at my table." A Miriam disguised as a doctor. What a relief to have a partner of that caliber. But she sure had me fooled.

My last hospital in Ypres was busy, but nothing in comparison to this unit. It was clear from day one that our American boys were meeting enormous resistance, outgunned and outmaneuvered on the battlefield by more experienced German fighters. Scores of macerated Americans were transported to Base Hospital 30 every hour. The day was certain to be long. With this much gunning, the stretcher-bearers wouldn't be cleared to enter the field until after nightfall. That didn't bode well for the injured who would be left lying for hours in the fertile, manure-filled soil.

Dr. Caulfield didn't tire. Hour after hour, she stood, instruments in hand, picking out debris, pointing out anatomy, and retracting with perfect tension as if she'd been performing repairs her entire career.

"How'd you learn to operate like this?" I asked.

Her eyes never left the surgical field, "Women must be twice as good as men or else we're out on our asses." Caulfield chuckled, "I also had excellent teachers. They were flawless."

"I can see that. Keep up the great work, and I'll see to it you have your own table soon. We can't have too many American men heading back home with unnecessary amputations."

After expecting to find the new hospital transition difficult, the fresh determination of these Americans was exhilarating. Their enthusiasm was palpable, lifting my stamina and spirit. I could only hope the new soldiers brought the same energy to the trenches. The French and British fighters needed the support as badly as the Medical Corps. All of us were worn down with battle fatigue.

Later that evening, I found a letter from Ben set atop the blanket on my cot.

August 10, 1918

Dear Eli,

I hope this note finds you adjusting to your new assignment. It will be quite a change working with an American team and mobilizing the hospital together with the changing battlefields. The ease of communication with staff and wounded will be a great time saver. Were you able to bring anyone from your surgical team? It would be a shame to lose an inch of ground with your limb procedures.

As you must know, Miriam has been transferred out of The American to oversee nursing at one of the two Head and Face Evacuation Hospitals near the Front. We've learned much about facial reconstruction since the beginning of the war, perhaps the most delicate of all battle wounds. Back in New York, I steered clear of facial injuries, not knowing where to begin. But the face, so frequently injured, is a critical part of our identity, who we represent to others and to ourselves. These men suffer in ways we can hardly comprehend.

I huffed. Suffer? Ben must be kidding, sounding so lofty. There wasn't a soul in France and Belgium who wasn't miserable. Certainly, the German soldiers couldn't be any better off. War had destroyed our innocence. Did anyone still recognize themselves? None of us would return home the same as when we left. I continued reading.

Miriam and her team will help achieve better end results for our boys. The most important lesson I've learned has been about cleanliness and speed. I've seen the outcome of bad wound flushing, and trust me, it always ends up the same, later cutting away more flesh, reducing the success of reconstruction.

Gillies has introduced procedures with bone and skin grafts unknown before the start of the war. We've learned to rebuild noses, jaws, and cheekbones through a series of bone and skin graft surgeries, improving the final appearance of these men. It's miraculous! I'll wager that he'll be a name remembered for a long time.

Most important, I hope you're safe. Watch out for patients sick with the flu. Under no circumstances should they be mixed with your surgical patients in recovery. This influenza is proving to be dangerous, leading to pneumonia at lightning speed. So, create an isolation unit, and make sure the staff all wear masks. I'm terribly perplexed that the disease isn't receiving a proportionate attention from above, while we on the wards are witnessing terrifying respiratory symptoms and an uncommonly high frequency of death. Beware.

That's it for now. I look forward to writing letters filled with far better news once we end this damn war. I'm counting on our American boys to give it the heave-ho needed.

Ben

The regularity of Ben's letters suggested his anger at me was dissipating. It would be a relief to put that behind us.

Although I was happy to know Miriam was nearby, I worried about her safety so close to battle. The German army, intimidated by the American forces fortifying the trenches, was fighting as viciously as ever. They sent aircraft inland beyond the trench lines and shot at hospitals, trains, and ambulances, those unarmed or too injured to fight back. It brought back memories of the Lusitania and all the innocents who drowned. The Germans were cowards, demonstrating their force in a merciless manner. Imagining Miriam's hospital as a target to their aggression kept me up at night.

* * *

After two weeks at Hospital Base 30, I was finishing my last case at nine in the evening when an orderly came racing into the operating room, calling my name.

"What is it?" I answered, irritated at the disturbance.

He stood fidgeting at the foot of the operating table. "Are you done? You need to see a patient on the unit."

My feet were numb from the hours of standing, and my nerves were completely shot. I hadn't eaten anything in fourteen hours, and it was well past dinner. "What is it? Why can't someone else take care of it?" I lashed out.

His upper body squirmed. "He asked for you. I think he's family."

A piercing ripple of dread ran through my empty gut. Who could it be? I didn't know anyone in the infantry. I snipped the last suture. "Caulfield, finish closing and be sure to wrap the leg exactly how I showed you earlier."

I washed my hands in the nearby basin and followed the orderly out of the operating room into a large medical ward.

He handed a clean mask to me from the linen table. "You must cover your face on this ward. Flu patients are pouring in from the trenches. Many are dying."

I covered my nose and mouth and followed him. The air was saturated with humidity, and the cacophony of hundreds of soldiers, coughing. Men sitting, lying on their sides, all hacking convulsively, blood splatters covering every surface. The last time I looked in this ward was on arrival, during my hospital tour a few weeks ago. At that time, it was practically empty. Now it was packed. As many flu patients filled our hospital beds as artillery wounds. They were separated by a long sheet wall. My arm swept across the sick room. "When did this happen?" I asked loudly over the racket.

The orderly didn't answer. Instead, he led me to a cot in the middle of the room. A young man, barely more than a child, lay curled in a circle like a snail, caught in the clutches of a respiratory spasm. His forehead was wet and hot with fever, blood dripping from the corner of his mouth onto his pillow. The boy looked familiar, but I couldn't place him. I studied his face as he caught his breath. His eyes shifted to me, sputtering, "Uncle. Thank God you're here."

Goose bumps ran from my forehead to my toes while I digested his words, sorting through Miriam's family. I gasped as the realization struck. We slept in his bedroom on our honeymoon stop at Nate's farm. Good God, this was Nate's son. I leaned into the orderly's ear, my voice shaky with disbelief. "Confirm name."

The medic lifted the chart from the foot of the cot. "Jake Isaacson from New York."

My belly dropped with a great force. Just as I feared, Nate's oldest. I dragged a stool beside his cot, its legs scraping along the floor, and sat beside Jake, taking his hand in mine. "I'm right here with you, son."

He squeezed my hand, choking out, "Martin's still there...." His body crumbled in a fit of bloody coughing "...fighting. Tried to hang tough...but couldn't breathe." Jake's coughing flared with sharp, choking gasps. His skin, deprived of oxygen, was turning blue.

I gently rubbed his back, attempting to settle him, and turned to the orderly. "I'm glad you found me. Grab a second mask for me and a nurse. Let's see what we can do to make Jake more comfortable. Bring morphine."

I sat beside the bed, thinking about Ben's warning letter. This flu was a lethal plague, far worse than anything I could have imagined. Why in God's name weren't the brass talking about it? I listened to Jake's chest with my stethoscope. His lungs were rattling, air barely making it into his body through his tortured trachea and lungs. Death was near. Like so many other soldiers on this ward, he was dying from a microscopic disease. Dying without a scrap of shrapnel touching his young, perfect body. Was this another price of freedom? What a load of horse shit!

Tears filled my eyes. I'd seen more than my share of death, but this broke me. Jake was Miriam's family, my family. I ached with helplessness. How would I possibly find the right words to tell Nate, Jenny, and Miriam this evening that their worst nightmare had come true, one that would forever devastate their tight-knit family?

With a heavy heart, I sat beside Jake for the next hour until he gasped his final breath.

Chapter Forty-Two: Miriam

August 1918—Head and Face Hospital, The Front

Sobbing, angry, I was tempted to tear Eli's telegram to shreds, wishing I could turn back time. Just one day ago, my cousin, Jake, was still alive, fighting alongside his brother, Martin. But it was no use. He was dead, and there was no changing the horrible reality. That happy young man with a head of curls I remembered from childhood at the farm was gone now. I wiped my eyes and read the letter again, attempting to feel Eli's words on the paper as they flowed from his heart, filling mine with immeasurable sorrow.

Dearest Miriam,

It is with the absolute heaviest of hearts that I must share news of Jake's death. He passed last evening from the horrendous flu sweeping through the trenches. As Ben warned, it has a ferocity none of us has ever witnessed in our years of practice.

The ambulance workers brought Jake to Base Hospital 30, along with a half-dozen other soldiers, all delirious with fever, coughing up blood. Thankfully, Jake was still able to speak and asked the medic if I worked there. At the time, I was closing my last case and scrubbed out. You can't imagine my shock when I saw his withered body, completely decompensated, overcome with illness. I listened to his chest. He was already in the throes of death; pneumonia had set in. All I could do

245

was order comfort care while he struggled for air, then passed barely an hour after I arrived at his bedside.

Sometime in my last year in France, surrounded by this mad sea of death, I had trained myself to stop feeling sadness or horror. There was no other way for me to stay sane. But seeing Jake, his life cut short, broke me. He will never realize the excitement of his future, one I'm sure would have been full of family and vitality. I sat beside him while his body was prepared for burial, struggling to find words that could bring comfort to your family. There were none. I only imagined the unbearable loss for Nate and Jenny, the agony they would feel opening their telegram. I only wish I could be there with you now, to hold you in my arms, absorb your sadness.

I set the letter on my lap and drew a deep, shaky breath, releasing it slowly. Working close to the Front without the buffer of intermediate hospitals, receiving soldiers fresh off the field, I had a better picture of what Eli had been facing this last year. Although not so quick to excuse his behavior, I was understanding the well of horror he'd fallen into. An absolute nightmare of suffering. I picked up the letter and continued,

I know Hannah left the older children at the farm for the summer, so I will notify her by telegram today as well and leave matters in her capable, comforting hands. Knowing Nate as I barely do, I would guess the children may bolster him. But who knows? Death unravels each of us in different ways.

Sitting beside Jake's body, I reminisced about our days at the farm last spring on our honeymoon, sleeping in Jake and Martin's room, squeezing into their narrow beds while they were in training. At that time, our lives were filled with romance and happiness. I never could have imagined the carnage and disease awaiting us in France. How I wish I could rewind time and better protect those boys.

If I can find a break from my duties tomorrow, I'll try to hop a ride with the head wounds we're transferring to your unit. I know you'll be

up to your eyeballs, but in the very least, I can give you a comforting
hug and help share your burden, even a tiny bit, while you digest this
heartbreaking news.

    With everlasting love,

    Eli

After folding Eli's letter, I placed it in my suitcase, wondering if he had changed. Had he finally learned the precious value of love? The unwavering love between parents and children, between a husband and wife?

In August, a month after arriving at this dreadful hospital ten miles in from the trenches, I began to see the ways battlefield surgery could change a man or woman. In Paris, we faced large numbers of patients, but none had come to us straight from the trenches, faces caked with mud and manure, hemorrhaging from their open facial wounds. Difficult as it was to witness the disfigurations at The American, this was a far more extreme challenge, multiples more difficult; cleaning open wounds, stemming the bleeding from the intricate and fragile facial vessels, dealing with the immediate fear and emotions of the wounded. My admiration for Dr. Gillies grew hourly. His talent for expressing compassion while sorting out complex surgical plans with bone and body transplant tissue for a series of reconstruction procedures was nothing short of genius.

Here, close to the battle, our overriding goal was to avoid infection at all costs, stabilize the soldiers, and transfer them to the large head and facial specialty units in France and England. Ours was a short-stay unit only.

My position as head nurse was to train the nursing staff, assist in preliminary surgeries, and sign off on the condition of our patients before transport. I had a small army of some of the finest nurses on the continent: quick, smart, and brave, tending men who had sustained severe mutilation. In keeping with the standards of The American, we kept no mirrors in the hospital. These men would be comforted and reassured until they reached the next hospital in the chain of care, where they'd be educated about the long road of intricate surgeries and recovery. For now, our job was to sustain them so their bodies would withstand the trials ahead.

But the pressure to return soldiers with minor injuries back to the trenches posed a hiccup in the process, one which I was unaccustomed to. No soldier from The American Hospital returned to the battlefield, but here, the pressure was enormous to return men to the trenches.

After storing Eli's letter in my suitcase, I walked into the recovery unit to round on the newly treated and bandaged patients, offering support to the nursing staff. I was accosted by a maelstrom of six angry soldiers, cursing their nurse. They'd been grouped together for return to battle once their wounds were sufficiently scabbed over and their bodies stabilized. Their injuries ranged from a shot-off ear to superficial facial injuries.

One shaggy-haired soldier smoking a cigarette, cleaned and bandaged, sat up in his bed, shouting, "There's no way in hell I'm goin' back to that slaughterhouse. I've had enough!"

Another chimed in, his western drawl dragging out the words, "The Huns are gunning us down like we're prairie dogs peeping out of holes. We're lucky to get out with a whole face."

My nurse was speechless, at a total loss.

I stepped into the fray, walking up to each man, demanding answers. "What seems to be your problem? You will all be fit to fight in a matter of days and, from the looks of things, you have plenty of fight left in you."

A mixture of shouting and grunts lashed back at me, their crescendo rising.

I dug deep. There must be some way to persuade them. I began by blowing a whistle I had in my apron pocket, shouting, "Quiet! All of you." I waited until all eyes were upon me. "We're finally beginning to win this war. No one promised it would be easy or safe. But look around the ward at the men who can't go back to help. What message are you sending to all those brave men, or the ones still fighting at the Front?"

The air was still, their hostility idling.

"You'll stay here with us for a few days. We'll feed you like kings to help you get your full strength back. Then you'll go back as the same courageous soldiers who came to win. But you'll be smarter. Always, and I mean always, wear your helmets, and never, never, never pop your head over the edge of the trench unless your commander orders you to advance." I paused. "Now you're shrewder and you know better. Fool them. Put an empty helmet up first and see if they shoot. The Germans wait for easy, foolish targets."

Was I sending them to their deaths, to be buried beside my cousin Jake in the military cemetery? I could only pray for a quick ending to this vile war.

As I turned, looking to the doorway, a warmth spread through my body. Eli stood there watching me. I wondered if he'd heard me read these men the riot act or if he'd just arrived. It didn't matter. He held out his arms and I ran into them, allowing him to comfort me, feeling the hope that there would be a tomorrow.

Chapter Forty-Three: Hannah

August 1918—New York

I n the short span of one hour after receiving the dreadful telegram,
I had arranged for Sophie to stay at the apartment with Gilda for a
few days, cancelled my patient appointments for the rest of the week,
packed, and jumped in my car, heading for Nate's Farm. I crossed the
Hudson River on a ferry to Englewood and eventually merged onto the
Liberty Highway that would take me to Sullivan County, cleaving a line
from the turbulent city to the serene countryside. I held back my tears with
every ounce of resolve, refusing to break down until I was across the river,
in the privacy of my car. Then it hit like a firestorm. The sharp reality of
loss. Realizing Jake's life was no more. He'd never live to marry and become
a father. Instead, his body would rot in a military cemetery in France.

The tears came in thick, drenching waves, blinding my vision. No longer
able to drive safely, I pulled off the two-lane highway into a gasoline station
in New Jersey to let the tears pass. The pumps stood empty at the roadside.
No attendant in sight. How I ached for Nate and Jenny. I knew in a remote
part of my brain, as we all knew, that both boys might not return. The
reality was far more excruciating than I could have imagined. Nate and
Jenny had raised such fine men, always an enormous help on the farm and
dutiful to their country. Was anything worth the cost of their lives? Their
futures?

A lanky middle-aged man in a denim boiler suit edged up to my window.

250

"You all right in there, ma'am?"

I nodded, sniffling, wiping my nose on my handkerchief. "Yes…no, not really. I lost a nephew in France. Barely a man." I inhaled. "I just need a minute."

He bent his body to peer into the open driver's window, facing me, his eyes leveling with mine. "Sorry to hear it. Lost my eldest there six months ago. You're in no shape to drive. How about you come with me and have a cold drink with my wife? We live right out back."

Startled by his unexpected kindness, I grabbed my purse and keys and blindly followed him behind the gas pumps across the dusty gravel patch to a small, paint-chipped porch attached to a tiny white wooden house.

He called, "Gladys, come on out. I want you to meet someone. Just lost her nephew in France. Bring some cold drinks."

A tall, willowy woman emerged from the house wearing a green calico flowered housedress buttoned in the front, reminding me of the kits Tillie sold years ago. She approached me and, without a word, pulled me into her arms, holding me tightly.

A new reservoir of tears erupted. "My goodness. I'm so embarrassed, falling apart like this. With strangers, no less." I unwrapped the handkerchief still clenched in a tight ball in the palm of my hand, wiped my eyes, and blew my nose.

Gladys pulled back and viewed me through her own tear-covered eyes. "My dear, we're no strangers to loss. You go ahead and cry. There's no shame in grieving."

I gulped back a fresh onslaught of tears. "You see, I'm heading to my brother's farm to help them deal with this tragedy. Now I'm the one falling apart." Another round of tears broke through. "Some help I'll be."

Gladys pointed to the white painted rocking chairs. "Sit a little and tell me about your boy. Where are you from?"

I exhaled, welcoming her company. She understood. "I live in the city with my husband and our three children. The two older ones are at my brother's chicken farm this summer, helping out. That's where I'm heading. It's my oldest nephew who died." I set my head back and rocked, absorbing the shady warmth of the porch, taking deep breaths, steadying myself.

I continued to pour out my story. "My family came from Germany over sixty years ago. My husband and I are both doctors at Beth Israel. We all feel strongly about protecting our country and the boys abroad."

She startled, examining me carefully. "You say Beth Israel? You're Jewish? We've never met a Jewish person."

A laugh escaped my lips. "Now you have."

Her faint blond brows drew together in amazement. "I didn't know there were Jewish people in the army."

Outside New York City and our ethnic enclave, I reminded myself that the United States was a big country, the Jewish people comprising less than a tiny percent of the population. Half of us lived in New York. "Yes, of course. We're in this war together. My husband, niece, and her husband are all in the Medical Corps in France, two doctors and a nurse. My nephews are at the Front."

"My word," she said, her voice softening to a whisper. "I had no idea."

My lips turned into a soft smile. "We're all part of this great country, defending it, mending the injured, and now burying our precious boys."

She extended her hand, setting it on mine. "And here you are, keeping the home fires burning with all the young children, helping your brother in his time of grief. You brave, brave woman."

I relaxed, once again reminded of how short the bridge was between people. Jewish, dark-skinned, Christian people. We were all facing the same fears and challenges during these treacherous times. For the unlucky, we shared the ultimate loss of sons and husbands.

I swallowed the last of my lemonade and stood to leave. "I should be on my way. But first, I must thank you. I feel so much better. Your generosity, extending yourselves in this way, has restored me more than you realize. You are very kind people." I cupped my hands over my heart. "And I'm very sorry for the loss of your boy."

She smiled, lips together, and nodded. "And you will be there for others, too. There's bound to be many more before this ordeal is over."

* * *

Hours later, I pulled into Jake's farm. The sun was setting in the western sky, jetting streaks of pink and purple across the horizon. How was it that nature could be so beautiful and hideous at the same time? I took a deep breath and walked up the steps to the screened door. The sad melody of chanting poured out of the open windows and front door. The mourner's Kaddish. Its magnetic pull drew me inside. *Yitgadal v'yitkadash sh'mei raba b'alma di-v'ra....* The Hebrew verses were imprinted in my memory from childhood. Like a magnet, they drew my past losses forward to the present until I found myself reliving the deaths of Tillie and Abe and my parents, Sam and Sarah.

The Rabbi completed the service. The parlor, filled with a dozen or more people stood in silence, absorbing the gravity of the moment, then they surrounded Nate and Jenny with comforting hugs and words. In the rear of the room, standing closest to the front door, stood Albert. Hearing the click of the screen door, he captured me in his line of sight. Albert clasped Anna's arm, and they lunged toward me, seeking comfort as I pulled them together into my arms.

They sobbed into my shoulders while I rubbed their backs, smelling their essence, the perfume of life. The farm's fragrances of summer hay, flowers, and fresh air filled me with the purity of nature. In this rural setting, issues of life and death always seemed more natural, tied to the change of season, birth and death of plants and livestock. But losing a young man in war, especially without the trauma of a bullet, was jarring, an act of nature's evil.

Guests arranged desserts and drinks in the back yard as I wove the children through the kitchen and out the door. For now, I would give Nate and Jenny time with their visitors and sit with them once the Shiva guests left for home. My immediate concern was Anna and Albert. How were they handling the devastating news? Would I need to bring them back to the city?

I led the children past a knot of women, all wiping their eyes while arranging the table, then filling their plates with pastries and fruit, talking all the while.

"Let's take a walk and find a private place to sit and talk," I said.

We strolled in silence down the slope through the tall grasses into the thick fruit orchard. The green apples and pears hung heavily from their bent branches, on the brink of ripeness, but burdening the tree with their growing weight. In no way did I want Anna and Albert to add to my brother's and Jenny's grief.

We sat on the parched brown grass flattened with half-ripened fallen fruit beneath the trees. The bees buzzed as they scouted the area, seeming to fly out of our way as if perceiving our need for privacy. "I came as fast as I could. How are you both holding up?"

Anna began to sniffle. "It's so sad. Aunt Jenny said Jake was buried in France. They can't even send his body back. He's never coming home to them."

Albert's eyes were moist, but he held back his tears. Instead, words burst forth with anger. "I don't understand how he could have died. Jake was never shot. Damn, Mama, who dies from a cold?"

I sighed. They were nowhere near accepting Jake was gone forever, still struggling with the details: circumstances, burial, illness. How would they react when the permanence of death set in? "Yes, you are both right. Albert, it does seem very unfair. If Eli hadn't been at his side as a witness, I'd find his death hard to believe."

Anna asked, "Will he feel lonely in France, so far from his parents?"

How my heart ached for that child. I answered, "No, sweetheart, once we're dead, we no longer feel emotion. Now the concern is for your aunt and uncle, and how to help them pick up the pieces." I inhaled a slow breath. "I need to understand what you both want to do. But most importantly, we must honor Uncle Nate and Aunt Jenny's wishes. As for the burial, remember there isn't time or space on the ships to bring most bodies across the sea. But maybe someday we can visit his cemetery in France, when this horrible war is over. He was buried with other American soldiers in a special cemetery." I turned to face Anna, wiping away the tears on her cheeks with my handkerchief. "They will keep him company."

Anna asked, "Were they afraid he might get people on the ship sick, too?

I wrapped her in my arms. If these near adults were old enough to face death straight on, they could manage the truth. "Most likely. From the letters I've been getting from your Papa and Aunt Miriam, it seems there are many men coming in from the trenches with a very serious influenza, just like the one Jake had. It attacks the lungs, and as in Jake's case, turns to pneumonia. There's a growing concern the disease will travel to America on the boats and make people here sick."

Albert's eyebrows tightened together. "It makes no sense. First, we're told the soldiers die from the shrapnel, now this. How did the diseases get there in the first place? Did the Germans invent it, like the mustard gas?"

How I wish I had all the answers and could give Albert something to blame. "Aunt Miriam has told me the flu is making the German soldiers sick, too. At the hospital, they've set up separate wards for them, so they don't infect the other soldiers. This month, half of the patients in Uncle Eli's hospital had the flu, and so many died, like Jake."

Albert blurted out in frustration, "But why aren't they taking better care of the soldiers? They shouldn't be getting sick. Uncle Jake's been sending pallets of chickens over there. Don't they feed it to them?"

How do I explain the harshness of the trenches and nature's vengeance to a fourteen-year-old boy who is still fantasizing about war as some sort of thrilling life adventure? I tried not to dampen his zeal with my explanation. "The soldiers in trenches live close together in a very dirty area with little fresh water for washing. It's common for them to catch things from each other or from fleas and other creatures, even if they receive plenty of clothes and food. It isn't anywhere as clean as it is at home."

Albert leaned back against the tree trunk, his chin resting on his chest. When he spoke, I knew he'd heard enough, could not absorb one more detail. He changed the subject to life on the farm. "This summer, I've learned to ride horses. We sent forty to the pier last week, from just our farm. I'd like to stay and keep helping. Would that be all right with you?"

"No promises, Albert, until I speak to your Aunt and Uncle." I leaned my head toward Anna. "What are your thoughts, darling? You can certainly come back to the city with me if you'd like."

Albert interrupted, still fixed on his work with the horses. "Did you know those bastards at Quaker Oats wanted so much money for the horse feed that the army had to get it elsewhere? Uncle Nate gives the army chickens practically at cost. He makes nothing from it."

I had given no thought to the supply chain needed to feed an army and its horses. I was glad Albert had a conscience, smoking out the profiteers. Something good was clearly happening here in the country; real lessons he hadn't gotten in the city. It was a relief to see Albert's growing maturity.

Anna had been waiting patiently to answer me. She half-whispered, "If Aunt Jenny needs my help, I'd like to stay with her until school starts."

The children knew their aunt and uncle well enough by this point in the summer to predict their answers. Losing Albert and Anna on the heels of Jake's death might only shake them further. The children's natural enthusiasm and assistance on the farm would help channel their sadness. For me, with the fear of the influenza entering New York with the soldiers, I preferred having the children far from the densely populated city until I had a better idea of how to keep them safe.

* * *

Saturday evening, the night after Nate and Jenny's shiva, I left for home. Although the Shiva period lasted a week in most observant Jewish families, Nate and Jenny, in keeping with our German parents, practiced their own version of the religion, picking and choosing from the traditional guidance, following the rules that best suited their lives.

The next morning, I packed the car with tomatoes, beets, and cucumbers from Jenny's vegetable garden to bring back to the city. Sophie would be delighted to prepare dinner with freshly picked country vegetables, a rarity in our neighborhood markets. As for the apples, they still needed a few more weeks to ripen.

Jenny followed me out of the house with an armload of trays containing food and pastries. "Take these with you. There's far too much for us. Look at it all, stuffed cabbage, brisket, rugulah, honey cake. It will just spoil."

I put my hands out. "Wait a minute. There's only Gilda and me, and trust me, Gilda eats crumbs compared to Albert and Anna." I took the trays from her hands and walked back into the house. "Let's fix a small container for me to take. Then you can give the rest to your neighbor, where Albert works with the horses. He must be eating them out of house and home. It won't go to waste." I pointed in the direction of the horse farm, the smell of manure filtering through the morning air.

Just then, a loud hiccupping sound erupted from Jenny, her tears flowing anew. Her hands swept over the kitchen counters, laden with stacks of wrapped plates of cookies, strudel, and breads. "I can't look at this food. It makes me remember he won't ever come home." Another loud moan escaped her lips. "What if something happens to Martin, too? Then we'll be childless. I couldn't bear it."

Rocking her, absorbing her anguish, I attempted to prod her out of her dark thoughts. "No sense imagining more tragedy. You'll drive yourself mad. Remember, Jake's last word to Eli was that Martin was well, still in the trenches." I noticed Anna at the doorway, her eyes misted over. "Let the children help you. They can take the extra food next door and to the shul for other families. You try to think about happy memories. That way it won't go to waste, and you won't need to look at it."

Jenny opened her arms to Anna. "My sweet Annala. I'm so happy you're staying here with us. You are God's blessing."

* * *

That evening, I returned to New York City before Gilda's bedtime. She was bathed and ready for her book as I walked in the door. Joy filled me, holding my precious youngest. This was the medicine I needed. I rocked her, singing our favorite song that summer, Erie Canal. *"Low bridge, everybody down, low bridge, because we're coming to a town...."* It always set Gilda into a fit of laughter, the very elixir I needed after the sad, last few days of mourning.

My schedule the next day back at Mount Sinai was jam-packed with the patients I'd postponed from the week before. Even knowing it would be a long day, I still called the President's office to arrange a few moments for us to speak. The matter of the flu was of paramount importance. Before venturing to inquire at other hospitals, I must hear his thoughts about this influenza coming back to New York from France.

With so many young men overseas for the past year, my patient mix had rapidly shifted from young expectant mothers to women in their middle years and older presenting with change of life difficulties and more serious ailments, tumors, and failing health as Tillie had. Although these women brought back heartrending memories of Tillie in her final days, they were quickly referred to our surgical staff for care, and in some cases, to The New York Cancer Center on the West Side, a hospital entirely devoted to the care of cancer patients. As much as I was leery of the gilded set in New York, known for their open antisemitism, I had to hand it to them when it came to philanthropy. Between The American Hospital in Paris and this relatively new cancer hospital, they took the cake when it came to helping the sick, particularly the Astor, Morgan, and Vanderbilt descendants.

By 1:00, I was able to scramble downstairs to the administrative offices and catch a moment with Mr. Blumenthal, the hospital president. Ben and he had a familiar, first-name relationship, but as a woman, that degree of familiarity was not extended to me.

Mr. Blumenthal sat rigidly behind his desk when his secretary let me in. He finished scribbling on a pad of paper and lifted his eyes to me. "How can I help you today, Dr. Kahn? I hope all is well in Paris with your husband." He gestured to a seat opposite his desk.

I launched in, knowing I had fifteen minutes before a full afternoon schedule of patients. "Ben, thank God, is fine, but my nephew passed away last week from that terrible influenza. That's what I'm here to discuss."

Mr. Blumenthal's bushy eyebrows lifted upward, creasing his forehead. His balding head, barely covered by thin grey hair, was combed back over his chalky scalp. "I'm sorry to hear that. So many senseless losses."

I nodded. "It's why I'm here. Has the Medical Corps or Health Department sent any warnings about this flu? From what I've heard from Ben, it's worse than anything he's ever seen. The respiratory symptoms are so severe, patients die in a matter of days, some hours."

Mr. Blumenthal sat back, removed his wire-rimmed glasses, and studied me. "Dr. Kahn wrote to me a few months ago about building a designated Head and Face Unit, that there may be public money in play, plus philanthropy for such a project, but he didn't mention a flu."

It irked me that news coming from me, a woman, would be met with disregard. "He and my niece have both worked with the head and face injuries. A special unit serving patients with those injuries, as well as burn patients here at home, is critical for our returning soldiers. I agree that Mount Sinai would meet a great need. Of course, it would reinforce the hospital's reputation for excellence and their forward thinking." I paused, leaning forward, holding his eyes to mine. "But this influenza poses an immediate threat to citizens here in New York. I reached into my purse and pulled out Miriam's last letter. "Please listen to this. I'll only read the pertinent parts. It was written a few weeks ago, from my niece, a nurse in France."

Uncle Ben and I see men coming into the hospitals from the Front with a severe influenza. At first it was just a trickle, now the sick arrive non-stop with violent coughing and pneumonia, their skin bluish, struggling to breathe. The strangest part is that no one up the chain of command wants to hear about it. Sure, they've let us isolate them, and everyone in the room wears a mask, but they're ordering us to send the sick back to the States to make room for the newly wounded from the trenches. My fear is they will wreak havoc along the way, passing the disease to others in trains and ships. God knows what the spread might look like once it hits American shores.

... If you can convince your hospital president, set up an isolation ward for these poor men. I pray the illness turns out to be nothing like we are told, but from what I've seen on the ward, it's extremely dangerous. These patients and nurses become desperately sick, struggling for air, their ears and eyes bleeding from all the strain. As you can see, I'm

worried this is but a new chapter of this hideous war. If you begin to see an influx of admissions, please don't brush it off as a nasty cold. It's the next plague.

He sat with his fingers tented in front of his face, his thumbs tweaking the ends of his mustache. "Plague, now, isn't that a bit dramatic? That's the first I've heard anything. Certainly not enough evidence to invest in an isolation unit. Do you have any idea how much they cost?"

An anger burned in my chest. I knew he wanted to hear about it from a man. "Perhaps I'll ask Ben to send a letter verifying Nurse Miriam's report. But what troubles me most is that you're not receiving cautionary measures from outside the hospital, for instance, the war office, or the city health departments, and the papers are not mentioning it."

He replaced his glasses on his bulbous nose, signaling the meeting had ended. "I'll take your caution under advisement, and in the meantime, I am raising funds for the Head and Face Unit as Dr. Kahn recommended."

There would be no use attempting further persuasion. I rose to return to my patients, my next moves already formulating in my head. As with most hospital presidents, he was reliant on established channels for official warnings and would not take my word, Miriam's letter from the Front, or a family member's death, did not meet his threshold to take action. Of course, the fact that I was a woman only diminished my message. "Thank you for your time, sir." I walked to the door. On second thought, turning back to Mr. Blumenthal, I said, "I would suggest with the strongest urgency that your operating committee add a contingency plan in the event my nephew's death is an omen of what's yet to come in New York City. I am confident that a sharp leader like yourself would not want to be accused of unpreparedness."

Back in my office, I called Bellevue to arrange an appointment with the president. As the safety net hospital in the city, and in the absence of any designated military hospitals since the Civil War, Bellevue would be the first line of care for many sick and injured soldiers. I was curious to learn what they knew.

* * *

The air began to cool the next week. I decided to walk downtown to Bellevue a mile south from my apartment, mentally constructing the conversation I intended, hopeful their bad memories of me from years ago had vanished.

My last exchange took place close to a decade before, when I was released from Blackwell's Island Workhouse after a false arrest, together with an apology in the form of a healthcare grant from the State for the trumped-up charges. In that final visit to Bellevue, I crossed paths with the worst scoundrel of my past, Roger Holloway, a former medical student from Johns Hopkins Medical School, who lulled me into believing he was a gentleman and, once alone, accosted me. Holloway's actions against me and others culminated in an expulsion, but it didn't keep his parents from buying a medical school seat for him in New York City. It was no surprise that my meeting at Bellevue years ago culminated in embitterment.

But this influenza was an entirely different matter, one that could impact Bellevue more profoundly than any hospital in the city. As the only true charity hospital, they bore the brunt of city-wide epidemics: typhus, diphtheria, tuberculosis. Even with specialty hospitals sponsored by the State, City, and on Blackwell's Island, Bellevue was still the first point of care for many, especially the poor. Would they have the resources to meet an influenza of historic proportions?

The last time I walked through the hospital doors, I was twisted in knots trying to find my way to the President's office. But despite the decade between visits, I knew exactly where to go. In the ten years that had passed, I was pleased to see the interior had received a sprucing up with fresh paint and better signage, although all in English. When would they learn? Although it was 1918 and the influx from Europe had virtually come to a halt during the war, there were entire neighborhoods still speaking in their native European tongues.

Walking through the corridor to the Administrative Offices, photographs of past presidents hung on the wall. My breath caught. A picture of Roger Holloway hung at the end of a long eye-level row of photographs. Beneath the celluloid rendering were the words, "In memory of". My stomach knotted as I looked at his deceptively handsome face, wondering what took his life at such a young age. In the photograph, he looked strong and proud, with no signs of remorse or humility. What did I expect? The man was a narcissist, his privilege used to skirt any consequences for his atrocious behavior.

I was summoned into the President's office upon my arrival. Relieved to see a new face, I relaxed. The President, an older man by the name of Albert Sellenings, stood to greet me. "Thank you, sir, for taking the time to meet with me on such short notice."

His warm blue eyes absorbed me as he pointed to an upholstered chair beside a coffee table set with tea, coffee, and breakfast buns. His voice was breathy, full of surprise. "When I heard you were coming here, I'd assumed you were the Mister Dr. Kahn, the President of the Medical Staff, but it's a pleasure to meet you, too. Can I assume you are his wife?"

Getting pushed to the sidelines was not the opening I'd expected or hoped for. Flicking my hand, I dismissed his error and smiled, pasting a good-natured, albeit insincere smile on my face. I learned long ago I'd catch more flies with honey. "That happens all the time. I head the maternity services at Mount Sinai, and Dr. Ben Kahn is presently serving in France."

He sat opposite me and pointed to the coffee pot. "I see. Godspeed to him and all the brave Americans there now. Do you care for coffee? I'm eager to hear how I can help you."

To further soften the confusion and ensure I'd derive the greatest benefit from our meeting, I picked up the coffee pot and poured our drinks, handing him his cup and saucer as any well-bred woman would do. "Yes, I'm hoping you can. Based on the news I've received from physicians in my family serving at both the Front and The American Hospital in Paris, a substantial number of soldiers are coming from the trenches infected with a deadly respiratory flu. With the enormous push against the Germans and the need to open hospital beds for the newly injured, these soldiers are being rushed stateside for their convalescence and to make room for a wave of new casualties in France. I'm wondering what you're hearing and if you have plans for isolation units."

Mr. Sellenings sighed loudly; his entire demeanor slumped as he sank into his chair. "We already admitted a few sick soldiers and have lost one nurse. In August, we were warned about the Bergensfjord patients out of Europe, but we thought it might be an isolated incident. No one gave us ample warning of just how serious the infection was."

"I'm terribly sorry to hear that. What are the military, Red Cross, or Public Health Department telling you? Will it get worse? How does a city of our size prepare?"

He bent toward me, hands clasped on his knees. "I've seen a lot of dangerous diseases run their course at Bellevue, but this one is the worst yet. Patients who survive the first three days have a chance of beating it; that is, if they don't dehydrate. For the rest, it is a quick ride through hell. I've put together a medical and nursing committee to come up with a plan. Now, with one dead nurse, I will only staff the unit with volunteers. It's too dangerous to force anyone. We will repurpose a minimum of two units previously earmarked for other purposes."

Although I fully agreed with his plan, he hadn't answered my question. "But what are you being told? What are the projections, severity, and duration? You see, I just lost a nephew in France to this very same influenza." I drew a full breath. "I know it will be bad. It's a question of how bad."

Mr. Sellening's voice dropped. "I'm very sorry to hear that." He reached out to pat my hand. "I'm not getting all the answers I need either, but I have gotten reassurances Bellevue will be warned if the military is bringing infected soldiers here. That's all I know." He cleared his throat before continuing, "But we both are aware, once the disease spreads outside the hospitals' walls, into the city, all bets are off."

We sat silently drinking our coffee. My appetite for breakfast was gone. The next order of business was to construct a plan to present back to Mr. Blumenthal at Mount Sinai. I stood to leave. "Thank you for taking the time to share this important information. May I call on you in the future?"

He stood and walked me to the door. "Of course. I'll join you on your way to the lobby. My doctors tell me I need to spend time out of that desk chair and move around more, but they haven't a clue the time it takes to run this place."

As we approached Roger Holloway's picture in the outer hallway, I stopped and asked, "I was wondering what happened to this man. He must have died very young."

Mr. Sellenings grunted, "Oh, him. He got what he had coming, the useless worm. His parents made a substantial donation to get his picture on the wall. Once they pass, it's coming down."

Surprised he shared that information openly with me, I couldn't help but feel at ease that justice had been delivered.

Chapter Forty-Four: Ben

August 1918—Paris

T he orderly raced into the charting room, beads of sweat covering his face. "Doctor, we have twenty-two new patients outside in ambulances waiting for beds in your unit and no place to put them."

I rose from my chair, the oppressive August heat weighing me down, the seat of my pants damp from perspiration. "I'll round on the floor and see who can be discharged back to the States or sent to England." Patting his shoulder, I added, "We'll find room for everyone. For now, take them all to the preoperative area for assessment and fluids. Most will need debridement. That will buy us a few hours to open some beds."

One by one, my nurse and I moved through the ninety beds lined along the walls and center of the room. The occupancy of the Head and Face Unit at The American had doubled since the beginning of summer. I was confident Dr. Gillies would admit all stable British soldiers to Queen's Hospital in South-East London, where he would continue their lengthy care. He never turned anyone away. Besides, I was eager to hear his feedback on my work thus far. Dr. Gillies had convinced his government to invest in extensive resources, assembling a broad team of talent, dentists, feeding specialists, artists, mask makers, addressing the complex needs of each patient, a deep showcase for the finest head and face care in the world. I'd send a telegram to Dr. Gillies letting him know they were coming.

How I wished I'd been able to visit his hospital, an invitation he extended when we met a year ago. My one opportunity had been this past winter, but Miriam's crisis required my presence. I was determined to convince the Mount Sinai donors to replicate his unit for our soldiers' ongoing care, offering the exact same services.

My nurse and I walked through the ward, identifying twenty-one patients stable enough for transport across the Channel to London. Their mixture of delight and trepidation at the prospect of returning home left me without words. It was in times like these I missed Miriam the most. She knew the right things to say when a soldier was apprehensive, his face repelling those he loved. She might even tease him, "You were more unsightly the day you were born, all wrinkled and screaming. Your mama will love you even more now, you brave man." Of course, she'd have him laughing and crying but coping.

* * *

I'd become a frequent, unwelcome intrusion to the administrative wing. Today, I'd had my fill of evasive answers. I would throw down the gauntlet. Something must be done about this flu. Fortunately, I had one ally remaining in the Front office, the former Lance Corporal Morgan, now promoted to Corporal Morgan. He greeted me with a curious smile, one eyebrow lifted. "Good morning, sir. What brings you here today?" He paused, "Nothing good, I presume."

I chuckled. "I must speak to Sergeant Anderson. Is he still sober?" We both knew of Anderson's penchant for dark rum in the Officer Lounge and the poorly hidden bottles rattling around in his desk drawers.

Morgan chuckled, "I believe so, but there's still time. The day is young." He turned to grab the crutch, leaning on the wall behind him. "Let me announce you."

I waved my hand. "Sit, I'll announce myself."

Not only did we need more beds, but with the growing number of influenza patients and their need for isolation, every unit throughout the hospital was tight. The pressure to send the sick boys back to the States was mounting, and many of us had growing concerns that hospitals back home were not taking our warnings seriously. And for some mysterious reason, the newspapers had shirked their duty to provide up-to-date information to the public. Ample warning was paramount. The Spanish newspapers were alone in printing clear warnings. Was it because they'd remained neutral throughout the war, or did the flu originate in their country? We were beginning to hear the disease referred to as the Spanish Flu.

Anderson dropped his pen on the cluttered desktop, papers scattered from one end to the other. "Oh, dear God, what do you want, Kahn? Come to make my day?" He looked more disheveled than usual, his hair falling in oily tufts over his face, top shirt button open.

I shook my head, wondering how long the man could hang onto his position. His family must have had connections to procure his post. The army likely figured he would do less harm in an office job, away from guns and sharp, metal objects. I said, "Good morning, sir. I promise I won't be long."

Anderson jerked his hand, pointing to the guest chair. "Sit, for God's sake. What is it?"

I smiled, thinking about the British and their tight grip on manners, politeness at all costs. Quite the opposite from New York, where the message came first, manners second, typically delivered with a sarcastic edge. "First, I wanted to thank you for the additional beds in my unit. They filled fast with the increased fighting. As of this morning, we are discharging two dozen British face injuries to Queen's Hospital in London. This will open beds for incoming soldiers who are, as we speak, outside the hospital waiting to be admitted. But we are running at 100% occupancy and need another unit. The Germans are shooting at the Americans troops like they're target practice, a goddamn vaudeville pop-up game. Doesn't anyone tell these boys to keep their heads down?" I exclaimed, my hands open at my sides.

Anderson pulled a clean sheet of paper from his desk drawer and began writing. "I have a meeting with the Chief Nursing Officer in an hour. I'll bring it up." His bloodshot eyes drifted back to mine, most likely hungover from last evening's drinking. "We are tight as a drum with all the flu patients. They're taking up close to half the beds this week. The nursing staff is jittery. Afraid to care for them."

He'd led me directly to my next issue. "Speaking of the flu, have you gotten any official word from above? You must know we're sending contagious men out the door onto trains and boats along with the wounded."

Anderson sat back in his chair, playing with his cuff buttons. "Nothing official. We are counting on the medical staff to provide proper warning during patient hand-off."

I shook my head, my mouth ajar. "Good God, sir, you must know that's not adequate. Our death rate is close to twenty percent. I lost a nephew at the Front last week to this plague. The hospitals in the States should all be setting up infection wards ahead of time, keeping the sick isolated, away from visitors, staff, and others who are not masked and protected."

Anderson threw his hands up in frustration. "I have orders! Do what you can through back channels and don't tell anyone I instructed you to do so. They want the beds cleared for incoming, and if they're not in the throes of death or hemorrhaging, patients are to be moved home."

I left his office more discouraged than ever, wondering if the price of war could possibly be worth this level of recklessness. Who knew what disaster might await the cities receiving these men? With this degree of press censorship, there'd be no opportunity for newspapers and public information channels to adequately warn the public.

That evening, I wrote to Hannah, urging her to meet with George Blumenthal, the President of Mount Sinai, where we both practiced. Although I knew he was rallying the donors for the construction of my Head and Face Unit, the potential for a highly infectious influenza in a city as densely populated as New York was far more pressing. I also encouraged Hannah to meet with the New York City Health Department and the presidents of Beth Israel, the Jewish Maternity Hospital, and Bellevue, all located downtown. Their proximity to the shipping lanes and the tenements encompassing lower Manhattan left those institutions and neighborhoods most vulnerable. There was no telling how much devastation an epidemic of this severity could unleash.

Chapter Forty-Five: Eli

September 1918—The Front

Shortly after Jake's death, I caught a ride to Miriam's hospital near the Front. I stood in the shadows at the doorway, watching Miriam assume control of several surly soldiers, knowing it was against every moral fiber in her being to send them back to the trenches. But this was war, and after years of bloody combat, things were tipping ever so slowly in the Allied favor. There was no choice but to keep pushing our men with the greatest force possible.

Dark rings circled her eyes; she'd lost more weight, and her uniform hung loosely over her slim body. When was the last time she'd eaten or slept? I imagined that Miriam's fierce intensity pushed aside all human comforts to get her job done. Running a hospital, even a small one like this, was a herculean task. Miriam had always been a glutton for a challenge.

She swung around, taking a long step toward the canvas flap door, toward me, and stopped in her tracks. Her mouth fell open in surprise, her eyes wide.

I cocked my head to the side with a shy smile, trying to read her thoughts. But I could not. I used her official name. "Hello, Nurse Rosen. I caught a ride over to check on you."

She approached me, then quickened her steps, falling into my arms, pausing for a moment before regaining her poise. She then led me through the door flap into the grassy pasture outside. Catcalling from the patients clung to us like a tail as we walked. She shrugged them off. "Eli, I didn't expect to see you."

I turned to wink at the injured soldiers in the ward, craning my head around Miriam to humor them. The least I could do was add a dose of entertainment to their day. "You have worked your magic on them, too, but that's not why I'm here."

She squinted her eyes inquisitively.

I took her shoulders in my hands. "After burying Jake, I had to see you. All those memories of the farm…." My voice hitched. "I had to make sure you were all right."

She shook her head and whispered, "I'm anything but all right." Tears filled her eyes as she fell into my chest, her breathing jagged.

I cradled her in my arms, finally leading her away from the heavy canvas tent to a more private area where we could sit together. I found two folding chairs in front of the hospital and guided her onto one, forgetting the comforting lines I'd rehearsed, unable to string together any words. We sat for a long time, holding each other's hands, both digesting the horror of Jake's death in the ocean of losses across Europe and now America, leaving families untethered. The world would be changed forever in ways we couldn't begin to fathom. The U.S. war casualties had topped one hundred thousand in only eighteen months, young lives whose futures would never unfold.

Leaning my cheek to her forehead, I was startled by how warm she felt. "Darling, have you been feeling sick?" I asked. "If I'm not mistaken, I think you have a fever."

She sighed, "I'm sure it's nothing. Just a headache from the aggravation of moving men through here so quickly. Nothing to worry about." She stifled a cough.

But I was worried. After watching Jake's rapid decline in a ward full of fever and coughing, I knew she must be checked carefully. "Stay right here. I'm getting a thermometer."

* * *

271

Within the hour, Miriam's fever had kicked up to 104°. She was barely lucid, calling for her mama in her delirium. After moving her to a bed on the sick ward, I spent every waking moment beside her, terrified I'd lose her again, administering aspirin suppositories, gently sponging her body with cold rags, waiting for the tell-tale coughing to take its grip. By nightfall, she was panting in exhaustion, her coughing emerging with a vengeance, racking her thin, wasted body. I pleaded with God, "You must spare her."

The nurses on the floor tried to coax me to leave, believing that, like so many others on the ward, she was heading for her end, fearful I might catch the flu, too.

"Doctor, please have something to eat. We'll make a bed for you in the office where you can get rest. Would you like us to notify your unit or her family?"

* * *

Two days passed, sleeping on the floor beside her, waking every hour to sponge bathe her body in cool water. With every passing minute, my hope strengthened, watching her fight, the warrior within her fragile body wielding her sword. I rooted in her ear, "I'm here. You can beat this. You're turning a corner."

Hours later, fast asleep on the pallet beside her bed, I was awakened by a tickle on my nose. Those damn mice have gotten into the tent. Or had my mask slipped down? I reached up to reposition my mask and heard a faint laugh. Were my exhausted ears playing games? My head cleared, and I opened my eyes, sitting up to check on Miriam. She lay on her narrow cot, eyes open. A small, weak smile pulled at the corners of her mouth. A victor.

I gasped with relief. "Darling, you've come back to me." I ran my palms down her face and neck. The fever had broken, leaving her skin sticky and damp. "How would you like a sponge bath and some beef marrow soup?"

Miriam nodded, following my movements with her soft eyes. "Close call, wasn't it? You took care of me again," she whispered, still too weak for a conversation. She knew I wouldn't let her go without a fight.

Was that love I saw in her eyes? Lord, I hoped so. There was no way I could bear losing Miriam. I took her hands in mine, squeezing them gently. "I don't know if I could go on if you hadn't come back to me." My tears threatened to break through, but I held strong. "Right now we need to nurse you back to health and get that indomitable woman I love back to work."

* * *

A day later, I left Miriam in the attentive care of her nursing staff and caught a ride back to Base Hospital 30. After three days of abstaining from all food and most liquids, she was dehydrated, requiring intensive nursing care. But she was on the mend, and I knew my hospital needed me back. If anything, the fighting had continued to escalate, and all hands were critical.

Upon returning, I immediately jumped back into my surgical gown and scrambled to the field of wounded men waiting for triage. I saw Dr. Caulfield holding a rag over her face while she examined a soldier. "I'm back," I called out. "What's in the lineup??"

She straightened, walking briskly to me. "I'll be damned. Double trouble. Men with both the flu and injuries. Where do they fit in the triage protocol?"

After the up-close week I had with the flu, I didn't hesitate to order, "Get a mask on! Support care only until they survive the flu. If we must act fast, we'll amputate. They can't be recovering from surgery while fighting the flu. It's too much strain on their compromised bodies. Let's get the bleeding under control and get fluids in them, but nothing more until they rally."

Louise studied my face. "What are their chances of making it through the flu?"

"From what I've seen, about one in five. It's a plague like we haven't seen in centuries."

She watched me, hesitating before she spoke. "I heard your wife caught it."

I sighed, "She'll make it, but damn if it wasn't nick and tuck there for a few days. It hits like a firestorm."

That week, we amputated more limbs than I would have liked, but what choice did we have? A lengthier surgery would have compromised the men further, and they needed every ounce of strength to fight the dragon attacking their lungs. We pumped the sick full of liquids, knowing they'd become dehydrated and crossed our fingers.

Chapter Forty-Six: Hannah

October 1918—New York City

I was summoned to Mr. Blumenthal's office within moments of entering the hospital. He didn't want to listen to anything I had to say a month ago, but now, with a flood of influenza cases hitting Mount Sinai, his thirst for the latest scuttlebutt was insatiable.

I ran up the stairs to his office, entered the waiting area, and was directed straight in. Before opening Mr. Blumenthal's door, I asked the secretary if she'd mind fetching a strong cup of coffee. "It was a long, late night of new babies."

"Right away, Doctor. Happy to help."

I settled into the armchair across from Mr. Blumenthal's desk, waiting for him to lift his eyes and bombard me with questions. After sharing Ben's letter and the news from Bellevue, he had finally agreed to outfit a large unit in case flu patients were admitted. Now every bed was full. So was the morgue. It was a saving grace that, unlike the Christian faith, the Jewish people buried their dead within twenty-four hours, so the morgue cleared quickly.

With my connections around the city, I knew he'd want to hear how our competition was faring. Mr. Blumenthal pushed the stack of papers to the side and peered up at me. "Tell me what you're hearing. Will we need another unit? Is the hospital safe for other patients? For visitors? For me?" I pondered why he was asking me. Where were his connections? Wasn't it his job to have his ear to the ground?

I sighed, drained from managing this powerful man who didn't care a fig about me, one of his key practitioners who didn't get home until after one in the morning, on my feet for hours in the hospital with a difficult delivery. I was impatient for my coffee. Where was she? "As you know, I met with a Health Department official earlier in the week, and they're finally acknowledging the severity of this influenza, particularly since Spain's newspapers have been publishing front-page warnings. They formed a committee assigned to issuing public guidance about masks and spitting. Schools are open, but movie theaters are closed, and some businesses have staggered hours."

He shouted, "What do you mean, schools are open? They're not keeping the children at home?"

My head pounded, his voice grating me further. Where was that coffee? I took a deep breath to calm myself. "They want to get children out of the tenement buildings for as many hours as possible, so they don't catch it there."

He banged his hands on the desk, shooting up from his chair. "But they'll infect the entire city! There aren't enough pediatric beds in New York."

Just then, his blessed secretary walked in with a steaming cup of coffee, setting it down on his desk before me.

He looked at her. "I didn't ask for coffee."

I interrupted. "I did. I had a late night here with patients." I took a long sip, turning to offer a thank you nod, and continued, "One might think the children would be spreaders, but the fact is, this flu hits the healthiest adults hardest. Those in the prime of life do the worst. We don't know why. We've been reporting all flu patients to the Health Department, as required, and they're predominantly young adults. Every week, they report the data." Shouldn't he know this?

He harrumphed, changing the subject. Knowing his style, I braced for what was coming next. It was his pattern, a deceptive calm after he found himself to be incorrect, and then a tornado. "What's your friend, Sellenings, telling you at Bellevue?"

I took a long draw from my cup, emptying it, and set it back on the saucer. "It's very bad downtown, worse than here. The hospital can't keep up, and as part of their mission, refuses to turn anyone away. Patients are overflowing from beds onto floor pallets in their sick units, and some family members are sharing mattresses. They're trying to encourage the sick to stay at home with visiting nurse care, but the public is terrified, banging at their doors."

He dropped backward into his desk chair. "Good God, an apocalypse. Have you been on the flu units? I'm told the sick turn blue within hours, struggling to breathe, bleeding from their face, for God's sake!"

I kept my voice even, in control. "Of course I have. Around the city, there've been nurse and physician deaths as well. The flu is highly contagious." I paused, ever so thankful the older children were safe on the farm. As for Gilda, she was confined to the apartment until this horror show was over.

"What about the other hospitals?" he barked.

"Every hospital is picking up its share. Columbia, across the park, is opening a second ward. Elective surgeries are all cancelled."

"Damn it! We'll all go under if this keeps up."

Was that all he could think of? I sat silently, waiting for him to regain his calm. Although known for his torrential temper, Mr. Blumenthal was also a brilliant businessman. I was confident he'd come up with a way to offset any losses. The Head and Face Unit would be a great start, the first in the city. A hopeful thought occurred to me. "From what I'm hearing, if our soldiers keep up the pressure, the end of the fighting may be in sight. Once the boys come home, my maternity unit will be hopping, every young couple making up for lost time."

For the first time that hour, he smiled. "New babies. What an innocent image after so much carnage. Will it be a new generation with no war?"

I hoped so.

But the uplifting moment passed as suddenly as a gust of wind. "Keep your ear to the ground. I want to know immediately if you hear anything new, especially from your husband. It's time for some good news."

But I knew at this rate, we would not be hearing any good news right away.

Chapter Forty-Seven: Miriam

November 1918—The Front

My mobile hospital was straining at the seams, split evenly between those fighting the flu and others recovering from battle wounds. We furiously discharged anyone stable enough for transport, but the roads and rails were often choked, stopping traffic for hours, and we didn't want sick patients languishing on the open road. Autumn rain had turned the dirt and gravel roads to thick pelts of mud, making it near impossible to drive cars or horse-drawn wagons any distance without getting stuck. The train cars were constantly packed with more hospitals sending wounded west. Nurses often placed two men in a berth.

"Flexible, be flexible," were the orders from above. We set pallets on the floor between cots and requisitioned additional tents and nurses for expansion. Names of the dead were carefully recorded, their bodies transported to nearby military cemeteries.

Eli had been back to check on me twice since I fell ill with the influenza. Always warm and loving, I struggled to match his passion in the same measure. Would I ever fully forgive him? I did yearn for his love, but was it strictly a physical yearning or that all-encompassing desire from the heart, a year ago when we married? Back then, I believed our minds, bodies, and souls were welded together. How much damage to that bond could I reckon with?

I heard a man yelling outside the hospital tent. "Nurse Rosen. We need you immediately." Dashing out the flap, I saw a lineup of Model T ambulances grounded to a halt outside the hospital.

The first driver jumped from his car and ran to me. "We picked up face wounds from two different bandaging stations along the Front. Have twenty-two altogether. Where do you want them?"

Frustrated beyond hope, I pointed to a grassy area in the shade of a tree. "Set them up in lines in the shade. We'll clean their wounds there. But don't leave, I need to free up beds. You must take our transfers to the train depot before returning to the Front. Otherwise, we'll have no beds to give them."

The driver pulled his cap off his head, staring at me intently. "No can do, Nurse, we have orders to return directly to the Front."

I stepped closer to him, speaking through my teeth, "You damn well can and will do what I say." I let my words settle. "Your efforts getting to us will be in vain if these men die on the grass and there is nowhere to put them inside."

A head poked out of the second ambulance, a young soldier yelling, "What's the word? Where do we stack 'em up?"

Livid, I limped to the second car, the brace digging into my thigh with every step, holding my tongue until I reached his face. "These men are not cordwood! They're your countrymen. Take a good, hard look, because tomorrow it might be you in the back of one of these!"

He shriveled back into his cab and cleared his throat. "Yes, Nurse. No disrespect intended."

The other drivers had jumped out of their cars onto the dry grass, waiting for instructions. I gazed at them, pointing to the grove of trees. "Place every injured soldier in full shade under the tree, and once your ambulance is empty, fill them with the soldiers we are now bringing out from the hospital."

I turned around, speaking to the hospital orderly standing behind me, "You have a half hour to bring twenty-three patients out here to load for transport out. Make sure you have all papers in order."

An ambulance driver called out, "Where are we taking them?"

"To the railway station. They are all going to Paris for advanced care. We'll place their identification and patient charts beneath their backs on their stretchers and let you know if anyone needs to sit upright in the ambulance." I took a deep breath, pushing back the pain from my brace. "Do not, and I mean do not, leave the train station until you've handed every patient off to the ambulance train's medical personnel."

Another soldier interrupted, calling out, "But…."

I sliced off his words as fast as a guillotine. "That's a direct order, Soldier."

* * *

The next few weeks passed, all a repetition of the one before. A parade of bodies poured in, bodies dropped off for immediate care, prepared for burial, prepared for transport, and others who returned to the trenches. Always more bodies. Unlike Paris, there was no time to rise above the rapid-fire routine of cleaning wounds, administering medicines, and preparing the wounded for their next stop on the journey home. Home to family or God.

And unlike Paris, where I learned everything about each man, here only a few miles from the battlefield, I knew nothing about their backgrounds and dreams. I could no longer remember their names, only the extent of their mutilation. My hospital was a brief stop on the back side of the war machine, where the wounded were passed from hand to hand, from station to station.

I thought about Eli more and more, working at the Front for close to eighteen months. Could I have held up under those dehumanizing conditions if temptation crossed my path? He'd gone straight from Paris to the Armageddon of the Front, struggling with this madness. I had the benefit of six months in Paris to prepare. Did I know for certain I would have resisted temptation?

I knew the pace was exhausting me. My brace was cutting into my skin, creating deep sores that refused to heal. The staff noticed my discomfort. Nurses and doctors began placing a chair under me. "Sit, Nurse. Take a load off. We can handle matters for a while." I thought back to New York

City and what that dreadful Red Cross nurse told me in her office. She was spot on with her concern. The brace had become a hindrance. But it was too late for regrets. I had no choice but to finish the job I'd begun.

* * *

Days later, on November 11, the Commanding Officer for the division of American hospitals pulled up to my hospital in his mud-splattered Model T. He marched into the ward and pulled me aside. "I have an update from the War Office."

I couldn't bear to hear any more bad news. I knew it would be another notice to gear up for more wounded, that the fighting was escalating. I could already hear his words, "We must flex up."

But as I led him into my office and took relief in a chair, the Commander broke into a smile, half-shouting, "Good news, Nurse. The Armistice has been signed. The war is over. The German army has surrendered."

A dam broke inside me, relief flooding every artery and vein. After a moment, tears broke through my stoic facade. "It's finally over. It's over...." I chanted, rocking back and forth in my chair until I realized he'd walked out, leaving me alone in the room. I heard men's and women's cheers resounding from inside the hospital tents, bedpans banging together, joyous clamor filling the air.

Moments later the Commander returned, poking his head back in. "You all right in there? I brought a handkerchief to dry those happy tears." He handed me the white, starched fabric. "We need to review the final procedure for closing down the hospital."

I shook off my emotions, blowing my nose into the clean handkerchief with an embarrassing honk. "Sorry, sir, it was beginning to feel hopeless. You couldn't have brought better news."

* * *

But the tide of wounded did not ebb with the signing of the Armistice. For the next eighteen hours, German soldiers still shot at our men at the Front. Didn't the German brass bother to tell their sharpshooters it was over?

For the better part of a day, American wounded continued to enter every hospital along the Front. The last of the injured lay on the battlefield, waiting until dark when the stretcher-bearers could safely reach them. Command Central instructed us to stay on the ready until the last man was brought in for care.

In the meantime, we were consumed with transferring as many soldiers as we could from our unit to Paris so we could close down. As a steady stream of ambulances arrived, we packed the wounded carefully in the rear, then they left for the train station. The same ambulances returned hours later, reporting the bottlenecks along the way. There was a rush of patients leaving all the hospitals for points west, idling on the route until the roads cleared and waiting until more trains arrived. Finally, the flow ebbed, and we rested, feeding ourselves and the transport drivers leftover provisions. That way, there would be less to carry back to Paris or spoil.

I sat outside the tent with a group of nurses in the afternoon as the sun released its grip, slowly sinking below the horizon. We built a fire in one of the pits and sat wrapped in army green wool blankets, all wondering when we'd be sent stateside. Would it ever feel the same at home as it felt before the war? We were hearing more every day about the influenza sweeping across America, the sick pouring into every hospital. Would that be the next war the nurses fought?

I unfolded a letter that arrived from Ben the day before, scanning to the part where he outlined his plans.

"The medical advancements in plastic surgery have come at a grave human cost. The past year, first working with Dr. Gillies and then heading the unit here at The American, has provided me with an arsenal of new, innovative skills. Mount Sinai will be opening a unit for continued care, much like Dr. Gillies has at Queen's Hospital in London. There we will be able to continue the arduous steps of facial reconstruction, but more so, we'll be ready to offer modern surgery to

those at home suffering injuries, deformities, and burns in the years to come.

I don't know if you've given thought to your plans, if you are resuming your role at Beth Israel. But before deciding, please give serious thought to working with me at Sinai. I'll be in desperate need of experienced talent, and yours is hard to come by.

In the meantime, I plan to stay in Paris for a couple more months, sorting out the men on my unit, ensuring that I'm passing them into capable hands.

Please keep me posted on your immediate whereabouts, and we can discuss the future more when I see you in Paris.

Stay safe.

I refolded his letter, slipping it back in my pocket. Up to now, working seamlessly as Sarah Rosen for close to a year, I hadn't thought about Miriam Drucker. It might be easier if I worked in a new hospital where they'd hire me on Uncle Ben's recommendation. With over twenty thousand nurses returning from the war, the Red Cross paperwork could easily get mislaid. As for Eli, we still needed to figure out our future, our marriage. Eli could stay at Papa's apartment while I lived with Hannah uptown, and we could sort things out. Perhaps it would give us the time and space to fall in love again.

As I stood to walk inside the tent, an ambulance tore into our loading area, honking, screeching to a halt amidst a swirl of dust. I walked over to the vehicle. "What do you have?"

The driver screamed out, "I need help. A German sharpshooter got into an operating room and went bonkers, tearing up the place. We lost two nurses, and one of our surgeons was hit. It's bad."

I flew to the back of the ambulance, my body in knots, shouting, "What hospital? What's his name?"

"Hospital Base 30." The medic lifted his clipboard to check. "Dr. Eli Drucker."

284

* * *

A team of two doctors and two nurses worked nonstop for five hours cleaning Eli's face and preventing further blood loss. The team would not allow me to scrub in. I was left pacing in my anxious state, barking at anyone who had a bandage out of place. When permitted to watch the surgery, I forced myself to shift from my role as wife to that of army nurse, concentrating on watching the operating team remove specks of grime from the tissue, preparing Eli's face for the next surgical steps at The American. By two in the morning, we had him stabilized. He would live, but the shrapnel had turned his left eye to pulp, and most of the zygomatic bone beneath his upper cheek had been ripped straight off his face. I imagined his upper cheekbone could be rebuilt using the grafting techniques Dr. Gillies had developed, but the eye was irreplaceable. He would most certainly need a patch. The loss of depth perception spelled the end of his surgical career.

I sat beside Eli through the night, knowing he would be inconsolable when he regained consciousness, learning the extent of his injury. I held his hand, feeling the pulse of life in his wrist, aching for his loss. It was during these suspended moments of time that I realized that in this imperfect world, filled with seemingly insurmountable challenges, my love for Eli couldn't be shaken by his misstep or injury. I was joined to him forever, far more deeply than I had understood. I would nurse him back to health and bring him home. With that resolve, I kissed his fingers and rested my head on the back of the chair.

Hours later, I was awakened by Eli murmuring my name. "Miriam, is that you? What happened?"

I held his hand to my mouth and kissed it gently. "Yes, darling, it's me, Sarah or Miriam, whatever you prefer. You were shot, but you're going to recover."

He struggled with his words, speaking through the heavy gauze bandages wrapped around his head. "Were you hurt? Please tell me you're all right."

I rested my head on his right shoulder, whispering in his ear. "I'm fine, but you need to rest now."

He lifted his hand to his face, feeling the bandage across his eyes. "How bad is it? You must tell me exactly what happened."

I sat straight as if giving a report to a doctor and explained the damage and his condition, waiting as he digested the unbearable news.

He sighed deeply, "Will you be able to look at me, to still love me?"

My shoulders shuddered, surprised at his reaction. His first concern was us, our future together. Had it occurred to him that his career was in shambles? All that seemed to matter at this moment was our bond, to have me, his wife, his companion, at his side. "Eli, you are the most handsome man I've ever met. I have no intention of leaving you, now or ever."

He mumbled through the gauze, "Well, that's a relief. The rest will sort itself out." With those words, Eli drifted back to sleep.

I never considered the final test of our love would come in such a merciless form. In the short span of eighteen months, we had both suffered more than any humans should ever endure. All that mattered to me was that he lived. As he said, the rest we would figure out, day by day.

Epilogue: Miriam

April 2019, six months later—Sullivan County, NY

"Ow!" Eli howled, biting his thumb. "This damn hammer. I can't see anything properly."

"Darling, let me help." I took the sign, hammer, and nail from his hands. "Where do you want to hang it?"

Eli pointed to a spot, eye-level on the right of the front door of our newly shingled cottage. We had purchased the forty-year-old house a month before, three weeks after Eli's final surgery and discharge from Mount Sinai. He had endured close to six months of operations, one after another, first at Queens Hospital in London under Dr. Gillies' care, and then in New York City, where Uncle Ben had opened his Head and Face Unit after returning to New York.

"This is so much harder than I thought it'd be, every damn thing in life is," shouted Eli. He plopped into a rocking chair, sitting back, inhaling deeply. "Every day I'm reminded how much less I can do, how much less of a man I am. Are you sure patients will feel comfortable in my care?" The floorboards on the porch creaked as he rocked with a vengeance.

I sat in the matching chair, wrapping myself in a red plaid wool blanket, warding off the early spring chill, and waited for his frustration to pass. I inhaled the pure country air, absorbing the magnificent spring scenery, tree branches saturated with pea-sized buds. Pillowy white clouds hung in the air, breaking the sun's glare. I delighted in the newness of the musky

287

smell from the ground, invisibly nourishing the germinating seeds buried within, nourishing us. The city had nothing quite like it with its buildings and pavement.

His question hung in the air. The months since we left France had been the most difficult in my life. First, traveling with a terribly injured man to London, then the exhaustion of repeated surgeries to rebuild the lost bone in his face. After that, a late winter sea crossing as dreadful as the ones we both took to France. And, finally, a succession of skin grafts in New York City at Mount Sinai. My respect for other soldiers undergoing Eli's care grew by the minute once we began walking in their boots. It took mountains of fortitude, the temptation to quit lurking around every corner.

Back in New York City in January, with Dr. Gillies' underlying bone grafts firmly healed, Uncle Ben completed the balance of Eli's skin reconstruction. While Eli healed from the grafting, I spent my time training nurses for his Head and Face Unit. That kept me close to Eli and busy. After three months at Eli's side in England, the distraction of working was a welcome relief, as my reservoir of compassion was near depletion. There was no denying our future held tremendous uncertainty. Everything hinged on Eli regaining his physical and emotional strength. What were the odds?

Our frequent conversations drained us both, a circular exercise in futility. They'd follow the same pattern each time. I'd begin while changing his bandages. "What do you think you'd like to do next?"

Eli then said, "Hell if I know. There's not much I can do. Forget about my career as a surgeon. I can't even do labor work with my hands. Everything requires depth perception."

I'd typically answer, "Perhaps you should teach at one of the medical schools. Your brain is perfect."

He'd scoff at me. "I'd scare the students. Have you taken a good look at my face?"

At this point, the tears would erupt from his intact eye. My husband had become despondent, a toxic emotion, fertile soil for frustration and hopelessness. I couldn't let him sink, not after everything we'd been through.

Then I'd answer firmly, "You've been brave and strong. We will figure it out together, just as we promised. How about you get some rest, and we'll sort it out later."

This cycle continued for weeks until after his final surgery. Ben had completed a masterful job on Eli's face. Beyond the eye patch, he looked nearly the same as when we married two years earlier. I watched Eli's expression as he studied his face in the hand mirror. He stared expressionless for the longest time, finally speaking in a soft voice, "Yes, I can live with this."

We'd turned the crucial corner.

A few days later, we had the discussion that changed our lives.

* * *

I'd always had an inkling the two of us would leave the city after Eli healed. It would be too difficult to remain in Manhattan, with too many reminders of his rising surgical talent before the injury and his new gift for repairing limbs. Eli was no different from the men in Ben's unit at The American, forced to redefine his life, his profession, his purpose. It took months before he found clarity.

Although establishing a general medical practice together in Sullivan County wasn't obvious at first, all it took was a late winter trip to Nate's farm to visualize a future. This happened shortly after he left the hospital.

As usual, Nate and Jenny came running out of the house, screaming out their welcomes when we pulled up, Martin and Albert at their heels. Their normal eagerness was amplified, all behaving as if we could vanish in an instant. That's what the damn war and flu did, it made us realize how fleeting life was.

My heart soared when I saw the young men. Martin pulled Eli into a bear hug, crying into his shoulder, "I can't tell you how happy I am to see you. To thank you for helping Jake in his darkest hour." Eli's face crumbled, reliving Jake's final moments struggling to breathe.

They were soldiers of the most genuine form, both having fought in the thick of smoke and artillery, deeply affected by the fierceness of war, and the tragedy of lives robbed in their youth. Now they shared this without words, with a simple embrace, tears, a head nod. I understood. I had been there with them, right at their sides.

Albert watched Martin and Eli, standing close by to absorb their intense energy, but still a few feet apart, allowing them room for their unique kinship. Finally, Eli turned to Albert, reaching out, pulling him in, enlarging their embrace. "Thank you. I hear you sent ambulance horses to us, you wily young man. We would never have won the war without them."

Albert beamed back, lips pursed in solidarity, nodding his head. His eyes glistened. He turned to face me, "I'm staying here."

Eli reached out his hand to mine, drawing me into their circle. "We should, too. Here we can have our new beginning."

* * *

Mid-April, months later, we screeched to a stop in front of the farmhouse. Eli was driving, a big step in regaining his independence. He now made house calls to his patients and needed both a car and lessons to drive safely with one eye. The blue Model T brought a fresh wave of optimism and renewed energy to him. Without question, he loved living in the country—a simpler life, the smell of clean air, the fresh food, the unhurried pace. It had begun on our honeymoon when we arrived at the chicken farm two years earlier and never left us.

It took me no time for me to realize this slice of farmland had become the beating heart of our family. The Harlem farm had faded into the past, as did the years Mama and Papa lived in the Lower East Side. It was time to leave the city.

We needed a quieter, simpler place where we could regain our strength and rebuild. The war and flu had chipped out large wedges of our reserve, challenging our values, instilling a heightened appreciation for life. There was no doubt we both needed to forge ahead with a fresh start. I reflected on the extent my thoughts of a country life had changed. After anticipating an exciting career in the city, I'd had my fill of action in France to satisfy several lifetimes. The calm around me suited me just fine.

This evening, we joined the family for the first night of Passover. Our back seat was toppling with wrapped trays of roasted carrots, potato kugel, and honey cake, all straight from our new oven. Our hearts were full, celebrating Passover with family for the first time in years.

It was an atypically warm night. Walking up the front steps onto the porch, I peered through the front door into the house to the backyard. Martin was showing Albert how to build firepits. How lovely. We would eat our Passover meal outdoors. A first for me.

Eli dashed back to the car, reaching in and pulling out a round hat box. He handed it to me. "I saw this when I was shopping for supplies in Poughkeepsie last week. Thought it would look beautiful on you. I hear in the country, it's tricky keeping the sun off your face outside. Don't want you burning up that beautiful skin."

He was right. We were already spending more hours a day outdoors than we'd ever spent living in the city, and the fair skin on my nose was constantly reddened. I opened the box and pulled out a gorgeous, wide-brimmed straw boater hat with a thick black grosgrain ribbon wrapped around the base of the crown, finished with a smartly ironed bow in the back.

"This is stunning." I smirked back at him. "It's a lovely hat trick." I placed the hat on my head and pinned it to the back of my hair, setting the round cardboard container on top of boxes neatly piled on the grass. I pointed to two empty wine cases. "Looks like we are going to be drinking quite a bit of wine tonight."

Eli chuckled, "We might as well drink it now. It's crazy what's going on across the country with those Abolitionists."

"I can't imagine Passover without a good red wine. It just wouldn't be the same."

Hannah and Ben's car was already there, parked on the grass. I knew she was bringing Mama's Haggadahs to distribute around the table and special matzoh from a kosher bakery. We would all take turns reading passages, working our way through the ceremonial meal, celebrating the Jewish people's liberation from slavery in Egypt. It was a perfect holiday to follow the bloody defeat of Germany. Freedom from oppression.

Eli threw his free arm around my shoulder and with one sentence stirred a happiness I hadn't felt since before the war. "I know it's been an unthinkably difficult road for us these last two years, but now our life is perfect. I wouldn't change a thing."

I had planned to wait a few more weeks, but his gratifying words—words I had waited so long to hear, words that came from the depth of his heart after a journey through hell—made me surrender my plan. I set the food trays onto the landing and took his free hand. Curious, he gazed at me as I placed his hand on my belly. Looking at his face, I smiled, "Darling, don't get comfortable too fast. Because things *are* about to change, in about seven months."

A Note from the Author

The art of historical fiction requires a seamless blend of fact and fiction, allowing the reader to be accurately transported to the time and place of the story. To achieve this, I have taken the liberty to adjust certain facts while remaining true to the historical period. For example, the layout of the American Hospital in Paris and the exact locations of military hospitals along the front were modified to serve the needs of the story. Also, the movement of military forces, interactions with luminaries in the medical field, and the NYC hospital's preparation for the Spanish Flu. The limb-saving techniques were few and far between, chosen to illustrate the inherent struggle surgeons faced between performing arduous operations and saving time and lives.

War presents a challenge for any writer. Ensuring my words resonate with the realities of war while highlighting the characters and their emotions was essential. My beloved Isaacson family cherished their adopted country to such an extent that three fought as soldiers (Jake, Martin, and Julian), while three served to care for the wounded (Ben, Eli, and Miriam). My own family is also filled with veterans: two grandfathers who fought in World War I, and my father, along with his two brothers, served in World War II. All of them played courageous roles and, fortunately, returned. America endured. Deep emotions compelled me to acknowledge their willingness to risk their lives for our country, its democracy, and freedom. I hope that readers will be reminded of those who served and sacrificed to enable the remarkable lives we enjoy today and feel encouraged to honor the values and promises of America.

The following non-fiction bibliography helped craft the setting of the story and contains many of the lesser-known, spellbinding facts:

- *The 1918 Spanish Influenza Pandemic*, David Anversa
- *The 1918 Spanish Flu – The Tragic History of the Massive Influence Outbreak*, James Parker
- *Over Here, The First Word War and American Society*, David M. Kennedy
- *A World Undone – the Story of the Great War*, G.J. Meyer
- *Women Heroes of World War 1*, Kathryn J. Atwood
- *Veiled Warriors – Allied Nurses of the First World War*, Christine E. Hallett
- *The Facemaker, A Visionary Surgeon to Mend the Disfigured Soldiers of World War I*, Lindsey Fitzharris
- *Dress Codes, How Laws of Fashion Made History*, Richard Thompson Ford
- *Victorian and Edwardian Fashion, A Photographic Survey*, Alison Gernsheim
- *Our Crowd*, Stephen Birmingham
- *Bellevue, Three Centuries of Medicine and Mayhem at America's Most Storied Hospital*, David M. Oshinsky
- *Polio, An American Story*, David M. Oshinsky
- *The Gospel of Germs, Men, Women, and the Microbe in American Life*, Nancy Tomes
- *The Women's Suffrage Movement*, Sally Roesch Wagner

Acknowledgments

My love for research is a gift from my parents, Robert and Gilda Loeb. They were both passionate readers, often surprising us with historical tidbits at the dinner table and among friends. Our World Book Encyclopedia set was well-loved, a testament to our shared curiosity. As I grew older, I discovered the allure of history through travel, books, and movies. The past, when examined closely, reveals the profound impact of historical eras on individual lives. What a thrilling way to understand history!

In this journey, I owe a debt of gratitude to the historical museums and local library staff in NYC and New Jersey. Their assistance was invaluable, helping me unearth obscure maps, rare books, and periodicals. Their cheerful and unwavering support was a constant source of inspiration.

As a writer, I continue to immerse myself in coaching, independent critique groups, and friends who are enthusiastic about reading and providing feedback. Specifically, Harriette Sackler, formerly of Level Best Books, Michelle Cameron at The Writer's Circle in New Jersey, my writing critique partner, Linda Rosen, and my book club and personal friends, Patti Bleicher, Debra Spicehandler, Lisa Ozer, Ilene Rosenbaum, Sandy Sachs, and Heidi Frances. Thanks to my editor, Verena Rose, for her excellent feedback and Shawn Reilly Simmons for the stunning cover art.

In my biographical information, I share my truth. Cancer, a formidable adversary, became the catalyst propelling me to the keyboard. It heightened my awareness of the fleeting nature of time, urging me to shape the legacy I sought. Writing not only opened the door to my family's past but also allowed me to craft a narrative that resonates with my readers. And in this journey, I discovered the enduring power of historical fiction to illuminate all of our forgotten lessons.

My deepest thanks to my husband, David Rubin, for his unflagging encouragement and to the medical workers: physicians, physician assistants, and nurses in my family and professional life who helped fact-check and imagine the experience of injury and illness before contemporary medicine—the vaccines, treatments, and medications we now take for granted. I deeply appreciate my son, Ben Taylor, MD for quarterbacking my personal care. And an endless thank you to my trusty, tireless trio of exceptional daughters: Laura Johnson, PA, Laura Taylor, RN, and Caroline Hodge, PA, who generously shared hours reading, commenting, and exploring plot options.

The last expression of gratitude is the trickiest to express. I had every reason to relinquish hope in May 2009 when I received an incurable cancer diagnosis. But with the rapid advances in treatment over the past decade, a team of superbly talented physicians, the loving support of my husband, family, and friends, and finally, an unshakable belief in the power of hope, I was able to fulfill my lifelong dream of writing.

A peek at THE HAT TRICK

(WORKING TITLE)
A continuation of the Gilded City series, transporting the Isaacson family into the early years of the Borscht Belt and Prohibition!
Release Date: May 2026

Chapter One—June 1924—Ella

"I'm never going back!" I shouted at the menacing river, turning to grab Robbie's trembling hand. I squinted with determination. "Come hell or high water, we're going to Uncle Nate's farm."

When we left Brooklyn that morning, there was not a cloud to be seen. But now, the June sky was blanketed with dark grey shadows, sending a lacing chill through the air. We were in for a rough Hudson River crossing.

Robbie pulled on my hand, forcing me to turn my eyes away from the distant ferry, still a brown smudge on the water, chugging its way slowly east where we waited at the Dyckman Street Pier in New York City. I scrutinized his unwashed face.

Robbie's soulful brown eyes filled with tears. "I'm hungry, Ella."

I patted my satchel. "I made cream cheese and jelly sandwiches for the boat and tossed in a hunk of cheese. And I filled the Stanley with cold milk." I laughed brightly, attempting to lift his spirits. "It was a sheer miracle Pop had food in the icebox."

The sky was about to break open and rain. A rumble of thunder came from the west. Robbie's body trembled. Time to adjust my plan.

I pointed to a bench near the entrance. "I thought we'd eat on the ferry, but maybe we should sit and have lunch now. Not sure the rain is going to hold off much longer."

Moments later, the ferry's horn blasted as it approached. We'd gobbled down our sandwiches, and I'd dug out a sweater for each of us. "Let's get on the ticket line to board early and find a dry spot. The rain's gonna come down hard any minute." I slung my satchel over my shoulder, picked up the valise, and reached for Robbie's hand, hoping Uncle Nate and Aunt Jenny wouldn't mind a few surprise visitors. I'd assumed a lot.

Robbie pulled back; his brows drawn in concern. "We've never crossed the river. Does this make us runaways?"

I gave his small hand a reassuring squeeze. "It'll be fine. We're going to visit family." The fact we were not expected hung in the air.

Moments later, we boarded the ferry and located a low wood bench in the boat's center near the beverage bar, fully protected from the rain. I crossed my fingers, hoping the squall would pass before we reached the other side.

Robbie's face relaxed, his eyes glimmering with an excitement I hadn't seen on his innocent face in months. "Can you hold my seat so I can watch the cars drive onboard?"

"Of course, just stay on the ferry, and somewhere I can see you. Try not to get wet." I called out to him as he scurried to the bow of the boat where cars, one by one, were driven aboard.

I studied the people while Robbie drifted to the front of the ferry. Most were families with small children, watching the sky, probably hoping the squall would clear and not ruin their day. Holding blankets and picnic baskets, they were dressed for a day outdoors by the river. Women wore colorful calf-length, smartly belted gingham dresses, and straw wide-brimmed boater hats. Men dressed casually in open-collared shirts and loose pants. Some wore boaters, others felt work caps.

Digging back into my memory, I couldn't recall a happy outing in my family. From my earliest years, my parents seemed to barely tolerate each other, arguments flaring at minor missteps, clinging tightly to failed expectations they likely never shared. I hoped for these friendly folks, the bad weather would pass over quickly.

I had Uncle Nate's address in my pocket on a folded paper. It was time to think about how we'd get from the Englewood ferry dock to his Liberty, New York farm. I knew there were trains and buses to Monticello, but that was as close as we could get. From there, it was nearly an hour to Liberty by car. We'd need to call Uncle Nate or hitch a ride if there wasn't a bus. Fortunately, we were flush with a packet of one- and five-dollar bills beneath my blouse.

I startled when the ferry captain blasted the horn, pulling the boat away from the dock. My eyes searched for Robbie. Where did he disappear off to? I hated it when he didn't listen. I heard Robbie call my name just as I gathered our belongings to search for him.

"Ella, come look, an Austin Twenty!" All heads turned his way. "A real one, all the way from England. And it's *gigantic,* just like in the pictures."

I vigorously waved him over to my seat. "Come here and stop shouting. I told you to stay where I could see you. Almost had to give up our seats."

Robbie stood before me, bubbling excitedly, his eyes popping with the moment's thrill. "But, Ella, the man let me sit in the driver's seat and pretend I was driving. He said it can go seventy miles an hour!"

I smiled, relieved he wasn't still upset about running away. I let him ramble on. Robbie had been fascinated by anything with wheels since he could hold a toy in his hands. Now eleven, I watched his interests narrow to machines with motors. He collected every issue of Motor and American Motorist magazine he could lay his hands on. At twenty cents an issue, far too rich for our blood, it was common for him to reach into a barber shop when the operators were busy and nick one. Mama would punish him if he didn't find a good excuse, but Pop was another story. He would chuckle, seemingly amused by Robbie's mischief.

"Robbie, sit by me. You can show me the car when we dock on the other side." I leaned forward to peer through the ferry windows and saw the cloudy sky separating, hints of pale blue breaking through. "Take a look at that. Clear skies are coming our way."

The pitch of the ferry passengers' conversation lifted as they took notice, too. Voices shifted from impatient and concerned to jovial and relieved, laughter overtaking the din. Moments later, we were docked on the New Jersey side of the Hudson River.

Robbie jumped up and grabbed my hand. "Come with me, I want to show you the Austin before he leaves."

I grabbed our things and followed Robbie through a short, tight corridor to the front of the ferry, where several cars were lined up on a platform. I immediately spotted the Austin, which stood out among the unassuming Model Ts. It was grand, robust, ready to hit the road with a flourish. A middle-aged man of average height and brown hair was opening the driver's door to step in, lifting his fedora from his head and tossing it onto the passenger seat.

"Hey, mister!" Robbie shouted. "This is my sister. Can she see your car, too?"

I pulled Robbie back, speaking in a hushed voice. "What have I told you about speaking to strangers?"

The man turned his head our way, a cigarette hanging from the corner of his mouth. A broad smile crossed his face as he bit down on his smoke. "Hey, kid." His eyes scanned my body, taking it all in, smiling. "Now, aren't you a tall drink of water?"

Heat rushed to my face. I was accustomed to catcalling and whistling on the street, but the man's comment felt far more personal, smoldering, in fact. I cleared my throat, "I'm sorry if my brother was bothering you. He loves cars."

Robbie pulled me closer until we were standing beside the passenger door. "Can Ella look inside? It's swell!"

The man chuckled. "Sure, kid. Where're you headed?"

Robbie scrambled inside the car before I could stop him.

"Robbie, come out of there right now," I ordered, then turned my eyes to the man. "North to my uncle's farm. I'm sorry for his boldness. This is the first time he's traveled out of the city." I caught Robbie's eye and tilted my head, lips squeezed together in annoyance, letting him know I meant it.

The man, standing at my height, looked me in the eyes. "Let the kid have his fun. I'm heading north, too. I have a turkey farm of my own up there. What town are you heading to?"

My body untensed, knowing he owned a neighboring farm. But his suit and fancy car didn't fit my image of a farmer. I studied him a little closer, feeling emboldened. "You're a farmer? Pretty swanky car for a farmer."

He leaned back and guffawed at my comment, his mouth hanging open. "You're a feisty thing, ain't ya?" Collecting himself, he said. "My farm's a big business and regularly takes me to the city distributors. There's big money if you run the business right."

Somehow, his explanation made little sense; Uncle Nate had raised chickens his whole life and was an intelligent man. I was almost certain he didn't drive a car like this. But the man's lightheartedness was a welcome change from my worrying.

He cocked his head to the side, "How're you two planning on getting there? I'm happy to give you a lift. It'd be nice to have the company. I can even drop you off on my way."

Robbie interrupted, begging, "Oh, could we, Ella? Could we? Please? I want to see how fast the car goes."

I looked from Robbie to the man and sighed loudly, "I don't think we've been properly introduced. My name is Ella Levine."

He reached out his hand, winked, and shook mine. "Nice, so you're one of the tribe, too. Dutch Schultz here, but you can call me Dutch."

About the Author

"I sail with the wind at my back, outrunning my disease –living to the hilt, loving my family, writing—my life forces."

A cancer diagnosis unveiling a genetic defect, together with a lifelong fascination with the history of medicine, propelled Jane Rubin to put pen to paper. In 2009, then a healthcare executive, Jane poured her energy into raising research dollars for ovarian cancer research with the Ovarian Cancer Research Alliance (OCRA) while learning more about her familial roots. Her research led her to Mathilda (Tillie), her great-grandmother, who arrived in New York City in 1866 as a baby, at sixteen married a man twelve years her senior, and later died of "a woman's disease." Then, the trail ran cold. With limited facts, she was determined to give Tillie an exciting fictional life of her own. Jane was left imagining Tillie's life, her fight with terminal disease, and the circumstances surrounding her death.

Her research of the history of New York City, the plight of the immigrants, its ultra-conservative reproductive laws, medicine during that era, and the forces that drew the United States into World War 1 have culminated in a suspenseful, fast-paced, award-winning three-book historical series. Her engaging characters are confronted with the poverty in the Lower East Side of NYC, the shifting role of midwives, the dangers of pregnancy, the infamous Blackwell's Workhouse, and the perilous road to financial success. These themes resulted in the books, *In the Hands of Women*, 5/23 (Level Best Books), and its prequel, *Threadbare*, 5/24 (Level Best Books). *Over There*, the third in the trilogy, transports members of the Isaacson family into the heart of France during World War 1, challenging the family values they dearly cherish. *Over There* was shortlisted by the Historical Novel Society for the 2024 First Chapters Competition.

Jane's other publications include an essay memoir, *Almost a Princess, My Life as a Two-Time Cancer Survivor* (2009 Next Generation - Finalist), and multiple magazine articles. She writes a monthly blog, Musings, reflecting on her post-healthcare career experiences and writing journey.

Ms. Rubin, a graduate of the University of Michigan (BS, MS) and Washington University (MBA), retired from a 30-year career as a healthcare executive to begin writing full-time. She lives with her husband, David, an attorney, in Northern New Jersey. Between them, they have five adult children and seven grandchildren.

AUTHOR WEBSITE:
  https://JaneLoebRubin.com

SOCIAL MEDIA HANDLES:
  FB: Jane Loeb Rubin
  Instagram: @janeloebrubin
  LinkedIn: Jane Loeb Taylor Rubin

Also by Jane Loeb Rubin

Threadbare (2024 Level Best Books)

In the Hands of Women (2023 Level Best Books)

Almost a Princess, My Life as a Two-Time Cancer Survivor (2010 IUniverse)